感恩劉毅老師，感謝「一口氣英語」！

我們從幼兒園學英語，學到高中、大學，甚至博士畢業，會做很多試卷，可是一見到外國人，往往張口結舌，聽不懂，不會說，變成英語上的「聾啞人」！「聾啞英語」如同癌症，困擾了數代英語人！我們多希望有一種教材，有一種方法，有一種良丹妙藥，讓我們治癒「聾啞英語」頑症，同時又能兼顧考試。直到遇見台灣「英語天王」劉毅老師的「一口氣英語」。

劉毅老師頒發授權書給趙艷花校長

趙老師學校主辦，劉毅老師親授「一口氣英語萬人講座」

「劉毅英文」稱雄台灣補教界近半個世紀，「一口氣英語」功不可沒！劉毅老師前無古人，後無來者的英語功底，成就了「一口氣英語」的靈魂。「一口氣英語」從詞彙學到文法，從演講到作文，從中英文成語到會話，各種題材、各種形式，包羅萬象。

康克教育感恩劉毅老師

感恩劉毅老師發明「一口氣英語」，2014年5月河南省鄭州市「康克教育」孫參軍老師，在接受「一口氣英語會話、演講」師訓後，經授權迅速在中原四省──河南省、河北省、安徽省、山西省，20多個城市、30多個分校開班授課，人數由5,000人倍速增長至12,000人次。

孫參軍校長與劉毅老師

2016年11、12月，受邀到「中國少林功夫弟子武僧院」，推廣「一口氣英語」教學，實現500人大班授課，全場武僧將少林功夫與「一口氣英語」完美詮釋，為打造未來功夫明星堅實的語言功底。

贏在學習・勝在改變

　　福建省福州市「沖聰教育」劉偉老師接受「一口氣英語演講」師訓後，讓同學從害怕、緊張、不敢，到充滿自信，並勇敢參加第十三屆「星星火炬英語風采大賽」，32位學生於福建省賽中，取得優異的成績。評委表示，學生演講的內容很有深度，驚訝不已！同年「沖聰教育」學生人數快速激增！

「一飛教育」陳佳明校長主持，
由劉毅老師親授「一口氣英語全國師資培訓」

劉毅獲頒「中國教育聯盟終身成就獎」

　　牛新哲主席代表「中國教育培訓聯盟」感謝「一口氣英語」創始人劉毅老師，終身致力於英語教育之卓越成就，給與全方位的獎勵，奠定角色模範，繼而鼓勵後輩，投入更多心力於英語教育領域，特別頒發「中國教育聯盟終生成就獎」，劉毅老師成為首位獲此殊榮的台灣之光。

劉毅老師於2017年2月6日在台北舉行「用會話背7000字」講座

一、托福作文怎麼考

托福主辦單位 ETS（Educational Testing Service）在電腦化測驗一開始實施的時候，公佈 155 個英文作文題目，經過不斷的研發測試後，ETS 刪除其中的 7 篇作文題目，又新增 37 個作文題目，也就是考生目前所看到 185 個作文題目。考試時，電腦會隨機從中選出一個，讓考生寫作。例如，其中一道題目如下：

> Some people think that human needs for farmland, housing, and industry are more important than saving land for endangered animals. Do you agree or disagree with this point of view? Why or why not? Use specific reasons and examples to support your answer.

『有人認為人類農地、住屋和工業的需求，要比保留土地以拯救瀕臨絕種的動物來得重要。你同意或不同意這種看法？為什麼同意？為什麼不同意？舉出明確的理由和例子，來支持你的看法。』

二、考生對托福作文的恐懼

看到以上的題目，考生心中的恐懼約可分為四種：

（一）沒有足夠的詞彙和片語供作文使用；

（二）作文要求的內容不是很熟悉；

（三）即使勉強寫出一些東西，對文字的正確性沒有把握；

（四）不知所寫的內容是否符合 ETS 的評分標準。

三、準備托福作文的方法

（一）至少背誦 60 篇範文

　　準備托福作文最直接有效的方法，就是背誦範文。由於托福作文考題固定，所以直接背誦本書的範文即可。本書一百八十五篇範文如果不能全背，那麼至少背 60 篇。這樣做至少有兩個好處：第一，背誦一舉消除了上述的四種恐懼，如果考試題目是背誦過的，必得高分。第二，一個人的作文能力與背誦的文句之量成正比，故背誦可以提高寫作程度，增強信心。如果考試題目是沒背誦過的，有了這 60 篇的基礎，作文能力已經大為提高，只要事先對其他題目稍加練習，考試時就會有不錯的表現。

（二）事先練習

　　對於背誦過的範文，每過一段時間就要從中抽題試答，直到完全正確為止。對於沒有背誦過的範文，要精讀，如有不熟悉的詞彙和片語，要利用注釋或查字典，務必將之學會。要整理出範文內容綱要，將綱要熟記，然後模仿範文試寫。

四、本書的編排

　　本書是由受過良好教育的美籍老師執筆，依 185 個托福作文題目的要求，並參考 ETS 作文評分標準，寫成 185 篇托福作文範文。為方便讀者參閱，每篇範文均附中文翻譯，生字也酌加注釋。範文、翻譯及注釋均經再三校對，如仍有疏失，還望讀者不吝指正。

編者　謹識

CONTENTS

◆　　　◆　　　◆

什麼是TOEFL-iBT？

　　托福測驗（Test of English as a Foreign Language, TOEFL®）由美國教育測驗服務社（Educational Testing Service, ETS®）在全世界舉辦。托福測驗是測試母語非英語者之英語能力，此項測驗是計畫申請美加地區大學或研究所的學子，所必須參加的測驗。台灣地區的托福測驗自西元 2006 年 4 月起，由電腦測驗（CBT）改為網路化測驗（Internet-Based Testing, iBT），透過網際網路，即時連線至 ETS。

TOEFL-iBT考些什麼？

　　TOEFL-iBT 分為閱讀（Reading）、聽力（Listening）、口說（Speaking）以及寫作（Writing）四個部分。閱讀與聽力約 2 小時，中場休息 10 分鐘後，再考口說與寫作。

閱 讀	1. 題數：36～70 題 2. 內容：3～5 篇學術性文章 　　　　新增 2 個特殊功能：① Glossary ─ 簡單的單字解說 　　　　　　　　　　　　　② Review ─ 快速地檢視已填寫的答案 3. 測驗時間：60-100 分鐘 4. 題型：選擇題（包含完成表格、將句子插入文章中適當的位置、同義字、代名詞、看圖選項…等的單選題或複選題）
聽 力	1. 題數：34～51 題 2. 內容：2～3 段對話，包含兩個或兩個以上的對話者 　　　　4～6 篇演說，學術性演講或學生在課堂中討論的對話 3. 測驗時間：60-90 分鐘 4. 題型：選擇題（含單選及複選題）
口 說	1. 題數：6 大題 2. 內容：看完或聽完題目後，有一段準備時間，然後再回答問題。準備時間與作答時間皆有限制。 3. 測驗時間：20 分鐘 4. 題型：2 種題型── ① 聽一段對話或演說後作答 　　　　　　　　　　　② 先看一篇文章再聽一段說明或對話後，再作答
寫 作	1. 題數：2 題 2. 測驗時間：50 分鐘 3. 內容：應試者根據電腦所指定的題目，於電腦上打字作答。 4. 題型：2 種題型── ① 看一篇文章，再聽一段說明或對話後，寫一篇相關的文章。測驗時間 20 分鐘。 　　　　　　　　　　　② 就一個題目寫一篇文章，測驗時間 30 分鐘。

TOEFL-iBT 的計分方式

TOEFL-iBT 分數等級	
測　驗　項　目	分　數　等　級
1. 閱　讀	0～30
2. 聽　力	0～30
3. 口　說	0～30
4. 寫　作	0～30
總　　分	0～120
總分：1＋2＋3＋4	

TOEFL-iBT 與 TOEFL-CBT 的比較

	TOEFL-iBT	TOEFL-CBT
閱　讀	0～30	0～30
聽　力	0～30	0～30
口　說	0～30	
寫　作	0～30	
文法／寫作		0～30
總　分	0～120	0～300

新舊制 TOEFL 測驗成績換算表

網路測驗 （iBT）	電腦測驗 （CBT）	紙筆測驗 （PBT）	網路測驗 （iBT）	電腦測驗 （CBT）	紙筆測驗 （PBT）
120（滿分）	300（滿分）	677（滿分）	71	197	527-530
120	297	673	69-70	193	523
119	293	670	68	190	520
118	290	667	66-67	187	517
117	287	660-663	65	183	513
116	283	657	64	180	507-510
114-115	280	650-653	62-63	177	503
113	277	647	61	173	500
111-112	273	640-643	59-60	170	497
110	270	637	58	167	493
109	267	630-633	57	163	487-490
106-108	263	623-627	56	160	483
105	260	617-620	54-55	157	480
103-104	257	613	53	153	477
101-102	253	607-610	52	150	470-473
100	250	600-603	51	147	467
98-99	247	597	49-50	143	463
96-97	243	590-593	48	140	460
94-95	240	587	47	137	457
92-93	237	580-583	45-46	133	450-453
90-91	233	577	44	130	447
88-89	230	570-573	43	127	443
86-87	227	567	41-42	123	437-440
84-85	223	563	40	120	433
83	220	557-560	39	117	430
81-82	217	553	38	113	423-427
79-80	213	550	36-37	110	420
77-78	210	547	35	107	417
76	207	540-543	34	103	410-413
74-75	203	537	33	100	407
72-73	200	533	32	97	400-403

網路測驗 （iBT）	電腦測驗 （CBT）	紙筆測驗 （PBT）	網路測驗 （iBT）	電腦測驗 （CBT）	紙筆測驗 （PBT）
30-31	93	397	23	73	363-367
29	90	390-393	22	70	357-360
28	87	387	21	67	353
26-27	83	380-383	19-20	63	347-350
25	80	377	18	60	340-343
24	77	370-373	17	57	333-337

聽　力　成　績			口　説　成　績		
iBT	CBT	PBT	iBT	CBT	PBT
30	30	67-68	30	30	67-68
30	29	66	30	29	66
29	28	65	29	28	65
28	27	63-64	28	27	63-64
27	26	62	27	26	62
26	25	60-61	26	25	60-61
25	24	59	25	24	59
23	23	58	23	23	58
22	22	56-57	22	22	56-57
21	21	55	21	21	55
閱　讀　成　績			寫　作　成　績		
iBT	CBT	PBT	iBT	CBT	PBT
30	30	67	30	30	68
29	29	66	29	29	67
28	28	64-65	28	28	65-66
28	27	63	26	27	63-64
27	26	61-62	24	26	61-62
26	25	59-60	22	25	59-60
24	24	58	20	24	58
23	23	57	19	23	56-57
21	22	56	17	22	55
20	21	54-55	16	21	54

托福寫作評分介紹

　　作文將由兩位評分者評分，評分者彼此不會知道另一位評分者給幾分，取這兩個分數的平均值為作文的最後成績。若是兩位評分者的給分差異超過一分，將交由第三位評分者進行評分。

　　考生可能所得到的分數是6.0，5.5，5.0，4.5，4.0，3.5，3.0，2.5，2.0，1.5，1。雖然托福電腦化測驗的結構（Structure）和寫作（Writing）在測驗時是獨立的兩個部份，但兩者的成績併在一起計算，而作文成績大約佔此部分的一半，換句話說，寫作成績佔托福電腦化測驗總成績的六分之一，因此如果你的寫作成績不理想，將會影響你托福整體的成績。

　　在托福電腦化測驗結束時，你可以立即得知你所考的各個部份的分數，但是寫作部份的成績，就必須等「美國教育測驗服務社」（ETS）閱卷者完成評分後才會得知。如果你選擇用電腦輸入寫作部份，那考試結束後約兩個星期，成績單會從「美國教育測驗服務社」寄出，因此台灣考生收到成績單，需要大約三個星期的工作時間；若是用手寫寫作部份，則成績會在考試結束後的五個星期，從美國寄出，台灣考生收到成績單，需要大約六個星期的工作時間。另外，成績單上面會另外標明作文分數，提供考生申請學校參考用，美國某些學校會另外要求申請者的寫作成績。

托福寫作評分指南

6 分數達到此程度的作文特點：
- ── 有效完成寫作
- ── 結構嚴謹，充分闡明
- ── 運用適當細節，清楚闡述論點或闡明觀點
- ── 前後連貫，顯示運用語言的能力
- ── 句法上呈現多樣性，用字恰當

5 分數達到此程度的作文特點：
- ── 比其他人更有效完成寫作的某些部分
- ── 大體而言，結構嚴謹，充分闡明

—— 運用細節，清楚闡述論點或闡明某個觀點

—— 顯示運用語言的能力

—— 句法上呈現一些多樣性，用字範圍達某種程度

4　分數達到此程度的作文特點：

—— 算是針對寫作主題發揮，但可能只有某些部分達到要求

—— 算是有基本結構和闡明內容

—— 運用一些細節，闡述論點或闡明某個觀點

—— 在句法和語法方面，文章前後沒有一貫呈現此能力

—— 可能含有一些錯誤，有時造成意思的混淆

3　分數達到此程度的作文顯示一個或更多的下列缺失：

—— 結構或闡明內容不完整

—— 細節不適當或不足，無法支持或闡明觀點

—— 用字選擇或形式上有明顯的錯誤

—— 句子結構及／或語法上有許多錯誤

2　分數達到此程度的作文，嚴重顯示出一個或更多的下列缺失：

—— 結構嚴重不完整，或是闡明內容不充分

—— 細節很少或沒有，或是不相關

—— 句子結構或語法上有嚴重的、常見的錯誤

—— 焦點嚴重不集中

1　分數達到此程度的作文特點：

---可能前後不連貫

---可能說明不完全

---可能含有嚴重及持續的寫作錯誤

0　作文零分的情況如下：

—— 沒有作答

—— 只有抄寫題目

—— 離題，用英文以外的語言作答，或是只有用鍵盤亂按出
的字體

Quit	Writing	

WRITING

When finished reading directions click on the icon below

- Read the essay question carefully.

- Think before you write. Making notes may help you to organize the essay.

- It is important to write only on the topic you are given.

- Check your work. Allow a few minutes before the time is up to go over your essay and make changes.

- In the actual test, you must stop writing at the end of 30 minutes. If you continue to write, it will be considered cheating.

- If you finish your essay in less than 30 minutes, click on Next and Confirm Answer.

When you are ready to continue, click on Dismiss Directions.

Dismiss Directions

Click on this icon.

Time

Help
?

Confirm
Answer

Next

Quit　　　　　　Writing

People attend college or university for many different reasons (for example, new experiences, career preparation, increased knowledge) Why do **you** think people attend college or university? Use specific reasons and examples to support your answer.

▲

Cut

Paste

Undo

▼

Time

Help
?

Confirm
Answer

Next
➡

1. **Why People Attend College or University**

There are many advantages to a college or university education. Students have ample opportunity to explore a variety of interests, increase both their general and specific knowledge, prepare for a chosen career and develop independence. All of these are valuable goals to achieve, but it is my belief that most students today pursue higher education in order to prepare for their future careers.

In the past, only the rich and privileged had the opportunity to attend a university and their goals were very different. Coming from wealthy families, few of them would have to compete for a job after graduation, and most wished only to be considered well-educated. Today's students are more practical. They must be able to compete in a very competitive job market; *therefore*, a practical education is very important. *Furthermore*, higher education is a big investment and so most students want to get all they can out of it. For these students, it is better to have clearly defined career and education goals rather than to try and find themselves in college. *Of course*, all students want to increase their knowledge, but I believe that most students today want that knowledge to be relevant to their future careers.

The world has changed a great deal since universities were established. They are still wonderful places for acquiring broad knowledge and for personal development. *However*, in today's competitive world these pursuits must be balanced with the pursuit of more specific goals. That is why I think most students view higher education as a valuable tool in career preparation.

1. 人們為什麼要上大學

大學教育有很多優點，大學生能有充分的機會，去探索自己感興趣的各種事物、增加一般與特定的知識、為自己所選定的職業生涯作準備，並培養獨立的個性，這些全都是值得追求的寶貴目標，但是我認為，現今大多數的學生接受高等教育，目的是為了要對未來的職業生涯作準備。

在過去，只有有錢人及特權階級才有機會上大學，而且他們的目標非常不一樣。因為他們出身富有的家庭，所以畢業後，很少有人必須要和別人競爭，以取得工作機會，大多只是希望讓別人覺得，他們受過良好的教育。現在的學生則較實際，由於必須在競爭非常激烈的就業市場和別人競爭；因此，講求實用價值的教育就變得很重要。此外，高等教育是一項重大的投資，所以大多數的學生，都會竭盡所能，想從中得到一切。對這些學生而言，最好是有明確的職業生涯和教育目標，而不是在大學中，才自己試著去尋找。當然，所有的學生都想要增加知識，但是我認為，現在大多數的學生，都希望獲得跟未來職業生涯相關的知識。

自從大學設立以來，世界已有了重大的改變，然而大學仍然是獲得廣泛知識，和尋求個人發展的一個極佳的場所。然而，在這個競爭激烈的世界，追求這些目標的同時，還必須有更明確的目標來加以平衡，那就是為什麼我會認為，大多數的學生，都視高等教育為就業準備的一項寶貴的工具。

【註釋】

ample〔'æmpḷ〕adj. 充足的　　explore〔ɪk'splor〕v. 探索
a variety of 各式各樣的　　specific〔spɪ'sɪfɪk〕adj. 特定的
chosen〔'tʃozṇ〕adj. 選出來的　　pursue〔pɚ'su〕v. 追求
higher education 高等教育　　privileged〔'prɪvḷɪdʒd〕adj. 有特權的
practical〔'præktɪkḷ〕adj. 實際的
competitive〔kəm'pɛtətɪv〕adj. 競爭激烈的
furthermore〔'fɝðɚ,mor〕adv. 此外
investment〔ɪn'vɛstmənt〕n. 投資　　define〔dɪ'faɪn〕v. 界定；下定義
relevant〔'rɛləvənt〕adj. 有關連的　　acquire〔ə'kwaɪr〕v. 獲得
broad〔brɔd〕adj. 廣泛的　　pursuit〔pɚ'sut〕n. 追求
view A *as* B　視 A 為 B（= *see* A *as* B）

Quit　　　　　　**Writing**

Do you agree or disagree with the following statement? Parents are the best teachers. Use specific reasons and examples to support your answer.

▲

Cut

Paste

Undo

▼

Time

Help
?

Confirm
Answer

Next
➡

2. Parents Are the Best Teachers

We will all have many teachers in
our lives. They include not only our
teachers in school, but our classmates

and friends, our colleagues and our bosses and, most
importantly, our parents. Our parents are our first and
best teachers because they teach us the most important
things in life, teach us continually and always have our
best interests at heart.

First, our parents begin teaching us the moment we are
born, and what they teach us in those early years are the
most important things we can learn. They teach us what is
important in our own culture and how to get along with
other people. *In addition*, they teach us how to be
independent and how to learn. *Of course*, they also teach
us language and many other practical skills. *Second*, our
parents are always teaching us whether we realize it or not.
They teach us both in words and by example. *Finally*, our
parents are devoted teachers who always want the best for
us. Their only motivation for teaching us is to prepare us
for a good life in the future. No one wants our success
more than they do.

Throughout our lives we will learn from many people,
for there is something that we can learn from everyone we
meet. *However*, no teacher can take the place of our parents
because they are our most devoted and best teachers.

2. 父母是最好的老師

我們一生當中會有許多老師，其中不只包括學校的老師、同學和朋友、同事與老闆，最重要的是，還有父母。父母是我們最初、也是最好的老師，因為他們教導我們生活中最重要的事情，他們會不斷地教導我們，而且總是非常關心我們的利益。

第一，父母從我們出生的那一刻起，就開始教導我們，而且他們在最初的那幾年所教導的，都是我們必須學習的。父母告訴我們，在自己的文化中，什麼是重要的，以及如何與人相處。此外，他們也教導我們如何獨立，以及如何學習。當然，他們也教我們語言，以及很多其他實用的技能。第二，不管我們是否有察覺到，父母總是不斷地以言教及身教的方式教導我們。最後，父母是最盡心盡力的老師，總是想給我們最好的。他們教導我們的唯一動機，就是想幫我們為將來的美好生活做準備。沒有人比他們更希望我們成功。

在我們的一生中，我們會向很多人學習，因為在我們所遇到的每個人身上，一定都有可供學習的地方。然而，沒有老師可以取代父母的地位，因為他們是我們最盡心盡力，同時也是最好的老師。

【註釋】

colleague〔'kɑlig〕*n.* 同事（= *co-worker*）

continually〔kən'tɪnjʊəlɪ〕*adv.* 持續地

interest〔'ɪntrɪst〕*n.* 利益　　*have…at heart* 關懷；把…放在心上

the moment (*that*) 一…就～　　*get along with* 和～相處

in addition 此外　　practical〔'præktɪkl̩〕*adj.* 實用的

skill〔skɪl〕*n.* 技能　　independent〔͵ɪndɪ'pɛndənt〕*adj.* 獨立的

example〔ɪg'zæmpl̩〕*n.* 榜樣　　devoted〔dɪ'votɪd〕*adj.* 全心全意的

motivation〔͵motə'veʃən〕*n.* 動機

throughout〔θru'aʊt〕*prep.* 遍及

take the place of 取代（= *replace*）

Quit　　　　　　**Writing**

Nowadays, food has become easier to prepare. Has this change improved the way people live? Use specific reasons and examples to support your answer.

▲

Cut

Paste

Undo

▼

Time

Help
?

Confirm
Answer

Next
➡

3. Changing Food, Changing Lives

In the past, preparing a meal was a long and laborious process. The raw ingredients had to be found and purchased, often from a variety of places and often from far away. Some ingredients were not always available, and when they were, it was often a painstaking process to prepare them. Chickens had to be killed and plucked, fish had to be cleaned and peas had to be shelled. When it came time to cook the food, there were no labor-saving devices such as food processors and dishwashers available. Everything had to be done by hand. *As a result*, preparing three meals for a large family was almost a full-time job. It certainly required a lot of skill and knowledge.

Now, all that has changed. There are many convenience foods such as instant soups and even entire frozen meals ready for the microwave oven, and they are all available in nearby supermarkets. Meals can now be prepared in a matter of minutes rather than hours, which means that a family's cook, usually the mother, no longer has to spend hours in the kitchen. *As a result*, many women work outside the home or pursue other interests. *Furthermore*, cooking is no longer a mystery and many more people feel competent in the kitchen. Even children can prepare simple meals for themselves. *Most importantly*, because food preparation is no longer such a time-consuming process, people have more time for other things.

3. 不同的食物，不同的生活

　　以前做飯是個費時又辛苦的過程，必須先知道並且購買做菜的材料，而且經常要到各個不同的地方採買，通常要離家很遠。有些材料還不一定買得到，如果買到的話，準備的過程也是很耗費心力的，要殺雞、拔雞毛，將魚洗乾淨，還要剝掉豌豆的豆莢。烹調食物時，也沒有像是食物處理機及洗碗機，這一類省力的裝置，每件事情都必須用手工處理。因此，為一個大家庭準備三餐，幾乎是個全職的工作。做飯必須需要具備許多的技術和知識。

　　現在情況完全不同了。有很多便利的食品，像是速食湯，甚至是全套的冷凍餐，只要放入微波爐即可食用，這些全都在住家附近的超級市場，就可以買得到。現在做菜只需要大約幾分鐘的時間，而不是好幾個小時，這就表示，家裡負責做飯的人，通常是媽媽，就不用再花幾個鐘頭的時間，待在廚房裡。因此，許多婦女會出外工作，或從事其他自己感興趣的活動。此外，做菜不再是令人難以理解的事，而且有更多人覺得，自己可以勝任廚房的工作，甚至連小孩都能夠自己準備簡單的飯菜。最重要的是，因為準備飯菜的過程，不再那麼耗費時間，所以人們就有更多的時間，可以做其他的事。

【註釋】

meal〔 mil 〕*n.* 一餐　　laborious〔 lə'borɪəs 〕*adj.* 辛苦的

raw〔 rɔ 〕*adj.* 生的　　ingredient〔 ɪn'gridɪənt 〕*n.* 材料

purchase〔'pɝtʃəs 〕*v.* 購買　　***a variety of*** 各式各樣的

available〔 ə'veləbļ 〕*adj.* 可獲得的

painstaking〔'penz,tekɪŋ 〕*adj.* 費力氣的　　pluck〔 plʌk 〕*v.* 拔毛

pea〔 pi 〕*n.* 豌豆　　shell〔 ʃɛl 〕*v.* 剝殼

labor-saving〔'lebɚ,sevɪŋ 〕*adj.* 省力的　　device〔 dɪ'vaɪs 〕*n.* 裝置

food processor 食物處理機　　dishwasher〔'dɪʃ,wɑʃɚ 〕*n.* 洗碗機

full-time〔'ful'taɪm 〕*adj.* 全職的　　***convenience food*** 便利食品

instant〔'ɪnstənt 〕*adj.* 立即的；速食的　　frozen〔'frozn 〕*adj.* 冷凍的

microwave oven 微波爐　　***a matter of*** 大約（ = about ）

mystery〔'mɪstrɪ 〕*n.* 難以理解的事物

competent〔'kɑmpətənt 〕*adj.* 能勝任的

time-consuming〔'taɪmkən,sjumɪŋ 〕*adj.* 費時的

Quit   **Writing**

It has been said, "Not everything that is learned is contained in books." Compare and contrast knowledge gained from experience with knowledge gained from books. In your opinion, which source is more important? Why?

Cut

Paste

Undo

4. **Book Knowledge vs. Experience**

Knowledge can be acquired from many sources. These include books, teachers and practical experience, and each has its own advantages. The knowledge we gain from books and formal education enables us to learn about things that we have no opportunity to experience in daily life. We can study all the places in the world and learn from people we will never meet in our lifetime, just by reading about them in books. We can also develop our analytical skills and learn how to view and interpret the world around us in different ways. *Furthermore*, we can learn from the past by reading books. *In this way*, we won't repeat the mistakes of others and can build on their achievements.

Practical experience, *on the other hand*, can give us more useful knowledge. It is said that one learns best by doing, and I believe that this is true, whether one is successful or not. *In fact*, I think making mistakes is the best way to learn. *Moreover*, if one wants to make new advances, it is necessary to act. Innovations do not come about through reading but through experimentation. *Finally*, one can apply the skills and insights gained through the study of books to practical experience, making an already meaningful experience more meaningful. *However*, unless it is applied to real experiences, book knowledge remains theoretical and, in the end, is useless. That is why I believe that knowledge gained from practical experience is more important than that acquired from books.

4. 書本知識與實際經驗

　　可以獲得知識的來源有很多，其中包括書本、老師，以及實際經驗，而每一種都有其優點。從書本及正規教育所獲得的知識，使我們知道在日常生活中，沒有機會親身去體驗的事。藉由讀書，我們可以研究世界各地的資料，還可以向不曾謀面的人學習。我們也可以培養分析的技巧，並學習如何以不同的方式，去觀察並理解周遭的世界。此外，我們可以藉由讀書，從歷史中獲取教訓。如此一來，就不會再重複別人的錯誤，並且能夠以他人的成就，做為我們行動的基礎。

　　另一方面，實際的經驗能夠給我們更多有用的知識。大家都說，從做中學的效果最好，我也認為的確如此，無論一個人成功與否都一樣。事實上，我認為犯錯是最好的學習方式。此外，如果想要有新的進展，就必須要付諸行動。想要創新，只靠閱讀是不夠的，必須要實際去驗證。最後，我們可以將藉由讀書所獲得的技巧及見解，應用在實際的經驗中，使得原本有意義的經驗，變得更有意義。不過，除非我們能將書本的知識，運用在實際的經驗中，否則書本的知識終究仍只是理論，毫無用處。那就是為什麼我會認為，從實際經驗獲得的知識，比從書本所得到的知識更為重要。

【註釋】

acquire〔ə'kwaɪr〕v. 獲得　　source〔sors〕n. 來源
practical〔'præktɪkḷ〕adj. 實際的　　gain〔gen〕v. 獲得
formal〔'fɔrməl〕adj. 正規的　　study〔'stʌdɪ〕v. 研究
lifetime〔'laɪf,taɪm〕n. 一生　　analytical〔,ænḷ'ɪtɪkḷ〕adj. 分析的
view〔vju〕v. 考慮；觀察　　interpret〔ɪn'tɝprɪt〕v. 解釋
repeat〔rɪ'pit〕v. 重複　　**build on** 以～為行動的基礎
achievements〔ə'tʃivmənts〕n. pl. 成就
on the other hand 另一方面　　**it is said that** 據說（= *people say that*）
advance〔əd'væns〕n. 進步　　innovation〔,ɪnə'veʃən〕n. 創新
come about 產生　　experimentation〔ɪk,spɛrəmɛn'teʃən〕n. 實驗
apply〔ə'plaɪ〕v. 應用 < *to* >　　insight〔'ɪn,saɪt〕n. 洞察力；見識
meaningful〔'minɪŋfḷ〕adj. 有意義的
theoretical〔,θiə'rɛtɪkḷ〕adj. 理論的　　**in the end** 到最後；終究

Quit   **Writing**

A company has announced that it wishes to build a large factory near your community. Discuss the advantages and disadvantages of this new influence on your community. Do you support or oppose the factory? Explain your position.

Cut

Paste

Undo

5. A Factory in the Neighborhood

Having a factory near where one lives brings with it both advantages and disadvantages. An obvious advantage   is an increase in the number of available jobs, and many people in the community might find employment in the new factory. The factory would bring money into the community in other ways as well. It would have to pay some taxes to the local government, and workers might go shopping or eat at a restaurant in the area before or after their shifts.

However, the factory would bring some disadvantages, too. Depending on what kind of factory it is, it might pollute the environment and bring down property values. It would be sure to increase traffic in the area, causing congestion and making it unsafe for children to play outside. *Finally*, the neighborhood would become a noisy, busy place. *For all of these reasons* I would be opposed to the construction of a new factory near my community. While the employment opportunities would help the community, I believe it would be better for residents to commute to work and preserve the peace of our neighborhood.

5. 住家附近的工廠

　　住家附近有工廠，有優點也有缺點。一項明顯的優點就是，工作機會會增加，社區內有許多居民，可能可以在新的工廠找到工作。工廠也會以其他的方式，為社區帶來收入。它必須繳給當地的政府一些稅金，工人可能會在輪班工作的前後，在當地購買東西，或在餐廳用餐。

　　然而，工廠也會帶來某些缺點，這就取決於工廠的性質，它可能會污染環境，造成房地產價格下跌。工廠一定會增加當地的交通流量，導致交通阻塞，使得小孩在外面玩，變得不安全。最後，附近地區會變得既熱鬧又吵雜。基於這些理由，我反對在社區附近興建新的工廠。雖然就業機會能造福社區，但我認為居民通勤上下班，保有居家附近環境的安寧，還是比較好。

【註釋】

factory〔'fæktrɪ〕 n. 工廠
neighborhood〔'nebɚ͵hʊd〕 n. 鄰近地區
increase〔'ɪnkrɪs〕 n. 增加　available〔ə'veləbḷ〕 adj. 可獲得的
community〔kə'mjunətɪ〕 n. 社區
employment〔ɪm'plɔɪmənt〕 n. 工作　　**as well** 也 (= *too*)
tax〔tæks〕 n. 稅　　local〔'lokḷ〕 adj. 當地的
shift〔ʃɪft〕 n. 輪班　　**depend on** 視～而定；取決於
pollute〔pə'lut〕 v. 污染　　**bring down** 使降低
property〔'prɑpɚtɪ〕 n. 房地產　　value〔'væljʊ〕 n. 價值
congestion〔kən'dʒɛstʃən〕 n. 阻塞
be opposed to 反對 (= *oppose*)
construction〔kən'strʌkʃən〕 n. 建造
resident〔'rɛzədənt〕 n. 居民　　commute〔kə'mjut〕 v. 通勤
preserve〔prɪ'zɝv〕 v. 保存　　peace〔pis〕 n. 安寧

Quit　　　**Writing**

If you could change one important thing about your hometown, what would you change? Use reasons and specific examples to support your answer.

Cut

Paste

Undo

6. Changing My Hometown

My hometown is a large city with a dense population. Because it is crowded with people and their vehicles, the environment is not as clean as I would like it to be. Too many cars and buses pollute the air and people also create a lot of garbage that is not always disposed of properly. If I could change just one thing about my hometown, it would be the environment. I would make it a cleaner and less polluted place to live.

I believe that such a change is important because a person's living environment can greatly affect both his physical and mental health. Bad air quality can contribute to many health problems such as asthma, and improperly discarded garbage can spread bacteria that are dangerous to health. *In addition*, the environment can greatly affect the way a person feels. When in clean, attractive surroundings we always feel more optimistic. For these reasons I think the people of my hometown should work together to make it a cleaner place to live.

In order to accomplish this goal we have to not only enact laws to limit pollution, but also take personal responsibility for our own actions. Only when people realize the effect that the environment has on their well-being will they take such proposals seriously. *Therefore*, we must first inform people of the dangers of a poor environment. *Then* I believe we can all live happier, healthier lives.

6. 改變我生長的城市

　　我的家鄉是個人口密集的大城市，因為擠滿了人和車輛，所以環境沒有我所希望的那麼乾淨。過多的汽車及公車污染了空氣，人們也製造了許多垃圾，卻不一定能夠妥善處理。如果我只能改變家鄉的其中一樣東西，我想改變的就是環境。我想使它成為一個更乾淨，更少污染的居住場所。

　　我認為這樣的改變是很重要的，因為居住環境可能會大大地影響人們的身體及心理的健康。不良的空氣品質，可能會導致許多健康方面的問題，例如氣喘；而隨意丟棄的垃圾，也會散播有害健康的細菌。此外，環境對於人們的感受會有相當大的影響。在乾淨且吸引人的環境裡，我們一定會覺得更樂觀。基於這些理由，我認為家鄉的居民應該共同合作，讓它成為更乾淨的居住場所。

　　為了達成這項目標，我們不僅要制定法律來限制污染，還必須為自己的行為負責。唯有了解環境對健康的影響，人們才會認真考慮這些提議。因此，我們必須先讓大家知道，不良的環境可能造成的危險，我相信這樣一來，我們都能過著更快樂，而且更健康的生活。

【註釋】

hometown〔'hom'taʊn〕 *n.* 出生的故鄉；生長的城市
dense〔dɛns〕 *adj.* 密集的　　***be crowded with*** 擠滿了
vehicle〔'viɪkḷ〕 *n.* 車輛　　***not always*** 不一定（ = *not necessarily* ）
dispose of 處理　　properly〔'prɑpəlɪ〕 *adv.* 適當地
contribute〔kən'trɪbjut〕 *v.* 促成＜ *to* ＞
asthma〔'æsmə〕 *n.* 氣喘　　discard〔dɪs'kɑrd〕 *v.* 拋棄
spread〔sprɛd〕 *v.* 散播　　bacteria〔bæk'tɪrɪə〕 *n. pl.* 細菌
optimistic〔͵ɑptə'mɪstɪk〕 *adj.* 樂觀的
accomplish〔ə'kɑmplɪʃ〕 *v.* 完成　　enact〔ɪn'ækt〕 *v.* 制定（法律）
well-being〔'wɛl'biɪŋ〕 *n.* 健康　　***take~seriously*** 把~看得很認真
proposal〔prə'pozḷ〕 *n.* 提議

Quit　　　　　**Writing**

How do movies or television influence people's behavior?　Use reasons and specific examples to support your answer.

Cut

Paste

Undo

Time

Help
?

Confirm
Answer

Next
➡

7. The Influence of Television and Movies

There is no doubt that watching television and movies can influence the way that people behave. ***Moreover***, it seems that people are spending more and more time watching some sort of visual entertainment, whether it is television, a video tape or a DVD. ***Therefore***, the effects of visual media cannot be ignored.

One obvious effect of these media is that watching them induces people to buy certain products. Television advertising is widespread and, nowadays, even movie theaters permit advertisements. Another way TV and the movies affect people is that they give people either a broader view of the world or a distorted one, depending on what type of programming they watch. Those who watch news and educational programming can learn many new things while those who watch primarily entertainment shows may come to believe that most people in the world possess great wealth and good looks. It may make them become dissatisfied with their own lives. ***Finally***, perhaps the most susceptible viewers are children, who may be unable to tell fact from fiction and may try to imitate acts that they see on TV or in the movies.

With the ever-increasing popularity of video entertainment, society must pay attention to these effects. Television and movies, while entertaining and informative, cannot take the place of real experience.

7. 電視和電影的影響

　　無疑地，看電視和看電影，可能會影響人們的行為舉止。此外，人們似乎是花愈來愈多的時間，去觀賞某種視覺娛樂，無論是電視、錄影帶，或是 DVD。因此，視覺媒體的影響是不容忽視的。

　　在這些媒體所造成的影響中，最明顯的就是，觀賞之後，會誘使人們去購買某些產品。現在電視廣告非常普遍，即使是電影院，也允許播放廣告。另外一個電視及電影會影響人們的方式就是，它們能使人們對世界有更廣闊的見解，或是扭曲的看法，而這就要看人們所觀賞的，是什麼樣的節目。凡是觀賞新聞性及教育性節目的人，可以學習許多新事物，而主要是看娛樂節目的觀眾，可能就會認為，世界上大多數的人都很有錢，而且都長得很好看，這可能會使他們對自己的生活感到不滿意。最後，兒童可能是最容易受影響的觀眾，他們可能無法分辨真實與虛構，而且可能會試著模仿在電視或電影中所看到的行為。

　　由於視覺娛樂愈來愈普遍，所以社會大眾必須注意其可能造成的影響。儘管電視及電影兼具娛樂性和知識性，但還是無法取代實際的經驗。

【註釋】

behave〔 bɪ'hev 〕*v.* 行為舉止　　visual〔'vɪʒʊəl 〕*adj.* 視覺的
DVD 數位影音光碟（*= digital visual disk*）
media〔'midɪə 〕*n. pl.* 媒體　　induce〔 ɪn'djus 〕*v.* 勸誘
advertising〔'ædvɚ,taɪzɪŋ 〕*n.* 廣告
widespread〔'waɪd'sprɛd 〕*adj.* 普遍的
view〔 vju 〕*n.* 看法　　distorted〔 dɪs'tɔrtɪd 〕*adj.* 扭曲的
depend on 視~而定　　programming〔'progræmɪŋ 〕*n.* 節目
primarily〔'praɪ,mɛrəlɪ 〕*adv.* 主要地　　possess〔 pə'zɛs 〕*v.* 擁有
wealth〔 wɛlθ 〕*n.* 財富　　susceptible〔 sə'sɛptəbḷ 〕*adj.* 易受影響的
viewer〔'vjuɚ 〕*n.* 觀眾　　***tell*** A ***from*** B 分辨 A 與 B
fiction〔'fɪkʃən 〕*n.* 虛構的事　　imitate〔'ɪmə,tet 〕*v.* 模仿
ever-increasing〔,ɛvɚɪn'krisɪŋ 〕*adj.* 不斷增加的
video〔'vɪdɪ,o 〕*adj.* 電視影像的
informative〔 ɪn'fɔrmətɪv 〕*adj.* 能增進知識的　　***take the place of*** 取代

Quit　　　　　　**Writing**

Do you agree or disagree with the following statement? Television has destroyed communication among friends and family. Use specific reasons and examples to support your opinion.

▲

Cut

Paste

Undo

▼

Time

Help
?

Confirm
Answer

Next
➡

8. The Effects of Television on Communication

There is no doubt that the television has greatly changed people's lives. After its invention, it became an almost indispensable part of most households within the space of just a few years. Nowadays, many families have two or even three television sets so that every member of the family can watch what he wants whenever he wants. *In my opinion*, this has significantly reduced the amount of time that family and friends spend communicating with each other.

Before the invention of television, people spent their leisure time in more active and social pursuits. They often played cards or other games, listened to the radio together or went out to see friends. *But* now television is widely available and it offers a variety of program choices that appeal to almost every interest. People no longer have to look to others for entertainment. *Also*, television can be like a sedative. Studies have shown that watching a great deal of television makes people more passive. *Finally*, people are simply watching increasing amounts of television. *And* with two or three TV sets in the house, there is no need for them to even watch it together.

Although television has reduced the amount of time that family and friends spend together, it doesn't have to be this way. People can make the choice to turn off the TV and do something more active. *Or*, if they really want to watch TV, they can find a thought-provoking program that they would all like to watch and discuss afterwards.

8. 電視對溝通的影響

　　電視已經大大地改變人們的生活，這一點是毋庸置疑的。電視在發明後的短短幾年內，幾乎就成爲大多數家庭中，不可或缺的一部份。現在許多家庭擁有兩台，甚至三台電視機，每個家庭成員，隨時可以看自己想看的節目。我認爲這樣已使得家人和朋友之間，溝通的時間大爲減少。

　　在電視發明之前，人們有空就會做一些比較積極的消遣，並從事社交活動。人們會經常玩撲克牌，或是其他遊戲，一起聽收音機，或出去拜訪朋友。但是現在電視很普及，有各式各樣的節目可供選擇，幾乎能讓每個人都很感興趣，於是人們便不再尋求其他的娛樂。而且，電視就好像鎮靜劑一樣，有研究指出，觀看大量的電視節目，會讓人變得比較消極。最後，人們看電視的時間變得愈來愈多，而且有兩台或三台電視機的家庭，家人甚至都不需要一起看電視。

　　雖然電視已使家人和朋友之間，相聚的時間變少，但這並非是必然的結果。人們可以選擇關上電視，去從事一些更積極的活動。或者如果眞的想看電視，也可以找一個大家都想看的思考性的節目，看完之後，可以一起討論。

【註釋】

indispensable〔ˌɪndɪsˈpɛnsəbl̩〕adj. 不可或缺的
household〔ˈhausˌhold〕n. 家庭　　space〔spes〕n. 期間
significantly〔sɪgˈnɪfəkəntlɪ〕adv. 相當大地
leisure time 空閒時間　　pursuit〔pɚˈsut〕n. 工作；消遣
a variety of 各式各樣的（= various〔ˈvɛrɪəs〕）
appeal〔əˈpil〕v. 吸引＜ *to* ＞　　*look to* 指望；依靠
sedative〔ˈsɛdətɪv〕n. 鎮靜劑　　passive〔ˈpæsɪv〕adj. 被動的
active〔ˈæktɪv〕adj. 主動的；積極的
thought-provoking〔ˈθɔtprəˌvokɪŋ〕adj. 發人省思的
afterwards〔ˈæftɚwɚdz〕adv. 後來

Quit　　　　　**Writing**

Some people prefer to live in a small town. Others prefer to live in a big city. Which place would you prefer to live in? Use specific reasons and details to support your answer.

Cut

Paste

Undo

Time

Help
?

Confirm
Answer

Next

9. The Advantages of City Life

There are undeniable advantages to both life in a big city and in a small town. The former offers more excitement and convenience while the latter offers a cleaner, quieter and often friendlier place to live. *However*, despite the advantages of small town life, I prefer to live in a big city for several reasons.

First, life in the city is more convenient. More goods are available and stores are open later. *Also*, there is better public transportation so it is easier to get around. I can find almost anything I want easily in the city. *Second*, there are more ways to spend leisure time in the city. There are many places I can go to meet friends and have fun. *Finally*, *and most importantly*, the city offers more educational and career opportunities. The city often attracts the best teachers and the best companies. There is also a wider choice of jobs so it is easier to move up the career ladder.

For all of these reasons, I prefer to live in the city. Although I sometimes miss the fresh air and quiet life of a small town, nothing can make up for the opportunities that the city offers me. If one wants to be successful, I believe the best place to live is the city.

9. 都市生活的優點

在大都市和在小城鎮生活各有優點，這是不可否認的。前者提供人們比較多的刺激及便利，而後者則提供一個比較乾淨、安靜，而且通常較舒適的居住場所。然而，儘管小鎮生活有這些優點，但基於某些理由，我還是比較喜歡住在大都市。

首先，都市生活比較方便，可以買到比較多商品，而且商店營業時間比較晚。此外，都市裏有較好的大衆運輸工具，要到哪裏都比較容易。在都市，我幾乎可以輕易地找到任何我想要的東西。其次，在都市有比較多的方法，可以消磨休閒時間。有很多地方可以讓我去認識朋友，並且玩得很開心。最後一項要點是，都市提供更多教育及就業的機會。都市往往能吸引最好的老師以及最好的公司。因爲工作機會比較廣泛，所以要升遷也比較容易。

基於上述種種理由，我比較喜歡住在都市。雖然有時候我會想念小鎮新鮮的空氣及安靜的生活，但沒有什麼可以彌補都市提供給我的機會。如果想要成功，我認爲最好的居住地點就是都市。

【註釋】

undeniable〔͵ʌndɪ'naɪəbl̩〕*adj.* 不可否認的

the former 前者　　***the latter*** 後者

friendly〔'frɛndlɪ〕*adj.* 舒適的　　goods〔gʊdz〕*n. pl.* 商品

available〔ə'veləbl̩〕*adj.* 可獲得的

public transportation 大衆運輸工具

get around 到處走動（= *get about*）

leisure time 空閒時間（= *spare time*）　　***have fun*** 玩得愉快

career〔kə'rɪr〕*adj.* 職業的　　***move up*** 升級

ladder〔'lædə〕*n.* 階梯；發跡的途徑　　fresh〔frɛʃ〕*adj.* 新鮮的

make up for 彌補（= *compensate for*）

Quit　　　　　**Writing**

"When people succeed, it is because of hard work. Luck has nothing to do with success." Do you agree or disagree with the quotation above? Use specific reasons and examples to explain your position.

Cut

Paste

Undo

10. The Role of Luck in Success

It has been said that when people succeed, it is because of hard work and that luck has nothing to do with success. Although I believe that hard work is very important and is the surest way to success for most people, I must disagree with this statement. It cannot be denied that luck often plays an important role in success. *For example*, many important discoveries have been made by accident. There have been many cases of researchers and inventors making major breakthroughs while they were actually trying to solve another problem or create a different device. *Furthermore*, there is something to be said for simply being in the right place at the right time — perhaps meeting someone by chance who can offer a good job or rare opportunity. *And* of course, there are the rare examples of gamblers and lottery winners who beat the odds and achieve sudden and unexpected success.

While the influence of luck cannot be ignored, this is not to say that one should depend on it and ignore the value of hard work. If one is willing to work hard, I believe that success will eventually be achieved, with or without the added benefit of luck. *Moreover*, hard work is often an essential ingredient of luck because it enables one to take advantage of a lucky encounter. If the scientist has not worked hard to develop his knowledge and skills, he may not recognize that lucky breakthrough when it comes along. *Therefore*, my suggestion is not to count on luck to bring you success. *Instead*, work hard and keep your eyes open for that lucky opportunity.

10. 運氣在成功裡所扮演的角色

　　有人說一個人會成功，是因為努力，而運氣和成功則是一點關係也沒有。雖然我相信努力很重要，而且對大部份的人來說，努力是成功最明確的方法，可是我也不得不反對這種說法。能否成功，運氣扮演著一個很重要的角色，這是不可否認的事實。例如，很多重要的發現，都是在偶然的情況下發生的。有很多實例指出，有重大突破的研究人員和發明家，原本是要試圖解決其他問題，或是發明別的儀器。而且，光是天時地利這方面也有一些關係——也許是偶然碰到，能提供好的工作機會和珍貴機會的人。當然也有極少數賭徒和樂透彩得主，很難得地得到突如其來、意想不到的成功。

　　儘管運氣的影響力不容忽視，但也不表示，人就應該完全靠運氣，而忽視努力的價值。如果一個人願意努力，不論有沒有運氣這額外的助力，我相信終究還是會成功。此外，因為努力能讓人充份利用幸運的機會，所以努力通常也常是運氣的必要因素。如果科學家沒有努力培養自己的知識和技巧，那麼當某個幸運的突破出現時，他可能也看不出來。因此，我建議大家不要指望運氣能帶來成功。相反地，應該努力，並隨時密切注意，不要錯過任何的好機會。

【註釋】

have nothing to do with 與～無關　　deny〔dɪ'naɪ〕v. 否認
by accident 偶然地　　researcher〔rɪ'sɝtʃɚ〕n. 研究人員
breakthrough〔'brek͵θru〕n. 突破　　device〔dɪ'vaɪs〕n. 裝置
furthermore〔'fɝðɚ͵mor〕adv. 此外　　rare〔rɛr〕adj. 罕見的
gambler〔'gæmblɚ〕n. 賭徒　　lottery〔'lɑtərɪ〕n. 彩券
odds〔ɑdz〕n. pl. 勝算；成功的可能性　　beat〔bit〕v. 擊敗
beat the odds 獲得出乎意料的成功　　added〔'ædɪd〕adj. 附加的
benefit〔'bɛnəfɪt〕n. 利益　　essential〔ə'sɛnʃəl〕adj. 必要的
ingredient〔ɪn'gridɪənt〕n. 要素　　encounter〔ɪn'kaʊntɚ〕n. 遭遇
recognize〔'rɛkəg͵naɪz〕v. 認出　　*come along* 偶然出現
count on 依靠；指望　　*keep one's eyes open* 留心；注意

Writing

Quit

Do you agree or disagree with the following statement? Universities should give the same amount of money to their students' sports activities as they give to their libraries. Use specific reasons and examples to support your opinion.

Cut

Paste

Undo

Time

Help
?

Confirm
Answer

Next

11. **Money for Sports Activities**

A student's education does not only consist of learning academic subjects. It is also important for students to develop other skills, such as teamwork, and healthy habits that will last them a lifetime. One way to do this is to encourage more participation in sports activities. Although it is important to provide adequate funding for academic services such as the school library, I believe it is important to fund sports activities equally.

A student's primary education goal is to pursue knowledge. *Therefore*, the school library is very important. *However*, the resources that a library buys are long-lasting. *In addition*, students now have resources other than the school library to support their studies. *For example*, many have their own computers and access to the Internet. Sports activities, *on the other hand*, require some investment every year. Equipment wears out and needs to be replaced more often than library resources. *Furthermore*, a school that provides good athletic equipment for its students will find that they are more willing to participate in physical activities. Since these activities are also an important part of their education, the importance of good equipment cannot be ignored.

Ideally, a school should provide its students with a well-balanced education that helps them develop all of their skills. *For this reason*, it is important that schools do not ignore sports activities. Setting aside more money for these activities will help schools to develop better physical education programs and encourage more students to participate in them.

11. 資助體育活動

　　學生的教育不是只有學科的學習而已，對學生而言，培養其他技能也是很重要的，例如團隊合作，以及可終身受益的健康習慣。要達成此項目標的方法之一，就是鼓勵學生多參加體育活動。雖然提供充足的經費資助學術性的設施，如圖書館，是很重要的，但我認為，資助體育活動也是同樣重要。

　　學生受教育的主要目標是追求知識，因此，學校圖書館非常重要。然而，圖書館所購買的資源是可長期使用的。此外，現在學生除了學校圖書館之外，也有其他的資源可協助他們的學業，例如，許多學生自己都有電腦，並且可以使用網際網路。而另一方面，體育活動則每年都需要一些經費投資，因為運動器材會耗損，比圖書館的資源，更需要經常更換。此外，學校若為學生提供良好的運動器材，就會發現學生，會比較願意參加體育活動。因為這些活動也是教育很重要的一部份，所以良好的運動器材的重要性，是不容忽視的。

　　理想的做法是，學校應該提供學生非常均衡的教育，以幫助他們培養各項技能。基於這項理由，學校不能忽視體育活動，這一點是很重要的。撥出更多的經費資助這些活動，可以幫助學校發展更好的體育課程，並鼓勵更多學生參與。

【註釋】

sports〔sports〕*adj.* 運動的　*consist of* 由～組成
academic〔,ækə'dɛmɪk〕*adj.* 學術的
teamwork〔'tim,wɝk〕*n.* 團隊合作　last〔læst〕*v.* 夠…之用
lifetime〔'laɪf,taɪm〕*n.* 一生　participation〔pɑr,tɪsə'peʃən〕*n.* 參加
adequate〔'ædəkwɪt〕*adj.* 足夠的　funding〔'fʌndɪŋ〕*n.* 資助
service〔'sɝvɪs〕*n.* 公用設施　equally〔'ikwəlɪ〕*adv.* 同樣地
primary〔'praɪ,mɛrɪ〕*adj.* 主要的
long-lasting〔'lɔŋ'læstɪŋ〕*adj.* 持久的　*other than* 除了～之外
access〔'æksɛs〕*n.* 使用權　equipment〔ɪ'kwɪpmənt〕*n.* 裝備
wear out 耗損　replace〔rɪ'ples〕*v.* 更換
athletic〔æθ'lɛtɪk〕*adj.* 運動的　willing〔'wɪlɪŋ〕*adj.* 願意的
ideally〔aɪ'diəlɪ〕*adv.* 合乎理想地　*set aside* 撥出

Quit　　　　　　　**Writing**

Many people visit museums when they travel to new places. Why do you think people visit museums? Use specific reasons and examples to support your answer.

▲

Cut

Paste

Undo

▼

Time

Help
?

Confirm
Answer

Next

12. Why People Visit Museums

Museums are great repositories of mankind's historical artifacts and achievements in art. From them we can learn a great deal about the people of the past and their link to the people of the present. We can also learn about cultures other than our own. I believe this last advantage is the main reason many people visit museums when they travel.

When someone chooses to visit a new place, he often does so because he is interested in seeing a different environment and a different way of life. To gain a better understanding of this new culture, many travelers will go to a history or cultural museum. Even those who never visit museums at home may be inspired by the new sights around them and want to find out more. Other people choose to visit museums abroad in order to see things that they cannot see at home. They may have read of famous works of art and look forward to the chance to see them with their own eyes. Still others may have a specific interest, such as butterflies or eighteenth century furniture. It is not possible for every community to support a museum devoted to every field of study, but travelers can take advantage of the opportunity to pursue their interests.

No matter why one travels, the journey often offers the opportunity to visit a new museum. It is an activity that will provide the traveler with a better understanding of the world, no matter what his specific interest is. This is why I think most people choose to visit museums when they travel to a new place.

12. 人們爲什麼要參觀博物館

　　博物館是人類歷史文物，及藝術成就的偉大寶庫。我們可以從中學習到，很多與過去的人們有關的事，和他們與現代人之間的關連。我們也可以了解其他不同的文化。我認爲最後這項優點，是許多人旅行時會去參觀博物館的主要原因。

　　當某人選擇造訪一個新的地方，他這樣做的原因，是因爲對不同的環境，以及不同的生活方式有興趣。爲了更加了解這個新的文化，許多遊客會去參觀歷史或文化博物館。即使是在國內從不去博物館的人，也可能受到周遭景物的啓發，而想要發掘更多東西。有些人在國外選擇參觀博物館，是爲了要看國內所看不到的東西。他們可能已經閱讀過一些有名的藝術作品的資料，而期待這個可以親眼目睹的機會。還有些人可能有某項特定的興趣，如蝴蝶、或十八世紀的家具，而並非每個地區都能資助與每一種學術領域有關的博物館，所以遊客就可以利用這個機會，去追求自己的興趣。

　　無論一個人是爲了什麼去旅行，旅行常能提供參觀新博物館的機會。這項活動能讓旅行者更加了解這個世界，不管他的特殊興趣爲何。這就是我認爲，大部分人到新的地方旅行，都會選擇參觀博物館的原因。

【註釋】

repository〔rɪˈpɑzəˌtorɪ〕n. 寶庫　　artifact〔ˈɑrtɪˌfækt〕n. 手工藝品
achievements〔əˈtʃivmənts〕n. pl. 成就　　link〔lɪŋk〕n. 關連
other than 和…不同的　　inspire〔ɪnˈspaɪr〕v. 啓發
abroad〔əˈbrɔd〕adv. 在國外（↔ *at home*）
read of 讀到；獲悉　　*work of art* 藝術品
look forward to 期待　　specific〔spɪˈsɪfɪk〕adj. 特定的
furniture〔ˈfɜnɪtʃə〕n. 家具　　community〔kəˈmjunətɪ〕n. 社區
devoted〔dɪˈvotɪd〕adj. 專門的〈*to*〉　　field〔fild〕n. 領域
take advantage of 利用　　pursue〔pəˈsu〕v. 追求

Quit　　　　　　**Writing**

Some people prefer to eat at food stands or restaurants. Other people prefer to prepare and eat food at home. Which do you prefer? Use specific reasons and examples to support your answer.

Cut

Paste

Undo

Time

Help 　Confirm Answer 　Next

13. Home Cooking

My country is famous for its good food. There is a wide variety of delicious food available at food stands and restaurants in every price range. Despite this, although I do enjoy eating out occasionally, I really prefer to cook and eat at home with my family.

Although the food we prepare may not be as elegant as that which can be found in a fine restaurant, I like the taste of my mother's cooking because it tastes like home. She is the head chef at our house, but we all help in the kitchen when we can. Preparing food together is fun and brings us closer. We also talk more around the dinner table when we eat together at home because the atmosphere is quieter and more personal. We are all relaxed and can say whatever comes to mind. *Lastly*, when we are finished we do not have to worry about who will pay the bill.

I love to eat, and I love to eat with my family. We all feel comfortable having dinner at home and really enjoy the quiet time that we can spend together. Eating out is great on a special occasion or for a change of pace, but nothing can replace the joy I find in eating at home.

13. 在家做飯

　　我國以美食聞名，小吃攤和各種不同價位的餐廳，都有各式各樣好吃的食物可供選擇。儘管如此，雖然我確實喜歡偶爾出去吃飯，不過我還是比較喜歡在家中做飯，和我的家人一起吃飯。

　　雖然我們所做的飯菜，也許不像高級餐廳那麼精緻，但我喜歡我媽媽烹調的口味，因爲嚐起來有家的味道。媽媽是我們家的主廚，不過只要情況允許，我們也會在廚房幫忙，一起做飯很有趣，而且讓我們更加親密。當我們在家一起圍坐餐桌吃飯時，因爲氣氛比較安靜，而且更隱密，所以會聊得更多。我們可以很輕鬆，並且想到什麼就說什麼。最後，當我們用餐完畢時，並不需要擔心誰要付帳。

　　我喜歡吃東西，而且喜歡和我的家人一起吃。在家吃晚餐，會讓我們每個人都感到很自在，而且也眞的很喜歡可以一起共度的安靜時光。如果是因爲特別的場合，或是爲了改變生活步調，外出用餐是很好的選擇，但是沒有什麼東西，可以取代我在家中吃飯所獲得的樂趣。

【註釋】

a variety of 各式各樣的（= various〔'vɛrɪəs〕）

available〔ə'veləbḷ〕*adj.* 可獲得的　*food stand* 小吃攤

range〔rendʒ〕*n.* 範圍　　*eat out* 外出用餐（= *dine out*）

occasionally〔ə'keʒənḷɪ〕*adv.* 偶爾

prepare〔prɪ'pɛr〕*v.* 做（飯菜）

elegant〔'ɛləgənt〕*adj.* 精緻的　　*head chef* 主廚

close〔klos〕*adj.* 親密的　　atmosphere〔'ætməsˌfɪr〕*n.* 氣氛

relaxed〔rɪ'lækst〕*adj.* 輕鬆的

sth. ***comes to*** *one's* ***mind*** 某人突然想到某事

lastly〔'læstlɪ〕*adv.* 最後

occasion〔ə'keʒən〕*n.*（重大或特殊的）場合

pace〔pes〕*n.* 步調　　replace〔rɪ'ples〕*v.* 取代

Quit	**Writing**

Some people believe that university students should be required to attend classes. Others believe that going to classes should be optional for students. Which point of view do you agree with? Use specific reasons and details to explain your answer.

Cut

Paste

Undo

14. Class Attendance Should Not Be Compulsory

It is undoubtedly true that students should take their studies seriously. This means not only doing the required work, but also actively pursuing every opportunity to learn. *So of course* they should attend their classes to receive the maximum benefit. *However*, I do not believe that there is a need to make class attendance mandatory at the university level.

By the time they reach university, students are no longer children. They are young adults and should be able to take responsibility for their actions. Attending their classes is of benefit to them, and while it may be tempting to skip them once in a while, it is not the responsible choice. Adults must be able to manage their time on their own and to make their own decisions. If a student misses too many classes and so does poorly in a course, he will have to accept the consequences and learn from his mistake. *Finally*, non-compulsory class attendance may not only lead to improvements in the students, but also in the teaching. *Of course*, every professor likes to see full attendance at his classes. If students are not coming to class, the professor should ask himself why. Perhaps the students do not understand the relevance of the material to their studies.

In conclusion, I believe that class attendance should not be required for university students. They should learn to make the right decisions for themselves, and this is one way to encourage the development of independence and responsibility.

14. 不應該強制規定上課必須出席

　　學生應該認眞看待自己的學業，這無疑是正確的，這也就意味著，學生不只要完成學校所要求的功課，也要主動尋求各種學習機會。所以，學生當然應該去上課，以得到最多的益處。然而，我認爲，到了大學的階段，就沒有必要強制規定，學生上課一定要出席。

　　學生上了大學就不再是小孩子了，他們是年輕的成人，應該有能力爲自己的行爲負責。上課對他們是有益的，雖然偶爾翹課頗令人心動，但這並不是負責任的選擇。成年人必須能夠管理自己的時間，自己做決定。如果學生缺課太多，因而某個科目考得很差，就必須接受後果，從自己的錯誤中學習。最後，不強制上課，可能能夠使學生進步，也可改善教學。當然，每位教授都樂於見到自己在上課時，學生出席率百分之百。如果學生不來上課，教授應該捫心自問爲什麼會如此。或許是因爲學生們不了解，上課的內容和課業之間有何關連。

　　總之，我認爲不應該強制規定，大學生上課必須出席。他們應該學習自己做正確的決定，而這正是鼓勵學生，培養獨立和責任感的方法之一。

【註釋】

attendance〔əˋtɛndəns〕*n.* 出席

compulsory〔kəmˋpʌlsərɪ〕*adj.* 強制性的

undoubtedly〔ʌnˋdautɪdlɪ〕*adv.* 無疑地　　*take ~ seriously* 認眞看待~

required〔rɪˋkwaɪrd〕*adj.* 被要求的；必須的

pursue〔pɚˋsu〕*v.* 追求

maximum〔ˋmæksəməm〕*adj.* 最大的；最高的（↔ *minimum*）

benefit〔ˋbɛnəfɪt〕*n.* 益處　　mandatory〔ˋmændəˌtorɪ〕*adj.* 必要的

level〔ˋlɛvḷ〕*n.* 程度　　tempting〔ˋtɛmptɪŋ〕*adj.* 誘人的

skip〔skɪp〕*v.* 翹（課）　　*once in a while* 偶爾

consequence〔ˋkɑnsəˌkwɛns〕*n.* 後果

relevance〔ˋrɛləvəns〕*n.* 關連　　*in conclusion* 總之

independence〔ˌɪndɪˋpɛndəns〕*n.* 獨立

Quit · **Writing**

Neighbors are the people who live near us. In your opinion, what are the qualities of a good neighbor? Use specific details and examples in your answer.

Cut

Paste

Undo

---

15. Good Neighbors

Unless we live in a remote area, we all have neighbors. We are not usually able to choose our neighbors. We can only hope that those who live near us will be people we can get along with. *However*, *in my opinion*, that is the minimum requirement of a good neighbor. The best neighbors should not only be able to live side by side without quarreling, but also help each other.

The first requirement of a good neighbor is that he does not disturb others in the neighborhood. *For example*, he should not be too noisy or block others' parking spaces. *Second*, a good neighbor should cooperate in the care of the neighborhood. Everyone should work together to keep the place clean. *Third*, neighbors should watch out for each other's security by reporting suspicious people who may be trying to steal something and dangerous conditions such as a broken slide on the playground. *Finally*, the best neighbors help each other when they are in trouble. Recently, my neighborhood was affected by a strong typhoon. It caused a lot of damage, but all my neighbors showed their concern for each other by sharing food, water and candles, and helping in any way they could.

Some people say that "Good fences make good neighbors." *But* I believe that kindness is repaid with kindness. *Also*, when we show respect for people it is more likely that they will do the same for us. *Therefore*, if we want to have good neighbors we first have to be good neighbors.

15. 好鄰居

除非我們住在偏遠的地區，否則都會有鄰居。我們通常無法自己選擇鄰居，只能希望住在附近的，是容易相處的人。然而，我認爲容易相處，是好鄰居須具備的最起碼的條件。最好的鄰居，不只是住在一起時不會吵架，而且也必須要能互相幫助。

成爲好鄰居的首要條件，就是不會打擾住在附近的其他人。例如，不會製造噪音，或是堵住別人停車的地方。其次，好的鄰居必須要能與別人合作，一起管理附近的地區。大家應該合作，共同維護環境的整潔。第三，鄰居應該注意彼此的安全，發現想偷東西的可疑人士，或是有危險的狀況出現，像是遊樂場中的滑梯毀損時，都要告訴大家。最後，最好的鄰居，是在有困難時，能彼此互相幫助。最近，我們的住家附近受到強烈颱風的影響，造成了十分重大的損害，但是所有的鄰居，都能互相表達關心，分享食物、飲用水，以及蠟燭，並盡可能地幫助其他鄰居。

有些人說：「籬笆築得牢，鄰居處得好。」但是我相信，好心一定會有好報。而且，當我們對別人表示尊敬，別人就比較可能，用同樣的方式來對待我們。因此，如果我們想要有好鄰居，自己就必須先成爲別人的好鄰居。

【註釋】

remote〔rɪ'mot〕*adj.* 偏遠的　　***get along with*** 相處

minimum〔'mɪnəməm〕*adj.* 最低限度的 (↔ *maximum*)

requirement〔rɪ'kwaɪrmənt〕*n.* 必要條件　　***side by side*** 一起

neighborhood〔'nebə,hud〕*n.* 鄰近地區

block〔blɑk〕*v.* 阻塞　　***parking space*** 停車的地方

cooperate〔ko'ɑpə,ret〕*v.* 合作 (= *work together*)

watch out for 留意　　security〔sɪ'kjurətɪ〕*n.* 安全

report〔rɪ'port〕*v.* 報告；告知　　suspicious〔sə'spɪʃəs〕*adj.* 可疑的

slide〔slaɪd〕*n.* 滑梯　　playground〔'ple,graund〕*n.* 遊樂場；運動場

concern〔kən'sɝn〕*n.* 關心　　fence〔fɛns〕*n.* 籬笆

kindness〔'kaɪndnɪs〕*n.* 親切的行爲　　repay〔rɪ'pe〕*v.* 報答

Quit　　　　　　**Writing**

It has recently been announced that a new restaurant may be built in your neighborhood. Do you support or oppose this plan? Why? Use specific reasons and details to support your answer.

Cut

Paste

Undo

Time

Help
?

Confirm
Answer

Next

16. A New Restaurant

In my opinion, restaurants serve a vital purpose in any community. They provide people with a place to meet and enjoy their leisure time. They can also be a convenience to those who have no time to prepare a meal at home. *For these reasons*, I would support a plan to build a new restaurant in my neighborhood.

Eating together is an important social activity. It gives people time to relax and catch up with what their family or friends have been doing. Restaurants can provide a special atmosphere for a meal and add variety to a nightly routine. *Furthermore*, in this busy society, it is often difficult to find the time and energy to prepare a meal after working hard all day. At times like this dining out can really be a big help, and having a restaurant located in the neighborhood only makes it more convenient.

Of course, there may be some disadvantages to a new restaurant. It may cause noise or traffic problems. *But* I believe such problems can be worked out amicably between the residents and the restaurant managers. *After all*, the restaurant owner wants to keep his customers happy. *To sum up*, I believe the advantages of having a restaurant in the neighborhood outweigh the disadvantages, and so I would support this proposal.

16. 一家新餐廳

　　我認爲社區裏的餐廳，具有非常重要的功能。它們能提供讓人們見面，以及享受閒暇時間的場所。餐廳對那些沒時間在家做飯的人而言，也非常方便。基於這些原因，我贊成在我家附近開一家新餐廳。

　　和他人一起用餐是一項重要的社交活動，這樣能讓人們有時間放鬆，並知道家人或朋友的近況。餐廳可以提供特殊的用餐氣氛，在晚上的例行事務中增添變化。此外，在這個忙碌的社會中，在一整天努力工作之後，常常很難有時間和精力準備飯菜，在這種時候，出外用餐眞的是一大幫助，而住家附近就有餐廳，是最方便的了。

　　當然，新餐廳或許有一些缺點，可能會導致噪音或交通問題。但我相信，這些問題都可以經由居民和餐廳經營者，共同和睦地解決。畢竟，餐廳老板就是想要讓顧客愉快。總之，我認爲住家附近開餐廳，其優點勝過缺點，因此，我支持這項提議。

【註釋】

serve〔sɝv〕v. 適合（目的）　　vital〔'vaɪtḷ〕adj. 非常重要的
community〔kə'mjunətɪ〕n. 社區　　*leisure time* 空閒時間
neighborhood〔'nebɚ͵hʊd〕n. 鄰近地區　　*catch up with* 趕上
atmosphere〔'ætməs͵fɪr〕n. 氣氛　　variety〔və'raɪətɪ〕n. 變化
nightly〔'naɪtlɪ〕adj. 夜間的　　routine〔ru'tin〕n. 例行公事
furthermore〔'fɝðɚ͵mor〕adv. 此外　　energy〔'ɛnədʒɪ〕n. 精力
dine out 出外用餐（= *eat out*）　　locate〔lo'ket〕v. 設立
disadvantage〔͵dɪsəd'væntɪdʒ〕n. 缺點　　*work out* 解決（= *solve*）
amicably〔'æmɪkəblɪ〕adv. 友好地；和睦地
resident〔'rɛzədənt〕n. 居民　　*to sum up* 總之
outweigh〔aʊt'we〕v. 勝過　　proposal〔prə'pozḷ〕n. 提議

Quit   **Writing**

Some people think that they can learn better by themselves than with a teacher. Others think that it is always better to have a teacher. Which do you prefer? Use specific reasons to develop your essay.

_____

_____

_____

_____

_____

_____

_____

_____

_____

_____

_____

_____

_____

_____

_____

_____

_____

_____

_____

_____

_____

_____

Cut

Paste

Undo

Time

Help
?

Confirm
Answer

Next

17. Learning with a Teacher

It is possible to learn on one's own as well as with a teacher. Which method is better may depend on what is being learnt and on the character of the learner. For myself, I prefer to learn with a teacher because I think that this method is more effective for me.

The advantages of studying with a teacher are many. Perhaps the most important is that a teacher can help me interpret and better understand what I am studying. By discussing the material with the teacher I can gain more than I would if I just memorized facts. *In addition*, I can benefit from the teacher's greater knowledge of and experience with the subject. My teacher may know not only the material found in the textbook, but also have valuable practical working experience. I also believe that a teacher can help me develop good learning skills so that I will be able to continue to learn independently in the future. *Finally*, a teacher can direct my studies so I can learn more efficiently. That is important at this time in my life when I have a great deal of important material to learn.

For all these reasons, I prefer to study with a teacher than on my own at this time. In the future, when the pressures of my studies are lessened and I am learning only in order to pursue my own interests, I may prefer to do so independently.

17. 跟著老師學習

　　我們可能會自己獨自學習，或是跟著老師一起學習。哪一種方式比較好，可能必須取決於學習的內容，以及學習者本身的性格。就我自己而言，我比較喜歡跟著老師學，因為我認為，這個方法對我比較有效。

　　跟著老師學習有很多優點。最重要的，或許就是老師可以幫我解釋，或使我更加了解自己正在學習的內容。藉由和老師討論資料，我得到的比只是死背還要來得多。此外，我可以從老師對於該科目，所擁有的較淵博的知識，以及更豐富的經驗中，獲益良多。老師知道的，可能不只是教科書中的內容，老師還會有珍貴的實際工作經驗。我也相信，老師能幫助我，培養良好的學習技巧，如此一來，以後我就能夠繼續獨立地學習。最後，老師能協助指導我的課業，使我更有效率地學習，那在我這段時期是非常重要的，因為我有許多重要的資料必須學習。

　　基於這些理由，我目前比較喜歡跟著老師學，而比較不喜歡自己學。以後，當我的課業壓力減輕，而且只是為了追求自己的興趣而學習時，我可能就會比較喜歡自己摸索學習了。

【註釋】

on one's *own* 靠自己　　　*as well as* 以及

depend on 視～而定　　character〔ˈkærɪktɚ〕*n.* 性格

effective〔ɪˈfɛktɪv〕*adj.* 有效的　　interpret〔ɪnˈtɝprɪt〕*v.* 解釋

memorize〔ˈmɛməˌraɪz〕*v.* 背誦；記憶　　*in addition* 此外（ = *besides* ）

benefit〔ˈbɛnəfɪt〕*v.* 獲益 < *from* >　　textbook〔ˈtɛkstˌbuk〕*n.* 教科書

valuable〔ˈvæljuəbl〕*adj.* 珍貴的　　practical〔ˈpræktɪkl〕*adj.* 實際的

independently〔ˌɪndɪˈpɛndəntlɪ〕*adv.* 獨立地

direct〔dəˈrɛkt〕*v.* 管理；指導　　efficiently〔əˈfɪʃəntlɪ〕*adv.* 有效率地

lessen〔ˈlɛsn̩〕*v.* 減輕　　pursue〔pɚˈsu〕*v.* 追求

Quit　　　　　　Writing

What are some important qualities of a good supervisor (boss)? Use specific details and examples to explain why these qualities are important.

▲

Cut

Paste

Undo

▼

Time

Help
?

Confirm
Answer

Next
➡

18. The Important Qualities of a Good Supervisor

A company's success depends on all of its employees, from low-level clerks to supervisors. As the leader of a team, a supervisor plays an especially important role. He must not only do his own job well, but elicit the best results from those he supervises. *Therefore*, good supervisor should possess certain important qualities.

Most importantly, a supervisor must be very knowledge-able about his company's business. The better understanding he has of the company as a whole and the industry, the better able he will be to anticipate problems and deal with unexpected events. *Another* important quality is the ability to delegate. A good supervisor must be willing to entrust some tasks to members of his team rather than try to control every detail. This will not only save him time, but offer his employees room to develop their skills. *Last but not least*, a good supervisor must be even-tempered and able to offer constructive criticism. It is of no use to blame an employee for his failure without offering any useful suggestions for improvement.

With the above qualities I believe that a supervisor can perform his job well and inspire those he leads to make their best effort. *In this way* the team will be efficient, effective and, no doubt, successful.

18. 優秀的主管應具備的重要特質

　　一家公司成功與否，視其全體員工而定，從最低層的職員到主管，都包括在內。身為一個團隊的領導者，主管扮演了特別重要的角色，不僅要做好自己份內的工作，還要激發下屬有最好的表現。因此，一位優秀的主管，應該具備某些重要的特質。

　　最重要的是，主管必須對公司的業務非常了解，對公司整體及企業走向愈了解，就愈能夠預測問題，並能應付突發的事件。另一個重要的特質，就是授權的能力。優秀的主管必須願意，將工作委託給其他的團隊成員，而不是想要掌控每一個細節。這樣做不僅能節省自己的時間，也能給下屬培養技能的空間。最後一項要點是，優秀的主管必須性情平和，並能夠提供建設性的批評，光是責怪員工的過錯，而沒有提供任何有益於改善的建議，是沒用的。

　　若具有上述的特質，我相信這樣的主管一定可以把工作做得很出色，並且激勵他領導的下屬盡心盡力。如此一來，整個團隊將會更有效率以及績效，而且無疑地，一定會成功。

【註釋】

quality〔'kwɑlətɪ〕*n.* 特質　supervisor〔ˌsjupɚ'vaɪzɚ〕*n.* 主管
depend on 視～而定　elicit〔ɪ'lɪsɪt〕*v.* 引出
supervise〔ˌsupɚ'vaɪz〕*v.* 管理；主管　possess〔pə'zɛs〕*v.* 具有
knowledgeable〔'nɑlɪdʒəbḷ〕*adj.* 有知識的　***as a whole*** 整體而言
anticipate〔æn'tɪsəˌpet〕*v.* 預料　***deal with*** 應付
unexpected〔ˌʌnɪk'spɛktɪd〕*adj.* 意外的
delegate〔'dɛləˌget〕*v.* 授權　willing〔'wɪlɪŋ〕*adj.* 願意的
entrust〔ɪn'trʌst〕*v.* 委託　***last but not least*** 最後一項要點是
even-tempered〔'ivən'tɛmpɚd〕*adj.* 性情平和的；不易激動的
constructive〔kən'strʌktɪv〕*adj.* 有建設性的
perform〔pɚ'fɔrm〕*v.* 做　inspire〔ɪn'spaɪr〕*v.* 激勵

Quit   **Writing**

Should governments spend more money on improving roads and highways, or should governments spend more money on improving public transportation (buses, trains, subways)? Why? Use specific reasons and details to develop your essay.

Cut

Paste

Undo

Time

Help
?

Confirm
Answer

Next
➡

19. **Improving Public Transportation**

Good transportation is very important to the success of both individuals and a city. Without efficient means of transportation, people will waste a great deal of time going to and from work. This will make them tired and less productive in their jobs. People may rely on either private or public transportation to get them to and from work. If a choice has to be made between spending money on improving the roads for private vehicles or improving public transportation, I would choose the latter for the following reasons.

First of all, better public transportation systems, including buses, trains and subways, will encourage more people to use them rather than drive their own cars. This will reduce the total amount of traffic on the roads and make travel quicker for everyone. *Second*, using public transportation saves energy. A bus which carries 60 people is a far more efficient use of fuel than 60 individual cars driving the same route. *And last but not least*, greater use of public transportation causes less pollution and will keep the environment cleaner.

There are many reasons to support spending money on public transportation. Good transportation systems make a city cleaner, more efficient and more convenient. This improves everyone's quality of life and can make the city more prosperous. Therefore, I support spending money on public transportation systems rather than improving roads.

19. 改善大眾運輸工具

好的運輸工具，對於個人和整個都市的成功，都非常重要。如果沒有有效率的運輸工具，人們上下班，會浪費很多時間，這會使他們疲倦，因而降低工作生產力。人們上下班可以依賴私人或大眾運輸工具，如果要在花錢為私人車輛改善道路，和花錢改善大眾運輸工具之間做選擇，我會選擇後者，原因如下。

首先，較好的大眾運輸系統，包括公車、火車和地下鐵，會鼓勵更多民眾搭乘，而不會自己開車，如此便能減少道路上整體的交通流量，讓大家往來的速度更快。其次，使用大眾運輸工具可節省能源。一輛公車搭載六十個人，比六十輛私人汽車行駛相同的路線，更能充分、有效率地使用燃料。最後一項要點是，多使用大眾運輸工具，可以減少污染，使環境更乾淨。

有許多理由都支持，該把經費用在大眾運輸工具上。好的運輸系統能使城市更乾淨、更有效率，而且更便利。這樣可以改善每個人的生活品質，並讓整個都市更繁榮。因此，我支持將錢用在大眾運輸系統上，而非改善道路。

【註釋】

transportation〔͵trænspə'teʃən〕 *n.* 運輸工具

individual〔͵ɪndə'vɪdʒʊəl〕 *n.* 個人　 means〔minz〕 *n.* 方法；工具

productive〔prə'dʌktɪv〕 *adj.* 有生產力的

rely on 依賴（= *depend on*）　 private〔'praɪvɪt〕 *adj.* 私人的

the latter （兩者中）後者（↔ *the former*）

energy〔'ɛnədʒɪ〕 *n.* 能源　 fuel〔'fjuəl〕 *n.* 燃料

carry〔'kærɪ〕 *v.* 運送　 route〔rut〕 *n.* 路線

last but not least 最後一項要點是　 ***quality of life*** 生活品質

prosperous〔'prɑspərəs〕 *adj.* 繁榮的

Quit　　　　　　**Writing**

It is better for children to grow up in the countryside than in a big city.
Do you agree or disagree?　Use specific reasons and examples to
develop your essay.

▲

Cut

Paste

Undo

▼

Time

Help　Confirm　Next
?　Answer　→

20. Childhood in the Countryside

Both the countryside and an urban environment have many things to offer. Many important museums and cultural venues can be found in the city. There is also often good access to educational resources and a wide variety of job opportunities. *However*, the countryside offers a more relaxed and peaceful way of life. Communities are often close-knit and secure. Although both environments offer good opportunities for development, *it is my opinion that* life in the countryside is more beneficial for children.

One important advantage of raising children in the countryside is that the environment is cleaner and healthier. With fresh air to breathe, less crowded living conditions, and more chances to take part in physical exercise, children in the country are usually healthier than those in the city. *Another* advantage of country living is safety. There is not only less crime in the countryside, but also fewer traffic accidents. Parents do not need to worry so much when their children are playing outside. A *third* advantage is the stronger sense of community in the country. Children know their neighbors and learn to care about others at an early age. *Finally*, a country upbringing allows children to experience a more natural environment without all the distractions of entertainment places in the city. *Thus*, they can concentrate on their schoolwork and their families.

Due to the great number of advantages in raising children in the country, I believe it is better for children to grow up there rather than in a city. Without all the dangers and distractions of city life, they will grow up healthier and better grounded in the moral values of their culture.

20. 在鄉下度過童年

　　鄉下和都市環境都有許多優點。許多重要的博物館,以及文化活動地點,都位於都市。雖然在都市有良好的教育資源可利用,以及各式各樣的工作機會,然而,鄉間卻能給人較輕鬆而且平靜的生活方式。社區之間通常是緊密結合,較爲安全。雖然兩種環境都能提供良好的發展機會,但依我之見,鄉下生活對孩子而言,是比較有益的。

　　在鄉下養育小孩的優點之一是,整個環境比較乾淨、健康。有新鮮空氣可呼吸,生活環境較不擁擠,並且有更多讓身體運動的機會,所以鄉下小孩通常比都市小孩健康。鄉下生活的另一個優點是安全。鄉下不只犯罪事件較少,交通事故也較少。孩子們在外面玩的時候,父母比較不用擔心。第三個優點是,在鄉下有較強烈的社區觀,孩子們都認識鄰居,所以從小就能學習關心他人。最後,在鄉下長大,能夠讓孩子體驗更自然的環境,而不會因都市裏各種娛樂場所而分心。因此,他們可以更專注於學校的課業和家庭生活。

　　由於在鄉下養育小孩有這麼多優點,所以我認爲,孩子在鄉下成長,比在都市好。沒有都市的各種危險和令人分心的事物,他們可以更健康地長大,並且在他們的文化道德價值觀方面,奠定更好的基礎。

【註釋】

countryside〔ˈkʌntrɪˌsaɪd〕 *n.* 鄉村地區　　urban〔ˈɝbən〕 *adj.* 都市的

venue〔ˈvɛnju〕 *n.* 舉行地點　　access〔ˈæksɛs〕 *n.* 使用權 < *to* >

close-knit〔ˈklosˈnɪt〕 *adj.* 緊密結合的　　secure〔sɪˈkjur〕 *adj.* 安全的

beneficial〔ˌbɛnəˈfɪʃəl〕 *adj.* 有益的　　raise〔rez〕 *v.* 養育

take part in 參加 (= *participate in*)

sense of community 社區觀 (守望相助、敦親睦鄰的觀念)

upbringing〔ˈʌpˌbrɪŋɪŋ〕 *n.* 養育;教養

distraction〔dɪˈstrækʃən〕 *n.* 使人分心的事物

entertainment〔ˌɛntəˈtenmənt〕 *n.* 娛樂

ground〔graʊnd〕 *v.* 奠定基礎　　moral〔ˈmɔrəl〕 *adj.* 道德的

values〔ˈvæljuz〕 *n. pl.* 價值觀

Quit **Writing**

In general, people are living longer now. Discuss the causes of this phenomenon. Use specific reasons and details to develop your essay.

Cut

Paste

Undo

Time

Help

Confirm Answer

Next

21. Living Longer

In the past it was not uncommon for a man to die at forty, having lived a full life. *But* now we consider a lifespan of forty years to be very short. It is not unusual for people to live into their eighties and nineties, and some even reach 100. *What's more*, people are living long, healthy lives and are active well into their "golden years."

Mankind's longevity is due mainly to advances in science and technology. Medical breakthroughs have eradicated many fatal diseases that were once common. Perhaps more importantly, better general health means that people are less likely to contract infections in the first place. Better health also helps people prevent slowly debilitating conditions, such as heart disease, which can take their lives at an early age. *And* as civilization has advanced, our living environment and sources of food have become more sanitary. *Furthermore*, work is now safer and not as taxing on the human body. We do not wear out after just a few years of very hard work.

There are many reasons why people are now living longer than ever before. *But* what is more important is that they are living better as they live longer. *It is my opinion that* we have scientific and technological developments to thank for this progress.

21. 活得更久

以前的人活到四十歲，就過完一生而死亡，是很平常的。但是現在，我們認爲四十歲的壽命很短，人們活到八十幾歲、九十幾歲，有些甚至到一百歲，是很平常的。而且，人們還能活得久而且又健康，精力充沛地邁入他們的「黃金時代（退休期）」。

人類會長壽，主要是因爲科學及科技的進步。醫學上的重大突破，已經根除了以前十分普遍的致命疾病。而也許更重要的是，大衆健康的改善，首先就意謂著，人們比較不可能得傳染病。人們變得較健康，也有助於預防罹患一些會使身體狀況日益衰弱的疾病，例如心臟疾病，這些疾病常會奪走年輕的生命。又因爲文明的進步，我們的生活環境以及食物來源已經變得比較衛生。此外，現在的工作比較安全，且對人體而言，沒有那麼繁重。我們不會因爲只辛苦工作幾年，就疲憊不堪。

現代人比以前長壽的原因有很多，但更重要的是，人們活得愈久，而且也活得愈好。我的看法是，拜科學和科技的發展所賜，我們才能有如此的進展。

【註釋】

lifespan〔ˈlaɪfˌspæn〕*n.* 壽命　　***what's more*** 而且

golden years 黃金時代；退休期（多指 65 歲以上）

mankind〔mænˈkaɪnd〕*n.* 人類　　longevity〔lɑnˈdʒɛvətɪ〕*n.* 長壽

advance〔ədˈvæns〕*n., v.* 進步　　breakthrough〔ˈbrekˌθru〕*n.* 突破

eradicate〔ɪˈrædɪˌket〕*v.* 根除　　fatal〔ˈfetl̩〕*adj.* 致命的

contract〔kənˈtrækt〕*v.* 感染　　infection〔ɪnˈfɛkʃən〕*n.* 傳染病

debilitate〔dɪˈbɪləˌtet〕*v.* 使衰弱　condition〔kənˈdɪʃən〕*n.* 身體狀況

civilization〔ˌsɪvl̩əˈzeʃən〕*n.* 文明　　sanitary〔ˈsænəˌtɛrɪ〕*adj.* 衛生的

taxing〔ˈtæksɪŋ〕*adj.* 累人的；繁重的

wear out 使筋疲力盡　　progress〔ˈprɑgrɛs〕*n.* 進步

Quit　　　　　**Writing**

We all work or will work in our jobs with many different kinds of people. In your opinion, what are some important characteristics of a co-worker (someone you work closely with)? Use reasons and specific examples to explain why these characteristics are important.

Cut

Paste

Undo

Time

Help
?

Confirm
Answer

Next

22. **Important Characteristics of a Co-worker**

Almost every type of job requires us to work with other people. In order to work effectively and efficiently, we must be able to get along with our co-workers and depend upon them. In an ideal work environment our co-workers would have the following characteristics.

Number one, a good co-worker is responsible and dependable. In most workplaces, the work that employees do is interdependent. If one employee fails to do his or her job, it can affect everyone. *Number two*, a good co-worker must be a team player. We all want to get ahead in the workplace, but we should not attempt to do so by treating others unfairly. If the team succeeds, everyone will benefit, but if one employee puts his interests ahead of those of the team, everyone will suffer. *Number three*, a good co-worker should have a pleasant personality and be easy to get along with. No one wants to spend the greater part of the day with someone he dislikes. If we can get along with our colleagues, we will enjoy our jobs more.

The above are only a few of the characteristics that an ideal co-worker should have, but I feel that they are among the most important. *Of course*, we will not always be able to work with ideal colleagues. *Therefore*, while we should treasure good co-workers, we must also learn how to get along with all kinds of people in the workplace.

22. 同事的重要特質

　　幾乎做每一種類型的工作，我們都必需和別人一起合作，為了讓工作有成果而且有效率，我們必須要能和同事相處，並且依賴他們。在一個理想的工作環境裡，我們的同事會有下列的特質。

　　第一，優秀的同事必須是負責任，而且可靠的。在大部份的工作場所中，員工所做的工作是互相依存的。如果某位員工未能完成份內的工作，將會影響全體。第二，優秀的同事必須注重團隊合作。雖然我們全都想在職場上領先別人，但我們不應該試圖以不公平的方法對待別人，來達到目的。如果團隊成功了，每個人都會獲益，但是如果某個員工把自己的利益，放在團隊利益之上，那大家都會受害。第三，優秀的同事應該有親切的個性，容易相處。沒有人想要把一天當中大部份的時間，用來和他不喜歡的人相處。如果我們能夠和同事處得好，將會更喜愛工作。

　　上述只是一些理想的同事應該具備的特質，但我覺得它們是最重要的。當然，我們未必能夠和理想的同事一起工作，因此，在我們珍惜優秀同事的同時，也必須學會如何在工作場所中，和各種不同的人和睦相處。

【註釋】

characteristic〔ˌkærɪktəˈrɪstɪk〕*n.* 特性

co-worker〔koˈwɜkə〕*n.* 同事　　*get along with* 與～和睦相處

depend upon 依賴（ = *depend on* ）

dependable〔dɪˈpɛndəbḷ〕*adj.* 可靠的

workplace〔ˈwɜkˌples〕*n.* 工作場所

employee〔ˌɛmplɔɪˈi〕*n.* 員工

interdependent〔ˌɪntədɪˈpɛndənt〕*adj.* 互相依賴的

get ahead 領先；獲得成功

colleague〔ˈkɑlig〕*n.* 同事（ = *co-worker* ）

not always 不一定（ = *not necessarily* ）

treasure〔ˈtrɛʒə〕*v.* 珍惜

| Quit | **Writing** | |

In some countries, teenagers have jobs while they are still students. Do you think this is a good idea? Support your opinion by using specific reasons and details.

▲

Cut

Paste

Undo

▼

| Time | | Help | Confirm | Next |
| ? | Answer | ➡ |

23. Teenagers and Part-time Jobs

In many countries it is common for teenagers to take part-time jobs while they are still in high school, while in other societies this is virtually unheard of. In the latter situation, students are expected to spend all of their time on their studies and consider schoolwork their "job". *In my opinion*, students benefit more from a more balanced lifestyle, which may include working at a part-time job. *Therefore*, I believe that it is a good idea for students to work while studying.

While it is true that a student's most important goal must be to learn and to do well at his studies, it does not need to be the only goal. *In fact*, a life which consists of only study is not balanced and may cause the student to miss out on other valuable learning experiences. In addition to bringing more balance to a student's life, part-time work can broaden his range of experience. He will have the opportunity to meet people from all walks of life and will be faced with a wider variety of problems to solve. *Furthermore*, work helps a student to develop greater independence, and earning his own pocket money can teach him how to handle his finances. *Finally*, a part-time job can help a student to develop a greater sense of responsibility, both for his own work and for that of the team he works with.

For all these reasons, I firmly believe that most students would benefit from taking a part-time job while they are in high school. *Of course*, they must be careful not to let it take up too much of their time because study is still their primary responsibility. *In sum*, living a balanced life is the best way to be successful.

23. 青少年與打工

在許多國家，青少年普遍會在高中時期打工，然而在有些國家，這幾乎是前所未聞。如果是後者的情況，那是因為一般認為，學生應把所有的時間花在課業上，把課業當作是自己的「工作」。我認為，生活方式愈均衡，對學生就愈好，而均衡的生活則須包含打工。所以我認為，在就學期間打工，是個不錯的想法。

雖然學生最重要的目標，的確必須是學習，而且功課要好，但這不必是學生唯一的目標。事實上，只重視課業的生活並不均衡，可能會使學生錯過其他珍貴的學習經驗。打工除了使生活更均衡外，還可拓展學生的經驗。學生可以有機會見到各行各業的人，而且會面臨更多各種不同的問題，需要解決。此外，工作幫助學生更加獨立，而且自己賺零用錢，還可以教導他如何處理自己的財務。最後，打工可以幫助學生，不只是對自己的工作，而且也對團隊工作培養更大的責任感。

基於這些理由，我堅決相信，大多數學生在高中時期打工，都能獲益。當然，也必須小心，不要讓打工佔據太多時間，因為課業仍然是青少年首要的責任。總之，過均衡的生活，才是最佳的成功之道。

【註釋】

take a part-time job 打工 (= *work part-time*)

virtually 〔'vɜtʃʊəlɪ〕 *adv.* 幾乎 (= *almost*)　　**hear of** 聽說

latter 〔'lætɚ〕 *adj.* (兩者中) 後者的 (↔ *former*)

benefit 〔'bɛnəfɪt〕 *v.* 獲益　　balanced 〔'bælənst〕 *adj.* 均衡的

consist of 由～組成　　**miss out on** 錯過 (良機)

broaden 〔'brɔdn̩〕 *v.* 拓展　　range 〔rendʒ〕 *n.* 範圍

all walks of life 各行各業　　**be faced with** 面對 (= *face*)

a variety of 各式各樣的　　furthermore 〔'fɜðɚ͵mor〕 *adv.* 此外

pocket money 零用錢 (= *allowance*)　　finance 〔'faɪnæns〕 *n.* 財務

take up 佔據　　primary 〔'praɪ͵mɛrɪ〕 *adj.* 主要的

in sum 總之

Quit　　　　　**Writing**

A person you know is planning to move to your town or city. What do you think this person would like and dislike about living in your town or city? Why? Use specific reasons and details to develop your essay.

Cut

Paste

Undo

Time

Help
?

Confirm
Answer

Next

24. Advantages and Disadvantages of My Town

Every place has its advantages and disadvantages, including my hometown. A newcomer to my town would find not only several things to enjoy, but also a few drawbacks. Among the good points of my town are the friendly people. The residents here are very kind and will make a new neighbor feel welcome. *Also*, my hometown is very convenient. Stores and businesses keep long hours and the public transportation is very good. *Last but not least*, there are many places to spend leisure time in my town. They range from cinemas and pubs to public parks. Whatever a newcomer's interests might be, I believe he would find something to enjoy in my town.

Unfortunately, there are also a few things about my town that a new neighbor probably wouldn't like. *For example*, because it is a crowded place, it is often noisy here. Someone who is used to the peace of the countryside may be disturbed by the sound of traffic. *In addition*, life here is very fast-paced and competitive. Most people do not have many opportunities to just take it easy. A newcomer might find the pressure difficult to deal with. *And finally*, because I live in a big city, it is necessary to travel to the suburbs or the countryside to really experience nature. *But* despite these disadvantages, I think that anyone who moves to my town will find much to enjoy. *In conclusion*, we should all concentrate on the benefits our living environment provides.

24. 我居住的城鎮的優缺點

　　每個地方有它的優缺點，我的家鄉也不例外。初次到我居住的城鎮的人，可以發現一些不錯的事情，但也會發現一些缺點。關於我的家鄉的優點之一，就是人們很友善，這裏的居民非常親切，而且會讓新搬來的鄰居覺得受歡迎。同時，我的家鄉很方便，商店和公司行號的營業時間都很長，而且大眾運輸也很便利。最後也值得一提的是，在我的家鄉，有很多地方可以消磨休閒時間，從電影院、小酒館，到市立公園都有。無論初來者的興趣是什麼，我相信他在這裏，一定會找到他喜歡的東西。

　　遺憾的是，我的家鄉也有一些新來的鄰居可能會不喜歡的地方。例如，因為這裡十分擁擠，所以常常很吵鬧。習慣鄉村寧靜的人，可能會受到交通噪音的干擾。此外，這裏的生活步調非常快速，而且競爭激烈。大多數的人並沒有很多機會可以放鬆。初來者可能會覺得，要應付這些壓力很困難。最後，因為我住在大城市，所以必須到郊區或鄉下去，才能真正體驗大自然。儘管有這些缺點，我認為任何搬到我的家鄉的人，都能找到許多樂趣。總之，我們應該把注意力，集中在我們的生活環境所具有的優點。

【註釋】

advantage〔əd'væntɪdʒ〕*n.* 優點（= *good point* = benefit〔'bɛnəfɪt〕）

disadvantage〔‚dɪsəd'væntɪdʒ〕*n.* 缺點（= drawback〔'drɔ‚bæk〕）

newcomer〔'njuˈkʌmɚ〕*n.* 新來的人　　resident〔'rɛzədənt〕*n.* 居民

hours〔aʊrz〕*n. pl.*（工作、營業的）時間

last but not least 最後一項要點是　　range〔rendʒ〕*v.*（範圍）包括

unfortunately〔ʌn'fɔrtʃənɪtlɪ〕*adv.* 遺憾的是

crowded〔'kraʊdɪd〕*adj.* 擁擠的　　disturb〔dɪ'stɝb〕*v.* 打擾

in addition 此外　　fast-paced〔'fæst'pest〕*adj.* 步調快速的

competitive〔kəm'pɛtətɪv〕*adj.* 競爭激烈的

take it easy 放輕鬆　　pressure〔'prɛʃɚ〕*n.* 壓力

suburbs〔'sʌbɝbz〕*n. pl.* 郊區　　***in conclusion*** 總之

Quit **Writing**

It has recently been announced that a large shopping center may be built in your neighborhood. Do you support or oppose this plan? Why? Use specific reasons and details to support your answer.

Cut

Paste

Undo

25. A Shopping Center in the Neighborhood

Large shopping centers are very convenient because we can find almost everything we need there. They are also good places to spend free time because they usually offer some form of entertainment such as movie theaters. However, large shopping centers can also bring some disadvantages, and for this reason I would oppose the building of one in my neighborhood.

One disadvantage of having a large shopping center in the neighborhood would be a great increase in traffic. More cars would not only bring traffic congestion, but also noise and parking problems. *Another* disadvantage is that a large shopping center requires a lot of space. In order to build one in my neighborhood, some open space would have to be sacrificed. We might no longer have room for a park or sports ground. *And finally*, if there were a shopping center in the neighborhood, people might visit it every day. They would no doubt spend too much money and ignore other ways of spending their leisure time.

Due to the above disadvantages, I would oppose any plan to build a large shopping center in my neighborhood. Although I enjoy visiting shopping centers on occasion, I don't need to go very often. I would rather spend some time traveling to one than live next door to one. My neighborhood is a peaceful and quiet place and I hope it will stay that way.

25. 住家附近的購物中心

　　大型購物中心非常方便，因為我們在那裏幾乎可以買到所需要的任何東西。大型購物中心也是可以度過閒暇時間的好地方，因為通常會有如電影院等娛樂設施。然而，大型購物中心也有一些缺點，因此，我反對在我們的住家附近興建大型購物中心。

　　住家附近有大型購物中心的缺點之一是，交通流量會大增。車輛增加不僅會造成塞車，也會製造噪音和停車問題。另一個缺點是，大型購物中心需要很大的空間。若要在住家附近興建，勢必要犧牲掉一些空地，那我們就可能不會有公園或運動場的空間了。最後，如果住家附近有大型購物中心，人們可能會天天去，這樣，無疑地會花費過多，並且忽視了其他度過閒暇時間的方式。

　　由於以上的缺點，我反對任何在我們住家附近興建大型購物中心的計劃。雖然我也喜歡偶爾逛逛購物中心，但我不需要常常去。我寧願多花點交通時間去購物中心，也不願住在購物中心隔壁。我們家附近是個寧靜安詳的地方，我希望永遠保持這樣。

【註釋】

neighborhood〔'nebɚ͵hʊd〕*n.* 鄰近地區

entertainment〔͵ɛntɚ'tenmənt〕*n.* 娛樂

disadvantage〔͵dɪsəd'væntɪdʒ〕*n.* 缺點

oppose〔ə'poz〕*v.* 反對（ = *be opposed to* ）

congestion〔kən'dʒɛstʃən〕*n.* 阻塞　　require〔rɪ'kwaɪr〕*v.* 需要

sacrifice〔'sækrə͵faɪs〕*v.* 犧牲　　sports〔sports〕*adj.* 運動的

ignore〔ɪg'nor〕*v.* 忽視

leisure time 空閒時間（ = *free time* ）

on occasion 偶爾（ = *occasionally* = *sometimes* ）

would rather + V_1 + *than* V_2　寧願 V_1，也不願 V_2

Quit **Writing**

It has recently been announced that a new movie theater may be built in your neighborhood. Do you support or oppose this plan? Why? Use specific reasons and details to support your answer.

Cut

Paste

Undo

26. A New Movie Theater

Entertainment is an important part of everyone's life. We all need to take time to relax in order to live healthy lives and do our work efficiently. It is easier to relax when an appropriate form of entertainment is convenient and close by. *Therefore*, I would support a proposal to build a new movie theater in my neighborhood.

Entertainment places can bring some disadvantages to a community such as increased traffic and noise, but I believe the advantages of a new movie theater would outweigh these concerns. *For one thing*, the people in my neighborhood would save time. When they wanted to see a movie they could simply walk to the new theater rather than spend time traveling by bus or car. *In addition*, it would be safer for children to visit a nearby movie theater rather than one in some other part of the city. *And finally*, a new theater might attract other businesses, such as restaurants and coffee shops, where the people of my neighborhood could go to relax.

In short, a new movie theater in the neighborhood would increase the number of entertainment options for the residents. They could enjoy themselves more easily without spending a lot of time traveling to another part of the city. *For these reasons* I would support the building of a movie theater in my neighborhood.

26. 一家新的電影院

娛樂是每個人生活中一個重要的部分，我們全都需要時間放鬆，才能過健康的生活，並有效率地工作。在住家附近有適合而且便利的娛樂設施，能使我們更容易放鬆心情。因此，我贊成在住家附近興建一家新電影院的提議。

娛樂場所會爲社區帶來一些缺點，像是增加交通流量及噪音，但是我認爲新電影院的優點多於缺點。首先，可以節省附近居民的時間，當他們想看電影時，只要走路到電影院，而不需要花時間坐公車或開車。此外，對小孩而言，到附近的電影院，比到市區其他地方的電影院安全許多。最後，一家新的影院可能會吸引其他的商家前來，像是餐廳及咖啡廳，附近居民可以到這些地方輕鬆一下。

簡言之，住家附近興建新的電影院，可以增加居民娛樂上的選擇。居民可以更容易得到娛樂，而不用花很多時間前往其他地方。基於這些理由，我贊成在我的住家附近興建電影院。

【註釋】

entertainment 〔͵ɛntɚˈtenmənt 〕 *n.* 娛樂
appropriate 〔 əˈproprɪɪt 〕 *adj.* 合適的
proposal 〔 prəˈpozḷ 〕 *n.* 提議
disadvantage 〔͵dɪsədˈvæntɪdʒ 〕 *n.* 缺點 (↔ advantage 〔 ədˈvæntɪdʒ 〕)
outweigh 〔 autˈwe 〕 *v.* 勝過　　concern 〔 kənˈsɝn 〕 *n.* 擔心；憂慮
for one thing 首先　　nearby 〔ˈnɪrˈbaɪ 〕 *adj.* 附近的
in addition 此外 (*= besides = furthermore = moreover*)
in short 簡言之 (*= in brief*)　　resident 〔ˈrɛzədənt 〕 *n.* 居民
option 〔ˈɑpʃən 〕 *n.* 選擇

Quit   **Writing**

Do you agree or disagree with the following statement? People should sometimes do things that they do **not** enjoy doing. Use specific reasons and examples to support your answer.

Cut

Paste

Undo

Time

Help
?

Confirm
Answer

Next

27. Doing Things We Don't Enjoy

Everyone has certain likes and dislikes, and there is no denying that we all prefer to do the things that we like. *However*, sometimes

doing things we don't enjoy can be beneficial for us, and sometimes it is necessary. *Therefore*, I agree that people should sometimes do things that they do not enjoy.

One reason is that some of the things we don't enjoy are good for us. *For example*, not everyone likes to exercise, but exercise is good for our health and so we should all do it anyway. *Likewise*, not many people enjoy going to see a dentist or a doctor, but it is good for us to take care of ourselves, so we should all visit dentists and doctors regularly for a checkup. *Another* reason is that, at times, the things we dislike are necessary. Students must take tests in order to complete their studies, and everyone must work in order to make a living. *And finally*, doing things we dislike can also open up new possibilities for us. Most people can probably remember hating a certain food when we were children even though they enjoy that same food now. *So*, when we do things we dislike, we may discover something we do like along the way, or simply find a better way to deal with the things we must do.

No one likes to do things he doesn't enjoy, especially when there is no benefit in doing them. *But* doing things we don't like can be good for us at times, and so I believe that we should sometimes give them a try.

27. 做我們不喜歡做的事

　　每個人都有某些自己喜歡，以及不喜歡的事，而且不可否認的是，我們都比較喜歡做自己喜歡做的事。然而，偶爾做些我們不喜歡做的事，對我們有益，而且有時候這是必要的。因此，我同意人們應該偶爾做些自己不喜歡做的事情。

　　其中一個理由是，有些我們不喜歡的事，是對我們有好處的。例如，並非所有人都喜歡運動，但運動有益健康，所以無論如何，我們都應該做運動。同樣地，大部分的人都不喜歡看牙醫或醫生，但是注意自己的身體健康是件好事，所以我們都應該定期看牙醫及醫生，做健康檢查。另外一個理由是，有時候我們不喜歡的事情卻是必須要做的。學生必須考試才能完成學業，而每個人都必須工作才能謀生。最後一個理由是，做我們不喜歡的事情，能夠提供自己新的可能性。大部份的人可能都記得，自己小時候很討厭某種食物，雖然現在很愛吃那種食物。所以，當我們在做自己不喜歡的事情時，我們可能在做的過程中，發現自己喜歡的事，或者就找到更好的方法，來應付我們必須做的事。

　　沒有人喜歡做自己不喜歡的事，特別是從中得不到好處的時候。但是有時候，做我們不喜歡的事情卻對我們有好處，因此，我認為，我們有時候應該試試看不愛做的事。

【註釋】

likes and dislikes （個人的）喜好及厭惡
there is no V-ing …是不可能的（ = *it is impossible to + V.* ）
deny〔dɪˋnaɪ〕*v.* 否認　　beneficial〔ˏbɛnəˋfɪʃəl〕*adj.* 有益的 < *to* >
likewise〔ˋlaɪkˏwaɪz〕*adv.* 同樣地（ = *similarly* = *in the same way* ）
regularly〔ˋrɛgjələlɪ〕*adv.* 定期地　　checkup〔ˋtʃɛkˏʌp〕*n.* 健康檢查
at times 偶爾（ = *sometimes* = *occasionally* ）
make a living 謀生（ = *earn a living* ）
open up 提供　　benefit〔ˋbɛnəfɪt〕*n.* 好處

Quit　　　**Writing**

Do you agree or disagree with the following statement? Television, newspapers, magazines, and other media pay too much attention to the personal lives of famous people such as public figures and celebrities. Use specific reasons and details to explain your opinion.

Cut

Paste

Undo

Time

Help Confirm Next

28. The Media and Famous People

In almost every form of media, including television, newspapers and magazines, a great deal of attention is paid to the personal lives of celebrities. It seems that the public cannot get enough of this kind of news. *However*, I believe that the media have a responsibility to present a balanced view of the world, as well as respect the lives of public figures. *Therefore*, I believe that the media pay too much attention to the personal lives of famous people.

For people who are fascinated with the lives of public figures there are some forms of media devoted exclusively to this topic. They can satisfy their curiosity by buying fan magazines and watching TV shows devoted to entertainment news. The general media should present all types of information because people have different interests. *Furthermore*, the practice of dwelling on the private lives of celebrities can lead people to pay more attention to these matters than they otherwise would. Perhaps *most importantly*, the media should respect the privacy of every individual, including public figures. They may have chosen to be in the public eye, but that does not give the public the right to know everything about them. *Moreover*, many stories about celebrities are untrue; they are only gossip reported to increase sales of magazines and other media. They are unfair to the famous and mislead the public.

For all of these reasons, I believe that the media should pay more attention to matters other than the private lives of public figures. In this way, they can appeal to a wider audience and encourage people to develop other interests. *In my opinion*, the media currently pay too much attention to the private lives of public figures.

28. 媒體與名人

　　幾乎每一種媒體，包括電視、報紙及雜誌，都把許多焦點放在名人的私生活上。一般大衆似乎對這種新聞一直很感興趣。然而，我認爲媒體有責任，以公正無偏袒的觀點報導時事，以及尊重公衆人物的生活。因此，我認爲媒體的確過度關注名人的私生活。

　　因爲有些人對於公衆人物的私生活十分著迷，所以有些媒體就專做這個主題。藉由購買針對歌迷或影迷所發行的雜誌，和觀看電視節目的娛樂新聞，就能滿足這些歌迷或影迷的好奇心。一般媒體應該提供所有類型的資訊，因爲人們的興趣各不相同。此外，老是強調名人私生活，會使人們比平常更注意這些事情。或許最重要的是，媒體應該尊重個人的隱私，包括公衆人物的隱私。他們可能選擇公開露面或上傳播媒體，但那並不表示，大衆有權利知道他們的一切。此外，許多關於名人的報導並不眞實；那些報導只不過是被用來增加雜誌銷售量，以及其他媒體業績的八卦傳聞。那些不實的報導不僅對名人不公平，也會誤導大衆。

　　基於這些理由，我認爲媒體應該多注意公衆人物私生活以外的事情。如此一來，媒體就能吸引更廣大的觀衆群，並且鼓勵人們培養其他的興趣。依我之見，目前的媒體的確過度關注公衆人物及他們的私生活。

【註釋】

celebrity〔sə'lɛbrətɪ〕*n.* 名人　　balanced〔'bælənst〕*adj.* 平衡的

figure〔'fɪgjɚ〕*n.* 人物　　fascinate〔'fæsn̩ˏet〕*v.* 使著迷

devoted〔dɪ'votɪd〕*adj.* 專用的 < *to* >

exclusively〔ɪk'sklusɪvlɪ〕*adv.* 專有地；單獨地

curiosity〔ˏkjʊrɪ'asətɪ〕*n.* 好奇心　　***dwell on*** 老是想著；強調

privacy〔'praɪvəsɪ〕*n.* 隱私（權）

individual〔ˏɪndə'vɪdʒʊəl〕*n.* 個人

in the public eye （人）常在公開場合露面；在傳媒上頻頻出現

story〔'storɪ〕*n.* 報導　　gossip〔'gasəp〕*n.* 流言

mislead〔mɪs'lid〕*v.* 誤導　　***other than*** 除了（= *except*）

currently〔'kɝəntlɪ〕*adv.* 目前

Quit	**Writing**

Some people believe that the Earth is being harmed (damaged) by human activity. Others feel that human activity makes the Earth a better place to live. What is your opinion? Use specific reasons and examples to support your answer.

Cut

Paste

Undo

Time		Help	Confirm	Next
		?	Answer	→

29. Human Activity and the Earth

There is no doubt that human activity has an effect on the planet. We see the evidence of mankind's endeavors all around us. While some of man's accomplishments, such as the building of transportation systems and the consistent supply of potable water, have made Earth a better place for people to live, they have not come without cost. *Overall*, it seems that human activity harms the Earth more than it benefits it.

For example, the transportation systems that benefit mankind also create pollution and use up valuable energy resources. While we cannot do without transportation these days, we cannot ignore the fact that it has an adverse effect on the planet. *Furthermore*, those advances that benefit people do not benefit all the life on Earth. Deforestation endangers many animals, and mankind's great thirst for water and other resources leads to the extinction of many plant forms. *In addition*, accomplishments such as the supply of potable water to a community are only responses to problems that mankind created in the past. It was man that made the water unfit to drink in the first place. *Finally*, the damage that human activity causes will eventually have a negative effect on people. They will also suffer the effects of pollution and diminishing natural resources.

In conclusion, it seems apparent that man's activity benefits primarily himself, not the Earth. *Moreover*, those benefits are only short-term advantages, and man will also suffer the negative effects of his activity in the future. The Earth does not have an inexhaustible supply of resources, so every effort should be made to conserve resources and limit the impact of human activity on the planet.

29. 人類活動與地球

　　人類活動無疑會對地球造成影響。人類努力的證據，我們在周遭隨處可見。雖然人類有些成就，如運輸系統的建立，以及飲用水持續的供應等，使得地球成爲一個更適合人類居住的地方，但這些成就的完成，也付出了代價。大體而言，對地球而言，人類的活動似乎弊多於利。

　　例如，運輸系統對人類有利，卻會製造污染，並用盡珍貴的能源。現在我們雖然不能沒有運輸工具，卻也不能忽視，運輸工具會對地球有不良影響的事實。此外，使人類獲益的這些進步，不一定能使地球上所有生物都獲益。砍伐森林危及許多動物，而人類對水和其他資源的需求極大，因而導致許多植物絕種。再者，像供應社區飲水的這類成就，就只是人類在爲過去所製造的問題，做出回應而已。首先使得水不適合飲用的，就是人類自己。最後，人類活動所導致的損害，終究會對人類本身產生負面的影響。污染及日益減少的天然資源所造成的影響，也會使人類受害。

　　總之，人類的活動顯然主要只對人類自己有利，但卻對地球不利。而且，那些益處是短暫的，將來人類還是會因自己的行爲所造成的負面影響而受害。地球上的資源，並不是取之不盡、用之不竭的，所以我們應該要盡全力保存資源，限制人類活動對地球的衝擊。

【註釋】

consistent〔kən'sɪstənt〕adj. 一致的；持續不斷的

potable〔'potəbḷ〕adj. 可飲用的

overall〔,ovə'ɔl〕adv. 大體而言；整體地　　***use up*** 用完

cannot do without 不能沒有　　adverse〔əd'vɝs〕adj. 不利的

deforestation〔dɪ,fɔrɪs'teʃən〕n. 砍伐森林

endanger〔ɪn'dendʒɚ〕v. 危害　　thirst〔θɝst〕n. 渴望 < *for* >

extinction〔ɪk'stɪŋkʃən〕n. 絕種

response〔rɪ'spɑns〕n. 回應 < *to* >　　diminish〔də'mɪnɪʃ〕v. 減少

apparent〔ə'pɛrənt〕adj. 明顯的　　short-term〔'ʃɔrt'tɝm〕adj. 短期的

inexhaustible〔,ɪnɪg'zɔstəbḷ〕adj. 取之不竭的；無窮盡的

Quit　　　　　　**Writing**

It has recently been announced that a new high school may be built in your community. Do you support or oppose this plan? Why? Use specific reasons and details in your answer.

Cut

Paste

Undo

30. A New High School in the Community

Education is a top priority for every society, and the better the educational facilities are, the more likely it is that students will succeed. Their success will in turn be of benefit to the society as a whole. Because I support investment in education, I would welcome a new high school in my community. *Furthermore*, I believe a high school would benefit the community in the following ways.

First, the students who live in my community would no longer have to travel very far to attend school. This would save them a great deal of time, which they could then spend studying, relaxing, or helping their families. *Second*, with a redistribution of students between the school they used to go to and the new high school, both schools would be less crowded. This would enable students to receive more personal attention and a higher quality of education. *Third*, a high school can offer many advantages to the community as a whole. Residents may use some of its facilities, such as the sports ground, or attend concerts and other events in the auditorium.

In conclusion, I believe that a new high school would benefit any community. It would help not only the students and their families, but also other residents of the neighborhood. *Therefore*, I would wholeheartedly support the building of a new high school in my neighborhood.

30. 在社區裏興建新的高中

　　對每個社會來說，教育都是最優先考量的事，而且教育設備愈好，學生就愈有可能成功，而他們的成功對社會整體而言，必然是有利的。因為我支持投資教育，所以我會歡迎在我的社區內興建新的高中。此外，我認為一所高中在以下幾個方面，都對社區有利。

　　第一，住在社區裏的學生，不需要再到很遠的地方上學，這將會讓他們節省很多時間，而他們可以用這些時間讀書、放鬆，或幫忙家人。第二，由於他們以前唸的學校和新學校之間的學生會重新分配，這兩所學校將不再那麼擁擠，這會讓學生能夠得到更多的個人關注，以及品質較高的教育。第三，整體而言，興建一所高中，可以提供社區很多好處，居民可以使用學校的設施，如運動場，或是在禮堂參加音樂會或其他活動。

　　總之，我認為新的高中對任何社區都有利，它不但可以使學生及其家人獲益，還可有嘉惠鄰近地區的居民。因此，我由衷地支持，在我們住家附近興建新的高中。

【註釋】

community〔kə'mjunətɪ〕*n.* 社區
priority〔praɪ'ɔrətɪ〕*n.* 優先的事
facilities〔fə'sɪlətɪz〕*n. pl.* 設施　　***in turn*** 必然也
as a whole 整體而言　　investment〔ɪn'vɛstmənt〕*n.* 投資
benefit〔'bɛnəfɪt〕*v.* 使獲益　　furthermore〔'fɜðɚ,mor〕*adv.* 此外
travel〔'trævl̩〕*v.* 前進　　***a great deal of*** 大量的
redistribution〔,ridɪstrə'bjuʃən〕*n.* 重新分配　　***used to*** 以前
crowded〔'kraudɪd〕*adj.* 擁擠的　　quality〔'kwɑlətɪ〕*n.* 品質
advantage〔əd'væntɪdʒ〕*n.* 優點　　resident〔'rɛzədənt〕*n.* 居民
sports ground 運動場　　auditorium〔,ɔdə'torɪəm〕*n.* 禮堂
in conclusion 總之　　neighborhood〔'nebɚ,hud〕*n.* 鄰近地區
wholeheartedly〔'hol'hɑrtɪdlɪ〕*adv.* 由衷地；全心全意地

Writing

Some people spend their entire lives in one place. Others move a number of times throughout their lives, looking for a better job, house, community, or even climate. Which do you prefer: staying in one place or moving in search of another place? Use reasons and specific examples to support your opinion.

Cut

Paste

Undo

Time

Help
?

Confirm
Answer

Next
➡

31. Staying in One Place

It is often said that the grass is always greener on the other side of the fence. Perhaps this is why some people frequently move around, looking for better jobs, houses, and so on. ***No doubt*** it is possible to make some advances in this way, but I believe that staying in one place and putting down roots in a community also has many advantages. That is why I would prefer to spend my life in one place rather than constantly move around in search of a new home.

One advantage of spending a lifetime in the same community is that people can put down roots and enjoy long relationships with their friends and neighbors. As these relationships mature, the neighbors will come to trust and depend on each other more. In such a community, one never needs to worry when in trouble; someone is bound to give a hand. ***Another*** advantage is that people who live their lives in the same community care more about the neighborhood and work hard to improve it. This creates a nicer place for everyone to live. ***Finally***, while we should never stop trying to improve ourselves, it is sometimes better to appreciate the advantages we already have than constantly seek more. A person who is always seeking will never be content.

In brief, I would prefer to have a permanent home in one community rather than constantly uproot myself and my family in search of something better. I believe that when we care about the place where we live we can always find a way to improve it and ourselves. In the future I will remember to appreciate the grass on my side of the fence.

31. 一直住在同一個地方

　　人們常說，鄰家芳草綠，隔岸風景好，或許這就是有些人會經常到處搬家，尋找比較好的工作或住所等的原因。無疑地，這樣做可能會有所改善，但我認為，待在一個地方，在某個社區落地生根，也有很多優點。這就是為什麼我寧願一輩子住在同一個地方，而不願不斷地搬來搬去，尋找新家的原因。

　　一輩子住在同一個社區有個優點，那就是可以落地生根，享有和朋友、鄰居之間長久的關係。當這些關係成熟時，鄰居之間會更互相信任、互相依賴。在這樣一個社區中，有困難時也不必擔心，因為一定有人會願意伸出援手。另一個好處是，永久居住在同一個社區中，我們會更關心住家附近的環境，並努力加以改善，而這樣便能創造更好的居住環境。最後，雖然我們應該不停地努力自我改進，但有時候，欣賞我們自己已經有的優點，勝過不斷地追求更多優點。一個一直在追尋的人，是永遠不會滿足的。

　　簡言之，我寧願在一個社區裏建立永遠的家，而不願為了尋求更好的地方，帶著自己和家人不斷地搬家。我相信，當我們關心自己居住的地方時，我們總能找到改善住家，以及改進自己的方法。將來我會記得，要懂得欣賞自己家裡這邊的草。

【註釋】

grass〔græs〕*n.* 草　　fence〔fɛns〕*n.* 籬笆
The grass is always greener on the other side of the fence.
【諺】鄰家芳草綠；隔岸風景好；外國的月亮比較圓。
move around 四處搬遷　　advance〔əd'væns〕*n.* 進步
put down roots 落地生根
prefer to + V_1 + ***rather than*** + V_2 寧願 V_1，也不願 V_2
constantly〔'kɑnstəntlɪ〕*adv.* 不斷地　　***in search of*** 尋找
mature〔mə'tʃur, mə'tʃur〕*v.* 成熟　　***be bound to*** + *V.* 一定
give a hand 幫忙　　content〔kən'tɛnt〕*adj.* 滿足的
in brief 簡言之（= *in short*）　　permanent〔'pɜmənənt〕*adj.* 永久的
uproot〔ʌp'rut〕*v.* 連根拔起；遷移他處居住

Writing

Quit

Is it better to enjoy your money when you earn it or is it better to save your money for some time in the future? Use specific reasons and examples to support your opinion.

Cut

Paste

Undo

Time

Help
?

Confirm
Answer

Next

32. **The Advantages of Saving Money**

Everyone must work to live, but many people are fortunate enough to make more money than they immediately need. What should they do with this extra income? While it is tempting for people to spend it all on things they desire, I believe it is better to save at least a portion of the extra income for the future.

By saving money, people give themselves more security. They cannot predict the future; perhaps one day they will be jobless. At a time like this their savings can spare them a great deal of suffering and help to see them through the hard time. *In addition*, saving money allows people to build up a larger sum. They can then buy something more worthwhile than the small things they can buy if they spend the money right away. *For example*, they may be able to buy a house with their savings. *Finally*, the practice of saving helps people develop the habit of setting goals and planning for their future. In this way they are bound to lead more meaningful and successful lives.

Most people would like to enjoy their money immediately. Nobody likes to wait for the things that he wants. *However*, if we learn to save our money, we can gain more advantages in the future. We will lead more secure and, thus, happier lives. We will also be able to buy the things we truly want but cannot afford right now.

32. 存錢的好處

　　每個人都必須工作以求生存，但是有許多人很幸運，能夠賺得比他們立即需要的還多。他們應該如何處理這些額外的收入呢？儘管把錢全花在自己想買的東西上是很誘人的，但我認為最好至少把一部分的額外收入存起來，以備將來之需。

　　藉由存錢，人們能獲得更多的安全感。未來是無法預測的，或許有一天，我們會失業，碰到像這樣的情況，存款可以讓我們免去許多痛苦，幫助我們度過難關。此外，存錢使人可以累積較大筆的錢，可以買更有價值的東西，比馬上把錢花掉所能買到的東西更有用。例如，我們可以用存款買房子。最後，存錢能幫助我們培養設定目標及為未來作計畫的習慣。如此一來，我們一定會過著更有意義，並且更成功的生活。

　　大部分的人會想要馬上享用手邊的錢。沒有人想等到以後再買想要的東西。然而，如果我們學會存錢，未來可以獲得更多的好處。我們將過著更有安全感，而且更快樂的生活。我們也能購買我們真正想要，但現在無法負擔的東西。

【註釋】

immediately〔ɪˋmidɪɪtlɪ〕*adv.* 立刻

extra〔ˋɛkstrə〕*adj.* 額外的　　*do with* 處理

tempting〔ˋtɛmptɪŋ〕*adj.* 誘人的　　portion〔ˋporʃən〕*n.* 部分

security〔sɪˋkjʊrətɪ〕*n.* 安全感　　predict〔prɪˋdɪkt〕*v.* 預測

savings〔ˋsevɪŋz〕*n. pl.* 存款　　spare〔spɛr〕*v.* 免除

see through 幫助…度過　　*in addition* 此外

build up 增加　　sum〔sʌm〕*n.* 金錢　　*right away* 立即

practice〔ˋpræktɪs〕*n.* 習慣　　*be bound to* + *V.* 一定

lead a ~ life 過~生活　　meaningful〔ˋminɪŋfḷ〕*adj.* 有意義的

secure〔sɪˋkjʊr〕*adj.* 安全的　　afford〔əˋford〕*v.* 負擔得起

Quit	**Writing**	

You have received a gift of money. The money is enough to buy either a piece of jewelry you like or tickets to a concert you want to attend. Which would you buy? Use specific reasons and details to support your answer.

Cut

Paste

Undo

Time

Help
?

Confirm
Answer

Next

33. A Gift of Money

Like many people, I can think of several things I would like to buy if I had a little extra money. Should I receive a gift of money, it would be difficult to decide what to do with it. However, given the choice of buying a piece of jewelry or concert tickets, I would choose the former.

One reason for my decision is that if the piece of jewelry is very special, I may not be able to find another like it. If someone bought it before I did, it would be lost to me forever. Concerts, *on the other hand*, occur frequently, and I would surely have another chance to attend one in the future. *Another* important reason is that jewelry is long-lasting. It is an investment that will appreciate in value over the years, while the concert tickets will have no value once the show is over. *Most importantly*, I would be able to enjoy the piece of jewelry every day, whereas I could attend the concert only once.

The above reasons are why I would choose to purchase a piece of jewelry rather than attend a concert. Although I like both choices, jewelry is unique, longer-lasting and more valuable. Jewelry is always a good investment to make when we have a little extra money.

33. 別人送的一筆錢

　　和很多人一樣，如果我有一些額外的錢，我會想到好幾樣我想買的東西。如果別人送我一筆錢，我很難決定要如何處置這筆錢。然而，如果要在一件珠寶和演唱會門票之間作抉擇，我會選擇前者。

　　我做這個決定的理由是，如果這件珠寶非常特殊，我可能再也找不到一樣的了。如果有人早我一步買走，我可能就永遠失去它了。另一方面，演唱會經常舉行，以後我一定會有機會參加。還有一個重要的理由是，珠寶的價值是持久性的，買珠寶是種投資，幾年後珠寶會增值，而演唱會一旦結束了，門票就沒有價值了。最重要的是，我可以每天欣賞這件珠寶，但演唱會只能參加那麼一次而已。

　　上述就是為什麼我會選擇購買一件珠寶，而不是參加演唱會的理由。雖然我兩者都喜歡，但珠寶是獨特的，較能持久，而且更有價值。當我們有一點多餘的錢時，珠寶絕對是不錯的投資。

【註釋】

extra〔'ɛkstrə〕*adj.* 額外的　　should〔ʃud〕*aux.* 萬一

do with 處理　　given〔'gɪvən〕*prep.* 假如

jewelry〔'dʒuəlrɪ〕*n.* 珠寶

the former （兩者中）前者（↔ *the latter* ）

on the other hand 另一方面　　occur〔ə'kɝ〕*v.* 發生；出現

attend〔ə'tɛnd〕*v.* 參加　　long-lasting〔'lɔŋ'læstɪŋ〕*adj.* 持久的

investment〔ɪn'vɛstəmənt〕*n.* 投資

appreciate〔ə'priʃɪ,et〕*v.* 增值　　value〔'vælju〕*n.* 價值

whereas〔hwɛr'æz〕*conj.* 然而（= *while* ）

purchase〔'pɝtʃəs〕*v.* 購買　　unique〔ju'nik〕*adj.* 獨特的

Quit　　　**Writing**

Businesses should hire employees for their entire lives. Do you agree or disagree? Use specific reasons and examples to support your answer.

▲

Cut

Paste

Undo

▼

34. Lifetime Employment

Lifetime employment, guaranteeing employees a job for their entire working lives, was once common in some countries, such as Japan. The policy was seen as a means to promote loyalty among employees. If they saw their company as a paternal figure, they would be more likely to support its decisions without question and work hard for its success, or so the reasoning went. However, this business policy was proved to be impractical in the long-term, and I do not believe that companies should offer lifetime employment today.

Due to the rapid developments in most industries today, it is necessary for companies to remain on the cutting edge. If they offer lifetime employment, they may have no room in the organization for new members who possess the latest skills and knowledge. *Furthermore*, constant promotion means that such firms are often top-heavy with managers and do not efficiently utilize the managers' skills. *Finally*, there is the danger that employees, knowing that they are unlikely to be replaced, would become complacent and no longer work as hard or make an effort to improve their skills.

It is my belief that the time for guaranteed lifetime employment has passed. In the past, it seemed to work in young industries where there was a lot of room for growth. *But* in today's more competitive economy, it is no longer feasible. Companies cannot guarantee employment and remain flexible and innovative enough to succeed. *And* if they fail, there will be no employment for anyone.

34. 終身雇用

終身雇用能保障員工的職業，在某些國家曾經很普遍，例如日本。這項政策被視為是提升員工忠誠度的方法。如果員工將公司視為父親般的形象，就比較可能會毫無疑問地支持公司的決策，並努力工作，為公司創造成功，這是日本人以前的想法。然而，這項企業政策長期以來，被證明是不切實際的，我也認為現在公司不應該提供終身雇用的保障。

由於現今大部分企業的快速發展，公司必須保持領先的地位，如果提供終身雇用的保障，那公司的組織就沒有空間，讓擁有最新技術及知識的新成員加入。此外，不斷的升遷就意味著，這樣的公司常是頭重腳輕，經理級的人物很多，但他們的技術卻無法有效率地運用。最後，還有一項危險是，員工知道自己不可能被取代，可能會變得自滿，而不再如往常般認真工作，或努力改進自己的技術。

我認為有終身雇用保障的時代已經過去了，在過去，這項政策在那些成長空間還很大的新興行業中，似乎行得通。但在今日競爭更為激烈的經濟情況中，這項政策已不再可行了。公司不可能在保障員工職業的同時，還能夠保持足夠的彈性和不斷創新，以獲得成功。而且如果公司垮了，那麼大家就都會失業了。

【註釋】

lifetime employment 終身雇用　guarantee〔ˌgærənˈti〕v. 保證
means〔minz〕n. 方法；手段　promote〔prəˈmot〕v. 提升
loyalty〔ˈlɔɪəltɪ〕n. 忠誠　paternal〔pəˈtɝnḷ〕adj. 父親般的
figure〔ˈfɪgjə〕n. 人物；形象　reasoning〔ˈriznɪŋ〕n. 推理；理論
impractical〔ɪmˈpræktɪkḷ〕adj. 不實際的
long-term〔ˈlɔŋˌtɝm〕adj. 長期的　**cutting edge** 領先的地位
possess〔pəˈzɛs〕v. 擁有　promotion〔prəˈmoʃən〕n. 升遷
top-heavy〔ˈtɑpˌhɛvɪ〕adj. 頭重腳輕的　utilize〔ˈjutḷˌaɪz〕v. 利用
complacent〔kəmˈplesṇt〕adj. 自滿的
competitive〔kəmˈpɛtətɪv〕adj. 競爭激烈的
feasible〔ˈfizəbḷ〕adj. 可行的　flexible〔ˈflɛksəbḷ〕adj. 有彈性的
innovative〔ˈɪnoˌvetɪv〕adj. 創新的

Quit

Writing

Do you agree or disagree with the following statement? Attending a live performance (for example, a play, concert, or sporting event) is more enjoyable than watching the same event on television. Use specific reasons and examples to support your opinion.

Cut

Paste

Undo

35. Attending a Live Performance

As a student, I don't often have the chance to go to a live performance. *But* when I do, I enjoy it very much. Some people prefer to stay home and watch events on television because they believe that it is more comfortable, less expensive and safer. *But* I don't agree.

In my opinion, it is much better to see a play, concert or game in person for three main reasons. *Most importantly*, I enjoy the atmosphere of a live performance. Nothing can replace the energy of the crowd or the fun of being with so many people. *Next*, seeing an event live makes it a special occasion. You can always see your favorite singer on MTV or catch a game on ESPN. Going out is what makes it an event. *Finally*, when I go to a performance I am not distracted by anything else. There is no homework waiting for me in the next room and no little brother trying to change the TV channel.

In conclusion, I prefer going to a live event to watching it at home. Although it costs a bit more money, I believe it is worth it. The experience becomes a wonderful memory that I will have all my life.

35. 觀賞現場表演

　　身為學生，我不常有機會觀賞現場演出。但每當有機會觀賞時，我都會覺得很高興。有些人比較喜歡待在家裡看電視轉播，因為他們認為這樣比較舒適、比較不花錢，也比較安全。但是我不同意。

　　在我看來，親自到現場觀賞戲劇表演、演唱會或比賽，會比較好，主要原因有三點。最重要的是，我喜歡現場表演的氣氛。觀眾的熱情以及和許多人一同觀賞的樂趣，是其他東西所無法取代的。第二，現場觀看使得活動本身成為一種特別的場合。你隨時都可以在 MTV 頻道上，看到自己最喜愛的歌手，或是在 ESPN 體育台看球賽。就是因為在現場，所以才這麼令人高興。最後，到現場觀看演出，我就不會因為受到任何事物的影響而分心。沒有功課在隔壁房間等我寫完，也沒有弟弟一直要轉台。

　　總之，我比較喜歡到現場觀看，勝過在家裡看轉播。雖然錢會花得比較多一點，但是我相信那是值得的。現場觀看的經驗，將成為我一輩子都可以擁有的美好回憶。

【註釋】

　　live〔laɪv〕*adj.* 現場的

　　event〔ɪˋvɛnt〕*n.* 事件；（比賽、節目中的）項目；大事；令人高興的事

　　in one's opinion 依某人之見　　*in person* 親自；本人

　　atmosphere〔ˋætməsˏfɪr〕*n.* 氣氛

　　replace〔rɪˋples〕*v.* 取代　　energy〔ˋɛnədʒɪ〕*n.* 活力

　　crowd〔kraud〕*n.* 人群　　occasion〔əˋkeʒən〕*n.* 場合；大事

　　catch〔kætʃ〕*v.* 沒錯過；收看

　　MTV 音樂電視（節目）(= *Music Television*)

　　ESPN ESPN 體育台 (= *Entertainment and Sports Programming Network*)　　distract〔dɪˋstrækt〕*v.* 使分心

　　channel〔ˋtʃænḷ〕*n.* 頻道　　*in conclusion* 總之

　　prefer + V₁-ing + to + V₂-ing 喜歡 V_1 甚於 V_2

　　a bit 有點 (= *a little bit*)　　memory〔ˋmɛmərɪ〕*n.* 回憶

Quit　　　**Writing**

Choose **one** of the following transportation vehicles and explain why you think it has changed people's lives.
- automobiles
- bicycles
- airplanes

Use specific reasons and examples to support your answer.

▲

Cut

Paste

Undo

▼

36. The Automobile

The invention of the automobile has had a great effect on society. Although automobiles are not important in the daily life of every country, they are widely used in most developed societies. *In my opinion*, they have played a significant role in this development and have greatly affected the culture as well.

Before the automobile, goods and people were often transported by train or horse-drawn wagon. *However*, the trains did not run everywhere and horses were slow and could carry only limited loads. People rarely traveled far from home unless it was a necessity. Then the automobile made it possible for people to travel door-to-door at a reasonable speed and in relative comfort. This in turn made society more mobile. Traveling was no longer a time-consuming, uncomfortable ordeal and so many more people were willing to travel regularly from their hometowns.

The automobile also contributed to development in other areas. With its invention came a new form of manufacturing — the assembly line. This more efficient process forever changed the way that work was done. *In addition*, the automobile was a great labor and time-saving device, giving its owners more leisure time. Leisure pursuits, no longer solely for the very rich, became more important in developed countries. *In my opinion*, the automobile played an important role in equalizing society.

36. 汽　車

　　汽車的發明，對社會具有重大的影響。雖然汽車在各國的日常生活中，並非都是很重要的，但在大多數已開發社會中，汽車是很普遍的。我認為汽車在社會的發展方面，扮演著重要的角色，並且對文化也有相當大的影響。

　　在汽車發明之前，運送貨物和人，通常要靠火車或是馬車。可是火車並不是每個地方都有，而馬車的速度慢，載貨量也有限，所以除非必要，人們很少出遠門。後來，汽車讓人們可以直接到達目的地，速度較合理，而且也比較舒適。這種現象讓整個社會動了起來，因為旅行不再是耗費時間，而且又不舒服的折磨，所以有比較多的人，願意定期離開家鄉到別的地方。

　　汽車也促進了其他方面的發展。隨著汽車的發明，產生了一種新的生產模式 ── 裝配線，這種更有效率的製造過程，造成生產方式永久性的改變。此外，汽車這項發明，大大地節省了勞力和時間，讓汽車的擁有者有更多的空閒時間。消遣娛樂在已開發國家已愈來愈重要，不再只是很有錢的人才有的專利。我認為，汽車在促進社會平等這方面，扮演了很重要的角色。

【註釋】

automobile〔ˈɔtəməˌbil〕*n.* 汽車　　draw〔drɔ〕*v.* 拉

wagon〔ˈwægən〕*n.* 四輪馬車　　load〔lod〕*n.* 一車的載運量

door-to-door〔ˈdortəˈdor〕*adv.* 門到門地　　***in turn*** 必然也

mobile〔ˈmobḷ〕*adj.* 流動的

time-consuming〔ˈtaɪmkənˌsjumɪŋ〕*adj.* 費時的

ordeal〔ɔrˈdil〕*n.* 折磨　　***be willing to*** + ***V.*** 願意

regularly〔ˈrɛgjələ·lɪ〕*adv.* 定期地

contribute〔kənˈtrɪbjut〕*v.* 貢獻；有助於

manufacturing〔ˌmænjəˈfæktʃərɪŋ〕*n.* 製造業

assembly line（工廠的）裝配線　　pursuit〔pɚˈsut〕*n.* 消遣

solely〔ˈsollɪ〕*adv.* 唯一地　　developed〔dɪˈvɛləpt〕*adj.* 已開發的

equalize〔ˈikwəlˌaɪz〕*v.* 使平等

Quit   **Writing**

Do you agree or disagree that progress is always good? Use specific reasons and examples to support your answer.

▲

Cut

Paste

Undo

▼

Time

Help **?**

Confirm Answer

Next ➡

37. **Is Progress Always Good?**

It is impossible to stop the march of time, and likewise, it is impossible to stop progress. There is no doubt that progress has brought us many wonderful things, such as convenience, improved health, and more leisure time. ***However***, everything has its drawbacks and so I do not believe that we can say that progress is always good.

For example, while progress has brought us many time-saving machines, it has also brought us pollution. We can now live more convenient and productive lives, but our quality of life is reduced by the polluted environment. ***Another*** drawback of progress is that while progress has made it easier for us to work and to obtain more things, it has also made us want more things. When a product is invented or improved upon, people immediately feel that their old possessions are no longer good enough. This leads us to be continually dissatisfied. ***Finally***, progress has changed the way we live and the way we relate to other people. Some inventions, such as the telephone, make it unnecessary for people to meet face-to-face. ***And*** because of television, fewer people spend their free time talking or doing things together. Progress has made our society more impersonal.

These are just a few examples of the drawbacks of progress. That is not to say that we should fight against progress, for it brings us many wonderful advantages as well. We should simply be aware of the effects that progress has on us and strive to diminish its negative influences. ***After all***, progress is inevitable.

37. 進步一定是好的嗎？

　　要時間停下腳步是不可能的，同樣地，要阻止進步也是不可能的。無疑地，進步帶給我們許多很棒的好處，如方便、健康狀況改善，和有更多的閒暇時間。然而，凡事皆有缺點，所以我認為，我們不能說進步一定是好的。

　　例如，雖然進步帶給我們許多省時的機器，但也為我們帶來污染。我們現在的生活過得更加便利，生產力也提高了，但我們的生活品質，卻因環境受到污染而降低。進步的另一個缺點是，雖然進步使我們工作更輕鬆，更容易獲得更多東西，但也使我們想得到更多。當新產品被發明出來，或經過改良，人們立刻就覺得，自己所擁有的舊東西不夠好，這樣會使我們一直覺得不滿足。最後，進步改變了我們的生活方式，以及和別人的相處之道。有些發明，例如電話，使得人們不需要面對面交談，而且因為有了電視，較少人會把空閒時間用來和其他人一起聊天，或從事活動。進步已經使我們的社會，變得比較沒有人情味。

　　這些例子只是一些進步所帶來的缺點，但這並不表示，我們就應該對抗進步，因為它也帶給我們許多很棒的優點。我們只是應該注意進步對我們的影響，並努力減少其負面的影響。畢竟，進步是不可避免的。

【註釋】

progress〔'prɑgrɛs〕*n.* 進步　　march〔mɑrtʃ〕*n.* 行進

likewise〔'laɪk‚waɪz〕*adv.* 同樣地　　drawback〔'drɔ‚bæk〕*n.* 缺點

leisure time 空閒時間　　time-saving〔'taɪm‚sevɪŋ〕*adj.* 節省時間的

productive〔prə'dʌktɪv〕*adj.* 有生產力的　　obtain〔əb'ten〕*v.* 獲得

improve upon 對…加以改良（＝*improve on*）

possession〔pə'zɛʃən〕*n.* 所有物

dissatisfied〔dɪs'sætɪs‚faɪd〕*adj.* 不滿足的

relate〔rɪ'let〕*v.* 相處＜ *to* ＞

impersonal〔ɪm'pɜsṇḷ〕*adj.* 沒有人情味的　　***fight against*** 對抗

be aware of 知道；察覺到　　strive〔straɪv〕*v.* 努力

diminish〔də'mɪnɪʃ〕*v.* 減少　　negative〔'nɛgətɪv〕*adj.* 負面的

inevitable〔ɪn'ɛvətəbḷ〕*adj.* 不可避免的

Writing

Quit

Learning about the past has no value for those of us living in the present. Do you agree or disagree? Use specific reasons and examples to support your answer.

Cut

Paste

Undo

Time

Help
?

Confirm
Answer

Next

38. **Learning from the Past**

In these fast-paced times it seems that we are always looking toward the future, planning and hoping for a better tomorrow. It is true that advances are being made very quickly these days in almost every field, making it almost a full-time job just to keep up. *However*, none of these advances would have been possible without steps made in the past. *Therefore*, I disagree with the statement that learning about the past has no value for those of us in the present.

In my opinion, the past holds many lessons for us. If we neglect to learn about our past, we may unnecessarily repeat mistakes that our forefathers have already made. Most people would agree that we should learn from our mistakes. I further propose that we should learn from the mistakes of others. *Another* reason to study the past is that we can build upon the achievements of those who came before us. There is no need to repeat basic research or to reinvent the wheel. *Instead*, we should learn from the accomplishments made in the past and then improve upon them. *And last but not least*, the past has something very important to teach us about our culture and who we are. If we do not learn the values and beliefs of our ancestors, how can we pass them on to our children? If we do not study our past, we may lose our culture.

In our continual efforts to create a better future, it is some-times easy to forget about the importance of the past. *But* I believe that without studying the lessons of the past, we cannot obtain a better future. *Therefore*, let us not forget the value of learning from the past.

38. 從過去學習

　　在現在步調快速的時代裡，我們似乎總是前瞻未來，計畫並期望有更美好的明天。的確，現在幾乎每個領域都進展快速，光是不落後進展的速度，就幾乎是個全職工作了。然而，若沒有過去的一步一腳印，這些進步則不可能存在。因此，我不同意，從過去學習，對活在現在的我們，一點也不重要的說法。

　　依我之見，過去給我們很多教訓，如果我們不從過去學習，可能會重蹈前人犯過的錯誤，這原本是可以避免的。大多數的人都會同意，我們應該從自己的錯誤中學習，我更進一步地建議，我們應該從別人的錯誤中學習。要研究過去的另一個理由是，我們能夠以前人的成就為基礎，那就不須重頭做基礎研究，或重新發明輪子。相反地，我們應該從過往的成就中學習，然後加以改進。最後一項要點是，過去有某些非常重要的事物，能教導我們認識自己的文化和身份。如果我們不知道祖先的價值觀和信念，又如何能把它們傳給後代呢？如果我們不知道過去，可能就會失去自己的文化。

　　我們持續不斷地努力，想要創造一個更美好的未來，有時候就很容易會遺忘過去的重要性。但是我相信，若不學習過去的教訓，我們就無法獲得一個更美好的未來。因此，讓我們不要忘記從過去學習的重要性。

【註釋】

fast-paced〔'fæst'pest〕*adj.* 步調快速的
advance〔əd'væns〕*n.* 進步　　field〔fild〕*n.* 領域
keep up 不落後；並駕齊驅　　***make a step*** 走一步
hold〔hold〕*n.* 包含　　lesson〔'lɛsn̩〕*n.* 教訓
neglect〔nɪ'glɛkt〕*v.* 忽略　　repeat〔rɪ'pit〕*v.* 重覆
forefather〔'for,fɑðɚ〕*n.* 祖先；前輩
further〔'fɝðɚ〕*adv.* 更進一步地　　propose〔prə'poz〕*v.* 提議
build upon 建立在…基礎之上 (= *build on*)
achievements〔ə'tʃivmənts〕*n. pl.* 成就
improve upon 對…加以改良 (= *improve on*)
values〔'væljuz〕*n. pl.* 價值觀　　***pass on to*** 傳給

Quit　　　　　　**Writing**

Do you agree or disagree with the following statement?　With the help of technology, students nowadays can learn more information and learn it more quickly.　Use specific reasons and examples to support your answer.

Cut

Paste

Undo

Time

Help
?

Confirm
Answer

Next

39. The Effects of Technology on Learning

The technological advances of the last few years have been amazing. Never before have students had such a wide variety of resources to help them in their studies. Those who can take advantage of these resources have the opportunity to learn about more subjects and to acquire more in-depth knowledge. *In my opinion*, students can indeed learn more and learn more quickly with the help of modern technology.

The piece of technology most important as a learning tool must be the computer. Paired with the Internet, it allows students to research topics more quickly and thoroughly and to write up their findings more rapidly as well. *Furthermore*, advances in many fields are being made so fast these days that it is impossible for textbooks to keep up. Technology allows students to keep abreast of the latest developments. *Also*, it cannot be denied that many students enjoy using such resources in their studies. Because of this, they are more likely to pursue subjects in greater depth.

For all these reasons, I believe that technology is of great benefit to today's students. *Of course*, it is still possible to learn without the aid of such devices, but I believe that those students who are fortunate enough to have access to technological resources should take every advantage of them.

39. 科技對學習的影響

近幾年來，科技方面的進步相當驚人。學生以前從來沒有這麼多各式各樣的資源，來幫助他們學習。能夠利用這些資源的人，就有機會學習更多的主題，並獲得更深入的知識。依我之見，有了現代科技的協助，學生確實能夠學得更多，而且學得更快。

科技上最重要的學習工具非電腦莫屬，再搭配網際網路的使用，使得學生能夠更快速、更徹底地研究他們的主題，也能更迅速地詳細寫出他們所發現的資料。此外，目前許多領域都進步神速，教科書根本不可能跟得上，科技讓學生能夠跟得上最新的發展，並且，不可否認的是，許多學生在學習時，也非常喜歡使用這樣的資源，因為這樣，他們較有可能更深入地研究各種主題。

基於這些理由，我相信科技對現今的學生有極大的助益。當然，沒有這些設備的協助，也是有可能學習的，但我認為，那些有幸能夠使用科技資源的學生，都應該善加利用這些資源。

【註釋】

effect〔ɪˋfɛkt〕*n.* 影響　　technology〔tɛkˋnɑlədʒɪ〕*n.* 科技
technological〔͵tɛknəˋlɑdʒɪkḷ〕*adj.* 科技的
advance〔ədˋvæns〕*n.* 進步　　amazing〔əˋmezɪŋ〕*adj.* 驚人的
a wide variety of 很多各式各樣的　　resource〔rɪˋsors〕*n.* 資源
take advantage of 利用　　acquire〔əˋkwaɪr〕*v.* 獲得
in-depth〔ˋɪnˋdɛpθ〕*adj.* 深入的　　*be paired with* 和～搭配
Internet〔ˋɪntɚ͵nɛt〕*n.* 網際網路　　research〔rɪˋsɝtʃ〕*v.* 研究
topic〔ˋtɑpɪk〕*n.* 主題　　thoroughly〔ˋθɝolɪ〕*adv.* 徹底地
write up 更詳細地寫　　textbook〔ˋtɛkst͵bʊk〕*n.* 課本；教科書
keep up 跟上　　*keep abreast of* 跟上（= *keep up with*）
deny〔dɪˋnaɪ〕*v.* 否認　　aid〔ed〕*n.* 協助（= *help*）
device〔dɪˋvaɪs〕*n.* 裝置　　access〔ˋæksɛs〕*n.* 使用權 < *to* >

Quit　　Writing

The expression "Never, never give up" means to keep trying and never stop working for your goals. Do you agree or disagree with this statement? Use specific reasons and examples to support your answer.

Cut

Paste

Undo

40. **Never, Never Give Up**

We often hear people say, "Never give up." These can be encouraging words and words of determination. A person who believes in them will keep trying to reach his goal no matter how many times he fails. *In my opinion*, the quality of determination to succeed is an important one to have. *Therefore*, I believe that we should never give up.

One reason is that if we give up too easily, we will rarely achieve anything. It is not unusual for us to fail in our first attempt at something new, so we should not feel discouraged and should try again. *Besides*, if we always give up when we fail, we will not be able to develop new skills and grow as people. *Another* reason we should never give up is that we can learn from our mistakes only if we make a new effort. If we do not try again, the lesson we have learned is wasted. *Finally*, we should never give up because as we work to reach our goals, we develop confidence, and this confidence can help us succeed in other areas of our lives. If we never challenge ourselves, we will begin to doubt our abilities.

In short, it is important that we do not give up when working for our goals. Whether we succeed in the end or not, we will learn something, and what we learn will help us to become better, more confident people. *Furthermore*, if we give up, we have no chance of attaining our goals, but if we keep trying, there is always a chance that we will succeed one day.

40. 永遠，永遠不要放棄

我們常聽到人們說：「永遠不要放棄。」這句話可能是要鼓勵別人，也可能是要表示自己的決心。相信自己的人，不管經歷多少次失敗，都會不斷試著要達成目標。我認為，有成功的決心，是每個人都應該要有的重要特質。因此，我認為我們應該永不放棄。

其中一個理由是，如果我們太輕易放棄，就幾乎無法完成任何事。我們第一次嘗試新事物會失敗，這是很平常的事，所以我們不應感到氣餒，而應該要再試一次。而且，如果我們總是一失敗就放棄，就無法培養新技能，並且不斷地成長。我們應該永不放棄的另一個原因是，只有再努力一次，才能從錯誤中學習，如果我們不再試一次，那麼我們所學到的教訓就白白浪費了。最後，我們應該永不放棄，因為當我們努力達成目標的時候，就會培養出自信，而這種自信，將有助於讓我們在生活的其他領域中獲得成功。如果我們不挑戰自我，我們就會開始懷疑自己的能力。

簡言之，當我們努力追求目標時，永不放棄是很重要的，不管最後有沒有成功，我們都會學到一些東西，而我們所學到的東西，將會使自己成為一個更好、更有自信的人。而且，如果放棄的話，我們就沒有機會達成目標，但是如果能不斷地嘗試，總有一天，我們一定會有機會成功的。

【註釋】

give up 放棄　　encouraging〔ɪnˈkɜɪdʒɪŋ〕adj. 令人鼓舞的
determination〔dɪˌtɜməˈneʃən〕n. 決心
reach〔ritʃ〕v. 達到（目標）（= achieve = attain）
goal〔gol〕n. 目標　　quality〔ˈkwɑlətɪ〕n. 特質
attempt〔əˈtɛmpt〕n. 嘗試　　lesson〔ˈlɛsṇ〕n. 教訓
confidence〔ˈkɑnfədəns〕n. 信心　　area〔ˈɛrɪə〕n. 領域
challenge〔ˈtʃælɪndʒ〕v. 挑戰　　**in short** 簡言之（= in brief）
in the end 到最後　　furthermore〔ˈfɜðəˌmor〕adv. 此外

Quit

Writing

Some people think that human needs for farmland, housing, and industry are more important than saving land for endangered animals. Do you agree or disagree with this point of view? Why or why not? Use specific reasons and examples to support your answer.

Cut

Paste

Undo

41. **Saving Land for Endangered Animals**

There is only so much land on the earth, and so what we can do with it is limited. Some people believe that human needs for farmland, housing and industry should come first, while others believe that some land should be set aside for endangered animals. *I am of the opinion that* we should reserve some land for the world's animals for the following reasons.

First, mankind's need for land is constantly growing. If the demand is not checked in some way, humans will eventually develop all of the earth's available land. At that time, mankind will have no more room to grow, and all the wild animals will have disappeared, as well as other valuable resources. *Second*, humans are able to innovate and can use the land that they already possess in more efficient ways. Animals are unable to do this. Once their land is taken away from them they will die. *Third and last*, endangered animals are an important part of the biodiversity of our planet. If they disappear, we cannot predict what the effect will be. *Therefore*, we should treat such animals as a valuable resource to be protected.

To sum up, the world's endangered animals are an important resource and we should protect them by setting aside some land for them. Although mankind's need for land continues to grow, people are intelligent and inventive enough to put the land they have to better use. *In this way*, we can have enough land for farming, housing and industry, and preserve the biodiversity of the planet at the same time.

41. 保留土地給瀕臨絕種的動物

　　地球上的土地就只有這麼多，所以我們可以利用的方式有限。有些人認為人類對於農地、居住，以及工業的需求應該擺在第一位，但是有人則認為，有些土地應該留給瀕臨絕種的動物。我的看法是，基於下列的理由，我們應該保留一些土地給地球上的動物。

　　首先，人類對土地的需求不斷在增加，如果這些需求不以某種方式來加以抑制，人類最後將會開發完地球上所有可獲得的土地，到那時候，人類將沒有栽種作物的空間，而且全部的野生動物，將會和其他寶貴的資源一樣，消失殆盡。其次，人類可以創新，並且以更有效率的方式，來使用已經擁有的土地，動物則無法做到這一點，一旦土地被剝奪，牠們就會死亡。第三點，也是最後一點，瀕臨絕種的動物，是我們地球上物種多元性的重要部份，如果牠們消失了，我們無法預測，將會造成什麼樣的影響。因此，我們應該把這些動物，視為需要保護的珍貴資源。

　　總之，全世界瀕臨絕種的動物，都是一項重要的資源，我們應該加以保護，並且保留一些土地給牠們。雖然人類對於土地的需求持續在增加，但人類很聰明，而且具有創造力，能夠更充份利用所擁有的土地。如此一來，我們會有足夠的土地耕種、居住，並用來發展工業，而且能同時保存地球物種的多元性。

【註釋】

endangered〔ɪnˈdendʒəd〕*adj.* 瀕臨絕種的
do with 處理；利用　　come〔kʌm〕*v.* 位於
come first 位居第一位　　*set aside* （為某種目的）留給；撥出
reserve〔rɪˈzɝv〕*v.* 保留　　constantly〔ˈkɑnstəntlɪ〕*adv.* 不斷地
check〔tʃɛk〕*v.* 抑制　　available〔əˈveləbḷ〕*adj.* 可獲得的
resource〔rɪˈsors〕*n.* 資源　　innovate〔ˈɪnəˌvet〕*v.* 創新
biodiversity〔ˌbaɪodəˈvɝsətɪ〕*n.* 物種多元性
planet〔ˈplænɪt〕*n.* 行星　　predict〔prɪˈdɪkt〕*v.* 預測
to sum up 總之　　*treat* A *as* B 把 A 視為 B
inventive〔ɪnˈvɛntɪv〕*adj.* 有創造力的

Quit — **Writing**

What is a very important skill a person should learn in order to be successful in the world today? Choose **one** skill and use specific reasons and examples to support your choice.

▲

Cut

Paste

Undo

▼

42. An Important Skill

The world today is a very competitive place. ***Therefore***, it is necessary to develop some skills to increase one's chances of success. Many skills, ***for example***, leadership, a second language, and technical skills such as computer programming, are very useful today. ***However***, I believe that the most useful skill is the ability to communicate well with others.

It is impossible to overstate the importance of good communication skills. In today's society we have to work cooperatively with others. A good communicator finds it easier to put forth his ideas clearly. ***In this way*** there will be fewer misunderstandings, which can lead to bad feelings as well as lost time and effort. ***In addition***, a person with good communication skills is a good mediator and negotiator. He or she can play a valuable role in resolving disputes and enhancing cooperation. This means that a good communicator is often a natural leader. ***Finally***, with good communication skills, it is easier to persuade others to accept your point of view. Having your views and plans approved of by others is a vital step on the way to success.

For all the above reasons, it is my belief that strong communication skills are the most important to have. Good communication is important in all situations, so a skillful communicator will always be in high demand.

42. 一項重要的技能

　　現今的世界競爭十分激烈，因此，必須培養一些技能，以增加自己成功的機會。許多技能，如領導能力、第二種語言能力，和技術能力，如電腦程式設計等，現在都非常有用。然而，我認為最有用的技能，是擅長和別人溝通的能力。

　　良好的的溝通技巧，其重要性再怎麼強調也不爲過。在現今的社會中，我們必須與他人合作。擅長溝通的人，比較容易能將自己的意見清楚地表達出來，如此一來，便能減少誤會，以免造成不好的感覺，甚至浪費時間和力氣。此外，具有良好溝通技巧的人，會是一個優秀的調停者與協商者，在解決紛爭、加強合作時，可以扮演重要的角色。這就表示，善於溝通的人，常常就是天生的領導人才。最後，具有良好的溝通技巧，比較容易說服別人，接受你的觀點，而你的意見和計畫能被別人認同，是邁向成功很重要的一大步。

　　基於上述理由，我相信，卓越的溝通技巧是最重要的必備技能。在所有的情況中，良好的溝通都非常重要，所以，善於溝通的人，總是非常受歡迎的。

【註釋】

competitive〔kəmˈpɛtətɪv〕*adj.* 競爭激烈的
leadership〔ˈlidɚ͵ʃɪp〕*n.* 領導能力　　technical〔ˈtɛknɪkl̩〕*adj.* 技術的
programming〔ˈprogræmɪŋ〕*n.* 程式設計
overstate〔ˈovɚˈstet〕*v.* 誇張
cooperatively〔koˈɑpə͵retɪvlɪ〕*adv.* 合作地　　***put forth*** 提出
mediator〔ˈmidɪ͵etɚ〕*n.* 調解者
negotiator〔nɪˈgoʃɪ͵etɚ〕*n.* 談判者；協商者
resolve〔rɪˈzɑlv〕*v.* 解決　　dispute〔dɪˈspjut〕*n.* 爭論
enhance〔ɪnˈhæns〕*v.* 提升；加強　　persuade〔pɚˈswed〕*v.* 說服
approve〔əˈpruv〕*v.* 贊成　　***point of view*** 觀點
vital〔ˈvaɪtl̩〕*adj.* 非常重要的　　***in demand*** 有需要的；受歡迎的

Quit   **Writing**

Why do you think some people are attracted to dangerous sports or other dangerous activities? Use specific reasons and examples to support your answer.

_____   ▲   **Cut**
_____
_____   **Paste**
_____
_____   **Undo**
_____
_____
_____
_____
_____
_____
_____
_____
_____
_____
_____
_____
_____
_____   ▼

Time   Help   Confirm Answer   Next

43. The Attraction of Dangerous Activities

In the past, people often faced many dangers in their daily lives. They had to cope with not only natural disasters and frequent outbreaks of disease, but also dangerous animals and warfare. The need to hunt and to protect their territory from other people required them to be skilled in the use of weapons. *In addition*, any travel also involved great risk as there were few roads and bridges. Nowadays, people do not have to live with such dangers on a daily basis, and yet many people choose to involve themselves in risky activities such as dangerous sports. I believe the following reasons can explain the attraction of such activities.

One reason people are attracted to risky activities is that they crave excitement. The thrill of mountain climbing or bungee jumping can satisfy their need to break out of their routine. Without the excitement of such sports, they may feel bored with their lives. *Another* reason people like such activities is that these activities often require a certain amount of skill. Learning to drive a racecar or hang-glide may satisfy the desire to excel and give the participant a feeling of accomplishment and personal confidence in his abilities. A *final* reason that people may choose to engage in risky activities is that they want to stand out from the crowd. By developing a skill that others don't have, they can feel unique.

For all of these reasons, I believe that risky activities will continue to be popular with some people. *In fact*, it seems that as soon as one activity becomes safer or commonplace, thrill seekers come up with a new way to challenge their skills and courage.

43. 危險活動的吸引力

　　以前的人在日常生活中，常面臨許多危險，他們不僅要應付天災，和經常爆發的疾病，也要應付危險的動物和戰爭。由於必須打獵，以及保護自己的領土，免於他人的入侵，他們必須非常精通武器的使用。此外，因為道路和橋樑很少，任何旅行的危險性都很高。現在人們不必每天生活在這樣的危險當中，但仍然有許多人，選擇從事一些危險的活動，像是有危險性的運動。我認為下列的原因，能夠解釋這些危險的活動為何會有吸引力。

　　人們會受到危險活動的吸引，原因之一是渴望刺激。登山或高空彈跳的那種刺激感，可以滿足人們想要逃離常規的需求。如果沒有這些運動帶來刺激，他們可能會對生活感到厭煩。人們喜歡這種活動的另一個原因是，這些活動通常需要相當程度的技術。學習駕駛賽車，或飛滑翔翼，也許能滿足他們想要高人一等的渴望，使自己有成就感，並對自己的能力有自信心。人們會選擇從事危險活動，其最後一個原因在於，他們想要在人群中脫穎而出。藉著培養別人所沒有的技術，他們會覺得自己是獨一無二的。

　　基於以上這些理由，我認為危險的活動會繼續受到一些人的喜愛。事實上，某種活動似乎只要一變得比較安全或普通時，尋求刺激的人，就會再想出一種新的方法，挑戰自己的技術和勇氣。

【註釋】

cope with 應付　　*natural disaster* 天災

outbreak〔'aʊt,brek〕*n.* 爆發　　warfare〔'wɔr,fɛr〕*n.* 戰爭

territory〔'tɛrə,torɪ〕*n.* 領土　　skilled〔skɪld〕*adj.* 熟練的

on a daily basis 每天（= *every day*）　　*involve oneself in* 參與

risky〔'rɪskɪ〕*adj.* 危險的　　crave〔krev〕*v.* 渴望

thrill〔θrɪl〕*n.* 刺激　　*bungee jumping* 高空彈跳

break out 逃脫　　routine〔ru'tin〕*n.* 例行公事

hang-glide〔'hæŋ,glaɪd〕*v.* 飛滑翔翼　　excel〔ɪk'sɛl〕*v.* 勝過別人

engage in 從事　　*stand out* 突出 < *from* >

unique〔ju'nik〕*adj.* 獨特的　　commonplace〔'kɑmən,ples〕*adj.* 平常的

thrill seeker 尋求刺激的人　　*come up with* 想出

challenge〔'tʃælɪndʒ〕*v.* 挑戰

Quit　　　Writing

Some people like to travel with a companion. Other people prefer to travel alone. Which do you prefer? Use specific reasons and examples to support your choice.

Cut

Paste

Undo

Time

Help
?

Confirm
Answer

Next
➡

44. **Traveling with a Companion**

Traveling can be wonderful. It introduces us to new experiences, broadens our minds and helps us relax. *However*, not everyone likes to travel in the same way. Some people prefer to travel alone so that they can do what they like during their trip without having to worry about anyone else. Others like to have a companion to share the experience with. I am one of the latter, because I believe that traveling with someone has many advantages.

When I travel with a companion, I have someone with whom to share what I experience. We can talk over the day's events and discoveries, and this will make them more interesting. *In addition*, it is often comforting to have a familiar person around when we are in a strange environment. When I am traveling in a foreign country, I may be unable to speak the language or may be confused by the local customs. With a travel companion, I will always have someone to talk and share my feelings with. *Finally*, a travel companion can make the journey easier and safer. We can help each other to take care of our bags and get information, as well as keep each other company while waiting in long lines.

To sum up, I prefer to travel with a companion rather than travel alone. I believe it adds enjoyment and comfort to my trip. *And* when we return from our journey, my friend and I can share our wonderful memories.

44. 結伴旅行

　　旅遊是很棒的，它能帶給我們新的經驗，擴展我們的眼界，幫助我們放鬆身心。然而，並非每個人喜歡的旅遊方式都一樣。有些人比較喜歡獨自旅行，因為可以隨心所欲，不用擔心別人的感受，有些人則喜歡有個同伴一起分享經歷。我屬於後者，因為我認為結伴旅行有很多好處。

　　有個伴一起旅行，就有人可以分享我的經歷，我們可以討論當天的事件及發現，如此一來，會讓這些經歷更有趣。此外，身處陌生的環境裡，有個熟人在身邊，較令人安心。當我在國外旅行時，我可能不會說該國語言，或者可能不了解當地的風俗習慣，有個同伴在身邊，我就有人可以一起說話、一起分享我的感受。最後，結伴旅行可以讓旅行更自在，而且更安全，我們可以幫對方看行李，以及獲得資訊，還有在大排長龍時，可以彼此作伴。

　　總之，我比較喜歡結伴旅行，而比較不喜歡獨自旅行。我認為結伴旅行能夠為旅程增添樂趣及舒適，而且旅行回來後，我的朋友和我，就可以共同分享美好的回憶。

【註釋】

companion〔kəmˈpænjən〕*n.* 同伴
introduce〔ˌɪntrəˈdjus〕*v.* 使認識 *< to >*　　broaden〔ˈbrɔdn̩〕*v.* 拓展
the latter （兩者中）後者（↔ *the former*）
advantage〔ədˈvæntɪdʒ〕*n.* 好處（↔ disadvantage〔ˌdɪsədˈvæntɪdʒ〕）
talk over 討論　　***in addition*** 此外（= *besides*）
comforting〔ˈkʌmfətɪŋ〕*adj.* 令人欣慰的
local〔ˈlokl̩〕*adj.* 當地的　　***keep*** sb. ***company*** 陪伴某人
to sum up 總之（= *in conclusion* = *in sum* = *in summary*）
prefer to + *V₁* + ***rather than*** + *V₂* 寧願 V_1，而不願 V_2
enjoyment〔ɪnˈdʒɔɪmənt〕*n.* 樂趣　　memory〔ˈmɛmərɪ〕*n.* 回憶

Quit　　　　　Writing

Some people prefer to get up early in the morning and start the day's work. Others prefer to get up later in the day and work until late at night. Which do you prefer? Use specific reasons and examples to support your choice.

	Cut
	Paste
	Undo

45. Being an Early Bird

It is said that there are two kinds of people in this world — those who like to get an early start to the day and those who prefer to do their work in the afternoon and evening. I am definitely one of the former, a morning person, or early bird. I find that I can wake up easily in the morning and that I think most clearly at that time, too. By the afternoon I don't feel as energetic, and in the evening I cannot work at all. I prefer to relax in the evening and then go to bed early rather than try to be a night owl, or night person.

In my opinion, there are many advantages to being an early bird, or morning person. Getting up with the sun, I can take advantage of the cool, fresh morning air. *And* since I am more efficient in the morning, I can get my work done faster. *More importantly*, if I finish my work by the afternoon, I can then relax and enjoy the rest of the day. In the evening I can enjoy my leisure time without having to worry about unfinished projects and deadlines. *With all these advantages*, I really enjoy being a morning person.

45. 早起的人

　　有人說，這個世界上有兩種人 —— 一種是喜歡一大早就開始工作的人，另一種則是喜歡在下午或晚上工作的人，我當然是前者，是個喜歡早起的人。我覺得自己早上很容易就醒過來，而且那時候頭腦也最清楚。到了下午，我會覺得沒那麼有活力，到了晚上，我就根本無法工作。我比較喜歡晚上放鬆，然後早一點睡覺，而不會想要當個晚睡的夜貓子。

　　我認為，早起的好處很多。日出即起，我可以享受早晨涼爽清新的空氣。由於我早上比較有效率，所以就可以比較快把工作做好。更重要的是，如果我下午就把工作完成，那時就可以放輕鬆，享受一天中其餘的時間。在晚上，我可以享受空閒的時間，不需要擔心未完成的計劃和最後期限。因為有這麼多的優點，所以我真的很喜歡當個早起的人。

【註釋】

early bird 早起的人（ = *morning person* ）
it is said that 聽說（ = *people say that* ）
definitely（ˈdɛfənɪtlɪ ）*adv.* 確定地
the former （兩者中）前者（ ↔ *the latter* ）
energetic（ˌɛnəˈdʒɛtɪk ）*adj.* 充滿活力的
prefer to + V₁ + rather than + V₂ 寧願 V₁，而不願 V₂
night owl 夜貓子（ = *night person* ）
take advantage of 利用（ = *make use of* ）
fresh（ frɛʃ ）*adj.* 新鮮的　　efficient（ əˈfɪʃənt ）*adj.* 有效率的
leisure time 空閒時間（ = *free time* = *spare time* ）
project（ˈprɑdʒɛkt ）*n.* 計劃
deadline（ˈdɛdˌlaɪn ）*n.* 最後期限

Quit　　**Writing**

What are the important qualities of a good son or daughter? Have these qualities changed or remained the same over time in your culture? Use specific reasons and examples to support your answer.

Cut

Paste

Undo

Time

Help
?

Confirm
Answer

Next

46. A Good Son or Daughter

Family harmony is very important. We all hope to have good relationships with our family members, including our parents. *Therefore*, we should be good sons and daughters. *But* what makes a good son or daughter? This is a difficult question in our rapidly changing society, but I feel that the most important characteristics have and will remain constant. Among them are the following.

First of all, a good son or daughter should be loving. No matter what a child does, his parents will still love and care for him. *Likewise*, children should always keep their love for their family in mind. This attitude will help them to work out any differences they may have. *Second*, a good child should be respectful of his or her parents. Our parents have experienced much more than we have and can often offer good advice. *In addition*, children should respect the opinions of their parents, even if they do not agree with them. *Last but not least*, a good son or daughter should be level-headed. Children today are influenced by many outside pressures, including their friends and the media. If they can consider all these new ideas carefully rather than follow every fashion that comes along without thinking, they will not make their parents worry about them.

The above are only a few of the qualities of a good son or daughter, but I believe that they are important and always have been. The rapidly changing society today often leads to what is called a generation gap between children and their parents. *But* if children remember the love and respect that they have for their family, and think about things carefully, they will be better able to sort out their differences.

46. 孝順的兒女

　　家庭和諧是非常重要的，我們都希望能跟家人有良好的關係，當然也包括與父母的關係。因此，我們必須要當個孝順的兒子或女兒。但怎麼樣才算是孝順的兒女呢？在現在這樣快速變遷的社會中，這是一個難以回答的問題，但我認為，最重要的特點都是不變的。以下就是我認為重要的幾個特點。

　　首先，孝順的兒女必須能愛父母。不論小孩做了什麼，父母一樣會關心和愛護他們。同樣地，為人子女也必須時時將對家人的關愛銘記在心。如果能抱持這樣的心態，不論親子之間有多少歧見，都能一一克服。其次，孝順的兒女一定要尊敬父母。父母的經驗比我們豐富許多，因此通常都能給我們很好的建議。此外，即使不同意父母的觀點，仍然要尊重他們的看法。最後一項要點是，孝順的兒女應該要保持理智。現代小孩承受外界各種不同的壓力，其中有的壓力，是來自同儕或大眾傳播媒體。假如小孩都能對這些新事物仔細思考，而不盲目跟從、照單全收，就不會讓父母為他們擔憂。

　　上述幾點只是做為孝順的兒女，所須具備的幾個特點，但我認為，這些標準永遠都是非常重要的。現代社會的快速變遷，總是會造成所謂父母與小孩之間的代溝。但如果為人子女能牢記要尊重與關愛家人，而且能思慮周延，就更能排解家人之間的歧見紛爭。

【註釋】

harmony〔ˈhɑrmənɪ〕 n. 和諧　　rapidly〔ˈræpɪdlɪ〕 adv. 快速地

characteristic〔ˌkærɪktəˈrɪstɪk〕 n. 特色

constant〔ˈkɑnstənt〕 adj. 恆久不變的

loving〔ˈlʌvɪŋ〕 adj. 敬愛父母的　　*care for* 照顧

likewise〔ˈlaɪkˌwaɪz〕 adv. 同樣地　　*keep…in mind* 把…牢記在心

work out 解決（ = *sort out* = *solve* ）

last but not least 最後一項要點是

level-headed〔ˈlɛvl̩ˈhɛdɪd〕 adj. 理智的；頭腦冷靜的

media〔ˈmidɪə〕 n. pl. 媒體　　*come along* 突然出現

what is called 所謂的（ = *what we call* ）

generation gap 代溝

Quit	**Writing**

Some people prefer to work for a large company. Others prefer to work for a small company. Which would you prefer? Use specific reasons and details to support your choice.

▲

Cut

Paste

Undo

▼

47. The Advantages of Working for a Small Company

Many people prefer to work for large companies because these firms are often well-established and seem to be more secure. They also usually offer training programs for new graduates and lots of support for new employees. *Furthermore*, there may be a well-defined chain of command that offers the promise of steady advancement. Despite these advantages, I would prefer to work for a small company for the following reasons.

First, small companies are more flexible. While it can be argued that larger firms have well-established markets and are, *therefore*, more stable employers better able to deal with the ups and downs of the marketplace, in today's competitive society a smaller firm is often better able to weather changes in the marketplace. With its smaller size and often smaller investment, it is easier for such firms to change track when the market demands it. *Second*, although a smaller firm may not offer the same level of training and support that a larger firm does, new employees are usually given more responsibility and opportunities to grow. *Furthermore*, the smaller staff size means they will get more personal attention from senior managers and have more opportunities to demonstrate their skills and advance.

There is no denying that joining a small firm does entail some risk. The company may fail, leaving its employees suddenly jobless. *But* even if the worst should happen, the employees would have already gained valuable experience that makes them attractive to other employers. *In conclusion*, as a new graduate I believe that this is a proper time in my life to take risks and seek out learning experiences, so working for a small firm would be appropriate for me.

47. 在小公司上班的優點

許多人較喜歡在大公司上班，因爲大公司通常很穩固，似乎比較有保障。大公司通常也會提供訓練課程，給剛畢業的學生，並且大力支持新進人員。此外，大公司有很明確的行政管理系統，讓人覺得有穩定升遷的希望。但儘管大公司有這些優點，我還是寧願進小公司工作，我的理由如下。

首先，小公司較有彈性。雖然有人認爲，大一點的公司市場穩固，因此，員工穩定性較高，並且較能應付市場的起伏，但在現今競爭激烈的社會中，規模較小的公司，反而經常比較能夠因應市場的改變。公司規模較小，通常投資額也較小，當市場有需要時，要變換跑道比較容易。其次，小公司雖然可能無法提供像大公司一樣的訓練和支持，但新進人員通常會被賦與較多的責任和機會，因此成長更快。此外，員工人數較少，也就意味著資深主管給予員工個人的關注較多，員工有更多機會來表現自己的技能和進步。

不可否認地，加入小公司的確會有一些風險，公司可能會倒閉，使得員工突然失業。但即使最糟糕的情況發生了，員工也已經得到了寶貴的經驗，使得他們在其他雇主眼中，更有吸引力。總之，身爲一個初入社會的畢業生，我認爲在我人生的這個階段，正是適合冒險以及尋求學習經驗的時刻，所以，在小公司上班，對我而言，是很適合的。

【註釋】

well-established〔ˋwɛləˈstæblɪʃt〕adj. 穩固的

secure〔sɪˈkjur〕adj. 安全的   graduate〔ˋgrædʒuɪt〕n. 畢業生

well-defined〔ˋwɛldɪˈfaɪnd〕adj. 明確的

chain of command 行政管理系統   promise〔ˋpramɪs〕n. 希望

steady〔ˋstɛdɪ〕adj. 穩定的   advancement〔ədˈvænsmənt〕n. 晉升

flexible〔ˋflɛksəbḷ〕adj. 有彈性的   argue〔ˋargju〕v. 認爲；主張

stable〔ˋstebḷ〕adj. 穩定的   *ups and downs* 起伏

marketplace〔ˋmarkɪt͵ples〕n. 市場   weather〔ˋwɛðɚ〕v. 平安渡過

investment〔ɪnˈvɛstmənt〕n. 投資   track〔træk〕n. 軌道；跑道

demand〔dɪˈmænd〕v. 需要   staff〔stæf〕n. 全體員工

senior〔ˋsinjɚ〕adj. 資深的   demonstrate〔ˋdɛmən͵stret〕v. 表現

deny〔dɪˈnaɪ〕v. 否認   *There is no denying that~* 不可否認地，~

entail〔ɪnˈtel〕v. 使人承擔   *seek out* 找出

appropriate〔əˈproprɪɪt〕adj. 適當的

Quit   **Writing**

People work because they need money to live. What are some **other** reasons that people work? Discuss one or more of these reasons. Use specific examples and details to support your answer.

▲

Cut

Paste

Undo

▼

Time

Help
?

Confirm
Answer

Next

48. Reasons to Work

For most people in the world, work is necessary in order to survive. Without work they cannot support themselves and their families. *But* not everyone works just in order to survive. Some people work in order to help others, some for the respect and admiration their work brings them, and others for personal fulfillment and satisfaction.

People who work for charitable organizations usually do so because they want to help people in need. They may be volunteers, or they may be given a small stipend for their work, but whatever monetary benefit they receive, it is not as important as the fact that they have made a difference in someone else's life. *Another* reason some people work is because they enjoy the respect and esteem of others. Politicians are a good example. *Of course*, they often make a handsome salary, but in most cases, they could make more in a career in the private sector than in government. Other careers, such as that of an artist or musician, attract people who find their work personally fulfilling no matter what the monetary reward.

Although earning a living is a very important reason to work, and is probably the most common one, it is not the only reason. People may work for all kinds of reasons, including those described above or a combination of them. Whatever a person's reason for doing the work he does, he should be respected for his commitment and good work.

48. 必須要工作的理由

　　對世界上大部分的人而言,想求生存,就必須要工作,沒有工作,就無法養活自己和家人。但並非每個人都只是爲了生存而工作。有些人工作,是爲了幫助別人,有些人則是爲了工作所帶給他們的尊敬和讚賞,還有些人是爲了實現自己的抱負,讓自己感到滿足。

　　在慈善機構工作的人,通常是因爲他們想要幫助窮困的人。他們可能是義工,也可能獲得少許的薪資,但無論得到什麼金錢上的利益,都不如改變某個人的生活這件事來得重要。有些人工作的另一個理由是,他們喜歡別人的尊敬與重視,政治人物就是一個很好的例子。當然,他們的薪水相當高,但大部分的政治人物,如果在私人機構工作,得到的薪水會比在政府單位服務更高。還有一些職業,如藝術家、音樂家,吸引人的原因在於,人們可以從工作中實現自己的理想,而不在乎金錢上的報酬。

　　雖然謀生是工作的重要理由,可能也是最普遍的理由,但並不是唯一的理由。人們可能會爲各式各樣的理由而工作,包括上述所提及的理由,或是上述各項理由的結合。無論一個人工作的理由爲何,只要他夠投入,並且表現良好,就應該受到尊重。

【註釋】

survive〔səˈvaɪv〕*v.* 生存　　admiration〔ˌædməˈreʃən〕*n.* 讚賞
fulfillment〔fʊlˈfɪlmənt〕*n.* 實現
charitable〔ˈtʃærətəbl̩〕*adj.* 慈善的　　*in need* 貧困的
volunteer〔ˌvɑlənˈtɪr〕*n.* 義工　　stipend〔ˈstaɪpɛnd〕*n.* 薪水;津貼
monetary〔ˈmʌnəˌtɛrɪ〕*adj.* 金錢的　　benefit〔ˈbɛnəfɪt〕*n.* 利益
esteem〔əˈstim〕*n.* 重視　　handsome〔ˈhænsʌm〕*adj.* 相當多的
case〔kes〕*n.* 情況　　private〔ˈpraɪvɪt〕*adj.* 私人的
sector〔ˈsɛktɚ〕*n.* 部門;領域　　reward〔rɪˈwɔrd〕*n.* 報酬
earn a living 謀生 (= *make a living*)
describe〔dɪˈskraɪb〕*v.* 描述　　combination〔ˌkɑmbəˈneʃən〕*n.* 結合
commitment〔kəˈmɪtmənt〕*n.* 投入

Quit　　　Writing

Do you agree or disagree with the following statement? Face-to-face communication is better than other types of communication, such as letters, e-mail, or telephone calls. Use specific reasons and details to support your answer.

▲

Cut

Paste

Undo

▼

49. Face-to-Face vs. Other Types of Communication

When deciding between face-to-face communication and other types, such as e-mail and telephone calls, the kind of communication one thinks is better depends on the definition of "better". Face-to-face communication is usually the most effective form because there is the least chance for a misunderstanding to occur. *On the other hand*, letters, e-mail, and telephone calls are more efficient means of communication. *In my opinion*, the latter type of communication is better because efficiency is becoming increasingly important in the workplace.

There are times when information must be communicated with exactness, and at such times a face-to-face conversation would be better. *However*, this is not always necessary or feasible. Many times we have to communicate with people who are far away. Traveling to meet them would be both prohibitively expensive and take a great deal of time. In these cases other forms of communication, especially electronic communication, are more appropriate. *In addition*, letters and e-mail allow us to have a record of the communication. This can be referred back to later should any dispute arise. *Finally*, these are types of communication that allow us to send messages when it is convenient. We do not have to match the schedule of another person.

In conclusion, letters, e-mail, and telephone calls are more efficient means of communication than a face-to-face conversation. They allow us to save both time and money. In today's world I think these are very important factors to consider. *Therefore*, I believe that these forms of communication are better.

49. 面對面溝通與其他的溝通方式

在決定哪一種溝通方式比較好,是要做面對面溝通,或是使用其他的溝通方式,如電子郵件、打電話等,就要看個人對「比較好」的定義爲何。面對面溝通常是最有效的溝通方式,因爲發生誤會的機會最小。另一方面,信件、電子郵件和電話,則是較有效率的溝通方式。依我之見,後面這些溝通方式比較好,因爲效率在職場上,已變得愈來愈重要了。

有時當必須傳遞準確的訊息時,面對面的談話會比較好,然而這種方式不一定是必要或可行的。在許多情況下,我們必須和遠方的人溝通,而專程去見他們,費用可能貴得離譜,而且又要花費很多時間。在這種情況下,其他的溝通方式,尤其是電子的通訊方式就比較適合。此外,書信和電子郵件則能讓我們在通訊時留下記錄,以便日後萬一發生爭論時,可留做參考。最後,這些溝通方式,使我們可以方便地隨時傳送訊息,不需要特別去配合對方的時間。

總之,信件、電子郵件與電話,和面對面談話比起來,是更有效率的溝通方式,能讓我們節省時間和金錢。在現今的世界中,我想這些都是必須考慮的重要因素。因此,我認爲它們才是比較好的溝通方式。

【註釋】

communication〔kə,mjunə'keʃən〕 *n.* 溝通　　***depend on*** 視～而定
definition〔,dɛfə'nɪʃən〕 *n.* 定義　　effective〔ə'fɛktɪv〕 *adj.* 有效的
least〔list〕 *adj.* 最小的;最少的
misunderstanding〔,mɪsʌndə'stændɪŋ〕 *n.* 誤會
efficient〔ɪ'fɪʃənt〕 *adj.* 有效率的　　means〔minz〕 *n.pl.* 方式
latter〔'lætə〕 *adj.* (兩者中)後者的
increasingly〔ɪn'krisɪŋlɪ〕 *adv.* 愈來愈
exactness〔ɪg'zæktnɪs〕 *n.* 準確　　feasible〔'fizəbl〕 *adj.* 可行的
prohibitively〔pro'hɪbɪtɪvlɪ〕 *adv.* 非常貴地
electronic〔ɪ,lɛk'trɑnɪk〕 *adj.* 電子的
appropriate〔ə'proprɪɪt〕 *adj.* 適當的　　***refer to*** 參考;查詢
dispute〔dɪ'spjut〕 *n.* 爭論　　arise〔ə'raɪz〕 *v.* 發生
match〔mætʃ〕 *v.* 配合　　factor〔'fæktə〕 *n.* 因素

Quit	Writing

Some people like to do only what they already do well. Other people prefer to try new things and take risks. Which do you prefer? Use specific reasons and examples to support your choice.

▲

Cut

Paste

Undo

▼

Time			Help	Confirm	Next
			?	Answer	➡

50. The Advantages of Trying New Things

Everyone likes to succeed at what he does, and it is more likely that we will succeed at things we already know how to do well. *However*, to limit ourselves to doing only those things which we are good at will cause us to miss many opportunities to develop other interests and skills. *For this reason*, I believe that it is to our advantage to try new things and take risks.

When we try something new we may fail. That is the risk that we take. *But* we can still learn something from our failure, even if it is only how to cope with failing. We may also succeed at a new activity and this will bring us a feeling of accomplishment and greater self-confidence. We may also discover a new interest that will bring pleasure to our lives or lead to a new line of work. *Furthermore*, it is not always possible to play it safe and do only those things that we know. We cannot control every situation and no doubt we will someday meet with challenges. If we already have the experience of testing ourselves in an unfamiliar situation, we will be better able to handle any situation which arises.

To sum up, trying new things and taking risks allow us to develop both our skills and our personal interests. When we take a risk we cannot know beforehand what will happen, but if we try our best we are certain to gain something positive from the experience whether we win or lose.

50. 嘗試新事物的好處

　　每個人都希望所做的事情可以成功,而如果我們已經知道如何才能把事情做好時,就比較可能成功。然而,限定自己只做那些我們擅長的事,將會使我們錯過許多發展其他興趣和技能的機會。基於這個理由,我認為嘗試新事物及冒險,對我們有好處。

　　當我們嘗試新事物時,可能會失敗,這就是我們所要冒的風險。但是我們仍然可以從失敗中學習,即使學到的只是如何面對失敗。我們可能也會在新的嘗試中成功,而這會帶給我們成就感,並更有自信。我們也可能發現新的興趣,為生活增添樂趣,或使自己從事新的行業。此外,一直只做我們所了解的事,而不冒任何風險,是不可能的。我們不能掌控每個情況,而且無疑地,有一天我們一定要面對挑戰。如果我們已經有過在不熟悉的情況下,考驗自己能力的經驗,就比較能夠應付所發生的任何情況。

　　總之,嘗試新事物和冒險,能讓我們培養技能和個人的興趣。當我們冒險時,我們無法事先預知會發生什麼事,但如果我們盡力而為,不論結果是輸或贏,我們必定可以從這次的經驗中,獲得一些正面的啓示。

【註釋】

be good at 擅長　　　*to one's advantage* 對某人有利

take a risk 冒險　　　*cope with* 處理;應付 (= *deal with* = *handle*)

accomplishment〔ə'kamplɪʃmənt〕*n.* 成就

lead to 導致;引起　　line〔laɪn〕*n.* 行業

furthermore〔'fɝðə,mor〕*adv.* 此外

play (*it*) *safe* 不冒險;謹慎行事

meet with 面對 (= *face* = *be faced with*)

challenge〔'tʃælɪndʒ〕*n.* 挑戰　　arise〔ə'raɪz〕*v.* 發生

to sum up 總之

beforehand〔bɪ'for,hænd〕*adv.* 事先 (= *in advance*)

try one's best 盡力　　positive〔'pazətɪv〕*adj.* 正面的

Quit　　　　**Writing**

Some people believe that success in life comes from taking risks or chances. Others believe that success results from careful planning. In your opinion, what does success come from? Use specific reasons and examples to support your answer.

Cut

Paste

Undo

51. **Planning for Success**

Everyone hopes for success in life, but not everyone can succeed, even after years of hard work. *At the same time*, we often

hear about an "overnight success", someone who has achieved fame and fortune suddenly and through what seems little effort. So what is the best way to increase our chances of success? Is it to take every risk or chance that comes along and hope for the best? Some people certainly do achieve success this way, but I believe that they are rare. *In my opinion*, our chances of succeeding are much greater if we carefully plan for our success.

One reason we should plan is that by planning we more clearly identify our goals and the steps we must take to achieve them. If we don't know what we want to achieve, we are unlikely to make much progress. Planning also helps us keep our goal in mind and, *thus*, keep working toward it. *Another* benefit of careful planning is that we will not miss any opportunities or deadlines due to carelessness or inattention. *Finally*, by planning for our success, we will be sure to develop the skills and knowledge we need to achieve our goals. Opportunity will do us no good if we lack the ability to take advantage of it when it arrives.

In conclusion, although a certain amount of risk taking can help one to achieve success, it cannot replace the benefits of careful planning. Rather than spend our time looking for shortcuts to success, we should think about our goals carefully and take the proper steps toward achieving them. *In that way*, we will have the greatest chance of success.

51. 爲成功做計劃

　　每個人都希望在人生中能成功，但並非人人都做得到，即使是經過多年的努力之後。同時，我們也常聽到有人「一夜之間成功」，他們突然名利雙收，而似乎沒有經過多少努力。所以，要增加成功的機會，什麼方法最好呢？是要把握每一個冒險的機會，做最好的打算嗎？有些人的確是這樣成功的，但我認爲這些情形很罕見。依我之見，如果我們能爲成功做仔細的計劃，成功的機會就會大得多。

　　我們應該做計劃的原因之一是，藉由做計劃，能更清楚地確認自己的目標，以及要達成目標必須採取的步驟。如果我們不知道要達成什麼，就不可能有太大的進步。計劃也幫助我們牢記自己的目標，因而不斷朝目標持續努力。詳細計劃的另一個好處是，我們不會因爲疏忽，或沒有注意到，而錯過機會或最後期限。最後，爲成功做計劃，我們必須培養達成目標所需的技能和知識，否則當機會來臨時，如果我們欠缺利用機會的能力，那麼機會對我們而言，就沒有任何好處。

　　總之，雖然某種程度的冒險有助於成功，但還是不能取代詳細計劃的好處。花時間去尋找成功的捷徑，不如仔細思考自己的目標，並採取適當的步驟去達成。如此一來，我們才能擁有最大的成功機會。

【註釋】

overnight〔'ovɚ'naɪt〕*adj.* 一夜之間的

achieve〔ə'tʃiv〕*v.* 獲得；達成　　fame〔fem〕*n.* 名聲

fortune〔'fɔrtʃən〕*n.* 財富　　*take a risk* 冒險（= *take a chance*）

come along 突然出現　　*hope for the best* 作最好的打算

rare〔rɛr〕*adj.* 罕見的　　identify〔aɪ'dɛntə,faɪ〕*v.* 確認

take steps 採取步驟　　progress〔'prɑgrɛs〕*n.* 進步

keep…in mind 將…牢記在心　　*work toward* 努力達到；設法獲得

benefit〔'bɛnəfɪt〕*n.* 好處；利益

deadline〔'dɛd,laɪn〕*n.* 最後期限

inattention〔,ɪnə'tɛnʃən〕*n.* 不注意　　*do sb. good* 對某人有益

take advantage of 利用　　shortcut〔'ʃɔrt,kʌt〕*n.* 捷徑 < *to* >

proper〔'prɑpɚ〕*adj.* 適當的

Quit	Writing

What change would make your hometown more appealing to people your age?　Use specific reasons and examples to support your opinion.

Cut

Paste

Undo

---

52. A Change in My Hometown

My hometown is a large and densely populated city. It offers many conveniences to the people who live here but, *of course*, there are some drawbacks as well. These include heavy traffic, pollution, noise and crowds. *However*, I still think the advantages of my hometown outweigh the disadvantages. If I could change one thing in order to make my hometown more attractive to young people, it would be the following.

In my opinion, providing more outdoor recreation areas would make my hometown more appealing to people my age. There are many parks in and around the city already, but they are heavily used, especially on school holidays. *Furthermore*, they are not always easy to get to and many do not offer amusements suitable for teenagers. It is fine to provide playgrounds for children, but people my age would like to see more open fields where we can play games such as soccer or baseball. More tennis and basketball courts would also be welcome.

Providing such facilities would have many advantages. Most important among them is that it would encourage young people to spend more time outdoors. *As it is*, teenagers are more likely to be found playing computer games or hanging around shopping malls than doing outdoor activities. *Furthermore*, it would provide us with an alternative place to meet our friends and socialize, with the added advantage of being cost-free.

To sum up, although I am happy with my hometown and think that it is an interesting and convenient place to live, I believe that the above change would make it more appealing to people my age. Young people are very active and we should have clean, safe and healthy places in which to spend our leisure time.

52. 家鄉的一項改變

我的家鄉是個人口稠密的大都市，提供當地居民許多的便利，但是當然也有一些缺點，包括繁忙的交通、污染、噪音以及擁擠的人潮。然而，我仍然認為家鄉的優點多於缺點。如果我可以做一項改變，使家鄉更吸引年輕人，那麼以下就是我想做的。

在我看來，提供更多的戶外休閒場所，可以讓我的家鄉更吸引與我年齡相仿的人。雖然市內及周圍地區已經有很多公園了，但是這些公園都不敷使用，特別是學校放假的時候。此外，公園不一定到處都有，而且很多公園沒有適合青少年的娛樂設施。蓋遊樂場給小孩是件好事，但是跟我同年齡的人，會想要有更多空曠的場地，可以從事像踢足球，或打棒球等的運動。我們也樂於見到有更多的網球場及籃球場。

提供這些設施有許多好處，最重要的是，能夠鼓勵年輕人，多花時間從事戶外活動。實際上，我們可以發現，青少年比較會想去打電動玩具，或是在購物中心逗留，而不是從事戶外活動。此外，在地點方面，戶外休閒場所能提供我們和朋友見面，以及從事社交活動的其他選擇，而且也有不用花錢的附加優惠。

總之，雖然我很滿意我的家鄉，覺得它是個有趣，而且方便的居住地點，但是我相信，上述的改變將使它更吸引和我同年齡的人。年輕人活潑好動，因此我們應該有乾淨、安全和健康的地方，來度過閒暇時間。

【註釋】

hometown〔'hom,taʊn〕n. 家鄉　　densely〔'dɛnslɪ〕adv. 稠密地
populate〔'pɑpjə,let〕v. 使居住　　drawback〔'drɔ,bæk〕n. 缺點
outweigh〔aʊt'we〕v. 勝過　　recreation〔,rɛkrɪ'eʃən〕n. 娛樂
appealing〔ə'pilɪŋ〕adj. 吸引人的　　heavily〔'hɛvɪlɪ〕adv. 大量地
not always 不一定　　amusement〔ə'mjuzmənt〕n. 娛樂
playground〔'ple,graʊnd〕n. 運動場；遊樂場
open field 空曠的場地　　court〔kort〕n.（網球、籃球等的）球場
facilities〔fə'sɪlətɪz〕n. pl. 設施　　***as it is*** 實際上
hang around 徘徊；逗留　　alternative〔ɔl'tɜnətɪv〕adj. 替代的
socialize〔'soʃə,laɪz〕v. 交際；來往　　added〔'ædɪd〕adj. 附加的
cost-free〔'kɔst'fri〕adj. 免費的　　***to sum up*** 總之
active〔'æktɪv〕adj. 活躍的　　***leisure time*** 空閒時間

Quit   **Writing**

Do you agree or disagree with the following statement? The most important aspect of a job is the money a person earns. Use specific reasons and examples to support your answer.

Cut

Paste

Undo

53. Money Is Not the Most Important Aspect of a Job

When deciding what career to pursue, and which specific job to take, there are many things for us to consider. They include the work location and environment, chances for advancement, and of course the salary. Some would say that money is the most important aspect of a job, but I do not believe this is true. *In my opinion*, there are some other aspects which are more important.

First of all, we should engage in work in a field which interests us. *Then*, we will enjoy our work more and not dread going to our job every day. A large salary is not worth the daily discomfort of doing something we do not enjoy. *Second*, our job should give us a sense of personal satisfaction. When we feel that what we are doing is important and worthwhile, how much money we make is not as important. *Finally*, our job should allow us to live a balanced life. It should not be so time-consuming that we have no time for family, friends and personal interests. Nor should it give us so much pressure that we cannot relax in our free time.

The three aspects above, *in my opinion*, are more important than money when considering which job to take. There is no denying that money is important, but it is not the only important thing in life. *Certainly*, money does not always lead to happiness. *Therefore*, it should not be the only consideration when evaluating a job opportunity.

53. 金錢不是工作最重要的一部分

要決定從事什麼職業，或做什麼特定的工作時，我們要考慮的事情很多，包括工作地點與環境、升遷的機會，當然還有薪水。有些人認為，錢是工作中最重要的一部分，但是我並不同意這樣的說法。在我看來，有其他方面，比錢更重要。

首先，我們應該投身於自己有興趣的領域，這樣才能更喜歡我們的工作，而不會每天都害怕去上班。再多的薪水也不值得我們去做不喜歡的工作，讓自己每天都不舒服。其次，工作應該讓我們有成就感，當我們覺得自己的工作很重要，而且很有價值時，金錢的多寡就沒那麼重要了。最後，工作應該要能讓我們過著均衡的生活。我們的時間不應該被工作完全佔滿，讓我們沒有時間跟家人和朋友相處，或無法發展個人興趣。工作也不能有過大的壓力，使我們連在空閒時間也無法放鬆。

依我之見，當我們考慮從事何種工作時，以上所列舉的三個方面就比金錢更重要。不可否認地，金錢是非常重要的，但它並不是生命中唯一重要的東西，當然，金錢也未必會帶來快樂。因此，當我們在衡量工作機會時，不應該只考慮到金錢。

【註釋】

aspect〔ˈæspɛkt〕*n.* 方面　　pursue〔pəˈsu〕*v.* 從事 (= *engage in*)
specific〔spɪˈsɪfɪk〕*adj.* 特定的
advancement〔ədˈvænsmənt〕*n.* 晉升
first of all 首先 (= *first = firstly = in the first place*)
field〔fild〕*n.* 領域　　dread〔drɛd〕*v.* 害怕
daily〔ˈdelɪ〕*adj.* 每天的　　discomfort〔dɪsˈkʌmfət〕*n.* 不舒服
worthwhile〔ˈwɝθˈhwaɪl〕*adj.* 值得的
balanced〔ˈbælənst〕*adj.* 均衡的
time-consuming〔ˈtaɪmkənˌsjumɪŋ〕*adj.* 費時的
pressure〔ˈprɛʃə〕*n.* 壓力
There is no + V-ing ～是不可能的 (= *It is impossible to + V.*)
lead to 導致　　consideration〔kənˌsɪdəˈreʃən〕*n.* 該慎重考慮的事
evaluate〔ɪˈvæljuˌet〕*v.* 評估

Quit   **Writing**

Do you agree or disagree with the following statement? One should never judge a person by external appearance. Use specific reasons and details to support your answer.

Cut

Paste

Undo

54. **Judging a Person by His Appearance**

We all meet a variety of people every day. When we meet someone new, we soon form an opinion of that person. Many factors may influence our judgment, including the person's physical appearance, dress, speech, body language, and so on. Some people say that it is unfair to judge a person according to his appearance, for things such as character and ability are more important. *No doubt* this is true, but I cannot agree with the statement that one should never judge a person by his external appearance, because it is a factor we cannot ignore.

The way a person dresses can be an important clue, because people use such things as dress, hairstyle and so on to express themselves. Observing a person's appearance can often tell us a lot about him or her. It can tell us if the person identifies with a certain group and, *more importantly*, how he sees himself. *In addition*, we should notice whether a person has dressed appropriately for the occasion. If not, we know that he either does not respect the occasion or is careless. These can also be important clues to his character. *Finally*, although it is wrong to judge people according to stereotypes, we cannot ignore the fact that they are sometimes true. *In other words*, if a person looks dangerous, he might really be a threat, so we should be careful until we know him better.

In conclusion, I believe that we cannot ignore the importance of external appearance when forming a first impression of someone. It may not be the most important factor, but it can tell us a lot about the person's character. *Therefore*, we should not only notice others' appearances, but our own as well.

54. 以貌取人

　　我們每天都會遇到各式各樣的人，當我們初識某人，就會馬上有對此人的看法。影響我們判斷的因素很多，包括這個人的外貌、穿著、談吐、肢體語言等等。有人說，根據外表來評斷某人是不公平的，因爲像是性格、能力等特質更爲重要。無疑地，這樣的說法沒錯，但是我不同意絕對不能以貌取人的說法，因爲外表是我們無法忽略的因素。

　　一個人的穿著打扮可能是重要的線索，因爲人會利用像是服裝、髮型等特色，來表達自我。觀察一個人的外表，往往可以讓我們知道很多關於這個人的事情。我們可以知道這個人是不是認同某個團體，而且更重要的是，這個人對自己有何看法。此外，我們應該注意這個人的穿著，在當時的場合是否恰當，如果不恰當，我們可以知道，這個人並不尊重這個場合，或者是很粗心草率，這些都可能是觀察其個性的重要線索。最後，雖然根據刻板印象來看人的好壞是錯誤的，但有時候我們也不能忽視其可靠性。換句話說，如果某人看起來很危險，他可能眞的是個危險份子，所以在我們更了解他的爲人之前，應該要小心謹愼。

　　總之，我認爲當我們對某人形成第一印象時，不能忽略外表的重要性。外表可能並非是最重要的因素，但我們可以從一個人的外表，得知許多與其個性有關的事情。因此，我們不只要注意別人的外表，也要注意自己的外表。

【註釋】

a variety of 各式各樣的　　factor〔ˈfæktɚ〕 *n.* 因素

and so on 等等　　judgment〔ˈdʒʌdʒmənt〕 *n.* 判斷

unfair〔ʌnˈfɛr〕 *adj.* 不公平的　　external〔ɪkˈstɜnḷ〕 *adj.* 外在的

ignore〔ɪgˈnor〕 *v.* 忽視　　clue〔klu〕 *n.* 線索

identify〔aɪˈdɛntəˌfaɪ〕 *v.* 認同 < *with* >

appropriately〔əˈproprɪˌetlɪ〕 *adv.* 適當地

occasion〔əˈkeʒən〕 *n.* 場合　　*either…or* ~ 不是…就是~

stereotype〔ˈstɛrɪəˌtaɪp〕 *n.* 刻板印象

in other words 換句話說 (= *that is to say* = *that is*)

threat〔θrɛt〕 *n.* 危險的人；威脅　　*as well* 也 (= *too*)

Quit　　　　　　**Writing**

Do you agree or disagree with the following statement?　A person should never make an important decision alone.　Use specific reasons and examples to support your answer.

Cut

Paste

Undo

Time

Help
?

Confirm
Answer

Next
➡

55. Making Important Decisions

Throughout our lives, we will have to make many decisions. Some will be small and unimportant, but others, such as where to go to school, which career to pursue, and whether or not to buy a house, will be very important. It is this type of decision that we must be very careful about making. *In my opinion*, a person should never make such an important decision alone.

One reason for my opinion is that I believe "two heads are better than one." When we have an important decision to make we can benefit from the advice and experience of others. *In addition*, just talking the issue over with someone else might help us to see aspects of the problem we had not considered before. *Another* reason for not making big decisions alone is that often these decisions do not affect only us. If someone else is going to be affected by the decision, *for example*, our spouse or business partner, that person should be able to voice his opinion and take part in the decision-making process.

These are only two of the reasons for never making an important decision alone, but I feel that they are the most important ones. By involving others in our decisions, we not only show them respect but benefit from their knowledge and experience. *In this way*, we are bound to make better decisions.

55. 做重要的決定

　　我們在一生當中，要做很多決定，有些決定是微不足道的，但有些決定卻非常重要，例如要唸哪一所學校、要從事何種行業，或要不要買房子。做這一類的決定時，我們必須非常小心。我認為，絕對不要獨自一個人做如此重要的決定。

　　我的其中一個理由是，「三個臭皮匠，勝過一個諸葛亮」。當我們要做重要決定時，聽聽別人的建議與經驗，會有所助益。而且，就算只是跟別人討論這些問題，也可能會讓我們看到事情的另一面，而那是我們之前沒考慮到的。另一個不要獨自做重大決定的理由是，這些決定通常影響到的不只我們自己而已。例如，如果還有其他人，如配偶、事業夥伴等，會因這項決定而受影響，他們就應該有權表達意見，並參與決策的過程。

　　這些只是兩個我認為絕不能獨自做重大決定的理由，但我認為，它們是最重要的。讓別人參與決策，不僅能表現出我們對他們的尊重，而且也能從別人的知識與經驗中獲益。如此一來，我們就一定能做出更好的決定。

【註釋】

throughout〔θru'aʊt〕prep. 遍及　　pursue〔pə'su〕v. 從事

type〔taɪp〕n. 類型　　alone〔ə'lon〕adv. 獨自地

Two heads are better than one.

【諺】三個臭皮匠，勝過一個諸葛亮；集思廣益。

benefit〔'bɛnəfɪt〕v. 獲益　　***in addition*** 此外

talk over 討論　　issue〔'ɪʃjʊ〕n. 議題

aspect〔'æspɛkt〕n. 方面　　spouse〔spaʊz〕n. 配偶

voice〔vɔɪs〕v. 表達　　***take part in*** 參與 (= *participate in*)

process〔'prasɛs〕n. 過程　　involve〔ɪn'valv〕v. 使牽涉在內

be bound to + V. 一定 (= *be sure to* + V.)

Quit　　　　**Writing**

A company is going to give some money either to support the arts or to protect the environment. Which do you think the company should choose? Use specific reasons and examples to support your answer.

Cut

Paste

Undo

56. Money for the Environment

Both the arts and protecting the environment are important causes, and both are often underfunded. They depend on government grants and private donations in order to continue. If a company were to give a sum of money to one of these causes, it would be difficult to choose between them. *However*, I believe that the company should put the money toward protecting the environment for the following reasons.

First, the state of the environment affects everyone, and it affects people in a very important way. If mankind destroys the environment, we will not be able to survive. The arts are important to our quality of life, but the environment is important both to the quality of life and to life itself. *Second*, because industry causes much of the damage to the environment, I believe that companies have some responsibility to support conservation and cleanup efforts. *Finally*, protecting the environment is a bigger problem, and so requires a higher level of funding than the arts. A company's donation to the arts may be more visible, but one to the protection of the environment would be more meaningful.

In conclusion, while both the arts and environmental protection are worthy causes, I believe the company should make its donation to an environmental cause. The environment affects everyone in important ways and protecting it is a big job. Hopefully, private donations will help to improve both our environment and our lives.

56. 資助環保

　　藝術和環保都是值得努力的重要目標，但卻經常有資金不足的問題，它們必須仰賴政府的補助金，以及私人的捐贈，才能持續發展。如果有公司要提供一大筆錢給其中之一，將很難做抉擇，然而，我認為基於下列理由，公司應該把錢用來資助環保。

　　首先，環境會影響到每個人，並且影響重大。如果破壞了環境，人類將無法生存。藝術對我們的生活品質很重要，但是環境對生活品質及生活本身都很重要。第二，因為工業對環境造成重大的傷害，所以我認為，企業有責任，支持在環保及環境清潔方面的努力。最後，環保是個較嚴重的問題，比藝術需要更多的資金。公司捐錢資助藝術，可能引起較多的注意，但是捐錢資助環保，則更有意義。

　　總之，雖然藝術與環保都是值得努力的目標，但是我認為，企業應該捐錢資助環保。環境對每個人都有重大的影響，而且環保是一項大工程，但願私人的捐贈能協助改善我們的環境及生活。

【註釋】

cause〔kɔz〕*n.* 事業；（奮鬥的）目標
underfund〔ˌʌndəˈfʌnd〕*v.* 對…提供資金不足
depend on 依賴　　grant〔grænt〕*n.* 補助金；贈款
donation〔doˈneʃən〕*n.* 捐贈　　state〔stet〕*n.* 狀態
survive〔səˈvaɪv〕*v.* 生存　　industry〔ˈɪndəstrɪ〕*n.* 工業；企業
support〔səˈport〕*v.* 資助
conservation〔ˌkɑnsəˈveʃən〕*n.*（自然資源等的）保護；保育
cleanup〔ˈklinˌʌp〕*n.* 大掃除　　level〔ˈlɛvḷ〕*n.* 程度
funding〔ˈfʌndɪŋ〕*n.* 資助　　visible〔ˈvɪzəbḷ〕*adj.* 看得見的
hopefully〔ˈhopfəlɪ〕*adv.* 希望；但願

Quit   **Writing**

Some movies are serious, designed to make the audience think. Other movies are designed primarily to amuse and entertain. Which type of movie do you prefer? Use specific reasons and examples to support your answer.

Cut

Paste

Undo

57. Entertaining Movies

These days, movies are a popular form of entertainment. There seems to be an endless variety of films to appeal to everyone. Some people like thrillers, others romances and still others futuristic sci-fi films. Many viewers prefer movies that amuse and entertain, while others like films that are designed to make the audience think. As for me, I prefer the former, entertaining movies, when I go to the theater.

One reason I prefer to watch movies designed to entertain is that watching a film is a form of relaxation for me. I work hard at my studies and must face a great deal of pressure every day. *In addition*, the world is full of bad news and serious problems. When I go to see a movie, I would rather forget my troubles and be amused than dwell on a serious subject. *Another* reason I prefer entertaining films is that when I do want to find out about a serious matter, I would rather do so by reading a book or watching news reports. I feel I can get more in-depth information and seek out a variety of sources that way. *In this way*, I will get a more balanced view of the issue.

In conclusion, I prefer entertaining movies because I think entertainment is what movies are best at. When exploring more serious issues, I would rather get information from other sources. *But* when I want to forget the pressure of modern day life for a while, I like to go to an amusing and entertaining movie.

57. 娛 樂 片

　　現在看電影是一種很普遍的娛樂形式。似乎有數不清的各式各樣的電影受人喜愛。有人喜歡驚悚片,有人喜歡文藝片,還有人喜歡先進的科幻片。很多觀衆偏愛娛樂搞笑的電影,而有人則喜愛那些發人深省的影片。至於我呢,我看電影時則偏愛前者,也就是娛樂片。

　　我比較喜歡看娛樂片的原因之一,是因爲看電影對我來說,是一種消遣的方式。我每天埋首苦讀,必須面對許多壓力,而且,這個世界充滿了壞消息和嚴重的問題,所以,當我看電影時,我寧可忘卻煩惱,開心一下,也不願老是想著嚴肅的主題。我比較喜歡看娛樂片的另一個原因是,如果我眞的想了解某個嚴肅的主題,我寧可去看書,或看新聞報導,我覺得這樣才能得到更深入的資訊,以及找到更多樣化的資料來源。如此一來,我就能對此議題有更平衡的看法。

　　總之,我比較喜歡娛樂片,因爲我認爲電影最擅長的,就是製造娛樂效果。如果要深入了解比較嚴肅的議題,我寧可從其他的管道取得資訊。可是如果我想要暫時忘掉現代生活的壓力,我還是喜歡看能讓人發笑、娛樂效果十足的電影。

【註釋】

a variety of 各式各樣的　　appeal〔ə'pil〕*v.* 吸引 < to >
thriller〔'θrɪlɚ〕*n.* 驚悚片　　romance〔ro'mæns〕*n.* 愛情故事
futuristic〔ˌfjutʃə'rɪstɪk〕*adj.* 未來的;先進的
sci-fi〔'saɪ'faɪ〕*n.* 科幻小說(= *science fiction*)
viewer〔'vjuɚ〕*n.* 觀衆　　*as for* 至於
the former (兩者中的)前者(↔ *the latter*)
entertaining〔ˌɛntɚ'tenɪŋ〕*adj.* 有趣的　　*be designed to* 目的是爲了
relaxation〔ˌrilæks'eʃən〕*n.* 消遣;娛樂　　*a great deal of* 大量的
would rather + V_1 + *than* + V_2　寧願 V_1,而不願 V_2
dwell on 老是想著　　in-depth〔'ɪn'dɛpθ〕*adj.* 深入的
seek out 找出　　balanced〔'bælənst〕*adj.* 平衡的
issue〔'ɪʃju〕*n.* 議題　　*in conclusion* 總之
be good at 擅長　　explore〔ɪk'splor〕*v.* 探討

Quit	**Writing**

Do you agree or disagree with the following statement? Businesses should do anything they can to make a profit. Use specific reasons and examples to support your position.

Cut

Paste

Undo

58. Making a Profit

The first goal of any commercial business is to make a profit for itself and its shareholders. If it does not, it will soon cease to exist. *However*, this does not mean that a business should do anything it can to make a profit. *On the contrary*, business leaders must keep their long-term goals in mind and occasionally this will mean turning down the most profitable course of action. The following are some examples of this kind of situation.

First, a business must, of course, not do anything illegal, even if by doing so it can earn a large profit. Illegal business activities are not only morally wrong, but will eventually hurt the business when the law catches up with it. *Second*, some business activities are profitable in the short-term, but will lead to loss in the long run. *For example*, a logging company will make a great deal of money by simply cutting down all the trees it can, but if it does not preserve the land and plan for the future, the business will fail in the end. *Third and last*, a business should sometimes forego profitable business opportunities if they will lead to public condemnation. Public relations and customer goodwill are very important to the long-term health of a business.

To be brief, a business should not always do anything it can to make a profit. *Rather*, it should consider the future and make the best decisions for the long-term success of the firm. This may mean it has to make decisions that are unprofitable in the short-term, but bring greater benefits in the future.

58. 賺取利潤

　　營利事業的首要目標，就是要爲自己與股東賺取利潤。如果沒有利潤的話，很快就會關門大吉。然而，這並不表示，營利事業爲了獲利，就能無所不用其極。相反地，企業領導者必須時時謹記長程目標，這就意謂著，有時須放棄獲利最多的做法。以下就是關於這種狀況的一些例子。

　　首先，企業當然不能涉及任何不法的行爲，即使這樣做會帶來大筆利潤。不法的營利行爲不僅不道德，而且當罪行曝光時，必定會傷害到企業本身。第二，有些營利活動是短期獲利，但就長期而言，將會造成虧損。以伐木公司爲例，將所有能砍伐的樹木全砍光，會賺很多錢，但如果沒有保護土地資源，也沒有規劃未來，公司最後一定會倒閉。第三點，也是最後一點，有時企業必須放棄可能會引起社會大衆責難的一些獲利機會。公共關係以及給客戶良好的商譽形象，對企業長期的健全發展而言，是非常重要的。

　　簡言之，企業不該只是盡其所能地追求利潤。相反地，企業應該考慮到未來，以及爲了長遠的事業成功，做出最好的決策。這可能就意味著，這樣的決策，短期之內也許無法獲利，但未來則會帶來更大的利益。

【註釋】

profit〔'prɑfɪt〕*n.* 利潤

commercial〔kə'mɝʃəl〕*adj.* 以營利爲目的的

shareholder〔'ʃɛr,holdɚ〕*n.* 股東（= *stockholder*）

cease〔sis〕*v.* 停止　　exist〔ɪg'zɪst〕*v.* 存在

on the contrary 相反地　　***keep…in mind*** 把…牢記在心

long-term〔'lɔŋ,tɝm〕*adj.* 長期的（↔ *short-term*）

occasionally〔ə'keʒənḷɪ〕*adv.* 偶爾　　***turn down*** 拒絕

course of action 做法　　morally〔'mɔrəlɪ〕*adv.* 道德上

catch up with 逮捕；處罰　　***in the long run*** 到最後（= *in the end*）

logging〔'lɔgɪŋ〕*n.* 伐木　　preserve〔prɪ'zɝv〕*v.* 保存

cut down 砍伐　　forego〔for'go〕*v.* 放棄

profitable〔'prɑfɪtəbḷ〕*adj.* 有利可圖的（↔ *unprofitable*）

condemnation〔,kɑndɛm'neʃən〕*n.* 譴責　　***public relations*** 公共關係

goodwill〔'gʊd'wɪl〕*n.* 商譽；信譽　　***to be brief*** 簡言之（= *in brief*）

rather〔'ræðɚ〕*adv.* 相反地

Quit	Writing

Some people are always in a hurry to go places and get things done. Other people prefer to take their time and live life at a slower pace. Which do you prefer? Use specific reasons and examples to support your answer.

Cut

Paste

Undo

59. Living Life at a Slower Pace

It seems that everyone is in a hurry these days. In our fast-paced and competitive society many people feel that they must do things as quickly as possible or they will fall behind. *Certainly*, there are many things for us to do. *However*, I do not believe that it is necessary to always hurry to get them done. *In fact*, living life at a slower pace has many advantages.

First of all, slowing down allows us to think more clearly about what we must do. With careful consideration we will make better decisions and make fewer mistakes. *And* when we do not have to correct the mistakes that we make in haste, we will actually save time. *Second*, when we take our time we can do things more carefully and thoroughly. *And* when we do a better job we will feel more satisfied with our efforts. *Finally*, if we do not rush through life, we will have more time to enjoy the things that we do. *And* when we take pleasure in our work, we will live happier lives.

In sum, taking our time when we do things has several advantages. By always hurrying we may accomplish more in one day, but we will soon become tired and inefficient. *In the end*, we will waste time by making bad decisions and mistakes that need to be corrected. That is why I believe that living life at a slower pace is preferable.

59. 過著步調較緩慢的生活

　　現在好像每個人的生活都很匆忙。在我們這樣生活步調快速，而且競爭激烈的社會裡，很多人都認為，做事情必須愈快愈好，否則就會落後。當然我們要做的事情很多，但是我認為，並不是每件事都要很快做完。事實上，過著步調較緩慢的生活有很多好處。

　　首先，步調減慢能讓我們對於必須要做的事情，想得更清楚。謹慎考慮能讓我們做出更好的決定，並較少犯錯。而且，當我們不需要花時間改正匆促之間所犯下的錯誤時，實際上是節省了時間。第二，當我們不那麼匆忙行事時，我們做事情將會更小心、更徹底。而且，當我們把事情做得更好時，就會對自己的努力成果感到更加滿意。最後，如果我們不匆匆忙忙地過生活，將會有更多的時間，去享受我們所做的事。而且，當我們在工作中找到樂趣時，就會過得更快樂。

　　總之，做事時放慢腳步，對我們有很多好處。每天都匆匆忙忙，也許會完成很多事，但卻會使我們很快就感到疲倦，因而沒有效率。最後，我們還會因為必須彌補不當的決策，及修正所犯的錯誤，而浪費時間。這就是為什麼我會認為，緩慢的生活步調比較好的原因。

【註釋】

pace〔pes〕*n.* 步調　　***in a hurry*** 匆忙地
competitive〔kəm'pɛtətɪv〕*adj.* 競爭激烈的　　***fall behind*** 落後
first of all 首先　　***slow down*** 慢下來
consideration〔kənˌsɪdə'reʃən〕*n.* 考慮
in haste 匆忙地 (= *in a hurry*)　　thoroughly〔'θɝolɪ〕*adv.* 徹底地
hurry through life 匆忙過生活　　rush〔rʌʃ〕*v.* 匆忙行動 (= *hurry*)
take pleasure in 喜愛 (= *enjoy*)
in sum 總之 (= *to sum up* = *in summary* = *in conclusion*)
accomplish〔ə'kɑmplɪʃ〕*v.* 完成
inefficient〔ˌɪnə'fɪʃənt〕*adj.* 沒有效率的　　***in the end*** 到最後
correct〔kə'rɛkt〕*v.* 改正　　preferable〔'prɛfərəbḷ〕*adj.* 較好的

Quit　　　　　　　**Writing**

Do you agree or disagree with the following statement? Games are
as important for adults as they are for children. Use specific reasons
and examples to support your answer.

▲

Cut

Paste

Undo

▼

Time

Help
?

Confirm
Answer

Next
➡

60. Games Are Not Just for Children

Games are not only a popular form of entertainment, but also a valuable learning tool. Unfortunately, many people believe that playing games is a behavior only appropriate for children. *In my opinion*, this is not the case for the following reasons.

First of all, we can gain knowledge and learn new skills by playing games, and we often learn better and faster through games than we do through more conventional methods. This is just as true of adults as it is of children. *Second*, playing games can develop our thinking and reasoning abilities. Contrary to popular belief, the brain does not stop developing after childhood; *therefore*, it is important for all of us to continue to exercise our brains. *Last but not least*, playing games is a social activity that brings people closer together while helping them learn how to get along with each other. *For this reason*, games can be a very useful part of company training programs as well as family gatherings.

For the reasons stated above, I cannot agree with the opinion that games are merely "child's play." *On the contrary*, they can be of great value to people of all ages as well as a pleasant way to spend time with others. Adults should not ignore the advantages of playing games.

60. 不是只有小孩適合玩遊戲

　　遊戲不僅是一種普遍的娛樂形式，也是一項珍貴的學習工具。可惜的是，許多人認為玩遊戲是只適合小孩的行為。依我之見，基於下列的理由，事實並非如此。

　　首先，我們能夠藉由玩遊戲，獲得知識並學習新技術，而且透過遊戲，我們經常會比使用傳統方法學得更好、更快，這適用於大人，就像適用於小孩一樣。第二點，玩遊戲能夠培養我們思考和推理的能力。和一般人的想法相反的是，大腦在孩童時期過後，並沒有停止發展；因此，繼續運用我們的大腦是很重要的。最後一項要點是，玩遊戲是種社交活動，能讓人們彼此更接近，有助於學習如何和別人相處。基於這個理由，遊戲可能是公司訓練課程和家庭聚會中，很有用的一部分。

　　基於上述的理由，我不同意遊戲只是「小孩玩的」這樣的說法。相反地，遊戲對所有年齡層的人而言，都具有極大的價值，它還是一種和別人相處，十分令人愉快的方式。成人不應該忽視玩遊戲所帶來的好處。

【註釋】

unfortunately〔ʌnˈfɔrtʃənɪtlɪ〕*adv.* 可惜的是
appropriate〔əˈproprɪɪt〕*adj.* 適合的　　case〔kes〕*n.* 事實
conventional〔kənˈvɛnʃənḷ〕*adj.* 傳統的
be true of 適用於　　reasoning〔ˈriznɪŋ〕*n.* 推理
contrary〔ˈkɑntrɛrɪ〕*adj.* 相反的　　brains〔brenz〕*n.* 智力
last but not least 最後一項要點是　　**get along with** 與～相處
gathering〔ˈgæðrɪŋ〕*n.* 聚會　　state〔stet〕*v.* 陳述
merely〔ˈmɪrlɪ〕*adv.* 僅僅　　pleasant〔ˈplɛznt〕*adj.* 令人愉快的
ignore〔ɪgˈnor〕*v.* 忽視

Quit   **Writing**

Do you agree or disagree with the following statement? Parents or other adult relatives should make important decisions for their older (15 to 18 years old) teenage children. Use specific reasons and examples to support your opinion.

▲

Cut

Paste

Undo

▼

Time

Help
?

Confirm
Answer

Next
➡

61. **Helping Teenagers Make Decisions**

Parents take on a great deal of responsibility when they choose to have children. *Of course*, they want the best for their children and hope that they will make the right decisions and have a happy and successful life. When children are younger, parents usually make all important decisions for them. This is only natural as young children do not have the experience and ability to make good decisions. *However*, I believe that when a child is an older teenager, he should begin to make more decisions for himself.

Rather than make decisions for their teenagers, I believe that parents should advise them and help them to make the best decisions for themselves. *In this way*, the children will learn how to make decisions in the future, when they can no longer depend on their families for everything. *Furthermore*, these years are a time for teenagers to take more responsibility. If they make bad decisions they will have to live with the consequences. *Of course*, parents should not leave their children to make important decisions all alone, but instead give them the benefit of good advice and guide them in the right direction. While it may be hard for parents to see their child make a decision that they do not agree with, teenagers are old enough to know what they want and what is important to them. Just as children must learn to make decisions, their parents must learn to respect them.

All in all, letting older teenagers make their own decisions offers more advantages to the family than disadvantages. Children may indeed make some bad decisions and suffer as a result, but this is also a learning experience. By letting their teenagers develop their decision-making skills parents help them to become more mature and competent adults.

61. 協助青少年做決定

當父母選擇生小孩後，就承擔了重大的責任。當然，父母會想給小孩最好的，也希望小孩能做出正確的決定，擁有快樂成功的生活。小孩年幼時，父母通常為他們決定所有的重要事情，這是一般常情，因為年幼的孩童沒有經驗以及能力，可以做出好的決定。然而，我認為當小孩長大，成為年紀較大的青少年時，就應該開始為自己做更多的決定。

我認為，父母與其替他們十幾歲的小孩做決定，倒不如提供建議給小孩，協助他們為自己做出最好的決定。如此一來，小孩將學會以後當他們無法再凡事皆依賴家人時，如何做決定。此外，這幾年是青少年該承擔更多責任的時機，他們如果做出錯誤的決定，就必須承擔後果。當然，父母不應該讓小孩獨自決定重要的事情，而是應該提供他們好的建議，引導他們朝正確的方向前進。雖然對父母而言，眼看著小孩做出他們不認同的決定是很困難的，但青少年年紀已經夠大了，知道自己想要什麼，以及什麼對自己而言是重要的。就如同小孩必須學會如何做決定，父母也必須學習尊重小孩。

總之，讓較年長的青少年自己做決定，能為家人帶來的好處比壞處多。小孩的確有可能會做出錯誤的決定，並且嚐到後果，但這也是個可供學習的經驗。藉由讓青少年培養做決定的能力，父母能幫助他們變得更成熟，成為更有能力的大人。

【註釋】

take on 承擔　　*a great deal of* 許多 (= *much*)
advise〔əd'vaɪz〕*v.* 勸告　　*depend on* 依賴
consequence〔'kɑnsə,kwɛns〕*n.* 後果
guide〔gaɪd〕*v.* 引導　　*all in all* 總之
advantage〔əd'væntɪdʒ〕*n.* 優點 (↔ disadvantage〔,dɪsəd'væntɪdʒ〕)
as a result 因此　　mature〔mə'tjur,mə'tʃur〕*adj.* 成熟的
competent〔'kɑmpətənt〕*adj.* 有能力的

Quit   **Writing**

What do you want **most** in a friend --- someone who is intelligent, or someone who has a sense of humor, or someone who is reliable? Which **one** of these characteristics is most important to you? Use reasons and specific examples to explain your choice.

Cut

Paste

Undo

Time

Help
?

Confirm
Answer

Next

62. **Reliable Friends**

It is important to have friends, but it is also important to have good friends. The best friends are many things, including intelligence, dependability and fun to be with. It is difficult to say which is the most important quality, but if I had to choose just one, I would say it is reliability. To me, a reliable friend is more valuable than one that is intelligent or has a great sense of humor.

There are several reasons for my preference. *First of all*, a reliable friend will always stand by me. He may not always know the answer, but he will always have time for my question. He may not get the latest jokes, but neither will he make a joke out of me. *Second*, such a friend will never let me down. I know he will keep his promises and will never reveal my secrets. *Finally*, a reliable friend will be a friend forever. No matter where our lives may take us in the future, I know he will not forget me.

A reliable friend can be depended upon for help in times of trouble and for sympathy in times of sadness. He will also share your joys without envy. *In short*, this kind of friend is the best of all possible friends because he is your friend through both good times and bad.

62. 可靠的朋友

　　交朋友很重要，但結交好朋友也很重要。最好的朋友有很多特質，包括聰明、可靠，而且和他在一起很快樂。要說什麼特質最重要，並不容易，但如果一定要選一個，我會說可靠性最重要。對我來說，一個可靠的朋友勝過聰明或富有幽默感的朋友。

　　我會有這樣偏好，是基於好幾個理由。首先，可靠的朋友永遠都會在我身旁支持我。他不一定每次都知道答案，但隨時都有時間聽我說自己的問題。他可能聽不懂最新的笑話，但他也不會拿我當作開玩笑的對象。第二，這樣的朋友絕不會讓我失望。我知道他會遵守諾言，絕對不會洩露我的秘密。最後，一個可靠的朋友會是一輩子的朋友。不管未來我們的人生會走向何處，我知道他不會忘記我。

　　可靠的朋友可以讓我依賴，在我有困難的時候幫助我，或是在我悲傷的時候，同情我。他也會和我一起分享快樂，而不會心懷嫉妒。簡言之，這種朋友是所有朋友當中最好的一種，因為不論是好是壞，他都能陪我一起渡過。

【註釋】

reliable〔rɪ'laɪəb!〕 *adj.* 可靠的（ = *dependable* ）
intelligence〔ɪn'tɛlədʒəns〕 *n.* 聰明；智慧
dependability〔dɪ͵pɛndə'bɪlətɪ〕 *n.* 可靠性（ = *reliability* ）
quality〔'kwɑlətɪ〕 *n.* 特質　　valuable〔'væljəb!〕 *adj.* 珍貴的
preference〔'prɛf(ə)rəns〕 *n.* 喜歡；偏愛　　*stand by* 站在旁邊；支持
not always 未必；不一定　　*get the joke* 了解笑話的笑點
make a joke out of sb. 拿某人開玩笑　　*let* sb. *down* 使某人失望

keep one's *promise* 遵守諾言　　reveal〔rɪ'vil〕 *v.* 洩露
No matter where our lives may take us in the future…
　　（ = *No matter where we end up in the future…* ）
　　不管未來我們的人生會走向何處（如何發展）…
depend〔dɪ'pɛnd〕 *v.* 依靠；依賴＜ *upon / on* ＞
sympathy〔'sɪmpəθɪ〕 *n.* 同情　　envy〔'ɛnvɪ〕 *n.* 嫉妒
both good times and bad （日子）是好是壞

Writing

Do you agree or disagree with the following statement? Most experiences in our lives that seemed difficult at the time become valuable lessons for the future. Use reasons and specific examples to support your answer.

Cut

Paste

Undo

Time

Help
?

Confirm
Answer

Next
→

63. Difficult Experiences are the Best Lessons in Life

We have all experienced difficulty in our lives. At the time, we rarely see anything good in the situation. We only rue our bad luck and wish that things were different. *However*, once the problem has been solved or the challenge overcome, we often find that it was a valuable experience. From it we learned something that made us grow.

I had a difficult time when I was in junior high school. In the middle of my final year my family moved to another city. *As a result*, I had to attend a new school. Not only did I know no one in my new class, but I was under a great deal of pressure because of the approaching high school entrance exam. It seemed that things would never get better. But to my surprise, by July I had not only gained entrance to a good high school but had made several new friends. Without realizing it I had grown up in several ways. Forced to study by myself, I learned to be more independent. *Furthermore*, having to adapt to a new society made me more outgoing and confident. Now I no longer fear new environments and challenges.

This difficult experience seemed terrible at the time but, in the end, it was good for me because it made me a stronger person. *In my opinion*, that is true of most difficult situations. *Therefore*, next time I face trouble rather than despair I will try to imagine how the experience may benefit me.

63. 困難的經驗是人生最好的教訓

我們大家在人生中都曾經歷過困難。在那個當下,我們很少會看到整個情況中好的一面。我們只會悲嘆自己的不幸,期望事情有所轉變。然而,一旦難題解決了,或是挑戰被克服了,我們通常會發現,其實那是一個寶貴的經驗。從其中我們可以學習到讓我們成長的東西。

我唸國中的時侯,有過一段困難時期。在我國三那一年,我們全家搬到另一個城市。因此,我必須轉到新的學校就讀。我不但完全不認識班上的同學,也同時因為高中入學考試的逼近,而感到相當大的壓力。情況看起來似乎不會有任何好轉。但令我驚訝的是,到了七月,我不但考上了好學校,而且也交了許多新朋友。在不知不覺間,我已經在許多方面有所成長。因為被迫獨自唸書,我學會更加獨立。此外,因為必須適應新環境,我變得更加外向、更有自信。現在我再也不怕新環境和挑戰。

這個辛苦的經驗在當時看起來很糟糕,但終究對我是有益的,因為我因此變得更堅強。在我看來,大部分的困境都是如此。因此,下次遇到困難時,我不會感到絕望,反而會思考,這次的遭遇將會帶給我什麼樣的好處。

【註釋】

at the time 在那個時候　　rarely〔'rɛrlɪ〕 adv. 很少
rue〔ru〕v. 悲嘆　　challenge〔'tʃælɪndʒ〕n. 挑戰
overcome〔ˌovə'kʌm〕v. 克服　　valuable〔'væljəbl̩〕adj. 珍貴的
in the middle of 在⋯當中　　*under pressure* 承受⋯壓力
a great deal of 大量的　　approaching〔ə'protʃɪŋ〕adj. 即將來臨的
entrance〔'ɛntrəns〕n. 進入;入學　　*entrance exam* 入學考試

to one's surprise 令某人驚訝的是　　gain〔gen〕v. 獲得
force〔fors〕v. 強迫　　independent〔ˌɪndɪ'pɛndənt〕adj. 獨立的
furthermore〔'fɝðəˌmor,-mɔr〕adv. 此外
adapt〔ə'dæpt〕v. 適應 < *to* >　　society〔sə'saɪətɪ〕n. 團體
outgoing〔'aʊtˌgoɪŋ〕adj. 外向的　　*in the end* 最後
be true of 適用於　　*rather than* 而不是
despair〔dɪ'spɛr〕v. 絕望　　benefit〔'bɛnəfɪt〕v. 有益於

Quit　　　**Writing**

Some people prefer to work for themselves or own a business. Others prefer to work for an employer.　Would you rather be self-employed, work for someone else, or own a business?　Use specific reasons to explain your choice.

Cut

Paste

Undo

Time

Help
?

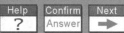
Confirm
Answer

Next

64. Self-employment

There are many types of careers from which we can choose. It is most important to choose work that is fulfilling for us, but it is also important to consider our preferred working style. Given the choice between working for someone else, owning a business or being self-employed, I would choose the last.

In my opinion, self-employment offers many advantages that the other two do not. *For one thing*, it would allow me to make my own decisions. While a business owner also makes decisions, he is constrained by his responsibilities to his employees. *For another*, the rewards are greater for those who are self-employed than for those who work for others. Granted there is more risk involved, but it would also be satisfying to know that any success was due to my own effort and was mine alone. *Finally*, self-employment is more flexible. I would be able to set my own hours and turn down any job I did not wish to do.

In short, self-employment offers more freedom than either owning a business or working for someone else, and that is why I would prefer it. *However*, these advantages do not come without cost, for while my success would belong solely to me, so would my failures. *Therefore*, being self-employed requires both courage and competence.

64. 自由業

　　有很多種職業供我們選擇。選擇能實現自我抱負的工作固然重要，但考慮到個人偏好的工作方式也很重要。如果要從受僱於他人、自己創業，或做自由業中做選擇，我會選擇最後一個。

　　在我看來，自由業提供許多前兩者沒有的好處。首先，做自由業可以自己做決定。雖然創業者也可以自己做決定，但他對員工有責任，因此會受到限制。另外，做自由業的報酬，也比受僱於他人高。就算風險可能會比較大，但知道成功完全歸因於自己的努力，會讓人很滿足。最後，做自由業較有彈性。我可以訂定自己的上班時間，也可以拒絕做不想做的工作。

　　簡言之，自由業比創業或受僱於他人更加自由，所以我比較喜歡自由業。然而，除了這些好處外，也要付出代價，因爲成功固然完全屬於我，但失敗也是要自己承擔。因此，做自由業同時需要具備勇氣及能力。

【註釋】

self-employment〔͵sɛlfɪm'plɔɪmənt〕*n.* 自由業

fulfilling〔fʊl'fɪlɪŋ〕*adj.* 能實現個人抱負的

preferred〔prɪ'fɝd〕*adj.* 偏好的　　given〔'gɪvən〕*prep.* 假如；考慮到

self-employed〔͵sɛlfɪm'plɔɪd〕*adj.* 自雇的；自由業的 (如作家等，不受雇
　　於別人的)　　advantage〔əd'væntɪdʒ〕*n.* 好處

for one thing 首先；一則　　constrain〔kən'stren〕*v.* 限制

employee〔͵ɛmplɔɪ'i, ɪm'plɔɪ-i〕*n.* 受雇者；員工

for another 另外；再者　　reward〔rɪ'wɔrd〕*n.* 報酬

granted〔'græntɪd〕*conj.* 假定；就算　　risk〔rɪsk〕*n.* 風險

involve〔ɪn'vɑlv〕*v.* 牽涉　　flexible〔'flɛksəbḷ〕*adj.* 有彈性的

set〔sɛt〕*v.* 安排　　hours〔aʊrz〕*n. pl.* 上班時間

turn down 拒絕　　*in short* 簡言之

either A *or* B 不是 A 就是 B　　cost〔kɔst〕*n.* 代價

solely〔'sollɪ〕*adv.* 完全　　*belong to* 屬於

competence〔'kɑmpətəns〕*n.* 能力

Quit

Writing

Should a city try to preserve its old, historic buildings or destroy them and replace them with modern buildings? Use specific reasons and examples to support your opinion.

Cut

Paste

Undo

Time

Help
?

Confirm
Answer

Next

65. Historic Buildings

It seems that a new building goes up every day in our city. People say that is progress. There is no doubt that the city is growing and that we need more buildings. *However*, I think an effort should be made to preserve old, historic buildings.

Historic buildings are a valuable part of our heritage. *For one thing*, they are a symbol of the past. They remind us of where we came from. *For another*, they may have historical significance. Some important events took place in some of these buildings. If they were lost, we might forget these events as well. *Still another*, they are unique. Buildings like these are not built nowadays because it would be too expensive. *Finally*, they are beautiful. Preserving them would make our city more attractive.

For all of the above reasons, I believe that we should preserve our historic buildings. We can still erect new buildings, but we should not destroy history in order to do so.

65. 具有歷史價值的建築物

在我們的都市裡，似乎每天都有新的建築物在興建。大家都說，那就是進步。無疑地，城市正在發展，我們需要更多建築物。然而，我認為應該努力保存古老的、具有歷史價值的建築物。

具有歷史價值的建築物，是我們的遺產中珍貴的一部份。首先，它們是過去的象徵。它們提醒我們自己的根源何在。再者，它們具有重大歷史意義。某些重要的事件，曾在其中一些建築物裡發生。如果它們消失了，我們可能也會將這些事件遺忘。此外，它們是獨一無二的。現在類似的建築物不再興建，因為成本可能過高。最後，它們具有美感，將它們加以保存會讓我們的城市更有吸引力。

基於上述種種理由，我認為我們應該保存具有歷史價值的建築物。我們仍然可以興建新的建築物，但是我們不應該為了如此而破壞歷史。

【註釋】

historic〔hɪsˈtɔrɪk〕*adj.* 有歷史性的；具有重大歷史意義的
go up （建築物）蓋起　progress〔ˈprɑgrɛs〕*n.* 進步
there is no doubt that~ 無疑地，~
preserve〔prɪˈzɝv〕*v.* 保存　valuable〔ˈvæljəbl̩〕*adj.* 珍貴的
heritage〔ˈhɛrətɪdʒ〕*n.* 遺產；傳統
for one thing 首先；一則　symbol〔ˈsɪmbl̩〕*n.* 象徵

remind *sb.* ***of*** *sth.* 提醒某人某事　***come from*** 來自
for another 另外；再者　historical〔hɪsˈtɔrɪkl̩〕*adj.* 歷史上的
significance〔sɪgˈnɪfəkəns〕*n.* 意義；重要性
event〔ɪˈvɛnt〕*n.* 事件；大事　***as well*** 也
unique〔juˈnik〕*adj.* 獨特的　nowadays〔ˈnɑuəˌdez〕*adv.* 現在
attractive〔əˈtræktɪv〕*adj.* 有吸引力的　erect〔ɪˈrɛkt〕*v.* 建立
destroy〔dɪˈstrɔɪ〕*v.* 破壞　***in order to*** *V.* 為了~（表目的）

Quit　　　　　**Writing**

Do you agree or disagree with the following statement? Classmates are a more important influence than parents on a child's success in school. Use specific reasons and examples to support your answer.

Cut

Paste

Undo

Time

Help
?

Confirm
Answer

Next

66. **Classmates as the Biggest Influence**

People say that we depend on our family when we are at home and on our friends when we are out. I believe that is true, especially in school. In school we depend on our friends and classmates a great deal. In fact, I would say that our classmates are an even more important influence than our parents.

Our classmates have a big effect on us for a number of reasons. Most importantly, they are our peer group. When we are in school it is very important for us to get along with our peers. ***Therefore***, we try to be like them. If our classmates are good students, we are more likely to be good students. Another reason is that we spend a lot of time with our classmates. When we are busy with our studies, the people who are closest to us are our schoolmates, and it is to them that we turn for advice. ***Finally***, some teenagers cannot communicate with their parents well. They feel their parents do not understand them because they are of a different generation.

There is no doubt that our classmates play a very important role in our lives and can affect our success. They are our role models, confidants and advisors. While our parents may know us better and certainly have more wisdom, we are less likely to listen to them than to our friends. That is why a child's classmates have such a great influence on him.

66. 同班同學影響最大

　　大家都說在家靠父母，出外靠朋友。我相信那是真的，特別是在學校的時候。在學校裡，我們非常依賴朋友和同班同學。事實上，我會說我們的同班同學比父母更具有影響力。

　　我們的同班同學對我們影響很大，基於幾個原因。最重要的是，他們是我們的同儕團體。當我們在學校時，和同儕處得好，是很重要的。因此，我們會努力想要和他們一樣。如果我們的同班同學是好學生，我們比較有可能成為好學生。另一個原因是，我們花很多時間和同學在一起。在我們忙碌於課業的同時，和我們最近的人，就是我們的同學，我們也是向同學尋求建議。最後，有些青少年無法和他們的父母做有效的溝通。他們覺得他們的父母不了解他們，因為他們是不一樣的世代。

　　無疑地，我們的同班同學在我們的生活中，扮演了非常重要的角色，而且會影響我們成功與否。他們是我們的模範、知己，和顧問。雖然我們的父母可能比較了解我們，而且肯定比較有智慧，但是我們可能比較不會聽從他們的意見，比較會聽朋友的話。那就是為什麼兒童的同班同學對他們有很大的影響的原因。

【註釋】

influence〔'ɪnfluəns〕 *n.* 影響　　*depend on* 依靠
a great deal 非常　　effect〔ɪ'fɛkt〕 *n.* 影響
a number of 許多；幾個　　*peer group* 同儕團體
get along with sb. 與某人和睦相處
close〔klos〕 *adj.* 接近的；(關係)密切的＜*to*＞　　*turn to* 求助於
advice〔əd'vaɪs〕 *n.* 勸告；建議　　generation〔ˌdʒɛnə'reʃən〕 *n.* 世代

there is no doubt that 無疑地，～
play a very important role in 在…(方面)扮演一個非常重要的角色
role model 榜樣；模範
confidant〔ˌkɑnfə'dænt, 'kɑnfəˌdænt〕 *n.* 知己；密友
advisor〔əd'vaɪzə〕 *n.* 提供意見者；顧問　　wisdom〔'wɪzdəm〕 *n.* 智慧
be likely to V. 可能～　　*listen to* 聽；聽從

Quit　　　**Writing**

If you were an employer, which kind of worker would you prefer to hire: an inexperienced worker at a lower salary or an experienced worker at a higher salary?　Use specific reasons and details to support your answer.

Cut

Paste

Undo

67. An Experienced Worker

When an employer has a job opening, he is likely to have a choice of candidates for the position. Often he will have to choose between hiring a well-qualified candidate at a high salary and an inexperienced one at a lower salary. *In my opinion*, it is better to hire the more experienced person.

A more experienced worker is a better investment than a less experienced one. While the employer will have to pay more for his services, he is bound to do a better job from the very start. By hiring a qualified employee, the boss will save not only the cost of training a new staff member but also the cost of the mistakes an inexperienced person is liable to make. *Furthermore*, an employee with a lot of experience will bring other benefits to the company. Based on his experience, he will be a better problem solver and will require less direction. Not only will he be a more independent worker, but he may have some new ideas that will benefit the company.

In conclusion, if I were an employer, I would choose to hire experienced workers. I believe that the success of the business as a whole is more important than saving a small amount on salaries.

67. 有經驗的員工

當雇主有職缺的時候，他可能要從該職位的應徵者中做選擇。通常他必須選擇僱用充分具備必要條件，但薪水要求高的人，或是比較沒有經驗，但薪水較低的人。依我之見，最好僱用較有經驗的人。

和經驗較少的人比起來，比較有經驗的員工是較好的投資。雖然雇主必須支付較多錢，來換取員工相對的服務，但是他一定從一開始，就會表現比較好。僱用夠資格的員工，老板不僅能省下訓練新員工的成本，也會省下沒有經驗的人可能犯下的錯誤所需的成本。此外，經驗豐富的員工將為公司帶來其他好處。因為他有經驗做基礎，他會比較擅長解決問題，比較不需要指導。他不僅是更具獨立性的員工，也會有一些對公司有幫助的新點子。

總之，如果我是雇主，我會選擇僱用有經驗的員工。我相信企業整體的成功，比省下一點點薪水來得重要。

【註釋】

experienced (ɪk'spɪrɪənst) adj. 有經驗的 (↔ inexperienced)
employer (ɪm'plɔɪɚ) n. 雇主；老板
opening ('opənɪŋ) n. (職位的) 空缺
candidate ('kændə,det ,-dɪt) n. 求職應徵者 < for >
position (pə'zɪʃən) n. 職位
well-qualified ('wɛl'kwɑlə,faɪd) adj. 充分具備必要條件的
in one's opinion 依某人之見　　investment (ɪn'vɛstmənt) n. 投資
one's services 某人的服務 (尤指需要專業知識的服務)
be bound to V. 必定~　　*from the very start* 從一開始

qualified ('kwɑlə,faɪd) adj. 具備必要條件的
employee (,ɛmplɔɪ'i , ɪm'plɔɪ-i) n. 員工　　train (tren) v. 訓練
staff (stæf) n. 全體工作人員　　liable ('laɪəbl̩) adj. 易於…的；可能…的
furthermore ('fɝðɚ,mor ,-,mɔr) adv. 此外
benefit ('bɛnəfɪt) n. 利益；好處　　v. 使受益
based on 根據；以…為基礎　　direction (də'rɛkʃən) n. 指導
independent (,ɪndɪ'pɛndənt) adj. 獨立性強的；獨立的
in conclusion 總之　　*as a whole* 整體而言

Quit	**Writing**

Many teachers assign homework to students every day. Do you think that daily homework is necessary for students? Use specific reasons and details to support your answer.

Cut

Paste

Undo

68. Homework

Like most students, I dislike having to do homework every day. Often I feel that the assignments I am required to do are not useful. Yet my teachers continue to assign them. *In my opinion*, homework is only beneficial if it can further the students' understanding of a lesson. *Therefore*, I don't think teachers need to assign it every day.

A student who is required to do homework every day won't necessarily learn more. *First of all*, daily homework is often assigned simply out of habit, whether or not it will actually help the students. *To my mind*, this busywork is a waste of time. *Second of all*, truly meaningful homework requires time and effort to complete. *Therefore*, it cannot be finished in one day. Students should be given enough time to do a good job. *Finally*, spending all their time on homework prevents students from pursuing other activities. Without hobbies and sports they become bored and lose their enthusiasm for learning.

In my opinion, a variety of activities is necessary for students. *Therefore*, they should not be required to do homework every day. *More importantly*, the homework that they are assigned should be meaningful.

68. 家庭作業

　　就和大部分的學生一樣,我不喜歡每天做功課。通常我覺得被要求做的家庭作業並不實用。然而我的老師仍然繼續指定作業。依我之見,家庭作業唯有在能夠增進學生對課程的了解,才算有用。因此,我認爲老師不需要每天指定作業。

　　被要求每天做家庭作業的學生,未必會學到比較多。首先,指定每天的家庭作業往往只是出於習慣,不論是否眞的對學生有幫助。在我看來,故意不讓學生閒著而出的作業,只是在浪費時間。第二點,眞正有意義的家庭作業,是需要時間和努力來完成的。因此,無法在一天之內完成。學生應該擁有足夠的時間把事情做好。最後一點,把所有的時間花在家庭作業上,使得學生無法從事其他活動。缺少嗜好和運動,學生會覺得很無趣,喪失學習的熱忱。

　　依我之見,各種不同的活動對學生而言是必需的。因此,不應該要求他們每天做功課。更重要的是,他們被指派的家庭作業也應該要有意義。

【註釋】

assignment〔ə'saɪnmənt〕 *n.* 作業;功課
require〔rɪ'kwaɪr〕 *v.* 要求　　assign〔ə'saɪn〕 *v.* 分派;指定
in one's opinion 依某人之見 (= *to one's mind*)
beneficial〔ˌbɛnə'fɪʃəl〕 *adj.* 有益的　　further〔'fɝðɚ〕 *v.* 促進
not necessarily 未必;不一定 (= *not always*)
first of all 第一;首先　　*out of* 由於;出於
actually〔'æktʃuəlɪ〕 *adv.* 實際上;眞地

busywork〔'bɪzɪˌwɝk〕 *n.* 外加作業 (使學生不致於空閒而故意外加的作業)
meaningful〔'minɪŋfəl〕 *adj.* 有意義的
prevent〔prɪ'vɛnt〕 *v.* 阻止;妨礙 <*from* >
pursue〔pɚ'su〕 *v.* 追求;從事　　hobby〔'hɑbɪ〕 *n.* 嗜好
enthusiasm〔ɪn'θjuzɪˌæzəm〕 *n.* 熱忱 <*for* >
a variety of 各種不同的

Quit　　　　　Writing

If you could study a subject that you have never had the opportunity to study, what would you choose?　Explain your choice, using specific reasons and details.

Cut

Paste

Undo

Time

Help
?

Confirm
Answer

Next
→

69. A Subject I like to Study

As a student, I have taken courses in a variety of subjects. ***However***, there remain many others that I know little about. If given the opportunity to broaden my curriculum with one course, I would choose to study world religions because I feel that is an important but neglected area of knowledge.

The advantages of knowing more about the religions of the world are many. ***To begin with***, a religion is a reflection of the culture that subscribes to it. By studying it we can learn many things about a people, including their history, social institutions, customs and values. A religion can tell us how people view themselves, the world around them and their relationship to the world. ***In addition***, religion often motivates political action. If we understand another people's religion, we can better understand what they do. ***Above all***, greater knowledge of world religions would lead to better communication.

Religion is such an important part of human society that it deserves careful study. Such study would promote understanding and respect among different nations and cultures. ***Therefore***, it would be a useful course for anyone who wishes to promote peace in the world.

69. 我想要唸的科目

身為學生，我已經修過各種不同的科目。然而，還是有很多其他的科目是我所不熟悉的。如果有機會選擇一門科目來擴展我的課程，我會選擇研讀世界宗教，因為我覺得那是一個重要但是被忽略的知識領域。

多認識世界宗教的益處很多。首先，宗教能反映出所代表的文化。藉由研讀宗教，我們可以知道很多關於某個民族的東西，包括他們的歷史、社會制度、習俗和價值觀。宗教可以告訴我們，人們是如何看自己、看待周圍的世界，還有他們和這個世界的關係。此外，宗教通常是政治活動的動機。如果我們了解別人的宗教，我們就可以更加了解他們的行為。最重要的是，增進對世界宗教的了解，會促成更良好的溝通。

宗教是人類社會非常重要的一部分，值得好好研究。這方面的研究能夠促進不同國家和文化之間的了解和尊重。因此，這門課程對任何想要促進世界和平的人而言，將會是非常有用的。

【註釋】

take a course 修一門課　　*a variety of* 各種不同的
given〔'gɪvən〕*prep.* 如果有；假如　　broaden〔'brɔdn〕*v.* 拓展
curriculum〔kə'rɪkjələm〕*n.* (學科的) 課程
religion〔rɪ'lɪdʒən〕*n.* 宗教　　neglected〔nɪ'glɛktɪd〕*adj.* 被忽視的
area〔'ɛrɪə〕*n.* 領域　　advantage〔əd'væntɪdʒ〕*n.* 好處
to begin with 首先　　reflection〔rɪ'flɛkʃən〕*n.* 反映
subscribe〔səb'skraɪb〕*v.* 同意；贊許 < *to* >

people〔'pipl〕*n.* 民族　　institution〔͵ɪnstə't(j)uʃən〕*n.* 制度
values〔'væljuz〕*n. pl.* 價值觀　　view〔vju〕*v.* 看
relationship〔rɪ'leʃən͵ʃɪp〕*n.* 關係 < *to* >
in addition 此外　　motivate〔'motə͵vet〕*v.* 給…動機；刺激
political〔pə'lɪtɪkl〕*adj.* 政治的　　action〔'ækʃən〕*n.* 活動
above all 最重要的是　　*lead to* 導致　　deserve〔dɪ'zɝv〕*v.* 應得
promote〔prə'mot〕*v.* 促進　　peace〔pis〕*n.* 和平

Quit　　　　　**Writing**

Some people think that the automobile has improved modern life. Others think that the automobile has caused serious problems. What is your opinion?　Use specific reasons and examples to support your answer.

Cut

Paste

Undo

70. The Automobile: A Most Important Invention

The automobile is arguably one of the most important inventions of recent times. There is no doubt that it has changed the way we live. *However*, as with all great changes there have been both good and bad effects. It is true that the automobile has caused some problems such as air pollution and traffic congestion for our society, but overall I believe it has improved modern life immensely.

The several benefits of the automobile outweigh its disadvantages. *For example*, the invention of the car has changed the way both goods and people are transported. By making transportation faster and cheaper it has decreased the cost of trade and given people much greater freedom of choice. We are now able to visit friends and family as well as travel for our work more easily. The congestion that many complain of is not nearly so time-wasting as traveling by horse and buggy. *Furthermore*, the invention of the automobile led to better public transportation systems.

Thanks to public buses and roadways, it is now possible for virtually every child to attend school. There are many more advantages to the automobile but, *in short*, without its invention our country would not have experienced the dramatic growth that it did in the twentieth century.

It is fair to say that the automobile has caused some problems for our society, but without it I think none of us would be as well off as we are now. The invention of the car has greatly affected our economic and social structures, primarily for the better. It is difficult to imagine what life would be like if it did not exist.

70. 汽車：一項最重要的發明

　　汽車大概是近代最重要的發明之一。無疑地，汽車已經改變了我們的生活方式。然而，儘管有了大幅度的改變，但所造成的影響好壞皆有。汽車已經引發某些像是空氣污染和交通阻塞的問題，這一點固然沒錯，但是整體而言，我認爲汽車大大地改善了現代生活。

　　汽車的好幾項優點勝過其缺點。例如，汽車的發明，已經改變了商品運輸和人類交通的模式。因爲交通變得更加快速和便宜，使得貿易成本降低，人類也獲得更多的選擇空間。我們現在要拜訪朋友和家人，以及去上班，都變得更加容易。多數人所抱怨的交通阻塞問題，遠遠不如騎馬或坐四輪馬車那麼費時。此外，汽車的發明，帶來了更加完善的大衆運輸系統。幸好有大衆巴士和馬路的出現，現在幾乎每個小孩都可以上學。汽車帶來的好處還有很多，但是簡言之，若是沒有此項發明，我們的國家在二十世紀，可能就無法經歷如此大幅度的成長。

　　公平而論，汽車爲我們的社會帶來了某些問題，但是若沒有汽車，我相信我們沒有人可以像現在這麼富裕。汽車的發明已經大大地影響我們的經濟和社會結構，主要是往好的方面發展。很難想像，如果沒有汽車的存在，我們的生活會變成什麼樣子。

【註釋】

automobile〔'ɔtəmə,bil , ,ɔtə'mobil〕*n.* 汽車（= auto〔'ɔto〕）

arguably〔'ɑrgjʊəblɪ〕*adv.* 大概（不會錯）

congestion〔kən'dʒɛstʃən〕*n.* 阻塞

overall〔,ovɚ'ɔl〕*adv.* 就整體來說

immensely〔ɪ'mɛnslɪ〕*adv.* 廣大地；非常

outweigh〔aʊt'we〕*v.* 勝過

transport〔trans'pɔrt ,-'pɔrt〕*v.* 運送；運輸

not nearly 一點也不　　buggy〔'bʌgɪ〕*n.* 輕便單座四輪馬車

thanks to 幸虧；由於　　roadway〔'rod,we〕*n.* 馬路；快車道

virtually〔'vɝtʃʊəlɪ〕*adv.* 實際上；幾乎

dramatic〔drə'mætɪk〕*adj.* 戲劇性的；引人注目的

well off 富裕的　　economic〔,ikə'nɑmɪk〕*adj.* 經濟的

structure〔'strʌktʃɚ〕*n.* 結構　　primarily〔'praɪ,mɛrəlɪ〕*adv.* 主要地

Quit　　　　　　**Writing**

Which would you choose: a high-paying job with long hours that would give you little time with family and friends **or** a lower-paying job with shorter hours that would give you more time with family and friends? Explain your choice, using specific reasons and details.

▲

Cut

Paste

Undo

▼

71. A Less Demanding Job

For most people, work is an important part of life. No matter what type of work we do, it involves giving our time and effort in exchange for some payment. Generally, the harder we work, the greater the reward will be. As income not only provides us with material goods and security but also affects our status in society, many people choose the highest paid careers and positions that they can attain. *In my opinion*, working solely for money at the expense of relationships with family and friends is not worth it. *Therefore*, I would prefer having a lower-paying job with shorter hours to being a high-powered executive who rarely sees his loved ones.

The advantages of a less demanding job are many but may not be obvious to some. *For one thing*, there is time. There is more personal time to spend with loved ones as well as on ourselves. We can maintain good relationships with others and pursue our own interests. Both will lead to a satisfying and fulfilling life. *To me*, these things are more important than monetary gain. *For another*, a less demanding job is usually less stressful. Therefore, we can be not only happier but also healthier. It is no secret that too much stress adversely affects our health. By keeping our job in perspective, we can live longer and better. *In short*, I believe it is better to control our job than let our job control us. Work is an important part of life, but it is only a part.

71. 要求較低的工作

　　對大部分的人而言，工作是人生當中一個重要的部分。不論我們做哪一種工作，都需要付出時間和努力，來換取一些報酬。一般而言，我們工作越努力，得到的報酬就越高。因為收入不僅能用來購買有形的物品，並能給我們安全感，也會影響到我們的社會地位，所以很多人選擇他們所能獲得的、報酬最高的職業和職位。依我之見，犧牲和家人、朋友的關係，只為了金錢而工作，是不值得的。因此，我寧願選擇薪水較低，工作時間較短的工作，而不要當高階主管，很少有時間看到自己的親人。

　　要求較低的工作好處有很多，但是對有些人而言，可能不是很明顯。一來，有時間。有更多個人時間和親人相處，以及留給自己。我們可以和他人維持良好的關係，並且追求自己的興趣。兩者都將會帶來令人滿意和有成就感的生活。對我來說，這些事情比金錢上的收益更重要。二來，要求較低的工作通常也比較沒壓力。因此，我們不僅可以更快樂，也可以更健康。太多壓力會產生負面的效果，影響我們的健康，這一點是公開的秘密。對工作抱持正確的眼光，我們可以活得更久、活得更好。簡言之，我相信能掌控自己的工作，比受制於工作好。工作是人生的一個重要部分，但也只不過是一部分。

【註釋】

demanding〔dɪ'mændɪŋ〕*adj.* 要求（過）多的

involve〔ɪn'vɑlv〕*v.* 包含；需要

in exchange for 作爲…的交換

payment〔'pemənt〕*n.* 報酬（= *reward*）

material〔mə'tɪrɪəl〕*adj.* 有形的

security〔sɪ'kjʊrətɪ〕*n.* 安全；安心

attain〔ə'ten〕*v.* 達到；獲得　　solely〔'sollɪ〕*adv.* 僅僅；完全

at the expense of 以…爲代價

relationship〔rɪ'leʃənˌʃɪp〕*n.* 關係

high-powered〔'haɪ'paʊɚd〕*adj.* 強有力的；（位階）高級的

executive〔ɪg'zɛkjʊtɪv〕*n.* 主管　　rarely〔'rɛrlɪ〕*adv.* 很少

loved ones 親人　　*for one thing* 首先；一則

fulfilling〔fʊl'fɪlɪŋ〕*adj.* 能實現個人抱負的

monetary〔'mʌnəˌtɛrɪ〕*adj.* 金錢的　　gain〔gen〕*n.* 收益

for another 另外；再者

stressful〔'strɛsfəl〕*adj.* 緊張的；壓力大的

adversely〔əd'vɝslɪ, æd-〕*adv.* 不利地

perspective〔pɚ'spɛktɪv〕*n.* 正確的眼光

keep sth. in perspective 以正確的眼光看待某事

Quit　　　**Writing**

Do you agree or disagree with the following statement?　Grades (marks) encourage students to learn.　Use specific reasons and examples to support your opinion.

Cut

Paste

Undo

Time

Help
?

Confirm
Answer

Next

72. Grades Encourage Students to Learn

Most students are concerned about their grades. They not only indicate our recent performance, but also can affect our future. They are the standard by which others judge our academic performance. But the question remains: do grades actually help us learn? *In my opinion*, they do.

The main effect of grades as a learning tool is as a motivating force. Since we all want high grades, we work hard to achieve them. If our work were never graded, perhaps we would not make as much effort. *Another* important benefit is our grades can tell us where our strengths and weaknesses lie. They let us know whether our performance is above or below standard. They could even help us decide in which course of study we want to major. *Finally*, they can provide positive reinforcement. Even if we don't have very high marks, our grades are a validation of the effort we have made.

In conclusion, grades are important and they are more than just a measure of our performance. *However*, it is important not to focus on our marks to the exclusion of all else. *After all*, it is what we actually learn that is important.

72. 成績鼓勵學生學習

　　大部分的學生都很關心自己的成績。成績不僅是最近表現的指標，也影響到我們的未來。成績是別人評斷我們學業表現的標準。但是問題依然還是存在：成績真的會有助於我們的學習效果嗎？依我之見，的確如此。

　　成績作爲學習工具的主要效果在於能促進學習動機。因爲我們全都想要得到高分，所以我們會努力達到。如果我們的努力沒有被評分，或許我們就不會那麼努力。另一個重要的好處是，我們的成績可以告訴我們自己的優缺點在哪裡。它們讓我們知道我們的表現是高於還是低於標準，甚至可以協助我們決定要主修什麼科目。最後，成績提供了正面強化的效果。即使我們沒有得到很高的成績，我們的成績能證明自己所做的努力。

　　總之，成績很重要，不僅僅只是作爲衡量我們的表現的基準。然而，話說回來，不要只注重成績，而把所有其他的事情排除在外，這是很重要的。畢竟，重要的是我們實際上學到了什麼。

【註釋】

grade〔gred〕 *n.* 分數；成績（= *mark*）　　*v.* 評分
be concerned about 關心　　indicate〔'ɪndə,ket〕 *v.* 指出；表示
performance〔pə'fɔrməns〕 *n.* 表現
standard〔'stændəd〕 *n.* 標準　　judge〔dʒʌdʒ〕 *v.* 判斷
academic〔,ækə'dɛmɪk〕 *adj.* 學術的；學業的
in one's opinion 依某人之見　　effect〔ɪ'fɛkt〕 *n.* 影響；效果
motivate〔'motə,vet〕 *v.* 使（學生等）產生學習興趣或動力；激勵

benefit〔'bɛnəfɪt〕 *n.* 好處　　strength〔strɛŋ(k)θ〕 *n.* 優點
weakness〔'wiknɪs〕 *n.* 缺點；弱點　　lie〔laɪ〕 *v.* 在於
major〔'medʒə〕 *v.* 主修 < *in* >　　positive〔'pɑzətɪv〕 *adj.* 正面的
reinforcement〔,riɪn'forsmənt〕 *n.* 強化
validation〔,vælə'deʃən〕 *n.* 確認　　***in conclusion*** 總之
more than 不只　　measure〔'mɛʒə〕 *n.* （判斷等的）尺度；基準
focus on 集中於　　***to the exclusion of*** 排除掉

Quit　　　　Writing

Some people say that computers have made life easier and more convenient. Other people say that computers have made life more complex and stressful. What is your opinion? Use specific reasons and examples to support your answer.

Cut

Paste

Undo

Time

Help
?

Confirm
Answer

Next

73. Computers

Perhaps the greatest advance of the last century has been the computer. There is no doubt that it has changed the way we work and communicate. But while it has made doing many tasks faster and more convenient, it has also caused problems for some people. *Therefore*, some believe the computer causes more trouble than it saves, but I don't agree with that opinion.

In my view, the invention of the computer has immeasurably benefited our society. Perhaps most importantly, it has made possible many advances in technological fields by assisting scientists in their work. It has also allowed businesses to function more efficiently and cheaply, thereby reducing costs to consumers. For the average home user, it provides access to a wealth of information as well as several convenient services such as email and online reservation systems and financial services. *In short*, it saves a great deal of time.

Although computers occasionally malfunction and cause inconvenience, this is no reason to disregard their advantages. Some people feel intimidated by technology and are uncomfortable working with computers. *However*, the wonderful thing about computers is that we do not have to be technically savvy in order to use them. I believe that as computers become more reliable and user-friendly, their advantages will win over even the most resistant of technophobes.

73. 電　腦

　　上個世紀最偉大的進步，或許就是電腦。無疑地，電腦已經改變了我們工作和通訊的方式。但是電腦雖然讓我們事情做得更快、更方便，電腦也造成了某些人的問題。因此，有些人認為，電腦造成的麻煩大過其免除的麻煩，但是我不同意那樣的說法。

　　依我看，電腦的發明為我們社會所帶來的好處，是無法衡量的。或許最重要的是，電腦協助科學家進行研究，讓許多科技領域的進步成為可能。它也讓商業運作更具效率、更省錢，因此降低了消費者的支出。對一般家庭個人電腦的使用者而言，電腦提供了能獲得豐富資訊的管道，以及好幾個便利的服務，像是電子郵件、線上預訂系統，以及金融服務。總之，電腦節省了大量的時間。

　　雖然電腦偶爾會故障，造成不便，但是沒有理由忽視其帶來的好處。有些人覺得科技令人畏懼，因此不習慣使用電腦。然而，關於電腦的一個絕佳優點是，我們不需要在技術上很專精才能操作。我相信當電腦變得越來越可靠，越來越好操作時，就連最抗拒的科技恐懼者，都會被電腦的好處說服。

【註釋】

advance〔əd'væns〕n. 進步　　***there is no doubt that*** 無疑地~
immeasurably〔ɪ'mɛʒrəblɪ〕adv. 不能衡量地；無法計量地
benefit〔'bɛnəfɪt〕v. 有益於　　assist〔ə'sɪst〕v. 協助
function〔'fʌŋkʃən〕v. 運作　　thereby〔ðɛr'baɪ〕adv. 因此
average〔'ævərɪdʒ〕adj. 一般的　　access〔'æksɛs〕n. 使用（權）< to >
wealth〔wɛlθ〕n. 豐富；大量< of >　　online〔'ɑn͵laɪn〕adj. 線上的
financial〔fə'nænʃəl, faɪ-〕adj. 金融的　　***in short*** 簡言之；總之
malfunction〔mæl'fʌŋkʃən〕v. 運作失常；發生故障
disregard〔͵dɪsrɪ'gɑrd〕v. 忽視
intimidated〔ɪn'tɪmə͵detɪd〕adj. 害怕的
technically〔'tɛknɪkl̩ɪ〕adv. 技術上
savvy〔'sævɪ〕adj. 精通的　　reliable〔rɪ'laɪəbl̩〕adj. 可靠的
user-friendly〔'juzɚ'frɛndlɪ〕adj. 容易使用的；（設計時）考慮使用者
　　需要的　　***win over*** 說服　　resistant〔rɪ'zɪstənt〕n. 抵抗者
technophobe〔'tɛknə͵fob〕n. 科技恐懼者；不喜歡機器設備者

Writing

Quit

Do you agree or disagree with the following statement? The best way to travel is in a group led by a tour guide. Use specific reasons and examples to support your answer.

Cut

Paste

Undo

74. Travel by Tour

Travel is a popular leisure time activity.
Many people like to get away to relax or to
see something new. *However*, it is often an
expensive undertaking. *Therefore*, I feel it is important to get
the most out of a trip. The way I do that is by going with a
group led by a qualified tour guide.

A tour guide can offer travelers many benefits. *One* is
that the guide will take care of all the practical arrangements.
This means that the travelers do not have to waste time
organizing transportation and accommodations. *Another* is
that the guide is knowledgeable about the place being visited.
Therefore, the group members can better appreciate what they
see. *Furthermore*, there are no language barriers because a
good guide will be a fluent translator. *Finally*, by traveling
with a group, tourists have the opportunity to meet more
people, many of whom will have similar interests. *As a result*,
new friendships may be formed and the trip will surely be
more enjoyable.

In my opinion, travel can be a meaningful activity. It
allows us to learn about new places and cultures, thereby
broadening our minds. *But* we can do this only if we are free
of worry. Traveling with a group and a guide lets us concentrate
on the new experience and learn more from it.

74. 跟團旅行

　　旅行是一種受歡迎的休閒活動。許多人喜歡出外旅行放鬆自己或是看看新的事物。可是那通常是一種昂貴的活動。因此，我覺得充分享有旅行的好處很重要。我的做法是參加由合格的導遊帶領的團體旅遊。

　　導遊可以提供旅客很多好處。其中一個好處是導遊會處理好所有實際層面的安排事項。這表示旅客不需要浪費時間安排交通和住宿。另外一個好處是導遊了解要參觀的地方。因此，團員可以更深入欣賞。此外，沒有語言隔閡，因爲好的導遊會是流利的翻譯者。最後，藉由跟團旅遊，旅客有機會認識更多人，其中有許多興趣相同的人。因此可能建立起新的友誼，旅行也一定會更有趣。

　　依我之見，旅行可以是一種有意義的活動。讓我們可以學習到不同的地方和文化，藉此擴展我們的心智。但是我們唯有在免除煩惱的時候，才能如此。跟團、有導遊帶的旅行讓我們專注於新的體驗，從中學習。

【註釋】

leisure time 空閒時間　　*get away* 出外（旅行、渡假等）

undertaking〔͵ʌndɚˋtekɪŋ〕*n.* 工作；事情

qualified〔ˋkwɑləͺfaɪd〕*adj.* 具備必要條件的；合格的

tour guide 導遊　　benefit〔ˋbɛnəfɪt〕*n.* 好處

take care of 處理　　practical〔ˋpræktɪkl̩〕*adj.* 實際的

arrangement〔eˋrendʒmənt〕*n.* 安排

organize〔ˋɔrgənͺaɪz〕*v.* 組織；安排

transportation〔͵trænspɚˋteʃən〕*n.* 交通運輸

accommodations〔əͺkɑməˋdeʃənz〕*n. pl.* 住宿

knowledgeable〔ˋnɑlɪdʒəbl̩〕*adj.* 有知識的；有見識的

appreciate〔əˋpriʃɪͺet〕*v.* 欣賞

furthermore〔ˋfɝðɚͺmor, -ͺmɔr〕*adv.* 此外；再者

barrier〔ˋbærɪɚ〕*n.* 障礙　　fluent〔ˋfluənt〕*adj.* 流利的

translator〔trænsˋletɚ〕*n.* 翻譯者

enjoyable〔ɪnˋdʒɔɪəbl̩〕*adj.* 愉快的　　thereby〔ðɛrˋbaɪ〕*adv.* 因此

broaden〔ˋbrɔdn̩〕*v.* 拓寬；開闊　　*be free of* 免除…；無…

Quit　　　　　　**Writing**

Some universities require students to take classes in many subjects. Other universities require students to specialize in one subject. Which is better?　Use specific reasons and examples to support your answer.

Cut

Paste

Undo

Time

Help
?

Confirm
Answer

Next

75. University Subjects

Universities that require students to take classes in many subjects are better than universities that require students to specialize in one subject. The reason why it is better to take classes in many subjects is that it will help students become well-rounded individuals who are well versed in many subjects and cultures.

In today's world it is not enough to just be familiar with your own field of specialty. *For example*, in today's business environment it is very likely that students will encounter people from different cultures. *One* of the main reasons for taking classes in many subjects is to learn about different cultures and peoples. Students that only know about their own field of specialty might be totally ignorant of the culture of their coworkers or business partners. *Another* reason is that in today's world people often change careers during their lifetime. If a student is only knowledgeable about one specialty it might become difficult to switch careers later on.

It is important to have a specialty in college or university. *However*, it is even more important for students to have a broad understanding of many subjects and the world they live in. This way students will be able to leave the university as a well-rounded individual.

75. 大學學科

　　大學要求學生修許多不同學科的課程，比要求學生專攻單一學科要來得好。爲什麼修不同學科的課程會比較好，原因是這將有助於讓學生成爲通才，精通許多不同的學科和文化。

　　在現今的世界裡，只熟悉自己的專業領域是不夠的。例如在現今的商業職場裡，學生很有可能會遇到來自不同文化背景的人。要修許多不同學科的其中一個主要原因，就是可以學習並認識許多不同的文化和民族。只了解自己專業領域的學生，可能會對其同事或生意上的夥伴的文化背景，一無所知。另一個原因是，現代人在一生當中，經常會更換職業。如果學生只具備一項專業知識，那麼以後要換工作，就會有困難。

　　在大學裡專攻一個專業科目是很重要的。然而，學生對於許多不同的學科以及自己所居住的世界，有廣泛的認識更爲重要。如此一來，學生將能夠在離開大學校園後，成爲具有多方面知識的人。

【註釋】

specialize〔'spɛʃə,laɪz〕v. 專攻 < in >

well-rounded〔'wɛl'raʊndɪd〕adj.（知識、經驗等）涵蓋多方面的；
　廣泛的

individual〔,ɪndə'vɪdʒʊəl〕n. 個人

versed〔vɜst〕adj. 熟練的；精通的 < in >

be familiar with 熟悉　　field〔fild〕n. 領域

specialty〔'spɛʃəltɪ〕n. 專長；專業　　encounter〔ɪn'kaʊntə〕v. 碰見

people〔'pipl̩〕n. 人（不可數名詞）；民族（可數名詞）

totally〔'totl̩ɪ〕adv. 完全　　ignorant〔'ɪgnərənt〕adj. 不知道的 < of >

career〔kə'rɪr〕n. 職業　　lifetime〔'laɪf,taɪm〕n. 一生

knowledgeable〔'nalɪdʒəbl̩〕adj. 有知識的 < about >

switch〔swɪtʃ〕v. 改變　　**later on** 以後

broad〔brɔd〕adj. 廣泛的

Quit	**Writing**

Do you agree or disagree with the following statement? Children should begin learning a foreign language as soon as they start school. Use specific reasons and examples to support your position.

▲

Cut

Paste

Undo

▼

Time

Help
?

Confirm
Answer

Next
➡

76. **Children Learning Foreign Languages**

I agree that children should begin learning a foreign language as soon as they start school. The main reason why I feel it is good for children to start learning a foreign language as early as possible is that childhood is the optimum time to learn a foreign language.

Many scientific studies have proven that the optimum time to learn a foreign language is during early childhood. During this period, a child's brain is still developing. *Therefore*, it is able to absorb and retain information such as a foreign language much better than adults. *Also*, during a child's early school years, he or she has more free time than adults. This is the best time to teach a child a foreign language. There are other benefits that come from teaching a child a foreign language early. One benefit is that a child will be able to make friends with children from another culture. *For example*, America is a multicultural society. Many languages are spoken in America.

Children should begin learning a foreign language as soon as they start school. As children, we naturally learned to speak our mother tongue without much guidance. *Therefore*, it is also very easy for a child to learn a foreign language while he is still young.

76. 小孩學習外語

我同意小孩應該一上學就開始學習外國語言。我覺得孩童應該儘早開始學習外語的主要原因,是因為童年時期是學習外語的最佳時間。

很多科學研究已經證實,學習外語的最佳時間是在童年時期的早期。在這段期間,小孩的頭腦仍處於發展階段。因此,小孩可以比成人更容易吸收並且記憶像是外語的資訊。此外,兒童在就學的早期,比大人有更多的空閒時間。這是教導小孩學習外語的最佳時間。讓小孩早點學習外語還有其他的好處。其中之一是可以和來自其他文化的小孩做朋友。例如,美國是個多元文化的社會,在美國會聽到許多不同的語言。

小孩應該一上學就開始學習外國語言。我們在兒童時期,不需要太多的指導,就很自然地學會說自己的母語。因此,在小孩年紀還小的時候,學習外語也是很容易的。

【註釋】

optimum〔ˈɑptəməm〕 *adj.* 最理想的

absorb〔əbˈsɔrb〕 *v.* 吸收

retain〔rɪˈten〕 *v.* 保留;記憶

benefit〔ˈbɛnəfɪt〕 *n.* 好處

multicultural〔ˌmʌltɪˈkʌtʃərəl〕 *adj.* 融合多種文化的

naturally〔ˈnætʃ(ə)rəlɪ〕 *adv.* 自然地

mother tongue 母語　　guidance〔ˈɡaɪdn̩s〕 *n.* 指導

Quit　　　　　Writing

Do you agree or disagree with the following statement? Boys and girls should attend separate schools. Use specific reasons and examples to support your answer.

Cut

Paste

Undo

Time

Help ?　Confirm Answer　Next ➡

77. Coeducation

I disagree with the statement boys and girls should attend separate schools. The primary reason why I disagree with the statement is that eventually boys and girls will have to learn how to interact with each other. By separating them it will deprive them of the chance to learn how to interact with the opposite sex.

The most common reason offered by supporters of separating boys and girls is that as children reach puberty they will become distracted by the opposite sex and will focus less on their education. I feel that it is important for teenagers to learn about the opposite sex. Human sexuality is something very normal and should not be taught as something bad. Teenage curiosity about the opposite sex is normal and attending the same school will teach boys and girls how to deal with each other when they become adults. *Also*, the argument that students will focus less on education is unfair. Students that are not interested in studying will not study regardless of the presence of the opposite sex.

It is important for boys and girls to learn how to interact with each other. If they do not interact with each other during their teenage years, they will be more likely to become awkward adults later in life. *Therefore*, it is beneficial for boys and girls to attend the same school.

77. 男女合校

　　我不同意男生和女生應該分校的說法。我不同意這項說法的主要原因是，男女生最後終究還是必須學習如何彼此互動。把他們分開來，將會剝奪他們學習和異性互動的機會。

　　男女分校的支持者最常用的理由就是，孩童到了青春期，會受到異性的影響而分心，較無法專心於他們的課業。我覺得青少年學習了解異性很重要。人有性慾是很正常的事情，不應該被教導成不好的事情。青少年對異性好奇是正常的事情，所以同校就讀可以教導男生和女生長大成人之後，如何對待彼此。此外，說學生會比較不專心於課業，也是不公平的說法。沒有興趣唸書的學生，不管周圍是否有異性存在，還是不會唸書。

　　男女生學習如何彼此互動是很重要的事情。如果他們在青少年時期，沒有產生互動，那他們將比較有可能在以後成為彆扭的成人。因此，男女同校對他們而言是有益的。

【註釋】

coeducation〔ˏkoɛdʒəˈkeʃən〕n. 男女合校

primary〔ˈpraɪˏmɛrɪ〕adj. 主要的　　interact〔ˏɪntəˈækt〕v. 互動

deprive〔dɪˈpraɪv〕v. 剝奪 < of >

opposite〔ˈɑpəzɪt〕adj. 相反的

opposite sex 異性　　puberty〔ˈpjubətɪ〕n. 青春期

distracted〔dɪˈstræktɪd〕adj. 分心的　　**focus on** 專注於

sexuality〔ˏsɛkʃuˈælɪtɪ〕n. 性慾　　normal〔ˈnɔrml̩〕adj. 正常的

curiosity〔ˏkjurɪˈɑsətɪ〕n. 好奇心　　**deal with** 處理；應付

argument〔ˈɑrgjəmənt〕n. 論點　　unfair〔ʌnˈfɛr〕adj. 不公平的

regardless of 不管　　presence〔ˈprɛzn̩s〕n. 存在；在場

awkward〔ˈɔkwəd〕adj. 笨拙的；彆扭的

beneficial〔ˏbɛnəˈfɪʃəl〕adj. 有益的

Quit **Writing**

Is it more important to be able to work with a group of people on a team or to work independently? Use reasons and specific examples to support your answer.

Cut

Paste

Undo

Time

Help ?

Confirm Answer

Next →

78. Teamwork

Teamwork gets things done faster, better and more efficient than individuals. Teams bring  together a group of talented and diverse individuals into a problem scenario. The individuals learn to use their skills with others to come to a solution for the problem. "Two heads are better than one" is an old proverb that is well known. Teamwork can build character and teaches each individual how to maximize their thinking so as to get the most out of their knowledge.

Teamwork is an important concept and almost a prerequisite to getting a job. Companies do not like to see lone wolves and will almost always ask a prospective employee in a interview to give an example of a time that he or she accomplished something through teamwork.

Teamwork does not necessarily mean giving up your individuality. *Rather*, it helps to hone your individual skills under a group setting. There are things you can always learn from others in a team and vice versa they can learn from you. So why not join a team today?

78. 團隊合作

　　和個人作業比起來，團隊合作能讓事情完成速度加快，而且做得更好、更有效率。團隊是把一群有才能、彼此互異的個人聚在一起，共同解決問題。個人學習如何運用技巧，與他人合作，共同解決問題。「三個臭皮匠勝過一個諸葛亮」是個眾所皆知的老諺語。團隊合作可以培養人格，讓個人學會如何將思考發揮至最大極限，以便於充分利用他們的知識。

　　團隊合作是一個重要的觀念，也幾乎是獲得工作的一個必要條件。公司不喜歡看到獨來獨往的人，也幾乎總會在面試的時候，要求來應徵的員工，舉例說明自己透過團隊合作的方式，完成過什麼事情。

　　團隊合作未必就表示要放棄個人特質。更確切地說，它反而有助於讓你在團隊的環境中，磨練個人的技巧。從團隊中的其他人身上，總有你可以學習的地方，而反之亦然，他們也可以向你學習。所以為何不今天就加入團隊？

【註釋】

teamwork（'tim,wɝk）*n.* 團隊合作
diverse（də'vɝs , daɪ-）*adj.* 不同的
scenario（sɪ'nɛrɪ,o , -nær- , -nɑr-）*n.* 情節；情況　　***come to*** 達成
Two heads are better than one. 【諺】集思勝於獨斷；三個臭皮匠勝過
　　一個諸葛亮。　　maximize（'mæksə,maɪz）*v.* 使增加至最大限度
so as to V. 以便~　　concept（'kɑnsɛpt）*n.* 概念
get the most out of 充分利用

prerequisite（pri'rɛkwəzɪt）*n.* 必要條件 ＜ *to* ＞
lone wolf 獨來獨往的人
prospective（prə'spɛktɪv）*adj.* 預期的；未來的
not necessarily 未必
individuality（,ɪndə,vɪdʒʊ'ælətɪ）*n.*（個人的）特性；特質
hone（hon）*v.* 磨鍊（技術等）　　setting（'sɛtɪŋ）*n.* 環境；背景
vice versa（'vaɪsɪ'vɝsə）*adv.* 反之亦然

Quit　　　　　**Writing**

Your city has decided to build a statue or monument to honor a famous person in your country.　Who would you choose?　Use reasons and specific examples to support your choice.

▲

Cut

Paste

Undo

▼

79. **Honoring Confucius**

If my city were to build a statue to honor a famous person in my country, I would choose Confucius. Confucius is the moral foundation of my country. His teachings have influenced not only my country but many other Asian countries such as Japan and Korea. Confucius is a person worth honoring because his philosophy is based on compassion for others.

Confucius was a famous Chinese scholar. He lived in ancient China. During that time China was divided into many small warring kingdoms. Due to all the constant fighting, the average person suffered tremendously. During this time many scholars came forward to teach their ideas on how best to rule a kingdom. *However*, only Confucius taught that compassion should be the guiding principle of a ruler. The goal of a ruler should be to avoid war and to be kind to his subjects. Even though during his lifetime his principles were not accepted, eventually his teachings became the foundation of Chinese culture and society.

If my city were to build a statue to honor a person, I would definitely choose Confucius. His teachings have greatly influenced my country and has brought a lot of good to our society.

79. 向孔子致敬

　　如果我的城市要興建一座雕像來向本國的某位名人致敬，我會選擇孔子。孔子是我國的道德基礎。他的學說不僅影響了我國，也影響了許多其他的亞洲國家，像是日本和韓國。孔子是一個值得尊敬的人，因為他的哲學是以對他人抱持憐憫心為基礎。

　　孔子是一位有名的中國學者。他生長於中國古代。當時的中國分為許多不同的小國，彼此交戰。因為戰爭不斷，平民百姓受到極大的痛苦。當時有許多學者挺身而出，傳授他們治國的理念。然而，只有孔子說憐憫心才應該是一國之君的指導原則。一國之君的目標應該是避免戰爭，並且仁慈對待他的子民。即使在他活著的時候，他的原則沒有被接受，但他的學說最後還是成為華人文化和社會的基礎。

　　如果我的城市要興建一座雕像向某人致敬，我一定會選擇孔子。他的學說已經大大地影響了我國，也為我們的社會帶來許多的好處。

【註釋】

honor（ˋɑnɚ）v. 向～表示敬意　　Confucius（kənˋfjuʃəs）n. 孔子
be to V. 預定；打算　　statue（ˋstætʃu）n. 雕像
moral（ˋmɔrəl）adj. 道德的　　foundation（faunˋdeʃən）n. 基礎
teaching（ˋtitʃɪŋ）n. 學說　　**be based on** 以…為基礎
compassion（kəmˋpæʃən）n. 憐憫；同情 < for >
ancient（ˋenʃənt）adj. 古代的　　divide（dəˋvaɪd）v. 使分裂 < into >
warring（ˋwɔrɪŋ）adj. 交戰的　　kingdom（ˋkɪŋdəm）n. 王國
constant（ˋkɑnstənt）adj. 不斷的　　average（ˋævərɪdʒ）adj. 一般的
tremendously（trɪˋmɛndəslɪ）adv. 極其；非常
come forward 自告奮勇；站出來　　rule（rul）v. 統治
guiding（ˋgaɪdɪŋ）adj. 指導性的；引導的
principle（ˋprɪnsəpl̩）n. 原則　　ruler（ˋrulɚ）n. 統治者
subject（ˋsʌbdʒɪkt）n. 臣民　　definitely（ˋdɛfənɪtlɪ）adv. 肯定地
good（gud）n. 利益；好處

Quit	**Writing**

Describe a custom from your country that you would like people from other countries to adopt. Explain your choice, using specific reasons and examples.

Cut

Paste

Undo

80. **A Good Custom from My Country**

A custom from my country that I would like people from other countries to adopt is respect for the elderly. I

choose this custom because in some societies the elderly are treated as a burden to society. *However*, in my country the elderly are treated as an asset.

The primary reason why I feel this custom will benefit other societies is because the elderly has a tremendous amount of experience that they can share with us. *For example*, in the old days, knowledge was often passed down by the oldest member of a tribe. His experience usually enabled their tribe to survive their environment. In today's society, the elderly still have a lot of knowledge, most of which has been gained through their life experiences. *Also*, the elderly are responsible for the world we live in. They are the ones who built many of the things that young people take for granted. Because of their hard work, our lives are much better than the lives that they lived.

Respect for the elderly is a custom that I feel will benefit all countries. *Therefore*, I would definitely want to share this custom with other countries. In every country, the elderly have contributed greatly to the betterment of their respective society.

80. 我國的一項好習俗

　　我希望其他國家人民採納的本國習俗，就是尊敬長輩。我選擇這項習俗，是因爲在某些社會裡，長輩被視爲是社會的負擔。然而在我國，長輩卻是被視爲資產。

　　爲什麼我會覺得，這項習俗會有益於其他社會，主要的原因就是因爲長輩擁有非常多的經驗可以和我們分享。例如在古代，知識的傳承往往是靠該部落最老的成員來執行。他的經驗通常使該部落可以在環境中生存。在現在的社會，長輩仍然具備許多知識，其中大部分是他們生活經驗的累積。此外，長輩造就了我們所居住的世界。是他們建立了許多年輕人視爲理所當然的事物。由於他們的努力，我們的生活遠比他們以前的生活進步許多。

　　尊敬長輩是我覺得會對所有國家都有益的一項習俗。因此，我當然要和其他國家的人分享這項習俗。在每個國家，長輩對於各自的社會都貢獻良多。

【註釋】

adopt〔ə'dɑpt〕*v.* 採用　　*the elderly* 年長者 (= *elderly people*)

be treated as 被認爲是　　burden〔'bɝdn̩〕*n.* 負擔

asset〔'æsɛt〕*n.* 資產；有利或有用的人

primary〔'praɪˌmɛrɪ〕*adj.* 主要的　　benefit〔'bɛnəfɪt〕*v.* 有益於

tremendous〔trɪ'mɛndəs〕*adj.* 極大的

pass down 傳下來　　tribe〔traɪb〕*n.* 部落

survive〔sə'vaɪv〕*v.* 生存下來；由…生存

be responsible for 是…的原因　　build〔bɪld〕*v.* 建造

take…for granted 視…爲理所當然

definitely〔'dɛfənɪtlɪ〕*adv.* 肯定地

contribute〔kən'trɪbjut〕*v.* 貢獻 < *to* >

betterment〔'bɛtəmənt〕*n.* 改善

respective〔rɪ'spɛktɪv〕*adj.* 個別的

Quit   **Writing**

Do you agree or disagree with the following statement?
Technology has made the world a better place to live. Use
specific reasons and examples to support your opinion.

Cut

Paste

Undo

81. Technology

I agree that technology has made the world a better place to live. *The primary reason* why technology has made the world a better place to live is the advancement of medicine. *The second reason* has to do with our ability to communicate with people around the world.

In the past people thought that diseases were caused by angry Gods. *However*, because of modern technological development, we now know it is not angry Gods but bacteria and viruses that cause diseases. One example is the discovery of the human Genome. With the help of modern computing, scientists have been able to completely map the human gene. This accomplishment has resulted in new treatment methods for genetic diseases that were previously incurable.

The second reason why I believe technology has made the world a better place to live has to do with our ability to communicate with people worldwide. In the past, communicating with someone from another country was very slow. *However*, modern technology has enabled people across the world to easily and quickly communicate with each other. The most obvious example would be the Internet. Today, an email can reach another country in less than a minute.

Technological advancement is something that all of mankind has benefited from. *Therefore*, I am confident that future technological development will bring even greater good to the world.

81. 科技

　　我同意科技已經讓這個世界成爲一個夠好的居住場所。科技讓這個世界成爲更好的居住場所，主要原因是醫學的進步，第二個原因和我們能和全世界的人通訊有關。

　　在過去，人們以爲疾病是憤怒的神明所帶來的。然而因爲現代科技的發展，我們現在知道不是憤怒的神明，而是細菌和病毒造成疾病。人類基因譜圖的發現就是一例。在現代電腦的幫助下，科學家已經能夠完全繪製人類的基因。這項成就導致新的遺傳疾病治療方法，這在以前是無法醫治的。

　　我相信科技已經讓這個世界成爲一個更好的居住場所的第二個原因，和我們能夠和全世界的人通訊有關。在過去，和別的國家的人通訊是非常耗時的。然而現代科技已經使全球人類可以輕易而迅速地彼此聯絡。最明顯的例子即是網際網路。現今的電子郵件，可以在一分鐘之內就寄到其他國家。

　　科技的進步讓所有人類都受益。因此，我確信未來的科技發展將爲全世界帶來更多的好處。

【註釋】

primary〔ˈpraɪˌmɛrɪ , -mərɪ〕*adj.* 主要的

advancement〔ədˈvænsmənt〕*n.* 進步　　***have to do with*** 與⋯有關

bacteria〔bækˈtɪrɪə〕*n. pl.* 細菌（單數形爲 bacterium〔bækˈtɪrɪəm〕）

virus〔ˈvaɪrəs〕*n.* 病毒　　Genome〔ˈdʒiˌnom〕*n.* 人類基因譜圖（將人類細胞內的細胞核中的組織內的 23 對染色體對上的十萬個左右的基因之位置繪製在圖譜上，以找出三億個人類遺傳配方的字母序列。）

computing〔kəmˈpjutɪŋ〕*n.* 使用電腦　　map〔mæp〕*v.* 繪圖

gene〔dʒin〕*n.* 基因　　accomplishment〔əˈkɑmplɪʃmənt〕*n.* 成就

treatment〔ˈtritmənt〕*n.* 治療　　genetic〔dʒəˈnɛtɪk〕*adj.* 基因的

previously〔ˈprivɪəslɪ〕*adv.* 以前

incurable〔ɪnˈkjʊrəbļ〕*adj.* 不能醫治的

worldwide〔ˈwɜldˌwaɪd〕*adv.* 在世界各地；在全世界

obvious〔ˈɑbvɪəs〕*adj.* 明顯的

benefit〔ˈbɛnəfɪt〕*v.* 受益於 <*from*>　　good〔gʊd〕*n.* 利益；好處

Quit　　　　　**Writing**

Do you agree or disagree with the following statement? Advertising can tell you a lot about a country. Use specific reasons and examples to support your answer.

_____
_____
_____
_____
_____
_____
_____
_____
_____
_____
_____
_____
_____
_____
_____
_____
_____
_____

Cut

Paste

Undo

Time

Help

?

Confirm
Answer

Next

82. **Advertising**

I agree with the statement that advertising can tell you a lot about a country. There are two major reasons why advertising can tell you a lot about a country. *The first reason* is that advertising can tell you what a country values. *The second reason* is that advertising often reflect the financial condition of a particular country.

What a country values can often be detected through the advertisements shown on their television. *For example*, if a country highly values patriotism, the advertisements seen on television will usually have the flag of that country as a part of their commercial. Another reason why advertising can tell you a lot about a country is because the type of product being sold can often tell you the income level of a country. *For example*, in poorer countries you rarely see commercials that advertise cars, overseas vacations, and other expensive luxury items.

Advertising can tell you a lot about a country. Principally what it values and how wealthy it is. Poor countries often won't have commercials for luxury items. In advertisements we also see values such as patriotism being used to attract customers. Both of these are important reasons why advertisement can tell us a lot about a country.

82. 廣　告

　　廣告可以告訴你許多關於這個國家的事情，我同意這樣的說法。為什麼廣告可以告訴你許多關於這個國家的事情，有兩個主要的原因。第一個原因是，廣告可以告訴你，這個國家重視什麼。第二個原因是，廣告通常能反映出該國的財經狀況。

　　一個國家所重視的東西，往往可以透過電視廣告一窺究竟。例如，如果這個國家非常重視愛國情操，電視上的廣告，就通常會有該國的國旗作為廣告的一部份。另外一個廣告為什麼可以告訴你很多關於這個國家的事情的原因，是因為販賣的產品類型，往往可以顯示該國的收入水準。例如，在比較貧窮的國家，你很少看到車子、海外渡假，和其他昂貴奢侈品的廣告。

　　廣告可以告訴你很多關於這個國家的事情。主要是該國重視什麼和富裕程度為何。貧窮的國家通常不會有奢侈品的廣告。在廣告中，我們也會看到像是愛國情操的價值觀，被運用來吸引顧客。這兩者都是為什麼廣告可以告訴你很多關於這個國家的事情的重要原因。

【註釋】

advertising (ˈædvɚˌtaɪzɪŋ) *n.* 廣告（總稱）

major (ˈmedʒɚ) *adj.* 主要的　　value (ˈvælju) *v.* 重視

reflect (rɪˈflɛkt) *v.* 反映　　financial (fəˈnænʃəl, faɪ-) *adj.* 財務的

condition (kənˈdɪʃən) *n.* 情況　　particular (pɚˈtɪkjələ) *adj.* 特定的

detect (dɪˈtɛkt) *v.* 發現；察覺　　highly (ˈhaɪlɪ) *adv.* 非常

patriotism (ˈpetrɪəˌtɪzəm) *n.* 愛國情操

commercial (kəˈmɝʃəl) *n.* （電視、廣播中的）商業廣告

income (ˈɪnˌkʌm, ˈɪŋˌk-) *n.* 收入

level (ˈlɛvḷ) *n.* 水準　　rarely (ˈrɛrlɪ) *adv.* 很少

overseas (ˈovɚˈsiz) *adj.* （在）海外的；（在）國外的

luxury (ˈlʌkʃərɪ) *adj.* 奢侈的；高級的　　item (ˈaɪtəm) *n.* 物品

principally (ˈprɪnsəpəlɪ) *adv.* 大部分；主要地

Quit　　　　　　**Writing**

Do you agree or disagree with the following statement? Modern technology is creating a single world culture. Use specific reasons and examples to support your opinion.

_____

_____

_____

_____

_____

_____

_____

_____

_____

_____

_____

_____

_____

_____

_____

_____

_____

_____

_____

_____

_____

_____

Cut

Paste

Undo

Time

Help ?

Confirm Answer

Next

83. Modern Technology and a Single World Culture

I agree that modern technology has created a single world culture. This is the case because modern technology has enabled the rapid transmission of information throughout the world. Modern technology has provided the medium through which different cultures are able to spread and blend.

Media technology has exploded in recent years. Technologies such as satellite TV and the Internet have spread different cultures around the world. *For example*, before the advent of satellite TV, many societies were isolated because of government or geography. *However*, the rapid development of satellite TV technologies has enabled peoples from different places to access information. In a mountainous country like Nepal, people can watch CNN on their satellite TV. The development of the Internet has a similar effect. People from all over the world can access the same information anytime they want. Young people all over the world can chat online and learn about each other's culture.

Modern technology has definitely created a single world culture. An event that happens in one part of the world is often known globally in a matter of minutes. Exchanges between people of different cultures are very frequent. All of this contributes to the creation of a single world culture.

83. 現代科技和單一的世界文化

　　我同意現代科技已經造就了單一世界文化的出現。事實會如此的原因,是因為現代科技已經使全世界的資訊能夠快速地流通。現代科技已經提供媒介,讓不同的文化可以傳播和融合。

　　近年來,傳媒科技已經迅速發展。像是衛星電視和網際網路的科技,將不同的文化,散播至世界各地。例如,在衛星電視發明之前,很多社會因為政治或地理因素而處於孤立狀態。然而,衛星電視科技的快速發展,已經使不同地區的民族可以獲得資訊。在像是尼泊爾這種多山的國家,人們可以觀看衛星電視的美國有線電視新聞網。網路的發展也有類似的效果。全世界的人都可以在任何時候取得同樣的資訊。全世界的年輕人可以上網聊天,學習彼此的文化。

　　現代科技肯定已經造就了單一世界文化的出現。世界某一地方所發生的事件,通常在幾分鐘之內就傳到全世界。不同文化背景的人互相交流的機會非常頻繁。這些全都促成單一世界文化的出現。

【註釋】

single〔ˈsɪŋḷ〕*adj.* 單一的　　case〔kes〕*n.* 事實;真相

transmission〔trænsˈmɪʃən , trænz-〕*n.* 傳播

medium〔ˈmidɪəm〕*n.* 媒介物　　blend〔blɛnd〕*v.* 混和;交融

media〔ˈmidɪə〕*n.* 傳播媒體　　explode〔ɪkˈsplod〕*v.* 激增;迅速擴大

satellite〔ˈsætḷ,aɪt〕*n.* 人造衛星　　***satellite TV*** 衛星電視

advent〔ˈædvɛnt〕*n.* 出現;到來　　isolated〔ˈaɪsḷ,etɪd〕*adj.*(被)孤立的

government〔ˈgʌvɚ(n)mənt〕*n.* 政體;政治

geography〔dʒiˈɑgrəfɪ〕*n.* 地理;地形

people〔ˈpipḷ〕*n.* 民族　　access〔ˈæksɛs〕*v.* 使用;接近

mountainous〔ˈmautṇəs〕*adj.* 多山的　　Nepal〔nɪˈpɔl〕*n.* 尼泊爾

CNN 美國有線電視新聞網(*= Cable News Network*)

anytime〔ˈɛnɪ,taɪm〕*adv.* 在任何時候　　online〔ˈɑn,laɪn〕*adv.* 在線上

definitely〔ˈdɛfənɪtlɪ〕*adv.* 肯定地　　globally〔ˈgloblɪ〕*adv.* 全球地

a matter of 大約　　frequent〔ˈfrikwənt〕*adj.* 頻繁的

contribute to 促成　　creation〔krɪˈeʃən〕*n.* 創造

Quit

Writing

Some people say that the Internet provides people with a lot of valuable information. Others think access to so much information creates problems. Which view do you agree with? Use specific reasons and examples to support your opinion.

Cut

Paste

Undo

Time

Help ?

Confirm Answer

Next ➡

84. The Internet and Valuable Information

The Internet provides people with a lot of valuable information. The bulk of the information is of high value. *However*, some media on the Internet are of very low quality and can create problems for society.

One reason why I feel that the Internet provides people with a lot of valuable information is because on the Internet, we can find a lot of helpful information. *For example*, on the Internet, people can quickly find information about a particular medical condition. If a child had accidentally ingested a particular medication, a parent will be able to find the proper treatment for this child on the Internet.

Even though the Internet provides people with a lot of valuable information, it also can create problems. Some information on the Internet can be misleading or harmful. *For example*, the Internet is filled with pornographic images and similar media. Children can potentially be exposed to this harmful information. *Therefore*, parental control of Internet content is very important.

Even though some of the information on the Internet can create problems, but overall, the spread of Internet technology has been very beneficial to society. A large amount of valuable information in fields such as medicine, education, and arts can be found on the Internet.

84. 網路和珍貴的資訊

網路提供人們很多珍貴的資訊。大部分的資訊都很有價值。然而，網路上有些媒體品質很差，可能會造成社會問題。

我覺得網路提供人們很多珍貴資訊的一個原因，是因為在網路上，我們可以找到很多有用的資訊。例如，在網路上，人們可以迅速找到關於某種身體不適的醫學資訊。如果小孩子誤食某種藥物，父母親就可以在網路上替孩子找到適當的治療方式。

雖然網路提供人們很多珍貴的資訊，但是也會造成問題。網路上有些資訊可能會誤導大眾或是有害的。例如，網路上充滿了色情圖片或類似的媒體。兒童很有可能會接觸到這種有害的資訊。因此，父母監控網路內容是非常重要的。

雖然網路上有些資訊會造成問題，但是就整體而言，網路科技的傳播，對我們的社會助益良多。在像是醫學、教育，和藝術等領域的珍貴資訊，皆可以在網路上獲得。

【註釋】

valuable〔ˋvæljəbḷ〕*adj.* 珍貴的
bulk〔bʌlk〕*n.* 大部分；大多數 <*of*>　　value〔ˋvælju〕*n.* 價值
media〔ˋmidɪə〕*n. pl.* 傳播媒體　　quality〔ˋkwɑlətɪ〕*n.* 品質
particular〔pəˋtɪkjələ〕*adj.* 特定的
medical〔ˋmɛdɪkḷ〕*adj.* 醫學的；醫療的
medical condition 身體不適；生病　　ingest〔ɪnˋdʒɛst〕*v.* 攝取
medication〔ˏmɛdɪˋkeʃən〕*n.* 藥物　　proper〔ˋprɑpə〕*adj.* 適當的
treatment〔ˋtritmənt〕*n.* 治療法　　misleading〔mɪsˋlidɪŋ〕*adj.* 誤導的

pornographic〔ˏpɔrnəˋgræfɪk〕*adj.* 色情文學或圖畫的
potentially〔pəˋtɛnʃəlɪ〕*adv.* 可能地
expose〔ɪkˋspoz〕*v.* 使接觸 <*to*>　　parental〔pəˋrɛntḷ〕*adj.* 父母親的
content〔ˋkɑntɛnt, kənˋtɛnt〕*n.* 內容
overall〔ˏovəˋɔl〕*adv.* 就整體來說
beneficial〔ˏbɛnəˋfɪʃəl〕*adj.* 有益的 <*to*>　　field〔fild〕*n.* 領域

Quit	**Writing**

A foreign visitor has only one day to spend in your country. Where should this visitor go on that day? Why? Use specific reasons and details to support your choice.

▲

Cut

Paste

Undo

▼

85. One Day to Spend in My Country

If a foreign visitor has only one day to spend in my country, I would strongly recommend him or her to visit the National Palace Museum. The reason why I would recommend it is because this museum contains many historical antiques from China.

The National Palace Museum in Taipei contains Chinese artifacts dating back thousands of years. In this museum it is possible to take in the whole scope of Chinese culture in a very short period. The artifacts in this museum include items from the Bronze Age to the modern era. Not only can a foreign visitor learn about Chinese art and history, he or she will also learn about Chinese architecture. This is because the National Palace Museum is built like an ancient Chinese palace with many different rooms for a foreign visitor to explore. In this museum a foreign visitor can explore on his or her own or he or she can join an English guided tour.

The National Palace Museum in Taipei is the best place to visit if a foreign visitor has only one day. After visiting the museum, I am sure the foreign visitor will leave with a greater understanding of my country.

85. 待在我國的一天

　　如果外國旅客只有一天的時間待在我國，我會強力推薦他或她去參觀國立故宮博物院。爲什麼我會推薦此處的原因，是因爲這間博物館有很多中國的歷史古物。

　　台北的國立故宮博物院，藏有可以追溯至數千年前的中國藝術品。在這間博物館裡面，你可以在非常短的時間內，對中國文化進行全盤的了解。這間博物館所收藏的藝術品，從青銅器時代到現代的物品都有。外國旅客不僅可以認識中國藝術和歷史，也可以認識中國建築。因爲國立故宮博物院的建築，就好像中國古代的皇宮，裡面有很多不同的房間，可供外國旅客探索。在這間博物館裡面，外國旅客可以自己進行探索，或是參加英文的導覽活動。

　　如果這名外國旅客只能待一天的話，那麼台北的國立故宮博物院是最佳的參觀地點。參觀博物館之後，我確信外國旅客在離開的時候，將會對我國有更進一步的了解。

【註釋】

recommend〔ˌrɛkəˋmɛnd〕v. 推薦

palace〔ˋpælɪs〕n. 皇宮；宮殿　　historical〔hɪsˋtɔrɪkl̩〕adj. 歷史的

antique〔ænˋtik〕n. 古物；古董

artifact〔ˋɑrtɪˌfækt〕n. 手工藝品；藝術品

date back 追溯至；始於（某一歷史時期）　　take in 接受；吸收

scope〔skop〕n. 範圍 < of >　　item〔ˋaɪtəm〕n. 物品

bronze〔brɑnz〕n. 青銅　　Bronze Age 青銅器時代

era〔ˋɪrəˌˋirə〕n. 時代；時期

architecture〔ˋɑrkəˌtɛktʃɚ〕n. 建築術；建築物

ancient〔ˋenʃənt〕adj. 古代的　　explore〔ɪkˋsplorˌ-ˋsplɔr〕v. 探索

on one's own 獨自地　　guided tour 導覽活動

Quit   **Writing**

If you could go back to some time and place in the past, when and where would you go? Why? Use specific reasons and details to support your choice.

Cut

Paste

Undo

Time

Help
?

Confirm
Answer

Next

86. Go back in Time

If I could go back to some time and place in the past, I would want to go back to the Italian renaissance. The reasons why I would choose this period is because many beautiful works of art were produced during this period.

The renaissance was a time of revival. Europe had just come out of the Dark Ages. Fields such as arts, science, and literature were flourishing. It would be great if one can travel back in time and be part of this wonderful period. During this time, great artists such as Michelangelo were creating their masterpieces. To be able to witness such great artists at work would indeed be fantastic. Better yet if one can go back in time one might even be able to participate in the creation of the great works of art that we see today. During this period, science also developed tremendously. People like Galileo discovered that the earth is round and not flat as many people thought before the renaissance.

If I could go back in time, I would want to go back to the renaissance. I would love to be part of the development of the modern world. Many great works of art and scientific ideas were created at this time.

86. 回到過去

如果我可以回到過去的某個時間和地方，我會想要回到義大利的文藝復興時期。爲什麼我會選擇這段時期的原因，是因爲當時創造出很多漂亮的藝術品。

文藝復興是一段再生的時期。歐洲才剛脫離黑暗時代。像是藝術、科學，和文學的領域，都在蓬勃發展。如果可以回到過去，成爲這段美好時光的一份子，那將會很棒。在這段時期，像是米開朗基羅等偉大的藝術家，創造出他們的代表傑作。能夠目睹這些偉大的藝術家進行創作，的確很棒。更棒的是，如果可以回到過去，甚至還可以參與我們今日所見的偉大藝術品的創作過程。在這段時期，科學也有驚人的發展。例如伽利略發現地球是圓的，而不是文藝復興之前大部分人所以爲是平的。

如果我可以回到過去，我會希望回到文藝復興時期。我希望能夠參與現代世界的發展過程。有很多偉大的藝術品和科學觀念，就在這段時期成形。

【註釋】

Italian〔ɪ'tæljən〕*adj.* 義大利的

renaissance〔͵rɛnə'zɑns〕*n.* 文藝復興（14世紀至17世紀時在歐洲發生的古典文藝及學術的復興）

work of art 藝術品　　revival〔rɪ'vaɪvl̩〕*n.* 再生；復興

Dark Ages 黑暗時代（大約自西元後476年至1000年間，是歐洲知識上的黑暗時代）　　flourish〔'flɜɪʃ〕*v.* 繁榮；興盛

Michelangelo〔͵maɪkl̩'ændʒə͵lo〕*n.* 米開蘭基羅（1475-1564，義大利雕刻家、畫家、建築家及詩人）　　masterpiece〔'mæstə͵pis〕*n.* 傑作

witness〔'wɪtnɪs〕*v.* 目擊；親眼目睹　　***at work*** 在工作

fantastic〔fæn'tæstɪk〕*adj.* 極好的；很棒的

participate in 參與　　creation〔krɪ'eʃən〕*n.* 創造

tremendously〔trɪ'mɛndəslɪ〕*adv.* 極其；非常

Galileo〔͵gælə'lio〕*n.* 伽利略（1564-1642，義大利天文學家及物理學家）

Quit　　　　　**Writing**

What discovery in the last 100 years has been most beneficial for people in your country?　Use specific reasons and examples to support your choice.

▲

Cut

Paste

Undo

▼

87. **The Most Beneficial Discovery**

The discovery that has most benefited the people of my country is penicillin. The primary reason why I feel the discovery of penicillin has been most beneficial is because before this discovery many people died needlessly from illnesses caused by bacteria.

Before the discovery of penicillin by Alexander Fleming, many people died from bacterial infections. The elderly and children were especially hard hit. Both the elderly and children have weaker immune systems and were more susceptible to infections caused by bacteria. One of the reasons why some people living in rural areas have lots of children was because often some of the children won't survive beyond their childhood. After the discovery of penicillin many of these bacterial infections became easily manageable. Children in general survived past their childhood and the elderly also recovered from illnesses sooner.

The discovery of penicillin ranks as one of the most important discovery for my country. Countless people benefited from this discovery. Parents no longer have to fear that a minor infection might cause their children to die. Sons and daughters don't have to worry as much about the health of their elderly parents. These are all due to the discovery of penicillin. I am sure not only my country but the whole world has been made better by the discovery of penicillin.

87. 最有益的發現

對我國人民最有益的發現，就是盤尼西林。爲什麼我覺得盤尼西林的發現是最有益的主要原因是因爲，在這項發現之前，很多人死於細菌所引起的疾病，這原本是不應該發生的。

在亞歷山大・佛來明發現盤尼西林之前，很多人死於細菌引起的傳染病。老人和兒童特別容易受到感染。老人和兒童兩者的免疫系統都比較差，比較容易受到細菌的感染。在鄉下地區，爲什麼有些人會生很多小孩，是因爲有些小孩在幼年時期就夭折了。在盤尼西林被發現後，很多細菌引起的傳染病就比較好控制。一般而言，兒童可以活過幼年時期，而老人生病之後，恢復健康的速度也更快。

盤尼西林的發現，被列爲是我國最重要的發現之一。有無數的人因爲此項發現而受益。父母不用再害怕，不嚴重的傳染病可能造成孩子死亡。兒女不用那麼擔心年長父母的健康。這些都要歸功於盤尼西林的發現。我很肯定，不只是本國，還有全世界，都因爲盤尼西林的發現而變得更美好。

【註釋】

beneficial〔,bɛnə'fɪʃəl〕*adj.* 有益的　　benefit〔'bɛnəfɪt〕*v.* 使獲益
penicillin〔,pɛnɪ'sɪlɪn〕*n.* 盤尼西林；青黴素
primary〔'praɪˌmɛrɪ〕*adj.* 主要的　　*die from* 因…而死
needlessly〔'nidlɪslɪ〕*adv.* 不必要地
bacteria〔bæk'tɪrɪə〕*n. pl.* 細菌（單數形爲 bacterium〔bæk'tɪrɪəm〕）
bacterial〔bæk'tɪrɪəl〕*adj.* 細菌（引起）的
infection〔ɪn'fɛkʃən〕*n.* 傳染病
be hard hit 受到重大打擊（= *be hit hard* ）
immune〔ɪ'mjun〕*adj.* 免疫的
susceptible〔sə'sɛptəbḷ〕*adj.* 容易感染…的 < *to* >
rural〔'rʊrəl〕*adj.* 鄉下的　　survive〔sə'vaɪv〕*v.* 存活
manageable〔'mænɪdʒəbḷ〕*adj.* 可控制的　　*in general* 一般而言
rank〔ræŋk〕*v.* 位居 < *as* >　　countless〔'kaʊntlɪs〕*adj.* 無數的
minor〔'maɪnɚ〕*adj.*（疾病等）不嚴重的；無生命危險的
as much 同樣多地

Quit　　　　　**Writing**

Do you agree or disagree with the following statement? Telephones and email have made communication between people less personal. Use specific reasons and examples to support your opinion.

Cut

Paste

Undo

88. The Effects of Telephones and Email

A hundred years ago, people communicated over long distances by mail and telegram. Fifty years ago came the telephone. Now, we have the Internet as a new means of communication. Many purists hark back to the days of traditional handwritten letters because they feel that email and telephones are less personal. I disagree and here's why.

If you are living in another country and during the middle of the night, you feel like talking to your parents, you can always pick up the phone and they are one call away. You do not want to wait two or three weeks for your letter to get there if you write to them and what if there is an emergency?

Nowadays, everybody is finding time to be a rare resource. If we are not busy with work, family, school and friends, then there are other distractions like getting in shape, keeping your apartment in order. People simply have a lot less time these days and email is an excellent alternative to keeping in touch with people. There are those that complain a phone call will only take two minutes, but other people might be too busy to take your call. So dropping friends a line via email lets them know that you are still thinking about them and gives them the option to read it at their leisure.

In conclusion, email and telephones have not made communication between people less personal, but simply more convenient.

88. 電話與電子郵件的影響

　　一百年前，人們透過信件和電報進行長距離的溝通。五十年前發明了電話。現在，我們有網路作爲溝通的新方式。很多純粹主義者懷念傳統的手寫信函，因爲他們覺得電子郵件和電話比較沒有人情味。我不同意，理由如下。

　　如果你住在別的國家，在三更半夜時，你想要和父母說話，你就隨時可以拿起電話筒，他們就在電話的另一頭。你不會想要寫信給他們，因爲他們會在兩、三個禮拜之後才收到信，而且如果有緊急狀況的話怎麼辦？

　　現在每個人都覺得時間是珍貴的資源。如果我們不是忙於工作、家庭、學業，和朋友，那還有其他讓人分心的事，像是健身和整理公寓等。人們現在簡直沒有時間，而電子郵件是和別人保持聯繫的極佳選擇。有人抱怨講電話只要花兩分鐘時間，但是有人則是忙到無法接聽電話。所以透過電子郵件寫封短信給朋友，可以讓他們知道你仍然掛念著他們，也讓他們有機會在空閒的時候讀信。

　　總之，電子郵件和電話並沒有讓人與人之間的溝通比較缺少人情味，反而只是更加方便。

【註釋】

telegram ('tɛlə,græm) n. 電報　　purist ('pjʊrɪst) n. 純粹主義者
hark back 談及過去的快樂回憶 < to >
traditional (trə'dɪʃənḷ) adj. 傳統的
handwritten ('hænd,rɪtṇ) adj. 手寫的　　**pick up** 拿起
what if…? 如果…的話怎麼辦？
emergency (ɪ'mɝdʒənsɪ) n. 緊急情況　　rare (rɛr) adj. 珍貴的
distraction (dɪ'strækʃən) n. 分散注意力的事物
in shape 處於良好的健康狀況；保持健美身材
keep…in order 把…整理好
alternative (ɔl'tɝnətɪv) n. （另外）可採用的方法；替代物 < to >
keep in touch with sb. 和某人保持聯絡
drop sb. **a line** 寫給某人一封短信　　via ('vaɪə) prep. 經由
option ('ɑpʃən) n. 選擇（自由）　　**at one's leisure** 某人有空時

Writing

Quit

If you could travel back in time to meet a famous person from history, what person would you like to meet? Use specific reasons and examples to support your choice.

Cut

Paste

Undo

---

89. Meeting a Famous Person from History

History is almost always a required curriculum in school. Whether you are in junior high school, high school or college, learning history is important because only those that know history are destined not to repeat it. If you are learning history and you could travel back in time to meet a famous person, which person would you like to meet?

I would choose to meet the astronomer Copernicus. He changed world history when he discovered that the earth and the other planets revolved around the sun rather than the other way around. He risked his life against the Inquisition of the church, which at that time was extremely powerful and influential. He was willing to shatter years of accepted belief and the norm for the truth. Copernicus did so because he believed in the irrefutable evidence that science provided. His discovery would alter the course of mankind because in one instant, it changed how people viewed the world and themselves. It's moments like these in history that when human beings stumbled upon a new truth, they will once again advance. It happened with Isaac Newton and the apple and Einstein with the atom.

Copernicus was a courageous man. It's not easy to be different and have vision beyond other's comprehension. But because he was determined to tell the truth and thus change history forever, I would like to meet him if I can travel back in time.

89. 和一位有名的歷史人物見面

　　歷史幾乎往往是學校的必修課程。不論你是讀國中、高中或是大學，學習歷史是很重要的，因爲唯有知道歷史的人，才不會注定要重蹈覆轍。如果你正在學習歷史，而且能夠回到過去，和一位名人見面，你會想要和誰見面？

　　我會選擇和天文學家哥白尼見面。他改變了世界歷史，當時他發現地球和其他行星繞著太陽旋轉，而非是相反的情況。他冒著生命危險，對抗教會的宗教裁判所，那在當時是非常權威、具有影響力的組織。他願意打破多年來所公認的信念和眞理的標準。哥白尼會如此，是因爲他相信科學證據是無法反駁的。他的發現改變了人類的發展進程，因爲在那一瞬間，人類看世界和自己的角度改變了。就是像這樣的歷史時刻，人類偶然發現新的眞理，又再次地進步。以撒‧牛頓的蘋果，還有愛因斯坦的原子都是如此。

　　哥白尼是個勇敢的人。抱持不同的看法，以及擁有超越他人理解的遠見，不是件簡單的事情。但是因爲他決心公開眞理，因此永遠改變了歷史，所以如果我可以回到過去，我希望能和他見面。

【註釋】

curriculum〔 kə'rɪkjələm 〕*n.* 課程　　***high school*** 高中

destined〔'dɛstɪnd 〕*adj.* 命中注定的

repeat〔 rɪ'pit 〕*v.* 重複做；再度經驗到

astronomer〔 ə'strɑnəmə 〕*n.* 天文學家

Copernicus〔 ko'pɜnɪkəs 〕*n.* 哥白尼（1473-1543，天文學家，主張地動說）

revolve〔 rɪ'vɑlv 〕*v.* 旋轉　　***the other way around*** 相反的情況

risk〔 rɪsk 〕*v.* 使遭受危險

Inquisition〔ˌɪnkwə'zɪʃən 〕*n.*（中世紀天主教審判異端的）宗教裁判（所）

extremely〔 ɪk'strimlɪ 〕*adv.* 非常

shatter〔'ʃætə 〕*v.* 使粉碎

accepted〔 ək'sɛptɪd 〕*adj.* 公認的

norm〔 nɔrm 〕*n.* 標準；規範

irrefutable〔 ɪ'rɛfjutəbḷ,ˌɪrɪ'fjutəbḷ 〕*adj.* 不能反駁的

alter〔'ɔltə 〕*v.* 改變　　course〔 kɔrs, kors 〕*n.* 過程；進程

instant〔'ɪnstənt 〕*n.* 瞬間　　view〔 vju 〕*v.* 看

stumble〔'stʌmbḷ 〕*v.* 偶然發現 < *upon* >

advance〔 əd'væns 〕*v.* 進步

Isaac Newton 牛頓（1642-1727，英國物理學家、數學家；發現萬有引力原理）

Einstein 愛因斯坦（1879-1955，生於德國的美籍物理學家，為相對論的提出者）

atom〔'ætəm 〕*n.* 原子　　vision〔'vɪʒən 〕*n.* 眼光

comprehension〔ˌkɑmprɪ'hɛnʃən 〕*n.* 理解

determined〔 dɪ'tɜmɪnd 〕*adj.* 堅決的；毅然的

| Quit | **Writing** | |

If you could meet a famous entertainer or athlete, who would that be, and why? Use specific reasons and examples to support your choice.

▲

Cut

Paste

Undo

▼

| Time | | Help
? | Confirm
Answer | Next
➡ |

90. Meeting a Famous Entertainer or Athlete

If I can meet a famous entertainer or athlete, I would have to choose the actor Orlando Bloom. The heartthrob thespian is currently one of the hottest and fastest rising stars in Hollywood having starred in films like Pirates of the Caribbean and The Lord of the Rings trilogy. But before his rise to fame, Orlando had to endure and overcome a life-changing experience.

Orlando Bloom got into a serious accident when he was a teenager challenging a dare from a friend. He was hospitalized and the prognosis was not bright. The doctor told him that it was highly likely he may never walk again. Determined to beat this minor setback, Orlando Bloom embarked on a routine of grueling physical therapy and he began walking within a year of his accident.

His temerity to beat the odds is inspirational. If he had accepted the doctor's prognosis and resigned himself to his fate, he would not be enjoying the fame and success he has today.

Never give up in the face of adversity. What does not kill you will only make you stronger. That is a life lesson that many people should learn.

90. 和一位有名的藝人或運動員見面

如果我可以和一位有名的藝人或運動員見面，我會選擇演員奧蘭多·布魯。這位偶像演員目前是好萊塢最熱門、竄起速度最快的明星之一，主演過像是「神鬼奇航」和「魔戒」三部曲的電影。但是在他成名之前，奧蘭多必須忍受並且克服一個改變他一生的經驗。

奧蘭多·布魯在青少年時期挑戰朋友的挑釁，因此導致了一場嚴重的意外。他住院治療，醫生預測他的情況不樂觀。醫生告訴他，他非常有可能再也無法走路了。雖然不至於有生命危險，但是奧蘭多·布魯下定決心不讓病情惡化，於是開始固定進行非常累人的物理治療，意外發生後的一年內，他就開始走路了。

他有向不可能挑戰的膽量，這一點非常鼓舞人心。如果他接受醫生的預測，順從命運的安排，就不可能享有今日的名聲和成功。

面對困境時絕對不要放棄。不會把你殺死的東西只會讓你更強壯。那是很多人應該學習的人生教訓。

【註釋】

heartthrob〔'hɑrt͵θrɑb〕*n.* 偶像（尤指異性的歌手、演員等）

thespian〔'θɛspɪən〕*n.* 演員　　currently〔'kɝəntlɪ〕*adv.* 現在

rising〔'raɪzɪŋ〕*adj.* 升起的　　Hollywood〔'hɑlɪ͵wʊd〕*n.* 好萊塢

star〔stɑr〕*v.* 主演　　pirate〔'paɪrət〕*n.* 海盜

Caribbean〔͵kærə'biən , kə'rɪbɪən〕*n.* 加勒比海

trilogy〔'trɪlədʒɪ〕*n.* 三部曲　　***rise to fame*** 成名

dare〔dɛr , dær〕*n.* 挑戰　　hospitalize〔'hɑspɪtl͵aɪz〕*v.* 使住院治療

prognosis〔prɑg'nosɪs〕*n.* 預後（對生病過程的預測）；預測

bright〔braɪt〕*adj.* 有希望的　　beat〔bit〕*v.* 打敗；勝過

minor〔'maɪnɚ〕*adj.*（疾病等）不嚴重的；無生命危險的

setback〔'sɛt͵bæk〕*n.*（疾病的）復發；變壞　　***embark on*** 開始做

routine〔ru'tin〕*n.* 例行公事　　grueling〔'gruəlɪŋ〕*adj.* 累垮人的

therapy〔'θɛrəpɪ〕*n.* 治療法　　temerity〔tə'mɛrətɪ〕*n.* 膽量

beat the odds 獲得出乎意料的成功

inspirational〔͵ɪnspə'reʃnḷ〕*adj.* 鼓舞人心的

resign *oneself to one's fate* 聽天由命　　***in the face of*** 面對

adversity〔əd'vɝsətɪ〕*n.* 逆境；厄運

Quit　　　　　**Writing**

If you could ask a famous person **one** question, what would you ask? Why? Use specific reasons and details to support your answer.

	Cut
	Paste
	Undo

---

91. Asking a Famous Person One Question

I would choose Neil Armstrong as a famous person to ask my question. I would ask him what he was thinking about when he first stepped off that lunar module and stepped onto the moon. Everyone knows the name Armstrong as the first person in history to walk on the moon. The significance of what he accomplished for humankind that day still cannot be fully articulated or written. I want to ask him if he was thinking about the future of human beings or if he was thinking about his wife and kids or simply just enjoying the view of earth from the moon. How many countless times have humans gazed towards the moon throughout the centuries and wondered what it would be like to be up there? Neil Armstrong is one of the few lucky ones to know that very answer.

That would be my question and Neil Armstrong would be my pick. Armstrong ushered in a new era of discovery and unprecedented progress for mankind when he took that first step. In the everlasting pursuit of finding our place in the universe, nothing says one step at a time better than Armstrong's first step.

91. 問名人一個問題

　　我會選擇問名人尼爾・阿姆斯壯一個問題。我會問他，當他首次走出登月艙，踏上月球的時候，他當時在想什麼。每個人都知道阿姆斯壯這個名字，他是歷史上第一個踏上月球的人。他當時為人類做出的貢獻，其重要性仍然沒有被完全明確地用言語或文字表達出來。我想要問他，他是在想人類的未來，或是在想他的太太和小孩，或者純粹只是從月球欣賞地球的景色。幾個世紀以來，有多少人注視著月亮，想在那上面會是個怎麼樣的情況？尼爾・阿姆斯壯是少數幾個可以知道答案的幸運兒之一。

　　那就是我的問題，而阿姆斯壯是我的選擇。阿姆斯壯在走了那第一步的同時，開啟了一個新的發現的時代和人類前所未有的進步。人類不斷在追尋自己在宇宙中的定位為何，這樣的過程中，阿姆斯壯的第一步，就是一步一腳印的最佳代表。

【註釋】

step〔stɛp〕v. 踏（出）　　n. 一步　　lunar〔'lunɚ〕adj. 月球的
module〔'madʒul〕n.（太空）艙　　*lunar module* 登月艙
significance〔sɪg'nɪfəkəns〕n. 意義；重要性
accomplish〔ə'kamplɪʃ〕v. 達到；完成
humankind〔'hjumən,kaɪnd〕n. 人類（= *mankind*）
articulate〔ɑr'tɪkjə,let〕v. 明確地表達
countless〔'kaʊntlɪs〕adj. 無數的　　gaze〔gez〕v. 凝視；注視

pick〔pɪk〕n. 選擇　　*usher in* 宣告…的到來
era〔'ɪrə,'irə〕n. 時代
unprecedented〔ʌn'prɛsə,dɛntɪd〕adj. 無先例的；空前的
progress〔'pragrɛs, pro-〕n. 進步
everlasting〔,ɛvɚ'læstɪŋ〕adj. 永遠的
pursuit〔pɚ's(j)ut〕n. 追求　　place〔ples〕n. 重要的位置或地位
universe〔'junə,vɝs〕n. 宇宙　　*at a time* 每次；一次
nothing says…better~ ~最適合說明或代表…

Quit	**Writing**

Some people prefer to live in places that have the same weather or climate all year long. Others like to live in areas where the weather changes several times a year. Which do you prefer? Use specific reasons and examples to support your choice.

Cut

Paste

Undo

92. Living in a Place with Changing Weather

Growing up in New York City, I was treated to a variety of different weather ranging from snowfall in

winters to cool breeze springs and hot and hazy summers. If I had to choose a place to live, I would choose New York because of its changing seasons.

Summers in New York are filled with fun in the sun activities. The weather gets hot and sometimes humid. You can go sunbathing in the parks or go tanning at the beaches. With the arrival of autumn, you exchange your bathing suits for scarves and hats and the tingling breeze of fall that hints at the arrival of winter. The greenery also changes in the fall. Trees whose leaves were a vibrant shade of green began to turn into fiery shades of yellow, orange and red. Upon the arrival of winter, the city is blanketed against the biting cold and snow. The city seems to get deserted and falls asleep. When spring comes around again, hints of life begin to show themselves in the blooming of flowers and tree leaves. Then summer comes around once again.

I prefer to live in a place with changing weather instead of the same climate all year round. The changing climate offers variety and different activities to do. *For example*, you can go swimming in the summers and go ice-skating in the winters. But one thing I don't like about New York is shoveling snow in the winter!

92. 住在天氣變化分明的地方

因為我生長於在紐約市,所以我感受到的天氣變化非常鮮明,從冬天下雪,到春天吹著涼爽的微風,而夏天則是熱到起霧的天氣。如果我要選擇一個居住的地方,我會選擇紐約,因為那裡的四季分明。

紐約夏天的時候,充滿了許多戶外活動的樂趣。天氣變得炎熱,有時候潮濕。你可以在公園裡作日光浴,或是在海邊曬太陽。隨著秋天的到來,泳衣換成圍巾和帽子,而吹起來讓人刺痛的微風,則暗示著冬天的到來。綠色植物到了秋天也換上了新的風貌。樹木原本翠綠的樹葉,開始轉為如火燃燒般的黃色、橘色、和紅色。等到冬天到,整個城市被包圍起來,躲避刺骨的寒意和降雪。整個城市變得很荒涼,好像進入了夢鄉。當春天再度降臨,萬物開始展現生機,百花盛開,樹木長出綠葉。然後又是夏天的到來。

我喜歡住在天氣變化分明的地方,勝過住在氣候終年不變的地方。例如,你可以在夏天的時候去游泳,冬天的時候去溜冰。但是紐約有一件事情是我不喜歡的,就是冬天要剷雪!

【註釋】

treat〔 trit 〕v. 款待;請客 < to >　　*a variety of* 各種不同的
range from A *to* B 範圍從 A 到 B 都有　　snowfall〔'sno,fɔl 〕n. 降雪
hazy〔'hezɪ 〕adj. 有霧的　　humid〔'hjumɪd 〕adj. 潮濕的
sunbathe〔'sʌn,beð 〕v. 做日光浴
tan〔 tæn 〕v. (皮膚) 曬成古銅色　　tingle〔'tɪŋl 〕v. 感到刺痛
hint〔 hɪnt 〕v. 暗示 < at >　　n. 微小的徵兆 < of >
greenery〔'grin(ə)rɪ 〕n. 綠色植物;綠葉
vibrant〔'vaɪbrənt 〕adj. (色彩) 鮮明的　　shade〔 ʃed 〕n. 色彩;色調

fiery〔'faɪrɪ 〕adj. 火一般的　　blanket〔'blæŋkɪt 〕v. (似用毯) 覆蓋
biting〔'baɪtɪŋ 〕adj. (寒風等) 刺骨的
deserted〔 dɪ'zɜtɪd 〕adj. 無人居住的;荒涼的
come around (季節等) 再來臨　　bloom〔 blum 〕v. 開花
all year round 一年到頭　　variety〔 və'raɪətɪ 〕n. 多樣性;變化
shovel〔'ʃʌvl 〕v. 用鏟子鏟起 (或除去)

Quit　　　　　　**Writing**

Many students have to live with roommates while going to school or university. What are some of the important qualities of a good roommate? Use specific reasons and examples to explain why these qualities are important.

▲

Cut

Paste

Undo

▼

93. **Important Qualities of a Good Roommate**

Going to university is a life-altering experience, especially for students moving away from home for the first time. Many students get roommates because it's cheaper and they get to meet new people. *However*, there are some important qualities in finding a good roommate and some traits to look out for.

First, make sure you at least share some common interests or traits with your roommates. *For example*, if your roommates smoke and you do not, that will make for an uncomfortable situation. *Second*, communicate with your roommates. Find someone you can speak freely to. If you are living under one roof with someone you do not want to talk to or associate with, it will be awkward and tense. *Third*, find a considerate roommate. Find somebody that is not selfish or rude. Find a roommate that will help out with the chores around the house like taking out garbage or cleaning the bathroom. *Finally*, find a roommate that is not dirty or sloppy and does not leave their stuff scattered all over the house.

There are many qualities to consider when finding a good roommate. There are also many things to look out for. But roommates are fun because they can provide a good learning experience on how to get along with others.

93. 好室友的重要特質

　　上大學是一個改變人生的經驗，特別是對第一次離家居住的人而言。很多學生會和室友合住，因為比較便宜，而且有機會認識他人。然而，在選擇室友方面，有一些重要的特質和一些特點要留意。

　　首先，要確定你和室友至少要有一些共同的興趣或特質。例如，如果你的室友會抽煙，但是你不抽煙，那樣就會讓生活變得不舒服。第二點，和你的室友溝通。找一個你可以說話不必顧忌的人。如果和你住在同一個屋簷下的人，是你不想交談或交往的對象，那會讓人覺得尷尬而且緊張。第三點，找一個體貼的室友。找一個不自私或粗魯的人。找一個會幫忙做家事的人，像是倒垃圾或清理浴室。最後，找一個不會骯髒或邋遢的人，不會把自己的東西在房子裡到處亂丟的人。

　　找室友時要考慮到許多特質。也有很多事情要留意。但是有室友是件有趣的事情，因為他們可以提供不錯的學習經驗，讓我們懂得如何和別人相處。

【註釋】

quality〔ˈkwɑlətɪ〕*n.* 特質　　alter〔ˈɔltɚ〕*v.* 改變
get to V. 有機會～　　trait〔tret〕*n.* 特點
look out for 當心；尋找　　***make sure*** 確定
share〔ʃɛr〕*v.* 共同擁有　　***make for*** 導致
associate〔əˈsoʃɪˌet〕*v.* 交往＜*with*＞
awkward〔ˈɔkwɚd〕*adj.* 尷尬的　　tense〔tɛns〕*adj.* 緊張的
considerate〔kənˈsɪdərɪt〕*adj.* 體貼的　　selfish〔ˈsɛlfɪʃ〕*adj.* 自私的
help out with （有困難時）幫助（某人）完成…
chores〔tʃorz, tʃɔrz〕*n. pl.* 家庭雜務　　sloppy〔ˈslɑpɪ〕*adj.* 邋遢的
stuff〔stʌf〕*n.* 東西　　scatter〔ˈskætɚ〕*v.* 散佈
all over 遍及　　***get along with*** *sb.* 和某人和睦相處

Quit　　　　　　**Writing**

Do you agree or disagree with the following statement? Dancing plays an important role in a culture. Use specific reasons and examples to support your answer.

Cut

Paste

Undo

94. Dancing Plays an Important Role in a Culture

There are many different cultures in the world. Cultural differences are defined by the unique dress, customs, art, language and even religion of a specific people. Out of all these traits, dancing plays an important role.

Dance is a way for a distinct culture to communicate with others. Depending on which culture, dancing can tell the history of an Indian tribe, a way of celebration for the Greeks or mourning for the Japanese. Dancing is a universal language that can speak volumes for a particular culture. *For example*, some tribes in Africa perform a rhythmic dance of high intensity and vigor. Legend has it that when these tribes were conquered by European settlers and were banned from carrying weapons, they invented a dance that simulates killing an enemy of war and at the same time keeping their bodies in shape so when the time comes they will be ready.

The Japanese mourn their dead by dancing a traditional dance using long bamboo ladders. The Greeks celebrate life at weddings with a dance that involves all the guests forming a long human chain.

Dance is just one of the ways a culture defines and expresses itself. Over the centuries, dance developed into what we regard as an art form but little does the audience know that when they watch a performance of New Zealand aboriginal dance that they are witnessing a telling of a story passed down for centuries.

94. 舞蹈在文化中扮演重要的角色

全世界有許多不同的文化。文化差異的界定，是由某個民族特有的服裝、習俗、藝術、語言，甚至宗教來做區別。在這些特點當中，舞蹈扮演了一個重要的角色。

舞蹈是某一特定文化和他人溝通的方式。根據不同的文化，舞蹈可以述說某個印地安部落的歷史，可以是希臘人慶祝的方式，或是日本人服喪的方式。舞蹈是世界共通的語言，可以充分說明某個特定的文化。例如，有些非洲部落跳富有強烈節奏、充滿活力的舞蹈。根據傳說，當這些部落被歐洲殖民者征服，禁止他們攜帶武器時，他們發明了一種舞蹈，模擬殺死作戰的敵人，同時也讓他們身體保持健壯，所以當機會來的時候，他們就準備好了。

日本人藉由搭配竹製長梯的傳統舞蹈，來哀悼亡者。希臘人在婚禮上跳舞慶祝人生，所有的賓客連在一起，形成一條長串。

舞蹈只是界定和表現文化的眾多方式之一。好幾個世紀以來，舞蹈已經發展為我們現今所界定的一種藝術形式，但是很少有觀眾知道，當他們在觀看紐西蘭土著舞蹈表演時，他們是在見證一個已經傳承數個世紀的說故事的方式。

【註釋】

define〔dɪˈfaɪn〕v. 界定；下定義　　people〔ˈpipl̩〕n. 民族
distinct〔dɪˈstɪŋkt〕adj. 獨特的　　*depend on* 視～而定
tribe〔traɪb〕n. 部落　　mourning〔ˈmɔrnɪŋ, ˈmɔr-〕n. 服喪
universal〔ˌjunəˈvɝsl̩〕adj. 普遍共有的
speak volumes for 充分說明　　rhythmic〔ˈrɪðmɪk〕adj. 有節奏的
intensity〔ɪnˈtɛnsətɪ〕n. 強度　　vigor〔ˈvɪgɚ〕n. 活力
legend has it that 傳說指出～　　conquer〔ˈkaŋkɚ, kɔŋ-〕v. 征服
settler〔ˈsɛtlɚ〕n. 殖民者　　ban〔bæn〕v. 禁止 <from>
simulate〔ˈsɪmjəˌlet〕v. 模仿　　*in shape* 身體狀況良好的；健康的
mourn〔morn, mɔrn〕v. 哀悼　　dead〔dɛd〕n. 死者
bamboo〔bæmˈbu〕n. 竹子　　involve〔ɪnˈvɑlv〕v. 需要；包含
chain〔tʃen〕n. 鏈條；一連串　　*regard as* 視為
aboriginal〔ˌæbəˈrɪdʒənl̩〕adj. 土著的　　*pass down* 傳下來

Quit　　　　**Writing**

Some people think governments should spend as much money as possible exploring outer space (for example, traveling to the Moon and to other planets). Other people disagree and think governments should spend this money for our basic needs on Earth. Which of these two opinions do you agree with? Use specific reasons and details to support your answer.

Cut

Paste

Undo

Time

Help
?

Confirm
Answer

Next

95. Spending Money on Earth

There are always many things that a government would like to spend its money on, but no government has unlimited resources, so choices must be made. One project that some people would like to give as much money as possible to is space exploration. They believe that by traveling to the moon and other planets, we can make great scientific advances and perhaps find an alternate place to live before our own planet becomes too crowded or uninhabitable. *No doubt* there is truth to what they say, but *in my opinion*, the money would be better spent on meeting the basic needs of people here on Earth.

One reason is that space exploration requires a great deal of money and offers little immediate return. Spending money on immediate human needs, *on the other hand*, can have a big effect with relatively little investment. *In other words*, the money will be more useful if spent here on Earth. *Another* reason for spending money at home is that space is not the answer to all our problems. Experiments done in outer space may lead to medical breakthroughs, but if we do not solve basic sanitation and other health problems, disease will continue to threaten human lives. *Finally*, space exploration is a long-term project, but the threat of some problems on Earth is immediate. If we do not solve our environmental and health problems soon, we may become extinct long before we find another habitable planet.

To sum up, although space exploration is a valuable endeavor and should be supported, it should not receive all the money available. There are many other areas of research and development on Earth that also require funding. *And* the benefit of giving money to them is greater and more immediate.

95. 把錢用在地球上

　　政府要花錢資助的事情有很多，但是政府的資源有限，所以必須有所選擇。有一項計畫是有些人想儘可能資助的，那就是太空探險。一般認為，藉由登陸月球及其他行星，我們就可以在科學上有重大的進步，或許在我們的地球過度擁擠，或再也不能居住之前，可以先找到可供替代的住所。無疑地，這樣的說法有其道理，但依我之見，把錢花在滿足地球人類的基本需求，是比較好的做法。

　　其中一個理由是，太空探險需要龐大的經費，但所能提供的立即的報酬卻很少。另一方面，把錢用在人類立即的需求上，會有顯著的效果，而且相較之下，所投資的金額也較少。換句話說，這筆錢若用在地球上，會更有用。要把錢用在地球的另一個理由是，太空並不是解決我們所有問題的方法。在外太空所做的實驗，可能帶來醫學上的重大突破，但如果我們無法解決基本的公共衛生，以及其他健康方面的問題，疾病仍然會持續對人類生命造成威脅。最後一個理由是，太空探險是長程的計畫，但地球上有些問題所造成的威脅，卻是需要立刻解決的。如果我們不儘快解決環境及健康方面的問題，我們可能早在找到另一個可居住的星球之前，就絕種了。

　　總之，雖然太空探險是重要的努力方向，而且應該加以資助，但不應該用掉所有的經費。地球上有很多其他領域的研究和發展，也需要資金，而且資助這些研究與發展，其投資報酬率更大，也更有立即性的效果。

【註釋】

space〔spes〕*n.* 太空　　exploration〔͵ɛkspləˈreʃən〕*n.* 探險
resources〔rɪˈsorsɪz〕*n.pl.* 資源　　advance〔ədˈvæns〕*n.* 進步
alternate〔ˈɔltə·nɪt〕*adj.* 可替代的
uninhabitable〔͵ʌnɪnˈhæbɪtəb!〕*adj.* 不適合居住的
return〔rɪˈtɝn〕*n.* 報酬；收益　　***on the other hand*** 另一方面
relatively〔ˈrɛlətɪvlɪ〕*adv.* 相對地；比較地
investment〔ɪnˈvɛstmənt〕*n.* 投資
answer〔ˈænsə·〕*n.* (問題的)解決之道 < *to* >　　***lead to*** 導致
breakthrough〔ˈbrek͵θru〕*n.* 突破
sanitation〔͵sænəˈteʃən〕*n.* 衛生　　extinct〔ɪkˈstɪŋkt〕*adj.* 絕種的
endeavor〔ɪnˈdɛvə·〕*n.* 努力　　funding〔ˈfʌndɪŋ〕*n.* 資助

Quit　　　　　**Writing**

People have different ways of escaping the stress and difficulties of modern life. Some read; some exercise; others work in their gardens. What do you think are the best ways of reducing stress? Use specific details and examples in your answer.

▲

Cut

Paste

Undo

▼

Time

Help
?

Confirm
Answer

Next
➡

96. The Best Way to Reduce Stress

Inevitably, we must all face a certain amount of stress in our lives. While modern life offers us many conveniences, it also requires us to deal with pressure and frustration in daily life. It is important for all of us to find a way to relieve this stress in order to live happy and healthy lives. Some people prefer to engage in physical exercise by running or playing a sport, and some feel more relaxed after watching TV or even sleeping. *As for me*, I find that the best way to reduce stress is to spend time with family and friends.

One reason I prefer to spend time with others is that their company is a pleasant distraction. When under stress, if I spend time alone, I may continue to dwell on my problems. Sharing good times with family or friends, *on the other hand*, helps me to forget my worries. *Another* reason is that I have an opportunity to discuss my problems. Their advice is often helpful because they can see my situation more objectively than I can. *Furthermore*, simply talking about my problems often makes me feel better. *Finally*, spending time with others reminds me of what is important in life and helps me to keep things in perspective.

For all of these reasons, I believe that the best way to reduce stress is to spend time with others. Because it helps me to relax and keep life in perspective, it is the method I prefer when faced with life's difficulties. *But* no matter what method we choose, it is important to find an appropriate way to relieve pressure. Only in this way can we lead well-balanced lives.

96. 減輕壓力最好的方法

　　我們在生活中，都難免必須面對某種程度的壓力。雖然現代生活的確使我們非常便利，但也讓我們在日常生活中，要應付很多的壓力與挫折。所以，為了要有快樂健康的生活，找到方法減輕這些壓力，是很重要的。有些人比較喜歡像跑步這樣的運動，或從事其他運動，而有些人則會覺得看完電視，甚至睡一覺之後，就輕鬆多了。至於我，我最喜歡跟家人及朋友在一起，來減輕壓力。

　　我比較喜歡跟別人在一起的原因是，因為有他們的陪伴，能讓我忘卻壓力，覺得很愉快。如果我在有壓力的情況下，仍然一個人獨處，就會一直想著自己的問題。另一方面，跟家人或朋友共度愉快的時光，能幫助我忘卻煩惱。另一個理由是，這樣會讓我有機會討論我的問題。因為他們能比較客觀地衡量我的情況，所以他們的建議通常都對我很有幫助。而且，就算只是聊聊我的問題，通常也會讓我覺得好很多。最後，跟他人相處，會提醒我人生真正重要的是什麼，進而幫助我以正確的眼光來看事情。

　　基於以上的理由，我認為減輕壓力最好的方法，就是和別人在一起。因為這能幫助我放輕鬆，並且以正確的眼光看待人生，所以這是我在面對生活中的困擾時，比較喜歡的方法。但不論我們選擇什麼方法，找到一個適當的減壓方法是很重要的。唯有如此，我們才能過著均衡的生活。

【註釋】

stress〔strɛs〕*n.* 壓力　　　inevitably〔ɪnˈɛvətəblɪ〕*adv.* 無法避免地

frustration〔frʌsˈtreʃən〕*n.* 挫折；沮喪

relieve〔rɪˈliv〕*v.* 減輕　　***engage in*** 從事

company〔ˈkʌmpənɪ〕*n.* 陪伴

distraction〔dɪˈstrækʃən〕*n.* 使人分心的事物　　***dwell on*** 老是想著

share〔ʃɛr〕*v.* 分享　　objectively〔əbˈdʒɛktɪvlɪ〕*adv.* 客觀地

remind〔rɪˈmaɪnd〕*v.* 提醒

keep *sth.* ***in perspective*** 以正確的眼光看待某事

be faced with 面對　　appropriate〔əˈproprɪɪt〕*adj.* 適當的

lead a~life 過著~生活

well-balanced〔ˈwɛlˈbælənst〕*adj.* 均衡的

Quit   **Writing**

Do you agree or disagree with the following statement? Teachers should be paid according to how much their students learn. Give specific reasons and examples to support your opinion.

Cut

Paste

Undo

Time

Help

Confirm Answer

Next

97. A Teacher's Pay

Education plays a great role in the advancement and success of every society. While there are many factors which affect how well a student learns, the teacher is no doubt one of the most important. Some people believe that teachers would be able to teach their students more if they were better motivated. *For this reason*, they suggest that teachers be paid according to how much their students learn. *In my opinion*, this is not a good idea for the following reasons.

First, although a teacher can have a great influence on students, he is not the sole determiner of the students' success. Other factors, such as the school curriculum and the home environment of the students, must be considered. *Therefore*, not only is the plan to pay teachers according to the success of their students unfair to the teachers, but it may lead the education authorities to disregard other important factors. *Second*, while basing their pay on how much their students learn might motivate teachers to teach better, it will certainly lead them to put too much pressure on the students. *Furthermore*, depending on how the students are evaluated, such a system might cause teachers to put too much emphasis on test scores and ignore other measurements of learning.

For these reasons, I think that paying teachers according to how much their students learn is not a good idea. It is unfair to both the teachers and the students and may be detrimental to the learning process. This, in turn, would be disadvantageous to the society as a whole.

97. 老師的薪水

　　教育在一個社會的進步與成功的發展上，扮演了重要的角色。儘管影響學生的學習情況的因素有很多，但毫無疑問的，老師是其中最重要的一個因素。有些人認為，如果老師能夠受到更多激勵的話，就能傳授更多東西給學生。有鑑於此，他們認為，應該以學生的學習成果，作為老師敘薪的衡量標準。但我認為，這並不是個好主意，以下就是我所持的理由。

　　首先，雖然老師對學生有很大的影響，但並不是學生學習成果的唯一決定因素，還有其他的因素，如學校安排的課程，以及學生的家庭環境，都必須加以考量。因此，老師的敘薪方式，若是根據學生的學習成果而定，則不僅對老師不公平，還會使得教育當局，忽視其他重要的因素。第二，當敘薪方式以學生的學習成果為基準時，也許會激勵老師要教得更好，但也一定會讓他們強加太多壓力在學生身上。而且，這種太依賴學生學習成果的評鑑制度，可能會讓老師過度重視考試成績，而忽略了其他評量學習成效的方法。

　　基於以上的理由，我認為根據學生學習成果，作為老師敘薪的根據，並不是個好主意。這不但對老師與學生都不公平，而且還會損害學習的過程。因此，整體而言，這必然也會對社會造成不良的影響。

【註釋】

advancement〔əd'vænsmənt〕 *n.* 提升

motivate〔'motə,vet〕 *v.* 激發；給予動機　　factor〔'fæktɚ〕 *n.* 因素

sole〔sol〕 *adj.* 唯一的　　determiner〔dɪ'tɜmɪnɚ〕 *n.* 決定因素

curriculum〔kə'rɪkjələm〕 *n.* 課程　　unfair〔ʌn'fɛr〕 *adj.* 不公平的

authorities〔ə'θɔrətɪz〕 *n.pl.* 當局

disregard〔,dɪsrɪ'gɑrd〕 *v.* 忽視 (= *ignore*)

base A ***on*** B　A 以 B 為基礎　　***depend on***　視～而定

evaluate〔ɪ'vælju,et〕 *v.* 評估

put emphasis on　強調 (= *emphasize*)　　score〔skor〕 *n.* 分數

measurement〔'mɛʒɚmənt〕 *n.* 衡量方式

detrimental〔,dɛtrə'mɛntḷ〕 *adj.* 有害的 < *to* >

disadvantageous〔dɪs,ædvən'tedʒəs〕 *adj.* 不利的

in turn　必然也　　***as a whole***　就整體而言

Writing

Quit

If you were asked to send one thing representing your country to an international exhibition, what would you choose? Why? Use specific reasons and details to explain your choice.

▲

Cut

Paste

Undo

▼

Time

Help
?

Confirm
Answer

Next
➡

98. A Representative Object

Every country and culture has at least one unique feature, such as a food, handicraft, music, art, sport, noted historical sight or innovative product. Choosing the one thing that best represents my country would be a difficult task. There are many objects that could convey a sense of my country's history and culture. *However*, I believe the best choice would be a fine piece of calligraphy.

In Chinese culture, calligraphy is not merely writing, but also art. The delicate brushwork is not only beautiful, but creates a feeling of harmony and balance, both of which are characteristics that are esteemed in our society. *Thus*, this representation of high achievement in art is also an indication of the values which are important in my country. *In addition*, calligraphy represents the importance of language and writing. Chinese writing is a unique system of pictographs, which is both very exact and expressive. *Furthermore*, calligraphic writing gives an indication of the history of my society. Chinese characters have been written for thousands of years, and have changed and adapted over time. *Therefore*, it is a living and dynamic form of communication.

For all of the above reasons, I believe that a piece of calligraphy would be the best object to send to an international exhibition as a representation of my country. It would give the attendees a sense of my country's history, culture and values. *Therefore*, I can think of no better symbol of my country.

98. 具有代表性的物品

　　每個國家和文化，都至少有一項獨一無二的特色，像是食物、手工藝、音樂、美術、運動、著名的歷史景點，或是創新的產品。選一件最具代表性的東西，來代表我國，是一項困難的任務。因為實在有太多東西，在某種意義上，能夠傳達我國的歷史和文化。然而，我相信一幅好的書法作品，會是最好的選擇。

　　在中國文化裡，書法不只是書寫方式而已，它也是一種藝術。書法優美的筆觸不但漂亮，更能創造出一種和諧平衡的感覺，兩者都是在我們社會中備受重視的特質。因此，書法除了代表藝術的頂尖成就之外，也象徵我國的重要價值觀。此外，書法也代表了語言和書寫的重要性。中文書寫系統是一套獨特的象形文字，不但非常精確，也富含意義。此外，書法也顯示出我國社會的歷史演變。中國字的使用已歷經幾千年，隨著時間而有所改變。因此，書法是一種非常具有生命力和活力的溝通形式。

　　因為以上種種的理由，我相信一幅書法，會是送至國際展覽會，代表我們國家的最佳物品。它會讓參觀展覽的人，感受到我國的歷史、文化，和價值觀。因此，我認為書法是最能代表我國的東西。

【註釋】

representative〔‚rɛprɪ'zɛntətɪv〕*adj.* 代表的

unique〔ju'nik〕*adj.* 獨特的　　feature〔'fitʃɚ〕*n.* 特色

handicraft〔'hændɪ‚kræft〕*n.* 手工藝　　noted〔'notɪd〕*adj.* 著名的

innovative〔'ɪno‚vetɪv〕*adj.* 創新的　　convey〔kən've〕*v.* 傳達

calligraphy〔kə'lɪgrəfɪ〕*n.* 書法　　delicate〔'dɛləkɪt〕*adj.* 優美的

brushwork〔'brʌʃ‚wɝk〕*n.* 書法　　harmony〔'hɑrmənɪ〕*n.* 和諧

esteem〔ə'stim〕*v.* 尊重　　indication〔‚ɪndə'keʃən〕*n.* 象徵

values〔'væljʊz〕*n. pl.* 價值觀　　*in addition* 此外

pictograph〔'pɪktə‚græf〕*n.* 象形文字　　exact〔ɪg'zækt〕*adj.* 精確的

expressive〔ɪk'sprɛsɪv〕*adj.* 意味深遠的

calligraphic〔‚kælɪ'græfɪk〕*adj.* 書法的

character〔'kærɪktɚ〕*n.* 文字　　adapt〔ə'dæpt〕*v.* 改變

dynamic〔daɪ'næmɪk〕*adj.* 充滿活力的　　attendee〔‚ətɛn'di〕*n.* 出席者

representation〔‚rɛprɪzɛn'teʃən〕*n.* 代表

Quit　　　**Writing**

You have been told that dormitory rooms at your university must be shared by two students.　Would you rather have the university assign a student to share a room with you, or would you rather choose your own roommate?　Use specific reasons and details to explain your answer.

Cut

Paste

Undo

Time

Help
?

Confirm
Answer

Next

99. **Choosing a Roommate**

It is common for university students to share their dormitory rooms with another student, and at some universities this is required. Because the two students will spend a great deal of time together and must share a small space, it is essential that they be able to get along. *For this reason*, if I had to share a room, I would rather choose my own roommate than let the university assign one to me.

By choosing my own roommate, I would be able to live with someone with whom I am already familiar. While I look forward to making many new friends at university, I know that not everyone is easy to live with. *Therefore*, I would rather live with someone I already know well. Choosing my own roommate would also allow me to live with someone whose habits are compatible with my own. This would make it easier for us to share the limited space of a dormitory room. *And* if some misunderstanding or problem should occur, I would be better able to deal with it if I knew my roommate well.

Letting the university choose my roommate might mean that I would have to live with someone I couldn't get along with. That could have a bad effect on my studies during my first year. *For this reason and all of those above*, I would prefer to choose my own roommate at university.

99. 選擇室友

　　對大學生來說，和另一個學生同住宿舍，是很常見的事，而且在有些學校，這還是明文規定的。因爲這兩個學生將要共度一段很長的時間，而且必須共同擁有一個小空間，所以能夠和諧相處是很重要的。因爲這個理由，如果我必須和別人同住一個房間，我寧可選擇自己的室友，也不要讓學校替我分配。

　　藉由選擇自己的室友，我可以和我熟悉的人一起住。雖然我期待在大學結交許多新朋友，但我知道，並不是每個人都可以成爲好室友。因此，我寧可和我很熟的人住在一起。我自己選擇室友，可以找生活習慣較相近的人同住，這會讓我們比較容易能夠一起共享有限的宿舍空間。而且萬一有誤會或問題產生，如果我和室友很熟，也會比較能夠處理這樣的情況。

　　讓學校選擇我的室友，可能就意味著，我必須和我無法相處的人一起住，那對我大一的學業會有不好的影響。因爲這個理由，以及上述的原因，唸大學時，我寧願自己選擇室友。

【註釋】

roommate〔'rum,met〕*n.* 室友
dormitory〔'dɔrmə,torɪ〕*n.* 宿舍
required〔rɪ'kwaɪrd〕*adj.* 被要求的；規定的
essential〔ə'sɛnʃəl〕*adj.* 必要的
get along 和睦相處 < *with* >
***would rather* + V_1 + *than* + V_2** 寧願 V_1，而不願 V_2
assign〔ə'saɪn〕*v.* 指派　　***look forward to*** 期待
compatible〔kəm'pætəbl̩〕*adj.* 能相容的
limited〔'lɪmɪtɪd〕*adj.* 有限的
misunderstanding〔,mɪsʌndə'stændɪŋ〕*n.* 誤會
occur〔ə'kɝ〕*v.* 發生　　***deal with*** 處理
effect〔ɪ'fɛkt〕*n.* 影響 < *on* >

Quit　　　　　　　**Writing**

Some people think that governments should spend as much money as possible on developing or buying computer technology. Other people disagree and think that this money should be spent on more basic needs. Which one of these opinions do you agree with? Use specific reasons and details to support your answer.

Cut

Paste

Undo

Time

Help
?

Confirm
Answer

Next

100. Money for Computer Technology

Every government must face a variety of demands from different groups of citizens. Almost all represent worthy causes but, unfortunately, there is only so much money to go around. *For this reason*, the government must make some decisions about how best to spend the funds available. Some people think that it should be spent on computer technology, whereas others would like to see it go toward more basic needs. I agree with the first group for the following reasons.

The most important reason is that we now live in a very competitive world which depends on technology to produce goods efficiently. In order to keep up with others, our country must be able to keep pace technologically. If we do not, we will soon fall behind, and then the economy will suffer and so will society as a whole. *Another* reason is that communication and trade are conducted on a global scale now, and this also requires up-to-date computer technology. *Last but not least*, investing in computer technology will allow our country to provide students with a better education and workers with more employment.

In short, the benefits of investing in computer technology are well worth the cost involved. With up-to-date technology our country can better educate its students, produce goods more efficiently, and compete more effectively with other countries. *In this way*, we will be able to provide a better life for everyone.

100. 資助電腦科技

　　每個政府都必須面臨，許多不同公民團體的各種要求。幾乎每個要求看來都是值得重視的目標，但不幸的是，就只有這麼多錢可供分配。因此，政府必須在使用現有的資金時，做些抉擇。有些人認為，應該將錢用在電腦科技上，而有些人，卻希望把經費用在更基本的需求上。基於以下理由，我贊成前者的看法。

　　最重要的理由是，我們生活在一個競爭非常激烈的世界，必須仰賴科技，以有效率的方式製造產品。為了與其他國家並駕齊驅，我們在科技方面一定不能落後，如果不這樣做，很快就會被拋在後面，經濟就會衰退，整個社會也會受害。另一個理由是，現今的通訊與貿易日趨全球化，即時的電腦科技也是必要的。最後一項要點是，投資在電腦科技上，能夠提供本國學生更好的教育，讓就業者有更多的工作機會。

　　簡言之，投資在電腦科技絕對是物超所值。有了最新的科技，國家就能讓學生受更好的教育、生產商品將更有效率，而且更有能力與其他國家競爭。如此一來，我們就能讓每個人過更好的生活。

【註釋】

a variety of 各式各樣的 (= various 〔'vɛrɪəs 〕)

citizen 〔'sɪtəzṇ 〕 *n.* 公民　　worthy 〔'wɝðɪ 〕 *adj.* 值得的

cause 〔 kɔz 〕 *n.* 目標　　*go around* 足夠分配 (= go round)

funds 〔 fʌndz 〕 *n. pl.* 錢　　whereas 〔 hwɛr'æz 〕 *conj.* 然而 (= while)

go toward 有助於　　competitive 〔 kəm'pɛtətɪv 〕 *adj.* 競爭激烈的

depend on 依賴　　efficiently 〔 ɪ'fɪʃəntlɪ 〕 *adv.* 有效率地

keep up with 跟上；與…並駕齊驅　　*fall behind* 落後

as a whole 就整體而言　　conduct 〔 kən'dʌkt 〕 *v.* 進行

global 〔'globḷ 〕 *adj.* 全球的　　scale 〔 skel 〕 *n.* 規模

up-to-date 〔'ʌptə'det 〕 *adj.* 最新的

last but not least 最後一項要點是　　invest 〔 ɪn'vɛst 〕 *v.* 投資 < *in* >

employment 〔 ɪm'plɔɪmənt 〕 *n.* 工作　　*in short* 簡言之；總之

involve 〔 ɪn'vɑlv 〕 *v.* 牽涉在內　　effectively 〔 ɪ'fɛktɪvlɪ 〕 *adv.* 有效地

Quit　　　**Writing**

Some people like doing work by hand. Others prefer using machines. Which do you prefer? Use specific reasons and examples to support your answer.

Cut

Paste

Undo

101. Working by Hand

Machines have made it possible for us to produce almost any kind of product more quickly and cheaply. There is no denying that they are essential in today's society. *However*, some things are still made by hand, and these goods are usually highly valued for their quality and uniqueness. If I had a choice between using a machine or using my own two hands in my work, I would choose the latter method because it has some unique advantages.

First of all, making something by hand would give me a greater sense of satisfaction than using a machine would. I would know that this product was a one-of-a-kind item that could never be exactly reproduced by another. *Second*, before a person can make something by hand, he must develop certain skills. *Therefore*, the product is the result of training and experience and so is an accomplishment the creator can take pride in. *Last*, because I live in a fast-paced society, I believe I would cherish the opportunity to take my time over my work and focus on quality rather than quantity.

Due to the advantages of working by hand, that is the method I would choose to employ. It may not be as fast and efficient as using a machine to accomplish my work, but it would give me a greater sense of satisfaction and accomplishment. Many people would much rather work with a machine, and our society needs such people to advance, but I believe working by hand is the best way for me.

101. 手工製作

　　機器使我們能夠更快速、更便宜地製造幾乎任何一種產品。不可否認的是，機器在現今的社會中，是非常必要的，然而，有些東西仍然是要靠手工製作，而且這些東西，通常都因其品質和獨特的風格，而受到高度的重視。如果在工作時，我可以選擇使用機器或使用雙手，我會選擇後者，因爲這個方法有其獨特的優點。

　　首先，用手工製作物品，會比用機器製作，給予我更大的滿足感。我會知道，這項產品是獨一無二的，不可能被別人完全複製。其次，要用手工製作物品之前，必須培養一些技術，因此，這項產品是訓練和經驗的成果，所以也會是製作者引以爲傲的成就。最後，由於我生活在一個步調快速的社會中，我認爲我要珍惜這個機會，可以從容不迫、不慌不忙地工作，而且重質不重量。

　　由於手工製作有這些優點，所以這正是我想要選擇使用的方法。用這個方法來完成工作，也許不如使用機器來得快而且有效率，但它能帶給我更大的滿足感和成就感。很多人工作時可能寧願使用機器，而且我們的社會要進步，也需要這些人，但我認爲，用手工工作，對我而言，是最佳的方式。

【註釋】

There is no + V-ing …是不可能的　　deny〔dɪ'naɪ〕*v.* 否認
essential〔ə'sɛnʃəl〕*adj.* 必要的　　value〔'væljʊ〕*v.* 重視
uniqueness〔ju'niknɪs〕*n.* 獨特
latter〔'lætɚ〕*adj.* (兩者中) 後者的 (↔ *former*)
on-of-a-kind *adj.* 獨一無二的　　item〔'aɪtəm〕*n.* 項目；物品
reproduce〔ˌriprə'djus〕*v.* 複製
accomplishment〔ə'kɑmplɪʃmənt〕*n.* 成就
creator〔krɪ'etɚ〕*n.* 創造者　　***take pride in*** 以～爲榮 (= *be proud of*)
fast-paced〔'fæst'pest〕*adj.* 步調快速的　　cherish〔'tʃɛrɪʃ〕*v.* 珍惜
focus on 專注於　　quantity〔'kwɑntətɪ〕*n.* 量
employ〔ɪm'plɔɪ〕*v.* 使用　　advance〔əd'væns〕*v.* 進步

Quit　　　　　Writing

Schools should ask students to evaluate their teachers.　Do you agree or disagree?　Use specific reasons and examples to support your answer.

_____
_____
_____
_____
_____
_____
_____
_____
_____
_____
_____
_____
_____
_____
_____
_____
_____
_____
_____
_____

Cut

Paste

Undo

Time

Help　?　Confirm Answer　Next ➡

102. Evaluating Teachers

In many universities, students are asked to evaluate their professors after each course, but this is not common practice in junior and senior high schools. The system has many advantages to the university, the students, and the teachers, and I believe that these same benefits can be brought to education at the junior and senior high school levels. *Therefore*, I agree that schools should ask students to evaluate their teachers.

One advantage of doing this is that this kind of feedback can be used to improve courses and teacher performance. The school will have a better idea of what students' needs are and can then design programs to meet them. *Another* advantage is that the process of writing evaluations will help the students think seriously about their education and what it means to them. A *third* benefit is that the students will feel that their teachers and school take their opinions seriously. Writing evaluations will give them some control over and responsibility for their education. *Finally*, when students evaluate their teachers, whether positively or negatively, they will realize that there is always room for improvement no matter what one does, and that we should always strive to better our performance.

For all of these reasons, I believe that student evaluations of teachers would be beneficial to schools, teachers, and students. *Of course*, the evaluations must be done responsibly, but when the students feel that their views are important and are listened to, I think they will do their best to contribute to improvement in education.

102. 教師評鑑

很多大學都會要求學生，在課程結束後，對教授進行評鑑，但在國中與高中，這樣的做法並不普遍。這樣的制度對大學、學生與教師，都有很多優點，而且我認爲，這些優點，也應該適用於國中與高中層級的教育。因此，我贊同校方應該要求學生對教師進行評鑑。

這樣做有個好處是，能採用學生的意見，來改善課程與教師的表現，校方能夠更了解學生的需求，進而設計符合需求的課程內容。另一個好處是，評鑑的過程可以幫助學生認眞思考何謂教育，以及教育對他們的意義。第三個好處是，學生會覺得教師與學校有認眞考慮他們的意見，進行評鑑能讓他們對上課內容，有一些掌控權與責任感。最後，學生在進行教師評鑑時，無論正面或負面的評價，都能使他們了解，不管教師怎麼做，都還是有改進的空間，而且應該要時時努力，以求有更好的表現。

基於這些理由，我相信學生進行教師評鑑，對學校、教師與學生，都有好處。當然，做評鑑時必須負責任，但當學生覺得他們的看法很重要，而且會受到重視時，我相信他們會盡力協助改善教育。

【註釋】

evaluate〔ɪ'vælju͵et〕v. 評估；評鑑
practice〔'præktɪs〕n. 慣例；做法　　advantage〔əd'væntɪdʒ〕n. 好處
level〔'lɛvḷ〕n. 層級　　feedback〔'fid͵bæk〕n. 回饋；意見反應
performance〔pə'fɔrməns〕n. 表現　　design〔dɪ'zaɪn〕v. 設計
meet〔mit〕v. 滿足（需求等）　　evaluation〔ɪ͵vælju'eʃən〕n. 評鑑
take～seriously 認眞看待～　　positively〔'pɑzətɪvlɪ〕adv. 正面地
room〔rum〕n. 空間　　improvement〔ɪm'pruvmənt〕n. 改善
strive〔straɪv〕v. 努力　　better〔'bɛtə〕v. 改善
beneficial〔͵bɛnə'fɪʃəl〕adj. 有益的
responsibly〔rɪ'spansəblɪ〕adv. 負責地；確實地
contribute〔kən'trɪbjut〕v. 貢獻；有助於 < *to* >

Quit	**Writing**

In your opinion, what is the most important characteristic (for example, honesty, intelligence, a sense of humor) that a person can have to be successful in life? Use specific reasons and examples from your experience to explain your answer. When you write your answer, you are not limited to the examples listed in the question.

Cut

Paste

Undo

Help 　Confirm Answer 　Next

103. Perseverance

Of all the advantageous characteristics to have, I think that perseverance plays the greatest role in one's success. Other characteristics, such as intelligence, confidence, and honesty, are no doubt important, but they do not necessarily guarantee success. Perseverance offers no guarantees either, but I believe that this trait offers one more opportunity to succeed.

There are several reasons why perseverance often leads to success. *First of all*, a man who has perseverance does not give up after a failure. He tries again and can, *therefore*, learn from his mistakes. *Second*, a persistent person is usually a hard worker, and hard work is an important ingredient in success. *Last*, with perseverance comes a certain amount of confidence — the confidence that one will eventually succeed.

For all of these reasons, I believe that perseverance is the most important characteristic to have. It is easily combined with other traits such as diligence and confidence to increase the chances of success. *However*, without perseverance, one's success may be more dependent on luck than anything else.

103. 毅　力

　　在我們所能擁有的優點中，我認為一個人是否能成功，毅力扮演了最重要的角色。雖然其他的特點，像是聰明才智、信心和誠實，無疑地，都很重要，但是並不能保證一定能使人成功。雖然有毅力也無法保證能成功，但是我相信，這個特質會讓人更有機會成功。

　　為何有毅力就容易成功，有好幾個理由。首先，有毅力的人，失敗之後，不會放棄，他們會再試一次，因此就能從錯誤中學習。其次，不屈不撓的人，通常都十分努力，而努力就是成功的重要因素。最後，有毅力就會產生一定程度的信心 —— 相信自己終究會成功。

　　基於這些理由，我認為毅力是必須擁有的最重要特質。毅力很容易就能和其他特點相結合，像是勤勉與信心，如此便能增加成功的機會。然而，如果沒有毅力，那麼一個人想成功，可能就會比較需要靠運氣，而不是其他特質。

【註釋】

　　perseverance〔,pɝsə'vɪrəns〕n. 毅力
　　advantageous〔,ædvən'tedʒəs〕adj. 有利的
　　characteristic〔,kærɪktə'rɪstɪk〕n. 特點 (= trait〔tret〕)
　　intelligence〔ɪn'tɛlədʒəns〕n. 聰明才智
　　not necessarily 未必 (= *not always*)
　　guarantee〔,gærən'ti〕v., n. 保證　　**lead to** 導致
　　first of all 首先 (= *first* = *in the first place*)　　**give up** 放棄
　　persistent〔pɚ'sɪstənt〕adj. 不屈不撓的
　　ingredient〔ɪn'gridɪənt〕n. 因素；成分
　　eventually〔ɪ'vɛntʃuəlɪ〕adv. 最後
　　combine〔kəm'baɪn〕v. 結合　　diligence〔'dɪlədʒəns〕n. 勤勉
　　be dependent on 依賴；視～而定 (= *depend on*)

Quit　　　　　**Writing**

It is generally agreed that society benefits from the work of its members. Compare the contributions of artists to society with the contributions of scientists to society. Which type of contribution do you think is valued more by your society? Give specific reasons to support your answer.

▲

Cut

Paste

Undo

▼

Time 🕐　　　　　　　　　Help ?　Confirm Answer　Next ➡

104. Science Versus the Arts

Society benefits from the work of all its members, from doctors to firefighters to garbage collectors. A person can make a contribution no matter what type of work he does. *However*, society does tend to value some kinds of work more highly than others. When it comes to scientists and artists, for example, I believe that my society places more importance on the work of scientists.

For one thing, my society is technologically advanced and is very competitive in technology industries. We require well-educated and skilled scientists to help us stay at the cutting edge. *Therefore*, many resources are put into the study of scientific subjects in my country. *Another* reason we tend to value the work of scientists more is that the discoveries they make often benefit many people. *For example*, a medical breakthrough can cure thousands, and a new product can bring convenience to many. *Finally*, the achievements of science are more concrete and, *therefore*, easier to understand than those of art. A machine either works well or it doesn't, but the success of a piece of art often depends on the opinion of the audience.

To sum up, both art and science are important in my society, but I believe that most people value the work of scientists more. They may do so because science benefits them more personally than art does, or simply because it is easier to understand. Whatever the reason, I believe that science will continue to be valued and supported in my society.

104. 科學與藝術

　　社會會因其所有成員的工作而獲益,從醫生、消防隊員,到清潔隊員,不論從事哪一種類型的工作,每個人都有其貢獻。然而,社會的確較重視某種類型的工作。例如,當我們提到科學家和藝術家的時候,我認為我們的社會較重視科學家的工作。

　　理由之一是,我們的社會是個科技進步的社會,在科技產業方面競爭非常激烈,我們需要受過良好教育,及擁有高技術的科學家,來幫助我們保持領先的地位。因此,在我國,很多資源都投入主題與科學相關的研究。我們傾向於較重視科學家的工作,另一個原因是,他們的發現經常讓很多人獲益。例如,醫學上的突破能夠治癒數千人,一項新產品,能為很多人帶來便利。最後一個原因是,科學的成就較為具體,也因此比藝術成就更容易讓人理解。機器的運作有好有壞,但是一件藝術品的成功與否,通常要視觀眾的意見而定。

　　總之,在我們的社會,藝術和科學都很重要,但我認為,大部份的人較重視科學家的工作。他們會這樣想,是因為就他們而言,科學帶來的好處比藝術多,或者只是因為科學成就較容易理解。不論是何種原因,我認為在我們的社會裡,人們將繼續重視並支持科學。

【註釋】

benefit〔'bɛnəfɪt〕v. 獲益 < *from* >
firefighter〔'faɪr,faɪtə〕n. 消防隊員
contribution〔,kɑntrə'bjuʃən〕n. 貢獻　value〔'vælju〕v. 重視
when it comes to 一談到　advanced〔əd'vænst〕adj. 進步的
competitive〔kəm'pɛtətɪv〕adj. 競爭激烈的
cutting edge 最頂尖的地位　breakthrough〔'brek,θru〕n. 突破
achievements〔ə'tʃivmənts〕n.pl. 成就
concrete〔'kɑnkrit〕adj. 具體的　work〔wɝk〕v. 運轉
depend on 視~而定　*to sum up* 總之

Quit　　　　　**Writing**

Students at universities often have a choice of places to live. They may choose to live in university dormitories, or they may choose to live in apartments in the community. Compare the advantages of living in university housing with the advantages of living in an apartment in the community. Where would you prefer to live? Give reasons for your preference.

Cut

Paste

Undo

Time

Help
?

Confirm
Answer

Next

105. University Housing

At most universities there is a variety of housing options for students to choose from. Two of the most common are university dormitories and off-campus apartments. Each of these options has its advantages, and so students should make their decision carefully.

When considering moving into a university dormitory, students will find the following advantages. *First*, it is usually located on the campus and so it is very convenient for students to get to their classes, the library, and other university facilities. They will save the time that they would have otherwise spent commuting to campus. *Second*, living in a campus dormitory offers students a convenient life. They do not have to worry about cooking meals or paying utility bills on time because all these services are included. They will be able to devote more time to their studies and extracurricular activities. *Finally*, living in a dormitory makes it easy for students to meet others and develop friendships. In addition to sharing living and recreation space, students can meet others through activities organized by the university or the dormitory itself. This is especially helpful to new students.

As for off-campus apartments, there are also several advantages. *First of all*, living away from the university allows students to develop more independence. Having more responsibility for their daily needs when they are students, they may find it easier to adjust to life on their own after graduation. *In addition*, the more independent lifestyle offers more freedom. Without university restrictions, the students can keep their own hours and set their own limits. *Finally*, students who live off-campus have more personal space. They do not have to share their bedrooms or bathrooms with many other people. This may allow them to better relax when not in class.

In conclusion, both university dormitories and off-campus apartments offer certain advantages to students. Which one a student should choose depends on what is important to him or her. As for me, I would choose to live in a university dormitory for the first year. This would allow me to make friends and get accustomed to school life without the distraction of having to worry about my daily needs. Later, I would move into an off-campus apartment in order to develop my independence and enjoy a freer lifestyle.

105. 上大學時的住所

大部分的大學，都有很多居住方式供學生選擇，其中最常見的兩種，就是大學宿舍與校外公寓，這兩種都各有優點，因此學生應該謹慎地選擇。

當考慮要搬進大學宿舍時，學生們可以發現有以下一些優點。首先，因為宿舍通常都在校園內，因此對學生來說，不論要去上課、去圖書館，還是要去使用其他校內設施，都很方便，可以省下住在其他地方所需的通勤時間。其次，住校內宿舍使學生生活很便利，他們不必擔心要煮飯，或按時繳水電費的問題，因為這些所有的公共設施都由宿舍包辦，他們可以花更多的時間在學業方面，或從事課外活動。最後，住在宿舍讓學生更容易認識其他人，並培養友誼。除了能與別人共享生活與休閒空間外，學生還能透過校方或宿舍所發起的活動，認識其他人，這對新生而言特別有幫助。

而住在校外公寓也有一些優點。首先，住在校外可以讓學生更獨立。使他們在學生時代，就能對自己的日常生活所需負責，畢業之後也許更能適應須自力更生的生活。此外，較獨立的生活方式，可以給學生更大的自由，由於沒有學校的束縛，學生就能安排自己的時間，並且自我約束。最後，住在校外的學生，能擁有較多私人空間，不需要和很多人共用寢室或浴室，這會讓他們在課餘時間更能放鬆。

總之，住在校內宿舍或校外公寓，對學生而言，都有一些好處。應該怎麼選擇，要看哪些好處對自己而言比較重要。對我來說，大一時我會選擇住在校內宿舍，這會讓我有交友的機會，並且熟悉校園生活，不用因為一些日常所需而分心。之後，我就會搬到校外公寓，這樣才能培養自己獨立，享受更自由的生活方式。

【註釋】

housing〔'haʊzɪŋ〕*n.* 住宅　　option〔'ɑpʃən〕*n.* 選擇

dormitory〔'dɔrmə,torɪ〕*n.* 宿舍　　campus〔'kæmpəs〕*n.* 校園

facilities〔fə'sɪlə,tɪz〕*n. pl.* 設施　　otherwise〔'ʌðɚ,waɪz〕*adv.* 否則

commute〔kə'mjut〕*v.* 通勤　　service〔'sɝvɪs〕*n.* 公共設施

utility〔ju'tɪlətɪ〕*n.* 公用事業（瓦斯、電力、自來水等）

extracurricular〔,ɛkstrəkə'rɪkjəlɚ〕*adj.* 課外的

adjust〔ə'dʒʌst〕*v.* 適應 < *to* >　　restriction〔rɪ'strɪkʃən〕*n.* 限制

be accustomed to 習慣於

distraction〔dɪ'strækʃən〕*n.* 使人分心的事物

Quit	**Writing**

You need to travel from your home to a place 40 miles (64 kilometers) away. Compare the different kinds of transportation you could use. Tell which method of travel you would choose. Give specific reasons for your choice.

▲

Cut

Paste

Undo

▼

106. Train Travel

Assuming that I had to travel to a place 40 miles away, I would have a choice of several means of transportation. *Of course*, I could drive my own car, which would give me the greatest flexibility and independence. I could leave at any time I liked and would be able to drive door-to-door. *However*, I would have to pay for the gas and for a parking place when I arrived. Another option would be to take a bus. This would be cheaper but not as comfortable or convenient. I could also take a train. This might cost about the same as a bus but departures would probably not be as frequent. *However*, I could relax on the train and travel in greater comfort. *Finally*, I could ride a motorcycle, but I feel the distance is too great to be comfortable, especially if the weather is bad.

In the end, I believe I would choose to travel by train. It is not the most convenient method, but it would allow me to relax during the trip. In contrast to driving my own car, if I took a train, I would not have to worry about getting lost or finding a parking place when I arrived. I could read the newspaper, do some work or just watch the scenery. *Also*, the set departure and arrival times would not be affected by traffic, so I could be sure of my schedule. This would be important if I were planning to meet someone at my destination. *Finally*, I believe that traveling by train is safer than traveling by bus or motorcycle. By choosing the train I could arrive at my destination in safety and in comfort.

106. 搭火車

　　假設我必須到四十英哩外的地方，有好幾種交通工具可供選擇，當然我可以自己開車，這樣最有彈性，而且不必依賴別人，我可以隨時出發，想開車去哪，就去哪。然而，我必須付汽油費，及到達後的停車費。另一個選擇是搭巴士，這樣會比較便宜，但比較沒那麼舒服或方便。我也可以搭火車，費用可能與巴士相同，但是班次可能沒有那麼頻繁，但是在火車上我可以休息，能更舒適地享受這段旅程。最後，我可以騎摩拖車，可是我覺得距離太遠，沒辦法很舒服，特別是如果天氣不好的話。

　　我想我終究會選擇搭火車，雖然不是最方便的方式，但卻能夠讓我在旅途中休息。和自己開車比起來，如果搭火車，就不用擔心迷路，或抵達後要找停車位。我可以在火車上看報紙，做些工作，或者就只是欣賞風景。此外，火車出發和抵達的時間都很固定，不受交通影響，所以我可以很確定自己的時間表，如果我預定和某人在目的地見面，這一點就很重要。最後，我認爲坐火車比搭巴士或騎摩拖車安全，所以選擇坐火車，我就可以安全而且舒適地到達目的地。

【註釋】

assuming (*that*) 假定　　flexibility〔ˌflɛksəˈbɪlətɪ〕*n.* 彈性

means〔minz〕*n.* 方式

transportation〔ˌtrænspɚˈteʃən〕*n.* 交通；運輸

independence〔ˌɪndɪˈpɛndəns〕*n.* 獨立

door-to-door〔ˈdɔrtəˈdɔr〕*adv.* 門到門地　　gas〔gæs〕*n.* 汽油

option〔ˈɑpʃən〕*n.* 選擇　　departure〔dɪˈpartʃɚ〕*n.* 出發

frequent〔ˈfrikwənt〕*adj.* 頻繁的

in contrast to 和…對比之下

set〔sɛt〕*adj.* 固定的　　schedule〔ˈskɛdʒʊl〕*n.* 時間表

destination〔ˌdɛstəˈneʃən〕*n.* 目的地

in safety 安全地 (= *safely*)　　*in comfort* 舒適地 (= *comfortably*)

Quit

Writing

Some people believe that a college or university education should be available to all students. Others believe that higher education should be available only to good students. Discuss these views. Which view do you agree with? Explain why.

Cut

Paste

Undo

Time

Help ?

Confirm Answer

Next

107. Higher Education for All

There is no denying that a college or university education is very beneficial. Those who receive higher education have more opportunities. They often hold better jobs, earn a higher income and enjoy a more comfortable and secure lifestyle. Unfortunately, places in university are often limited and reserved for "good" students. It is my belief that this practice is not only detrimental to those students denied a college or university education, but to the society as a whole. *Therefore*, higher education should be available to all students.

One reason that higher education should not be limited to good students is that not all secondary students study in equal circumstances. The facilities and teaching at some high schools are superior to those at others, and the students who study there enjoy a great advantage. *In addition*, a student's performance can be affected by his or her home environment or family financial pressure. It is often more difficult for a student from a disadvantaged environment and school district to perform well. *However*, this does not mean that the student would not appreciate and benefit from higher education if given the opportunity.

Another reason for making higher education available to all is to encourage less capable students to improve. If marginal students believe that they have no hope of entering university, they may feel that there is no point in studying diligently. *However*, if they see a more direct relationship between their academic performance and their future opportunities, they will be more motivated. *In this way*, a poor student may turn out to be a good one.

Finally, a better educated population contributes to the growth and prosperity of a society as a whole. *For this reason*, it is advantageous to educate as many young people as possible. *Furthermore*, by denying higher education to students who do not make their mark in secondary education, the country may be ignoring a future Einstein. When every person in the society is given the opportunity to reach his or her full potential, the society will benefit.

For all of these reasons, I believe that higher education should be available to all students, not only to those with good academic performance in high school. *Of course*, it is desirable to encourage good performance in students. This can be done by offering financial support in the form of scholarships to those who work hard. *In this way*, we can ensure that students have the ability to take advantage of the opportunities available to them.

107. 全民高等教育

　　大學教育非常有益，這是不可否認的。受過高等教育的人，會擁有更多的機會，通常也會有比較好的工作，賺比較多的錢，並享有比較舒適和安全的生活方式。可惜的是，大學的入學資格通常是有設限的，而且都是保留給「好」學生。我相信這樣的做法，不但對那些無法受大學教育的人是有害的，整體來說，對社會也不利。因此，高等教育應該開放給所有學生。

　　高等教育不應該只限於給好學生，原因之一是，並非所有的中學生都在平等的環境中學習。有些中學的設施和教學，比其他的學校好很多，這使得他們的學生佔了很大的優勢。此外，學生的表現也可能受到家庭環境，和家中經濟壓力的影響。對來自環境貧困和落後學區的學生來說，功課要好，通常比較困難。然而，這並不表示，如果這些學生有機會接受高等教育，他們不會心存感激，並且從高等教育中獲益。

　　另一個應將高等教育開放給所有人的原因，是為了鼓勵那些能力較差的學生力求進步。如果邊緣學生認為，自己沒有進大學的希望，那麼他們也許會覺得，用功讀書是沒有道理的。然而，如果他們知道，學業表現和未來的機會有很直接的關連，便會覺得更有動力唸書。如此一來，原本很差的學生，也可能會變成好學生。

　　最後，就整體而言，人們的教育程度較高，會促進社會成長與繁榮。因此，儘可能多讓年輕人受教育是有好處的。此外，國家如果不讓高中成績未達標準的學生受高等教育，可能會因此埋沒了一個未來的愛因斯坦。當社會中的每個人都有機會充份發展潛力時，整個社會都將獲益。

　　基於這些理由，我認為所有學生都應該接受高等教育，而不是只有那些在高中時期功課好的學生。當然，鼓勵學生有好的表現是可取的。我們可以藉由金錢上的資助，來達到目的，以提供獎學金的方式，鼓勵認真的學生。如此一來，我們就可以確保學生，有能力可以充分利用他們可獲得的機會。

【註釋】

beneficial〔͵bɛnə'fɪʃəl〕adj. 有益的　　income〔'ɪn͵kʌm〕n. 收入

secure〔sɪ'kjʊr〕adj. 安全的　　place〔ples〕n. 資格

reserve〔rɪ'zɜv〕v. 保留　　practice〔'præktɪs〕n. 做法；慣例

detrimental〔͵dɛtrə'mɛntḷ〕adj. 有害的＜to＞

deny〔dɪ'naɪ〕v. 拒絕給予　　*as a whole* 就整體而言

available〔ə'veləbḷ〕adj. 可獲得的＜to＞

be limited to 僅限於　　secondary〔'sɛkən͵dɛrɪ〕adj. 中學的

circumstances〔'sɜkəm͵stænsɪz〕n. pl. 情況；條件

facilities〔fə'sɪlətɪz〕n. pl. 設施　　*be superior to* 比～優秀

in addition 此外　　financial〔fə'nænʃəl〕adj. 財務的

disadvantaged〔͵dɪsəd'væntɪdʒd〕adj. 下層社會的

school district 學區　　perform〔pɚ'fɔrm〕v. 表現

appreciate〔ə'priʃɪ͵et〕v. 欣賞；感激

capable〔'kepəbḷ〕adj. 有能力的

marginal〔'mɑrdʒɪnḷ〕adj. 邊緣的；勉強夠格的

point〔pɔɪnt〕n. 道理　　diligently〔'dɪlədʒəntlɪ〕adv. 勤勉地

motivate〔'motə͵vet〕v. 使產生動機

academic〔͵ækə'dɛmɪk〕adj. 學術的

turn out 結果　　population〔͵pɑpjə'leʃən〕n. 國民

contribute〔kən'trɪbjut〕v. 促成　　prosperity〔prɑs'pɛrətɪ〕n. 繁榮

advantageous〔͵ædvən'tedʒəs〕adj. 有益的＜to＞

make one's mark 成功　　potential〔pə'tɛnʃəl〕n. 潛力

reach one's full potential 充分發揮潛力

desirable〔dɪ'zaɪrəbḷ〕adj. 可取的；有利的

scholarship〔'skɑlɚ͵ʃɪp〕n. 獎學金　　ensure〔ɪn'ʃʊr〕v. 確保

take advantage of 利用

Quit　　　**Writing**

Some people believe that the best way of learning about life is by listening to the advice of family and friends. Other people believe that the best way of learning about life is through personal experience. Compare the advantages of these two different ways of learning about life. Which do you think is preferable? Use specific examples to support your preference.

Cut

Paste

Undo

Time

Help
?

Confirm
Answer

Next
➡

108. Learning About Life

As we grow, we learn many things about life. Some of these lessons are easy and some are difficult. What is the best way to learn them? Some believe that they can learn best by listening to the advice of others, while some people believe that it is better to learn through personal experience. Both methods have their advantages.

In the first case, learning by listening to others, we have the benefit of learning from others' mistakes and are thus being able to avoid them ourselves. We can take advantage of the experience and wisdom of our friends and family. This will help us to make better decisions and avoid costly errors. *Furthermore*, the people who know us well can advise us effectively because they understand our strengths and weaknesses. *At the same time*, they are sometimes able to see situations more objectively than we are.

In the second case, learning through doing, we have the advantage of gaining meaningful experience. We will no doubt better remember the lessons we learn when we enjoy the rewards or suffer the consequences ourselves. *Moreover*, we can often develop other skills through personal experience and can learn from our mistakes.

Finally, no two people are exactly alike. *Therefore*, what family and friends think may be suitable for them, but not appropriate for us.

Given a choice between these two ways of learning about life, I would still choose the former, learning through the advice of others. This is because I believe I should take advantage of all the resources available, and the experiences of my family and friends are a valuable resource. *For example*, if I were preparing to take my first trip abroad on my own, the advice of others who have already experienced such a trip could only help me. Just as we can learn from history, we can learn from the past actions of those close to us.

In conclusion, I find advantages in both ways of learning. Although I prefer to learn by listening to the advice of others, that does not mean I will forgo learning through my own experiences. It does mean, *however*, that I will approach new experiences with the added benefit of my family and friends' good advice.

108. 學習人生

　　當我們逐漸成長時，我們會學習到許多生活中的事情。其中有些教訓很簡單，而有些卻很困難。什麼是獲取教訓最好的方法？有些人認為，他們可以藉由聽從別人的建議，而有最好的學習效果，而有些人卻認為，最好是藉由親身體驗來學習。這兩種方法都各有優點。

　　第一種方法，是聽從別人建議而學習，因為我們可以從別人所犯過的錯誤中學習，避免再犯相同的錯誤。我們還可以利用家人和朋友的經驗或智慧，幫助我們做出更好的決定，避免犯下代價高昂的錯誤。此外，因為他們了解我們，知道我們的優缺點，所以能提供有用的建議。同時，他們對於事情的看法，有時比我們客觀。

　　第二種方法，是從做中學，這樣我們可以因為得到寶貴的經驗而獲益。毫無疑問地，當我們因為自己所做的事情享受成果，或承擔後果時，會對這些教訓記憶更加深刻。此外，藉由親身體驗，可以培養其他的技巧，而且也能從錯誤中學習。最後，沒有兩個人是完全相同的，因此，家人或朋友的想法，也許只適合他們自己，不見得適合我們。

　　若要我從這兩種學習人生的方法中選一個，我仍然會選擇前者，也就是從別人的建議中學習。因為我認為，應該利用所有可獲得的資源，而家人與朋友的經驗，就是寶貴的資源。例如，如果我初次要準備自己出國旅行，那麼有類似出國旅行經驗的人，所提供的建議，對我就很有幫助。正如我們能從歷史中學習一樣，我們也能藉由周遭的人的經驗來學習。

　　總之，這兩種學習方法我認爲各有優點，儘管我比較喜歡聽從別人的建議，但這不表示我就不會親身去體驗。然而，這確實意味著我除了會體驗新的經驗，同時還要聽聽家人與朋友提供的忠告，才能獲得更大的益處。

【註釋】

lesson〔ˈlɛsn̩〕n. 教訓

advantage〔ədˈvæntɪdʒ〕n. 好處；優點（= benefit〔ˈbɛnəfɪt〕）

case〔kes〕n. 情況；例子　　**take advantage of** 利用

costly〔ˈkɔstlɪ〕adj. 代價高的；昂貴的　　error〔ˈɛrɚ〕n. 錯誤

furthermore〔ˈfɝðɚˌmor〕adv. 此外　　advise〔ədˈvaɪz〕v. 建議

effectively〔ɪˈfɛktɪvlɪ〕adv. 有效地

strength〔strɛŋθ〕n. 優點（↔ weakness）

objectively〔əbˈdʒɛktɪvlɪ〕adv. 客觀地

meaningful〔ˈminɪŋfl̩〕adv. 有意義的

reward〔rɪˈwɔrd〕n. 報酬

consequence〔ˈkɑnsəˌkwɛns〕n. 後果

suitable〔ˈsutəbl̩〕adj. 適合的（= appropriate〔əˈproprɪɪt〕）

given〔ˈɡɪvən〕prep. 如果考慮到

the former（兩者中）前者（↔ the latter）

resource〔rɪˈsors〕n. 資源

available〔əˈveləbl̩〕adj. 可獲得的

valuable〔ˈvæljʊəbl̩〕adj. 珍貴的

abroad〔əˈbrɔd〕adv. 到國外

on one's **own** 自行；獨力（= by oneself）

in conclusion 總之　　forgo〔fɔrˈgo〕v. 放棄

approach〔əˈprotʃ〕v. 處理；對待

added〔ˈædɪd〕adj. 附加的

Quit	**Writing**

When people move to another country, some of them decide to follow the customs of the new country. Others prefer to keep their own customs. Compare these two choices. Which one do you prefer? Support your answer with specific details.

▲

Cut

Paste

Undo

▼

Time

Help

Confirm
Answer

Next

109. Keeping Customs

When people move to another country, they not only face a different environment and language, but also different customs. Every culture has its own customs, and all of them are valuable. *However*, deciding how to deal with the problem of unfamiliar customs is a challenge for many immigrants. Some choose to follow the customs of their new country, while others prefer to adhere to their own customs. Each of these choices has some advantages as explained below.

When people choose to follow the customs of their adopted country, they may find that it helps them to adapt more quickly to the new society. They have something to discuss and share with their new neighbors, and sharing customs is one way for people to feel closer to one another. *Thus*, following the new customs may help immigrants feel more at home. It may also help them to see the positive things in their new environment and to forget their feelings of homesickness.

On the other hand, those who choose to continue following their own customs may also find that it helps them feel more at home. There are many things to adjust to in another country, and following their traditional customs may help people feel more secure in the new surroundings. *More importantly*, our customs are a part of us. They are an expression of the culture that has shaped us. This is something that most of us would like to pass down to our children and share with others. Sharing our old customs can also bring us closer to our new neighbors.

To sum up, our customs have value and are an important part of our culture. *Therefore*, I don't believe that we should abandon our traditional customs when we move to another country. *At the same time*, I believe that we should learn about the customs of our new home and follow those that appeal to us. *In this way*, we can remember and celebrate our old culture while adapting to our new one.

109. 保存習俗

　　當人們搬到另一個國家後，不僅要面對不一樣的環境和語言，還要面對不同的風俗習慣。每個文化都有其風俗習慣，而且都非常重要。然而，如何應付因不熟悉習俗所產生的問題，對許多移民者而言，都是一項挑戰。有些人選擇遵從新國家的風俗習慣，有些人則寧可堅守自己國家的風俗習慣。如以下所解釋的，這兩種選擇都有一些優點。

　　當人們選擇遵從他們移入國家的風俗習慣時，可能會覺得，這樣有助於更快適應新的社會。他們和新鄰居有話題可聊，有東西可以分享，而且擁有相同的風俗習慣，是能讓人們覺得更親近的一種方式。因此，遵從新的風俗習慣，有助於使移民者感到更舒服自在，也會幫助他們看到新環境的優點，忘掉思鄉的情緒。

　　另一方面，那些選擇堅持自己本國風俗習慣的人，也是因為覺得這樣做，有助於讓他們覺得更自在。要適應另一個國家，有很多事要做，而遵從傳統的風俗習慣，會讓人在陌生的環境中，覺得較有安全感。更重要的是，風俗習慣是我們的一部分，能表達出塑造我們的文化原貌，這是我們大多數人都想傳承給自己的小孩，並和他人分享的東西。和新鄰居分享我們的傳統習俗，也可以使我們和新鄰居更親近。

　　總之，風俗習慣有其價值，並且是我們文化中很重要的一部分。因此，我不認為當我們搬到新的國家時，就應該拋棄傳統習俗。同時，我認為我們應該學習新家園的風俗習慣，遵從那些我們所喜愛的。如此一來，我們一方面能夠適應新的文化，同時也能記得並頌揚自己舊有的文化。

【註釋】

deal with 處理　　immigrant〔ˋɪməgrənt〕n.（自外國移入的）移民
adhere〔ədˋhɪr〕v. 堅持 < to >　　adopted〔əˋdɑptɪd〕adj. 移居的
adapt〔əˋdæpt〕v. 適應　　***feel at home*** 覺得很舒服自在
positive〔ˋpɑzətɪv〕adj. 正面的
homesickness〔ˋhom͵sɪknɪs〕n. 思鄉　　adjust〔əˋdʒʌst〕v. 適應
shape〔ʃep〕v. 塑造　　***pass down to*** 把…傳給（後代）
abandon〔əˋbændən〕v. 放棄　　appeal〔əˋpil〕v. 吸引 < to >
celebrate〔ˋsɛlə͵bret〕v. 頌揚；讚美

Quit   **Writing**

Some people prefer to spend most of their time alone. Others like
to be with friends most of the time. Do you prefer to spend your time
alone or with friends? Use specific reasons to support your answer.

▲

Cut

Paste

Undo

▼

Time

Help
?

Confirm
Answer

Next

110. Spending Time with Friends

People like to spend their free time in different ways. Some like to do active things, like playing sports or going hiking. Others prefer to relax by reading a good book or listening to music. *Similarly*, some people like to spend time by themselves, while others would prefer to spend it with friends. As for me, I prefer to spend time with my friends for the following reasons.

First of all, when I am with my friends we can share our experiences. If I saw a beautiful sunset by myself and then tried to describe it to them, I don't think they would really understand how I felt. *However*, if we see it together, we can talk about how it made us feel and better understand one another. *And* sharing such experiences can bring us closer together and make our friendship more solid. *Second*, when I am with my friends I feel more courageous. I am willing to try more new things when I have company than when I am alone. I am not afraid of failure when I know my good friends can help me. *Finally*, some activities are just not much fun when I'm alone. Many sports and games require at least two players. *So*, when I am by myself, I am limited in what I can do.

There are many reasons why I like to spend time with my friends. The ones given above are just three of the most important. My friends are people that can help me, encourage me, console me and have fun with me. *Therefore*, I really enjoy spending most of my time with my friends.

110. 和朋友在一起

　　人們消磨空閒時間的方式各有不同，有人喜歡從事動態的活動，像是運動或健行，有人則較喜歡藉由看本好書，或聽聽音樂，來放鬆心情。同樣地，有些人喜歡獨處，而有些人則喜歡和朋友在一起。至於我，基於下列理由，我喜歡和朋友在一起。

　　首先，當我和朋友在一起時，我們可以分享經驗。假設我獨自看到夕陽美景，然後再跟朋友描述當時的景象，我想他們無法真正了解我的感受。然而，如果我們一起看到的話，就可以討論有何感受，因而更加了解彼此。而且分享這樣的經驗，可以讓我們更親密，使友誼更堅定。第二，當我和朋友在一起時，我會更勇敢，因為有伴時，我會比獨自一人更願意嘗試新事物。當我知道好朋友會幫我時，我就不怕失敗。最後一點，有些活動在獨自一人的情況下，就不好玩了。很多運動和遊戲，都需要至少兩個人參與。所以，當我獨自一人時，所能從事的活動就很有限。

　　我喜歡和朋友共度時光的理由很多，上述只是三個最重要的理由。朋友能夠幫助我、鼓勵我、安慰我，並跟我一起玩樂。因此，我真的很喜歡把大部分的時間，用來和朋友相處。

【註釋】

go hiking 去健行　　*as for* 至於
similarly〔'sɪmələ-lɪ〕 *adv.* 同樣地
solid〔'sɑlɪd〕 *adj.* 堅固的
courageous〔kə'redʒəs〕 *adj.* 勇敢的
be willing to + *V.* 願意
company〔'kʌmpənɪ〕 *n.* 同伴
console〔kən'sol〕 *v.* 安慰

Quit　　　　　**Writing**

Some people prefer to spend time with one or two close friends. Others choose to spend time with a large number of friends. Compare the advantages of each choice. Which of these two ways of spending time do you prefer? Use specific reasons to support your answer.

Cut

Paste

Undo

Time

Help
?

Confirm
Answer

Next

111. Small and Large Groups of Friends

Friends play a very important part in everyone's life. *And* each of our friends is special and unique. Some friends may be good advisors or confidants while others challenge our opinions or push us to try new things. *Therefore*, we may like to pursue different activities with different friends, and we may like to be with a large group of friends or spend time with just one or two. Each has its advantages.

One advantage of spending time with one or two close friends is that these friends usually know us well. We can communicate with them easily and are unembarrassed to share our feelings. We know that these good friends won't judge us. *In addition*, we are likely to share many of the same interests and will, *therefore*, find it easy to talk about many things. *Finally*, it is much simpler to arrange activities when only two or three people are involved.

Spending time with large groups of friends also has its advantages. *First*, being with a wider variety of people exposes us to many more new ideas. We may be introduced to new things and develop new interests as a result. *Also*, we will be more likely to find someone to do things with when we associate with many friends. *Last but not least*, being with a large group of people can be a fun and happy thing. There will always be enough people to play any game or make up a team.

As for me, although it can be fun to spend time with a large group of friends, I am more likely to find myself with one or two close friends. It is easier for us to match our schedules and arrange a time to meet. *Also*, we have a deeper relationship, so I find the time that I spend with them to be very valuable. No matter how we like to spend time with friends, there is no denying that friends are very important to us.

111. 一小群和一大群朋友

　　朋友在每個人的生活中，扮演著很重要的角色。我們的每個朋友都是特別而且獨一無二的。有的朋友可能是很好的顧問，或是心腹知己，而有的朋友，則會質疑我們的看法，或驅使我們去嘗試新事物。因此，我們可能會喜歡和不同的朋友，從事不同的活動，可能會喜歡和一大群朋友在一起，或和一兩個朋友一起消磨時間。每一種都各有其優點。

　　和一兩個好朋友消磨時間的好處之一就是，這些朋友通常很了解我們，我們可以輕易地和他們溝通，也不會不好意思分享自己的感受。因爲我們知道，這些好朋友是不會去評斷我們的好壞的。此外，我們也可能因爲分享許多共同的興趣，而找到更多能聊的事情。最後一個好處就是，要安排只有兩三個人的活動，眞是簡單多了。

　　和一大群朋友消磨時間也有它的好處。首先，和一大群各式各樣的人在一起，能讓我們接觸到更多新的想法，我們可能因此接觸到新的事物，或培養出新的興趣。此外，和很多朋友來往，也讓我們更容易找到，可以一起做事的夥伴。最後一項要點是，和一大群人在一起，本身就是一件有趣又快樂的事情，因爲永遠都有足夠的人可以玩遊戲，或是組個隊伍。

　　至於我呢，雖然和一大群朋友消磨時間很有趣，但我還是比較可能會和一兩個好朋友在一起，因爲規劃行程，或安排時間見面都比較容易。此外，因爲我們的關係較密切，所以會覺得和他們共度的時光格外珍貴。不論我們想要和朋友在一起的方式爲何，朋友對我們的重要性是不可否認的。

【註釋】

unique〔ju'nik〕*adj.* 獨特的　　advisor〔əd'vaɪzɚ〕*n.* 顧問

confidant〔ˌkɑnfə'dænt〕*n.* 密友；知己（= *confidante*）

challenge〔'tʃælɪndʒ〕*v.* 挑戰；反對

push〔puʃ〕*v.* 催促　　pursue〔pɚ'su〕*v.* 進行

advantage〔əd'væntɪdʒ〕*n.* 利益；好處

judge〔dʒʌdʒ〕*v.* 評斷　　*in addition* 此外

arrange〔ə'rendʒ〕*v.* 安排

involved〔ɪn'vɑlvd〕*adj.* 牽涉在內的

a wide variety of 很多各式各樣的

expose〔ɪk'spoz〕*v.* 暴露；使接觸 < *to* >

be introduced to 認識　　*be likely to* + *V.* 可能

associate〔ə'soʃɪˌet〕*v.* 結交；來往 < *with* >

last but not least 最後一項要點是　　*make up* 組成

as for 至於　　team〔tim〕*n.* 隊伍

match〔mætʃ〕*v.* 使一致；配合　　schedule〔'skɛdʒul〕*n.* 時間表

relationship〔rɪ'leʃənˌʃɪp〕*n.* 關係

valuable〔'væljuəbḷ〕*adj.* 珍貴的

There is no + *V-ing* ～是不可能的（= *It is impossible* + *to V.*）

deny〔dɪ'naɪ〕*v.* 否認

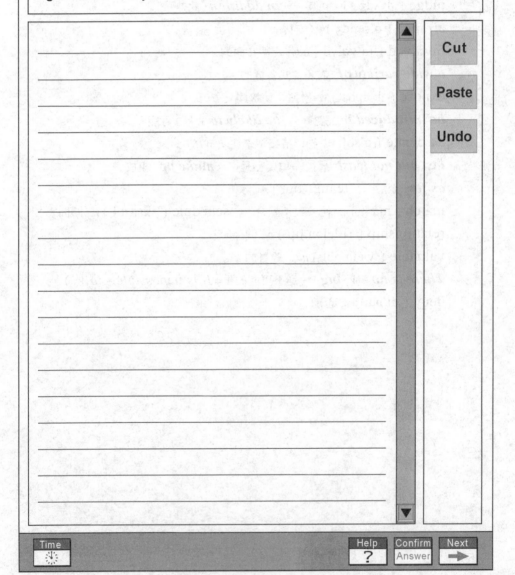

Quit   **Writing**

Some people think that children should begin their formal education at a very early age and should spend most of their time on school studies. Others believe that young children should spend most of their time playing. Compare these two views. Which view do you agree with? Why?

Cut

Paste

Undo

Time

Help Confirm Next
?   Answer

112. Young Children and Education

There is no denying that a child's education is very important. For this reason some people think that children should begin their formal education at a very early age. They believe that this will give them some advantage over those who do not enter school until the traditional school age. ***In my opinion, however***, young children should spend most of their time playing because it will offer them more advantages than will formal schooling at that age.

One advantage to a child of spending his early years outside of school is that he can learn many things that formal schooling does not teach, such as how to take care of himself and how to cope with an ever-expanding world. ***In addition***, he will have a better opportunity to develop a good relationship with his family. ***Another*** reason not to send a child to school too early is that he may not be ready. If he is not prepared to deal with the rules and the pressure of schoolwork, he may become discouraged and develop a negative attitude toward school. ***Last but not least***, children can learn many beneficial things through play. By having fun while learning, they not only gain knowledge, but develop curiosity and a desire to learn.

For all of these reasons, I believe that it is not beneficial to young children to begin formal education too soon. They need time to play and explore their world without being subject to the regulations and demands of formal schooling. With proper preparation, children will be active and confident learners when they do begin their education.

112. 兒童與教育

不可否認的，兒童的教育很重要。基於這個原因，有些人認為孩子在年紀還很小的時候，就應該開始接受正規教育，這樣會使他們比依照慣例，年紀夠大才入學的小孩，更具優勢。然而，依我之見，孩子大部份的時間應該用來玩樂，因為就那樣的年紀而言，玩樂所帶來的好處，比正規的學校教育多。

小孩年幼時，不入學就讀的一個好處是，他能夠學到很多正規學校教育沒有教的東西，像是如何照顧自己，如何面對日益開闊的世界。此外，他會比較有機會和家人發展良好的關係。另一個不要太早把小孩送到學校的理由是，孩子可能還沒準備好，如果還沒準備好要如何面對學校課業的規範和壓力，就可能會感到氣餒，對學校抱持負面的態度。最後一項要點是，孩子透過玩遊戲，可以學到很多有益的事情。藉由邊玩邊學的方式，他們不只會獲得知識，也能培養好奇心和學習的慾望。

基於上述的理由，我認為對年紀幼小的兒童來說，太早開始接受正規教育是沒有好處的。他們需要時間玩樂及探索他們的世界，而不必受限於正規教育的規範及要求。如果有適當的準備，孩子在開始接受教育時，將會主動，而且有自信地學習。

【註釋】

formal education 正規教育

advantage〔əd'væntɪdʒ〕*n.* 優勢＜ *over* ＞；好處

traditional〔trə'dɪʃənl̩〕*adj.* 傳統的　　schooling〔'skulɪŋ〕*n.* 學校教育

take care of 照顧　　*cope with* 處理；應付（ = *deal with* ）

ever-expanding〔ˌɛvɚɪk'spændɪŋ〕*adj.* 不斷擴張的

negative〔'nɛɡətɪv〕*adj.* 否定的；負面的（ ↔ *positive* ）

beneficial〔ˌbɛnə'fɪʃəl〕*adj.* 有益的

curiosity〔ˌkjʊrɪ'ɑsətɪ〕*n.* 好奇心　　desire〔dɪ'zaɪr〕*n.* 慾望

explore〔ɪk'splor〕*v.* 探索

subject〔'sʌbdʒɪkt〕*adj.* 受…支配的＜ *to* ＞

regulation〔ˌrɛɡjə'leʃən〕*n.* 規定　　proper〔'prɑpɚ〕*adj.* 適當的

confident〔'kɑnfədənt〕*adj.* 有信心的

Quit	**Writing**

The government has announced that it plans to build a new university. Some people think that **your** community would be a good place to locate the university. Compare the advantages and disadvantages of establishing a new university in your community. Use specific details in your discussion.

Cut

Paste

Undo

Time

Help
?

Confirm
Answer

Next
➡

113. A New University

A new university brings both advantages and disadvantages to the community in which it is built. If the government were to establish one in my community, we would have to consider both the benefits and the drawbacks carefully. *One* obvious benefit would be the advantage of having university facilities close by. A university would offer an excellent library and sports facilities, *for example*. *Another* benefit to the community would be that local students would not have to commute long distances or live away from home while they attended university. This would save them both time and money. *But* perhaps the most important benefit a university would bring to the community would be a younger, more dynamic atmosphere. Universities are exciting places filled with new ideas and hopes.

However, along with these benefits would come some drawbacks. *For example*, my community would become much more crowded if a university were established in it. There would be many students living in a small space and this would bring the problems of noise, traffic and trash. *In addition*, new businesses geared to the young would likely move into the community as well. There would be more coffee shops, stores and pubs. This would contribute to the growing congestion and might make some people feel the community had lost its family atmosphere. Despite these shortcomings, I still believe that a new university would be a beneficial addition to my community. The advantages far outweigh the disadvantages *in my opinion*.

113. 一所新大學

　　興建一所新的大學，會爲其所在的社區，同時帶來好處及壞處。如果政府預定在我居住的社區設立一所大學，我們就必須仔細考慮其優缺點。第一個明顯的好處是，附近就會有大學的各項設施了，例如，大學可以提供一流的圖書館及運動設施。能爲社區帶來的另一個好處是，當地學生就讀大學，可以不用長距離通勤，或離家居住在外，這樣可以讓他們同時節省時間及金錢。但或許興建大學帶給社區最重要的好處，就是營造出更年輕、更有活力的氣氛。大學充滿新思想和希望，是個令人興奮的地方。

　　然而，隨著這些好處而來的，還有一些壞處。例如，如果興建大學的話，我居住的社區就會變得更擁擠，會有很多學生住在狹小的環境中，這樣會帶來噪音、交通，以及垃圾方面的問題。此外，針對年輕人而開的新商店，也會進駐我們的社區，那就會有更多的咖啡店、商店，以及酒吧，這會導致日益嚴重的堵塞現象，也可能會讓人覺得，社區失去了家庭的氣氛。僅管有這些缺點，我仍然認爲，興建一所新的大學對社區有益。依我之見，其優點遠勝於過缺點。

【註釋】

advantage〔əd'væntɪdʒ〕*n.* 好處；優點（= benefit〔'bɛnəfɪt〕）
disadvantage〔,dɪsəd'væntɪdʒ〕*n.* 壞處；缺點
（= drawback〔'drɔ,bæk〕= shortcoming〔'ʃɔrt,kʌmɪŋ〕）
facilities〔fə'sɪlətɪz〕*n. pl.* 設施　　***close by*** 在附近
sports〔sports〕*adj.* 運動的　　local〔'lokḷ〕*adj.* 當地的
dynamic〔daɪ'næmɪk〕*adj.* 充滿活力的
atmosphere〔'ætməs,fɪr〕*n.* 氣氛
along with 伴隨（= *together with*）
space〔spes〕*n.* 場所；區域　　***be geared to*** 適合
contribute〔kən'trɪbjut〕*v.* 促成 < *to* >
congestion〔kən'dʒɛstʃən〕*n.* 阻塞
beneficial〔,bɛnə'fɪʃəl〕*adj.* 有益的
addition〔ə'dɪʃən〕*n.* 增加物　　outweigh〔aut'we〕*v.* 勝過

Writing

Quit

Some people think that the family is the most important influence on young adults. Other people think that friends are the most important influence on young adults. Which view do you agree with? Use examples to support your position.

Cut

Paste

Undo

Time

Help
?

Confirm
Answer

Next
➡

114. **The Influence of Friends on Young Adults**

We are all affected by the actions, opinions and beliefs of those around us. Some people feel that young adults are most affected by their families, while others believe that friends have the greatest influence. I believe that the latter is true for the following reasons.

First, in young adulthood people spend more time with their peers than their families. They may be attending school or working, but whatever they do, they will spend more time away from their families than with them. *Second*, the opinions and beliefs of their families are well-known to young adults; they have heard them for years. *In contrast*, those of their friends may be new and different. This will naturally be interesting to young adults and, *thus*, it is not unusual for them to become excited over one fad after another. *Third*, when they are young adults people want to express their individuality and independence. They may see differentiating their viewpoints from those of their families as a good way to do this.

From the above, we know that a young adult's friends can have a great influence on the things he does and believes. This is not to say that the family's influence no longer exists. *In fact*, the values and beliefs that a person acquires during childhood are more likely to stay with him throughout his life than are the short-lived enthusiasms of his young friends. *Therefore*, I believe that friends have a more obvious and immediate effect on a young adult but that a family's influence is deeper and longer-lasting.

114. 朋友對年輕人的影響

　　我們都會受周遭人的行為、意見與信念的影響。有些人認為年輕人受家庭的影響最大，而有些人則認為，朋友對年輕人的影響才是最大的。我認為後者才是正確的，以下就是我所持的理由。

　　首先，大部分的人在年輕時，與同儕相處的時間，比和家人相處的時間多。他們也許是上學或上班，但不管做什麼，與家人分開的時間，總是比相處的時間多。其次，家人的意見與信念，對年輕人而言，是再熟悉不過了，因為他們已經聽了好多年。相較之下，朋友的意見與信念，就顯得新奇而且不同，很自然地，這對年輕人而言是有趣的，所以一個接一個的流行風潮會讓他們興奮，也就不足為奇了。第三，年輕人會想要表達自我個性與獨立，他們可能會認為，跟家人的看法不同，是個不錯的表現方式。

　　基於以上的理由可知，朋友對年輕人的行為與信念，都有很大的影響，但這並不表示，家人的影響力就不存在了。事實上，一個人從小所接受的價值觀與信念，比較有可能影響他一輩子，而受朋友所影響的短暫熱情卻不會。所以，我認為朋友對年輕人的影響是較明顯而立即的，但家人的影響卻較為深入而持久。

【註釋】

the latter （兩者中）後者（↔ *the former*）

adulthood〔ə'dʌlthʊd〕*n.* 成年時期　　peer〔pɪr〕*n.* 同儕

well-known〔'wɛl'non〕*adj.* 熟知的

in contrast 相較之下　　fad〔fæd〕*n.* 一時的流行

individuality〔ˌɪndə͵vɪdʒʊ'ælətɪ〕*n.* 個人風格

independence〔ˌɪndɪ'pɛndəns〕*n.* 獨立　　***see…as~*** 視…為~

differentiate〔ˌdɪfə'rɛnʃɪ͵et〕*v.* 使有差別 <*from*>

viewpoint〔'vjuˌpɔɪnt〕*n.* 觀點　　***no longer*** 不再

exist〔ɪg'zɪst〕*v.* 存在　　values〔'væljuz〕*n. pl.* 價值觀

acquire〔ə'kwaɪr〕*v.* 獲得　　throughout〔θru'aʊt〕*prep.* 遍及

short-lived〔'ʃɔrt'laɪvd〕*adj.* 短暫的

enthusiasm〔ɪn'θjuzɪ͵æzəm〕*n.* 熱忱

obvious〔'ɑbvɪəs〕*adj.* 明顯的　　lasting〔'læstɪŋ〕*adj.* 持久的

Quit　　　　**Writing**

Some people prefer to plan activities for their free time very carefully. Others choose not to make any plans at all for their free time. Compare the benefits of planning free-time activities with the benefits of not making plans. Which do you prefer — planning or not planning for your leisure time? Use specific reasons and examples to explain your choice.

▲

Cut

Paste

Undo

▼

Time

Help
?

Confirm
Answer

Next

115. **Planning Activities**

In this busy society, our free time is very valuable to us. It is important that we take some time to relax and renew our energy in order to face the challenges ahead of us. Different people like to spend their leisure time in different ways. Some like to plan their activities so that they can make the most of the time available while others prefer not to plan anything. Both schools of thought have their advantages.

When people carefully plan their leisure time, they will not waste any time on decision making or last-minute preparations. This saves them time and, *therefore*, makes them feel that they have more free time to enjoy. Planning ahead also allows people to take advantage of the opportunity to participate in certain restricted activities. *For example*, by planning ahead, they can buy tickets for a concert or play that may later be sold out. *Finally*, being better prepared for an activity not only saves time but can make the outing more fun and more meaningful. It is not much fun to make a spontaneous trip to the beach only to find you have left your swimsuit at home.

However, unplanned leisure time also has its advantages. With no commitment to take part in a certain activity or meet a friend at a certain hour, the non-planner can take advantage of last minute changes and opportunities. *Furthermore*, he will not be disappointed should his plans fall through, because he has made none. *On the other hand*, if someone has looked forward to a baseball game all week, it is very disappointing if it is cancelled due to rain. *Last but not least*, unplanned leisure time can be more relaxing. During the workweek, we must all be punctual and face deadlines. Some people prefer to make their free time as different from that as possible.

Although both planned and unplanned leisure time have their benefits, I still prefer to plan my free time activities. My free time is limited, and so I want to make the best of it. By planning ahead, I can take part in the activities that I want and spend time with the people I want to see. *And* in case my plans should be changed by unforeseen circumstances, I can always go to Plan B.

115. 規劃活動

在這個忙碌的社會中，空閒時間對我們而言是非常珍貴的。找個時間放鬆一下，並且恢復精力，以面對接踵而來的挑戰，是很重要的。每個人喜歡的休閒方式各不相同。有些人喜歡規劃活動，以充分利用休閒時間，而有些人卻寧願不做任何規劃。這兩種想法都各有優點。

當人們仔細規劃休閒時間後，就不會浪費時間做決定，或是最後才匆促地準備，這樣做能節省時間，因此會讓他們覺得，可以享有更多的空閒時間。事先規劃也讓人們可以利用機會，去參加某些受限制的活動。例如，假如事先有規劃，就可以買到晚一點就買不到的音樂會，或戲劇演出的門票。最後，爲活動做好準備，不僅可以節省時間，還能讓旅遊更添樂趣和意義。當你一時興起去海邊玩，而到達之後才發現泳衣放在家裡，可能就不太好玩了。

然而，休閒時間不作任何規劃，也有好處。因爲沒有要參加特定活動，也沒有和朋友相約在某個時間見面，所以不作規劃的人，就能在最後一刻改變主意與利用機會。而且，如果計劃落空了，他也不會失望，因爲他根本沒有計畫。另一方面，假使有人一整個禮拜都在期待能去看棒球比賽，若球賽因雨取消，這實在是一件非常令人失望的事。最後一項要點是，不做計劃的休閒時間，能使人更加放鬆。在工作日，我們必須都很準時，且要面臨最後期限的壓力。有些人比較希望，空閒時間能儘可能和工作時有所不同。

　　雖然規劃或不規劃休閒時間都各有好處，但我還是比較喜歡規劃我的休閒活動。我的空閒時間有限，因此要儘量善加利用。我事先做好規劃，就能參加想要參加的活動，見我想要見的人。而且假如計劃因非預期的情況而有所改變，我還可以採用另一個替代方案。

【註釋】

valuable〔'væljuəbḷ〕*adj.* 珍貴的

renew〔rɪ'nju〕*v.* 恢復　　challenge〔'tʃælɪndʒ〕*n.* 挑戰

make the most of 充分利用（= *make the best of*）

available〔ə'veləbḷ〕*adj.* 可獲得的　　school〔skul〕*n.* 學派

advantage〔əd'væntɪdʒ〕*n.* 優點

last-minute preparations 最後一分鐘的準備工作

take advantage of 利用

participate〔pɑr'tɪsə,pet〕*v.* 參加< *in* >

ahead〔ə'hɛd〕*adv.* 事先　　restricted〔rɪ'strɪktɪd〕*adj.* 受限制的

sell out 賣完　　outing〔'autɪŋ〕*n.* 出遊

spontaneous〔spɑn'tenɪəs〕*adj.* 自發性的；一時衝動的

only to + *V.* 結果卻　　swimsuit〔'swɪm,sut〕*n.* 泳裝

commitment〔kə'mɪtmənt〕*n.* 承諾　　hour〔aur〕*n.* 時間

furthermore〔'fɝðə,mor〕*adv.* 此外　　***fall through*** 失敗

look forward to 期待　　***due to*** 由於

last but not least 最後一項要點是

workweek〔'wɝk,wik〕*n.* 一週工作日

punctual〔'pʌŋktʃuəl〕*adj.* 準時的

deadline〔'dɛd,laɪn〕*n.* 最後期限　　***in case*** 如果（= *if*）

unforeseen〔,ʌnfor'sin〕*adj.* 意料之外的

circumstances〔'sɝkəm,stænsɪz〕*n. pl.* 情況

Plan B 替代方案；另一個計劃（= *another plan*）

Quit

Writing

People learn in different ways. Some people learn by doing things; other people learn by reading about things; others learn by listening to people talk about things. Which of these methods of learning is best for you? Use specific examples to support your choice.

Cut

Paste

Undo

116. Learning by Doing

Learning is an essential part of growing, and there are many ways in which we can learn. We can learn from our parents, from our teachers in school and from our friends. In addition to learning by listening to others, we can also learn by reading or by doing things for ourselves. All of these learning methods have their advantages, but the one that is most effective for me is to learn by doing.

One reason I prefer to learn by doing things is because I believe that experience is the best teacher. Knowledge that I gain through experience is the knowledge that I remember best. *A second reason* is that practical knowledge is often more useful than theoretical knowledge when dealing with problems in everyday life. *Third*, I can learn from the process itself. Even when I make mistakes, I can learn something from them. *Finally*, learning by doing allows me to make my own discoveries and, *in this way*, I not only have a more meaningful learning experience, but often learn things I never expected.

In conclusion, learning through experience is the best method for me because I can acquire practical knowledge and remember my lessons well. *In addition*, the knowledge I gain is not only meaningful, but also wider than that I can get from other learning methods. *Therefore*, I will continue to try to learn as much as possible by doing things myself.

116. 從做中學

學習是成長中非常重要的一部分，而學習的方法有很多。我們可以向父母、向學校老師，和向我們的朋友學習。除了讓別人來教導我們之外，我們還能看書，或邊做邊學。這些學習方法都有優點，但對我而言，最有效的方法是從做中學。

其中一個讓我比較喜歡從做中學的理由是，我認為經驗是最好的老師，從經驗中所學到的知識，我記得最牢。第二個理由是，在日常生活中處理問題時，實際的知識比理論更有用。第三，我還能從過程中學習，即使犯錯，我還是可以學到一些東西。最後，從做中學讓我能自己發現新的事物，如此一來，我不僅能有更具意義的學習經驗，而且還能學到一些意想不到的東西。

總之，從經驗中學習，對我而言是最適合的，因為我能獲得實用的知識，而且會牢記所學到的教訓。此外，我所獲得的知識不僅有意義，而且範圍還比我用其他方法所學的還廣泛。因此，我會儘可能地從做中學。

【註釋】

essential〔ə'sɛnʃəl〕*adj.* 必要的
in addition to 除了…之外
effective〔ɪ'fɛktɪv〕*adj.* 有效的
practical〔'præktɪkḷ〕*adj.* 實際的
theoretical〔ˌθiə'rɛtɪkḷ〕*adj.* 理論的
process〔'prɑsɛs〕*n.* 過程
deal with 處理　　*in conclusion* 總之
acquire〔ə'kwaɪr〕*v.* 獲得　　wide〔waɪd〕*adj.* 廣泛的
lesson〔'lɛsṇ〕*n.* 教訓

Quit　　　　　**Writing**

Some people choose friends who are different from themselves. Others choose friends who are similar to themselves. Compare the advantages of having friends who are different from you with the advantages of having friends who are similar to you. Which kind of friend do you prefer for yourself? Why?

Cut

Paste

Undo

Time

Help
?

Confirm
Answer

Next
➡

117. Choosing Friends

Some people prefer to make friends with people who are very much like them while others prefer friends who are very different. There are advantages to both types of friendship. *First*, if a man chooses a friend similar to himself, there is no doubt that they will share many common interests. They may also have similar goals in life. This means that they will be able to help and encourage one another in the pursuit of their goals. *Finally*, two people who are very similar will feel comfortable with each other and may understand each other's feelings better. *So* their friendship may be deeper and last longer.

On the other hand, there are also many advantages to making friends with someone of opposite interests and even character. In this type of friendship, the two people complement each other. Where one is weak, the other is strong. *Moreover*, while two people with similar goals may find themselves in competition, those who want different things can always support each other without reservation. *In addition*, with different interests, they can introduce each other to new experiences and so broaden their knowledge. *Despite all this*, I find that I prefer the first type of friendship, that of a person who is more like me than unlike me. A dissimilar friend is challenging, but a similar friend is familiar and a friend for life.

117. 選擇朋友

　　有些人比較喜歡結交和自己類型很像的朋友，而有些人，則比較喜歡交一些和他們非常不同類型的朋友。這兩種友誼都有好處。首先，如果選擇和自己相似的朋友，無疑地，將可以分享許多相同的興趣。他們可能還會有類似的人生目標，這意謂著能夠在追求目標的過程中，相互幫忙、鼓勵。最後，兩個非常相似的人在一起，會覺得很自在，而且也更能了解對方的感受。所以，這樣的友誼會比較深厚而且持久。

　　另一方面，和興趣、個性相反的人交朋友，也有許多好處。在這種友誼當中，雙方會有互補的作用。一個在某方面弱，另一個就強。此外，兩個有相似目標的人，可能會彼此競爭，而追求不同東西的人，會毫不保留地互相支持。此外，有不同的興趣，就可以互相介紹新的經驗，增廣知識。儘管如此，我覺得我比較喜歡第一種類型的友誼，也就是和我較相似，而不是較不相同的朋友。有個和自己不同類型的朋友，是很有挑戰性的，但一個相似的朋友，則能帶給我們熟悉的感覺，而且會是一輩子的朋友。

【註釋】

advantage〔əd'væntɪdʒ〕n. 優點；好處

be similar to 與～相似　　**there is no doubt that** 無疑地

pursuit〔pə'sut〕n. 追求　　last〔læst〕v. 持續

on the other hand 另一方面　　opposite〔'ɑpəzɪt〕adj. 相反的

character〔'kærɪktə〕n. 個性

complement〔'kɑmplə,mɛnt〕v. 補充

moreover〔mor'ovə〕adv. 此外（= *in addition*）

competition〔,kɑmpə'tɪʃən〕n. 競爭

without reservation 毫無保留地　　broaden〔'brɔdṇ〕v. 增廣

despite all this 儘管如此　　dissimilar〔dɪ'sɪmələ〕adj. 不同的

challenging〔'tʃælɪndʒɪŋ〕adj. 有挑戰性的　　**for life** 終生的

Quit

Writing

Some people enjoy change, and they look forward to new experiences. Others like their lives to stay the same, and they do not change their usual habits. Compare these two approaches to life. Which approach do you prefer? Explain why.

Cut

Paste

Undo

Time

Help
?

Confirm
Answer

Next

118. Habit Versus Change

It has been said that man is largely a creature of habit. We all develop routines and habits in our everyday lives, whether we are aware of it or not. To some people these routines are very important and even a small change, such as missing the morning paper, can affect the way they feel all day. Other people dislike routine and change their habits often in order to ward off boredom. They may even go so far as to change their residence or job frequently. These two different approaches to life are extremes, but each has advantages and disadvantages.

In the first case, that of people who dislike change, a dependency on routines and habits can provide a sense of security and convenience, but it can also be limiting. Routines provide security because people do not have to wonder what will happen. In this rapidly changing world, it is sometimes reassuring to have a schedule to follow. Habits also make life more convenient because people do not have to think about what they must do next and do not need to worry about forgetting something. They can go through their daily routines automatically. *However*, this way of life is limiting when people are too dependent on their routine. They may not only be upset when things do not go according to plan, but also miss many good opportunities to try new things.

In the second case, that of people who seem to thrive on change, there are also advantages and disadvantages. *First of all*, this kind of person is usually more open to new ideas. He can, *therefore*, learn more and experience more. *In addition*, because he is not afraid to make changes in his life and take risks, he is more willing to take advantage of unexpected opportunities. This may lead him to a previously unforeseen success. *But* if a person is always seeking ways to change his life, he may not stick with things long enough to gain the most benefit from them. If he lacks the necessary determination and perseverance, it will be difficult for him to succeed by any means other than luck.

In my opinion, both of these lifestyles are extremes. Most people are not so dependent on their habits, nor are they addicted to change. For me, a lifestyle somewhere between these two is ideal. I find some habits and routines comforting and convenient, yet I do not want to be afraid to face changes or take advantage of unforeseen chances to improve my life. *Therefore*, I will continue to follow my routine in daily life, but keep my eyes open for opportunities.

118. 習慣與改變

　　一直以來，大家都說人類大多是習慣性的動物。不論我們有沒有意識到，在日常生活中，我們就是一直在做例行公事，並且養成習慣。對某些人而言，這些例行公事非常重要，就算像是沒看到早報這種微小的改變，也會影響到他們整天的心情，而有些人則討厭公式化，而且為了不無聊，經常改變習慣，甚至有些還會經常變換居住的地點或工作。這兩種生活態度都很極端，但也各有其優缺點。

　　第一種人不喜歡改變，依賴例行工作與習慣，能帶給他們安全感與便利，但卻也有所限制。例行公事帶給他們安全感，因為不需要猜想會發生什麼事，在這個快速變遷的世界中，有時預先知道要做什麼事情會讓人安心。習慣也讓人覺得生活更方便，因為這樣就不必去想下一步要做什麼，與擔心會忘掉什麼，如此他們就能習慣性地過每天一樣的生活。然而，當人們過於依賴例行公事，其生活方式就會受限，如果事情不按計畫進行，他們會不高興，而且也會錯失很多嘗試新事物的良機。

　　第二種人樂於改變，但也是有利有弊。首先，這種人通常較能接受新的想法，因此，就能學得更多，而且見識更廣。此外，這種人因為不怕改變生活與冒險，所以就更願意利用意想不到的機會，這也許就讓他獲得出乎意料的成功。但如果這種人一直不斷在尋求改變生活的方法，也許就因為不能長久堅持，而無法從中獲得最大的利益。如果缺乏必要的決心與毅力，那麼除了靠運氣之外，是很難有所成就的。

　　以我之見，這兩種生活方式都過於極端。大部分的人，既不會過於依賴習慣，也不會執著於改變。對我來說，介於這兩者之間的生活方式，是最理想的。我認為有些習慣與例行公事，能讓人覺得舒適而便利，但我卻不會害怕面對改變，或利用意想不到的機會去改善我的生活。因此，雖然我會繼續在日常生活中墨守成規，但還是會張大眼睛，尋覓機會。

【註釋】

largely〔'lɑrdʒlɪ〕*adv.* 大部份　　creature〔'kritʃɚ〕*n.* 動物

routine〔ru'tin〕*n.* 慣例；例行公事

aware〔ə'wɛr〕*adj.* 意識到的 < *of* >　　***ward off*** 避開；防止

go so far as to* + *V. 甚至　　residence〔'rɛzədəns〕*n.* 住處

approach〔ə'protʃ〕*n.* 處理方法 < *to* >

extreme〔ɪk'strim〕*n.* 極端的事物

advantage〔əd'væntɪdʒ〕*n.* 優點（= benefit〔'bɛnəfɪt〕）

disadvantage〔,dɪsəd'væntɪdʒ〕*n.* 缺點　　case〔kes〕*n.* 情況；例子

dependency〔dɪ'pɛndənsɪ〕*n.* 依賴 < *on* >

security〔sɪ'kjurətɪ〕*n.* 安全　　wonder〔'wʌndɚ〕*v.* 想知道

reassuring〔,riə'ʃurɪŋ〕*adj.* 令人安心的

automatically〔,ɔtə'mætɪkḷɪ〕*adv.* 習慣性地；自動地

upset〔ʌp'sɛt〕*adj.* 不高興的　　***thrive on*** 樂意做

first of all 首先（= *first* = *in the first place*）

in addition 此外（= *besides* = *furthermore* = *moreover*）

take a risk 冒險　　willing〔'wɪlɪŋ〕*adj.* 願意的

take advantage of 利用　　previously〔'privɪəslɪ〕*adv.* 以前

unexpected〔,ʌnɪk'spɛktɪd〕*adj.* 意想不到的

unforseen〔,ʌnfor'sin〕*adj.* 意料之外的　　seek〔sik〕*v.* 尋求

stick with 堅持　　determination〔dɪ,tɜmə'neʃən〕*n.* 決心

perseverance〔,pɜsə'vɪrəns〕*n.* 毅力　　means〔minz〕*n.* 方法

other than 除了（= *except*）

addicted〔ə'dɪktɪd〕*adj.* 上癮的 < *to* >　　ideal〔aɪ'diəl〕*adj.* 理想的

keep *one's* ***eyes open*** 提高警覺；注意

Quit　　　　　**Writing**

Do you agree or disagree with the following statement? People behave differently when they wear different clothes. Do you agree that different clothes influence the way people behave? Use specific examples to support your answer.

▲

Cut

Paste

Undo

▼

119. The Influence of Clothes

Most people wear different types of clothing for different occasions. They may wear a uniform to school or work, a formal suit to a party, and sportswear on the weekends. Does what people wear affect their behavior? I believe it does, as can be illustrated by the following examples.

First of all, more formal clothing reminds us that we must behave in a polite and formal way. When we wear a business suit, we may think about our actions more seriously. We can not only command more respect, but also give it. The example of "casual Fridays" at many companies shows us that more informal clothing can make us behave more informally as well. This practice encourages employees to relax at the office and express themselves more. *In addition*, when we attend a formal social occasion, such as a wedding, our special clothing makes the event seem more special. We are certain to behave in a more polite manner. *Finally*, wearing a costume allows us to behave in a completely different manner. We may take on the persona of the character we are dressed as, or just let ourselves go while we are "someone else."

Given the above examples, I think it is clear that our clothing influences the way that we behave. This may be because of the way we feel in the clothing itself, or because of the way our clothing leads others to treat us. Whatever the reason, there is no doubt that we feel more comfortable when appropriately dressed for the occasion.

119. 服裝的影響力

　　大部分的人在不同的場合，會穿不同類型的衣服。他們可能會穿著制服去上學或上班，穿著正式的套裝去參加宴會，週末時則穿運動服。穿著會影響人的行為嗎？我想是會的，下列的例子就可說明這一點。

　　首先，較正式的服裝提醒我們，行為舉止必須合乎禮儀。當我們穿著上班西裝，我們可能會更謹慎思考自己的行為，我們不但能贏得別人的尊敬，也尊重別人。很多公司有「星期五穿休閒服」的做法，顯示不正式的服裝，也會讓我們的行為較不正式。這樣的做法，能鼓勵員工在辦公室內放輕鬆，更能表現自我的風格。此外，當我們參加正式的社交場合，像是婚禮時，我們特別的服裝，能讓婚禮顯得更特別，我們的行為舉止，一定會表現得更有禮貌。最後，服裝穿著會讓我們的行為舉止完全不一樣，我們可能表現出，符合我們穿著打扮的角色的個性，或者是藉由扮演「別人」，來解放自己。

　　基於上面的這些例子，我認為，穿著會影響我們的行為，這是顯而易見的。這可能是因為穿著本身帶給我們的感受，或是因為我們的穿著，引導別人如何對待我們。不論理由為何，無疑地，穿著適合某種場合的服裝，我們會覺得比較舒服自在。

【註釋】

occasion〔əˈkeʒən〕n. 場合　　uniform〔ˈjunəˌfɔrm〕n. 制服
formal〔ˈfɔrml̩〕adj. 正式的（↔ informal）
suit〔sut〕n. 西裝；套裝　　sportswear〔ˈsportsˌwɛr〕n. 運動服
illustrate〔ˈɪləstret , ɪˈlʌstret〕v. 說明
business suit 上班時穿著的西裝　　command〔kəˈmænd〕v. 贏得
casual〔ˈkæʒuəl〕adj. 非正式的　　behave〔bɪˈhev〕v. 行為舉止
as well 也（= too）　　practice〔ˈpræktɪs〕n. 慣例；做法
event〔ɪˈvɛnt〕n. 大事；重要活動　　manner〔ˈmænɚ〕n. 態度
take on 呈現　　persona〔pɚˈsonə〕n. 性格
character〔ˈkærɪktɚ〕n. 角色　　**let go** 解放
given〔ˈɡɪvən〕prep. 考慮到
appropriately〔əˈproprɪɪtlɪ〕adv. 適當地

Quit	**Writing**

Decisions can be made quickly, or they can be made after careful thought. Do you agree or disagree with the following statement? The decisions that people make quickly are always wrong. Use reasons and specific examples to support your opinion.

Cut

Paste

Undo

120. Quick Decisions

Everyone must make many decisions every day of his life. They range from the trivial — tea or coffee for breakfast — to issues of life-changing importance, such as who to marry. Some people make decisions quickly, while others take as much time as possible to consider all their options. They tend to think that quick decisions are always wrong, but I disagree with this opinion.

As a matter of fact, quick decisions are sometimes the best ones. When faced with a difficult choice, it is often our first instinct that is the best. This is why people are sometimes told to "go with your gut." *Moreover*, when we think too long about a decision we may become confused. *And* if we worry too much we may become so anxious that we are unable to make any decision at all. *Last but not least*, some decisions are simply too trivial to spend any time worrying about. When the consequences of making the "wrong" decision are slight, whether our decision is right or wrong is irrelevant.

For all of these reasons, I cannot agree with the statement that quick decisions are always wrong. Long consideration does not guarantee that the choice we make will be the right one, and sometimes too much deliberation can even lead us astray. *Therefore*, I believe it is all right to make a quick decision now and then, for it cannot always be wrong.

120. 匆促的決定

　　每個人在一生當中，每天都要做很多決定，從一些瑣事——如早餐要喝茶還是咖啡——到可以改變一生的重要問題，例如和誰結婚。有些人匆匆做決定，而有些人則盡可能多花時間，考慮他們所有的選擇，這些人認為，匆促決定一定會出錯，但我不同意這種看法。

　　事實上，匆促決定有時候是最好的。當我們面對困難的抉擇時，我們的第一直覺經常是最好的。這就是為什麼別人會勸我們「跟著你的感覺走」。此外，當我們考慮一個決定太久時，可能會變得很困惑。而且如果我們太擔心，可能就會變得很焦慮，而完全無法做任何決定。最後一項要點是，有些決定太瑣碎了，根本不需要花費太多時間擔心。當做出「錯誤」決定的後果很微不足道時，無論我們的決定是對或錯，都無所謂。

　　基於以上種種理由，我不同意匆促決定一定是錯的這樣的說法。長時間的考慮並不能保證，我們所做的選擇一定是正確的，而且有時候過於深思熟慮，甚至會使我們迷失方向。因此，我認為偶爾匆促決定沒什麼關係，因為它不一定是錯的。

【註釋】

***range from* A *to* B** 範圍從 A 到 B 都有

trivial (ˈtrɪvɪəl) *adj.* 瑣碎的　　issue (ˈɪʃju) *n.* 問題；議題

option (ˈɑpʃən) *n.* 選擇　　***as a matter of fact*** 事實上 (= *in fact*)

be faced with 面對 (= *face*)　　instinct (ˈɪnstɪŋkt) *n.* 直覺

gut (gʌt) *n.* 內心

go with your gut 跟著你的感覺走 (= *go with your feelings*)

anxious (ˈæŋkʃəs) *adj.* 焦慮的　　***last but not least*** 最後一項要點是

consequence (ˈkɑnsəˌkwɛns) *n.* 後果

slight (slaɪt) *adj.* 輕微的；微不足道的

irrelevant (ɪˈrɛləvənt) *adj.* 不相關的；不重要的

statement (ˈstetmənt) *n.* 陳述　　guarantee (ˌgærənˈti) *v.* 保證

deliberation (dɪˌlɪbəˈreʃən) *n.* 深思熟慮

astray (əˈstre) *adv.* 迷路地　　***now and then*** 偶爾 (= *sometimes*)

not always 不一定

Quit　　　　**Writing**

Some people trust their first impressions about a person's character because they believe these judgments are generally correct. Other people do not judge a person's character quickly because they believe first impressions are often wrong. Compare these two attitudes. Which attitude do you agree with? Support your choice with specific examples.

▲

Cut

Paste

Undo

▼

121. First Impressions

When we first meet someone, we know nothing about his or her character. *However*, we often make some assumptions based on the impression that the person makes. Can these first impressions be trusted? Some people believe that our initial judgment of a person is usually correct, while others think it is often wrong. There are arguments to support both positions.

People who trust their first impressions believe that a person's appearance can be a good indication of not only his character, but also how he views himself and the people around him. It is true that we often send messages about our feelings without being aware of it. Body language is a good example of this. A person's posture, gestures and facial expression can tell us a lot about what he is thinking and feeling. *Furthermore*, dress and grooming can indicate whether someone cares enough about us to make a good impression.

On the other hand, first impressions can sometimes be misleading. People may be nervous around others they don't know well or in an unfamiliar situation. This may cause them to act in ways that do not reflect their true character. ***Likewise***, some people may give a false impression because they are trying too hard to impress. They may be consciously or unconsciously fooling the other person. ***In addition***, a new acquaintance might simply be in a bad mood or not at his best for other reasons.

Considering the arguments above, I believe that it is better not to judge a person's character too quickly. First impressions are, at best, an indication of how a person is feeling at the moment, and may not indicate his or her true character. ***However***, due to the importance that many people do place on first impressions, we should be aware of the impression that we make on others. ***To sum up***, I think we should not judge people according to first impressions, but we should take care to make a good impression ourselves.

121. 第一印象

當我們初識某人時，對於對方的個性一無所知，然而，我們卻經常根據對方給予我們的印象，做出一些假設。這些第一印象可靠嗎？有人認為，對人最初的判斷通常是正確的；而有人卻認為，最初的判斷經常是錯的。這兩種立場都有其支持的論點。

相信第一印象的人認為，一個人的外貌可以充份顯示其個性，以及他對自己和周遭人的看法。的確，我們經常不自覺地，透露自己的感覺，肢體語言就是最好的例子。人的姿勢、手勢及臉部表情，可以顯示出很多訊息，告訴別人他正在想什麼，有什麼感覺。此外，穿著打扮能表示，這個人是否在乎我們，想不想給我們留下好的印象。

另一方面，第一印象有時會讓人誤解。有人可能會因為跟周遭的人不熟，或處於不熟悉的環境，而心生緊張，這樣可能會使他們的表現，不符合真實的個性。同樣地，有些人可能因為過度想讓別人印象深刻，而造成不實的印象。他們可能在自覺或不自覺的情況下，欺騙對方。此外，初識者可能只是心情不好，或基於某種原因，而未能表現出最佳狀態。

基於上述論點，我認為最好不要太快評斷別人的個性。第一印象充其量只能告訴我們，當時某人的感受為何，無法顯示其真實的個性。可是，因為很多人非常重視第一印象，所以我們應該注意自己給別人的印象。總之，我認為我們不該憑第一印象來評斷別人，而且應該注重自己是否留給別人良好的印象。

【註釋】

assumption〔əˈsʌmpʃən〕*n.* 假設　***based on*** 根據

initial〔ɪˈnɪʃəl〕*adj.* 最初的

judgment〔ˈdʒʌdʒmənt〕*n.* 判斷

argument〔ˈɑrgjəmənt〕*n.* 論點

position〔pəˈzɪʃən〕*n.* 立場

indication〔ˌɪndəˈkeʃən〕*n.* 顯示　view〔vju〕*v.* 看待

aware〔əˈwɛr〕*adj.* 知道的 < *of* >

posture〔ˈpɑstʃə〕*n.* 姿勢　gesture〔ˈdʒɛstʃə〕*n.* 手勢

expression〔ɪkˈsprɛʃən〕*n.* 表情　groom〔grum〕*v.* 打扮

misleading〔mɪsˈlidɪŋ〕*adj.* 誤導的

likewise〔ˈlaɪkˌwaɪz〕*adv.* 同樣地

consciously〔ˈkɑnʃəslɪ〕*adv.* 有意識地（ ↔ *unconsciously* ）

fool〔ful〕*v.* 欺騙　mood〔mud〕*n.* 心情

be at *one's* ***best*** 處於最佳的狀態

place importance on 重視　***take care*** 注意

Quit

Writing

Do you agree or disagree with the following statement? People are never satisfied with what they have; they always want something more or something different. Use specific reasons to support your answer.

Cut

Paste

Undo

Time

Help
?

Confirm
Answer

Next

122. People Are Never Satisfied

No matter how much we have, it seems that there is always something more to strive for. It is a rare person who is truly content with his life just as it is. ***However***, I believe that a certain amount of dissatisfaction is a natural part of human nature and is actually beneficial to mankind. ***After all***, it is dissatisfaction with the way things are that pushes us to improve. ***In my opinion***, people will always want something more or something different than what they have.

Take Edison ***for example***. He was not satisfied with the knowledge he gained from the books and teachers of his time. He still had many questions to which he could not find satisfactory answers. This dissatisfaction led him to make many important discoveries and they, in turn, contributed greatly to the advancement of mankind. There are many other examples like Edison throughout history. ***In addition***, people are competitive. They like to keep up with others, so when one person acquires something desirable, those who know him will want to do the same. ***Furthermore***, people like to express themselves and differentiate themselves from others. This leads people to strike out on their own in some way and do or invent something new, which in turn leads to a new fad for the others to follow.

For all of the above reasons, I believe that people will never be truly satisfied with what they have. They will always be striving for something new or better, and it is this process that leads to progress. ***In the end***, some dissatisfaction can be good for us.

122. 人是永遠不會滿足的

不論我們已經擁有了多少，似乎總是努力想追求更多的東西。很少有人會真的對其生活現狀感到滿意。然而，我認為某種程度的不滿足，是人之常情，而且實際上對人類有益。畢竟，對事物現狀的不滿，是驅使人類進步的原動力。依我之見，人們總是想要擁有更多，或和自己所擁有的不一樣的事物。

以愛迪生為例，他從不滿足於他當時從書本與老師身上所得到的知識。他一直有很多問題，沒有找到令他滿意的答案。這樣的不滿足感，促使他有了很多重大的發現，進而對人類的進步貢獻良多。綜觀歷史，有很多像愛迪生這樣的例子。此外，人類會互相競爭，人們喜歡跟別人並駕齊驅，所以有人得到某個令人渴望的東西時，認識他的人，也會想要得到。而且，人們還喜歡表現自我，讓自己跟別人有所不同，這使人們自發性地去做某些事情，或發明某種新奇的事物，進而創造引領他人跟隨的新風潮。

基於以上理由，我認為人們永遠不會真的對現狀感到滿足。人們永遠都會努力追求更新或更好的事物，而這樣的過程，能促使我們進步。某種程度的不滿足，對我們而言，終究也算是好事。

【註釋】

strive〔straɪv〕v. 努力＜for＞　　rare〔rɛr〕adj. 罕見的

content〔kɑn'tɛnt〕adj. 滿足的　　*human nature* 人性

beneficial〔,bɛnə'fɪʃəl〕adj. 有益的　　*after all* 畢竟

push〔pʊʃ〕v. 催促　　*in turn* 必然也

contribute〔kən'trɪbjut〕v. 貢獻＜to＞

advancement〔əd'vænsmənt〕n. 進步

throughout history 自古以來　　*in addition* 此外（＝ *besides*）

competitive〔kəm'pɛtətɪv〕adj. 競爭的　　*keep up with* 與～並駕齊驅

desirable〔dɪ'zaɪrəbḷ〕adj. 值得要的；令人滿意的

differentiate〔,dɪfə'rɛnʃɪ,et〕v. 使不同＜from＞

strike out 從事新的活動　　*on one's own* 獨力；自行

lead to 導致　　fad〔fæd〕n. 一時的流行

in the end 最後；終究

Quit　　　**Writing**

Do you agree or disagree with the following statement?　People should read **only** those books that are about real events, real people and established facts.　Use specific reasons and details to support your opinion.

▲

Cut

Paste

Undo

▼

123. **The Value of Reading Widely**

It goes without saying that we can learn a great deal from factual books — those books about real events, real people, and established facts. This kind of reading material is an important part of a good education. *However*, it is not the only kind of material that people should read. Fiction, poetry and opinion pieces can also teach us a lot. My reasons for this argument are as follows.

First, reading non-factual material can help us develop our critical thinking skills. When an author states his or her opinion on something, we have to think about whether we agree or not, and why. *Second*, critical thinking teaches us not to accept everything we are told as the only possibility. Questions and curiosity are what lead to innovations. *For example*, Copernicus questioned the "factual" view of the universe at his time, and this led to important scientific discoveries. *Third*, reading fiction and poetry can inspire the imagination and add enjoyment to life.

In conclusion, I support the reading of non-factual material because it can broaden our minds. Reading factual material is important in developing an understanding of the world, past and present, but other types of material inspire us to dream of the future. Perhaps one day our questioning and exploration will lead to new facts.

123. 博覽群書的重要

　　不用說大家都知道，我們可以從有事實根據的書中，學到很多，這些書中記載的，都是眞人眞事，以及旣定的事實。這一類的閱讀資料，是良好教育中，很重要的一部份。然而，這並不是大家應該閱讀的唯一資料。小說、詩和評論，也可以敎我們很多東西。我會這麼認爲，理由如下。

　　首先，閱讀無事實根據的資料，可以幫助我們培養批判性思考的技巧。當作者說明他對某件事的看法時，我們必須思考，自己同不同意，以及理由何在。其次，批判性思考能敎導我們，不要把別人所說的，看作是唯一的可能。質疑和好奇，能讓我們不斷地創新。例如，哥白尼質疑當時大家所知道，關於宇宙的一些「事實」，因而產生了重大的科學發現。第三，閱讀小說和詩，可以激發想像力，並增添生活的樂趣。

　　總之，我贊成要閱讀一些與事實無關的資料，因爲這樣可以拓展我們的心智。閱讀寫實的資料，對於培養我們對全世界，以及古往今來的了解非常重要，但是其他類型的資料，卻可以激發我們，夢想未來。或許有一天，我們的質疑和探索，會創造出新的事實。

【註釋】

It goes without saying that~　不用說，~

factual〔'fæktʃuəl〕*adj.* 基於事實的　　event〔ɪ'vɛnt〕*n.* 事件

established〔ə'stæblɪʃt〕*adj.* 已確立的　　fiction〔'fɪkʃən〕*n.* 小說

opinion piece 評論性的文章　　argument〔'ɑrgjəmənt〕*n.* 論點

as follows 如下　　*critical thinking* 批判性思考

accept A *as* B　認爲 A 是 B　　curiosity〔,kjurɪ'ɑsətɪ〕*n.* 好奇心

innovation〔,ɪnə'veʃən〕*n.* 創新

Copernicus〔ko'pɝnɪkəs〕*n.* 哥白尼（1473-1543，波蘭天文學家）

inspire〔ɪn'spaɪr〕*v.* 激發　　*add* A *to* B　把 A 加於 B 中

enjoyment〔ɪn'dʒɔɪmənt〕*n.* 樂趣

in conclusion 總之（= *to sum up*）

broaden〔'brɔdn̩〕*v.* 拓展　　exploration〔,ɛksplə'reʃən〕*n.* 探索

Quit	**Writing**

Do you agree or disagree with the following statement? It is more important for students to study history and literature than it is for them to study science and mathematics. Use specific reasons and examples to support your opinion.

Cut

Paste

Undo

124. The Importance of Science and Mathematics

A classical education often emphasizes the importance of history and literature.

There is no doubt that these are important subjects for all students to study; ***however***, I do not believe that they are any more important than science and mathematics are today. Ideally, a student would receive a well-rounded education in which all of these subjects play an important part. ***Therefore***, I cannot agree with the statement that literature and history are more important than science and mathematics.

In fact, it can be argued that science and mathematics are becoming increasingly important. In today's society, technological advances occur rapidly and are usually the result of developments in the fields of science and mathematics. If they do not study these two subjects, students will not be able to contribute to the further development of technology. ***Furthermore***, technological advances affect everyone's life. Without a basic understanding of math and science, it is difficult for people to take full advantage of new products and tools. ***So*** no matter what one's field, it is important to study these two subjects.

In my opinion, all subjects can contribute to a good education. No matter what one's interests or future career, it is best to gain some basic knowledge in as many areas as possible. ***And finally***, given the rapid pace of technological advances in our society, the study of science and mathematics is essential.

124. 科學和數學的重要

　　傳統教育通常會強調歷史和文學的重要性。無疑地，這些科目非常重要，所有的學生都應該研讀，然而我認為，它們在今日，並不如科學和數學重要。就理想的情況而言，學生應該接受通才教育，因為這些所有的科目都扮演著重要的角色。因此，文學和歷史比科學和數學重要，這個說法我並不同意。

　　事實上，我們可以說，科學和數學已變得愈來愈重要了。在現今的社會中，科技進步快速，而這通常都是科學和數學領域的發展所導致的。如果學生不研讀這二個科目，他們就無法對科技進一步的發展有所貢獻。此外，科技的進步影響到每一個人的生活，如果對數學和科學沒有基本的了解，人們就很難充分利用新的產品和工具。所以，無論一個人的專門領域為何，研讀這二個科目都很重要。

　　依我之見，所有的科目都有助於良好的教育。不管一個人的興趣或未來的職業為何，最好儘可能在各種領域中，學得一些基本知識。最後，由於在我們的社會中，科技進步非常快速，所以研讀科學和數學，是十分必要的。

【註釋】

classical〔'klæsɪkḷ〕*adj.* 古典的；傳統的

emphasize〔'ɛmfə͵saɪz〕*v.* 強調　　literature〔'lɪtərətʃɚ〕*n.* 文學

ideal〔aɪ'diəlɪ〕*adv.* 理想地

well-rounded〔'wɛl'raʊndɪd〕*adj.* 通才的

statement〔'stetmənt〕*n.* 說法　　argue〔'ɑrgju〕*v.* 認為；主張

technological〔͵tɛknə'lɑdʒɪkḷ〕*adj.* 科技的

advance〔əd'væns〕*n.* 進步　　occur〔ə'kɝ〕*v.* 出現

rapidly〔'ræpɪdlɪ〕*adv.* 快速地　　field〔fild〕*n.* 領域

contribute〔kən'trɪbjut〕*v.* 貢獻；有助於 < *to* >

further〔'fɝðɚ〕*adj.* 更進一步的　　***take advantage of*** 利用

given〔'gɪvən〕*prep.* 考慮到；有鑑於　　pace〔pes〕*n.* 步調

essential〔ə'sɛnʃəl〕*adj.* 必要的

Quit　　　**Writing**

Do you agree or disagree with the following statement? All students should be required to study art and music in secondary school. Use specific reasons to support your answer.

_____

▲

Cut

Paste

Undo

▼

125. Art and Music Classes

School programs around the world differ in the type of classes they offer and those that they require students to take. *For example*, in some countries all students must study a foreign language, while in others language study is optional. *Similarly*, some schools don't offer courses in art and music while other schools offer them as an elective and still others require them. *In my opinion*, such courses should be available to interested students, but should not be required.

Students have different interests and abilities, and elective courses allow students to tailor their education to their personal interests and goals. *Of course*, all students must take a certain number of required courses such as mathematics and history, which make up the core of their education, but students in secondary school should be given some freedom of choice in non-academic courses. Art and music are interesting and beneficial subjects for many people, but not all, and some students may prefer to spend their time on other subjects. Giving students this choice will allow all of them to explore a variety of interests and to make the best use of their time.

All in all, I believe that students should be allowed to choose from a variety of non-academic courses. Although courses such as art and music can broaden the mind, uninterested students will probably not gain much benefit from them. Why not allow them to take courses that are to their advantage?

125. 藝術和音樂課程

　　在全世界的學校課程中，學校所開的課程種類，和規定學生必修的科目，都會有所不同。例如，在某些國家，所有學生都必須修一種外語，而在有些國家，語言學習則是選修課。同樣地，有些學校沒有提供藝術和音樂方面的課程，而有些學校則將它們列為選修科目，還有些學校規定這兩科為必修科目。依我之見，這些課程應該開放給有興趣的學生，但不應該列為必修。

　　每個學生都有不同的興趣和能力，而選修科目使學生所受的教育，更適合他們個人的興趣和目標。當然，所有學生都必須修某些必修科目，如數學和歷史，這些科目構成了他們的教育核心，但應該給中學生更多自由，來選擇一些非學術性的科目。藝術和音樂對許多人而言，不但很有趣，而且是有益的科目，但並非對所有人都是如此，有些學生可能寧願把時間花在其他的科目上。給學生這個選擇權，將可讓他們去探索各式各樣的興趣，並善用自己的時間。

　　總之，我認為應該允許學生，能選修各式各樣非學術性的課程。雖然像藝術、音樂等課程，可以拓展我們的心智，但不感興趣的學生，或許無法從中得到太多益處。何不讓學生選擇對自己有益的課程呢？

【註釋】

program〔'progræm〕 *n.* 課程
optional〔'ɑpʃənl̩〕 *adj.* 選修的（= *elective*）
similarly〔'sɪmələ˙lɪ〕 *adv.* 同樣地　　elective〔ɪ'lɛktɪv〕 *n.* 選修科目
required〔rɪ'kwaɪrd〕 *adj.* 必修的　　tailor〔'telə˙〕 *v.* 使適合< *to* >
make up 組成　　core〔kor〕 *n.* 核心；中心
secondary school 中學　　academic〔ˌækə'dɛmɪk〕 *adj.* 學術的
beneficial〔ˌbɛnə'fɪʃəl〕 *adj.* 有益的　　explore〔ɪk'splor〕 *v.* 探索
a variety of 各式各樣的（= various〔'vɛrɪəs〕）
make the best of 善用　　***all in all*** 總之（= *in conclusion*）
broaden〔'brɔdn̩〕 *v.* 拓展
uninterested〔ʌn'ɪntrɪstɪd〕 *adj.* 不感興趣的
to one's advantage 對某人有利

Quit　　　　　**Writing**

Do you agree or disagree with the following statement?　There is nothing that young people can teach older people.　Use specific reasons and examples to support your position.

Cut

Paste

Undo

Time

Help
?

Confirm
Answer

Next
→

126. The Young Can Teach the Old

Most of us have been brought up to respect our elders and pay heed to their advice, for there is much that they can teach us. This is undeniably true because older people have more experience and knowledge than the young. *However*, I believe that this learning process can be a two-way street, and that the old can also learn something from the young. *Therefore*, I disagree with the statement that there is nothing that young people can teach older people.

Young people may lack the experience and wisdom of their elders, but they are more likely to be flexible in their thinking and their approach to problems. They don't have as many preconceptions and habitual ways of dealing with things, so they are more open to new ideas. This is one valuable thing that older people can learn from the young. *In addition*, there have been many new developments in recent years and younger people are more likely to be familiar with them than older people. *For example*, a grandson may teach his grandfather how to use the Internet. *Finally*, the most important thing that older people can learn from the young is that there are still many things to learn. Curiosity is not limited by age and we should never stop trying to learn and to improve ourselves.

For all these reasons, I believe that young people do have some valuable lessons to teach their elders. We should look for teachers in everyone around us, not only our elders. Because we all have different kinds of knowledge, we can all learn something from everyone around us, even from a child.

126. 年輕人可以教導老年人

我們大多數的人從小就被教導，要尊敬年紀較大的人，要聽他們的勸告，因為他們可以教導我們許多事情。不可否認地，這一點是對的，因為老人家比年輕人更有經驗及知識。然而，我認為這種學習過程可以是雙向的，老年人也可以從年輕人身上學到東西。因此，年輕人就無法教導老年人的說法，我並不同意。

年輕人可能缺乏老年人的經驗和智慧，但是他們可能思考的方式較靈活，對問題的解決方法較具彈性。年輕人處理事情時，沒那麼多先入為主的觀念，和習慣性的做法，所以較能接受新想法，這一點很重要，老年人可以向年輕人學習。此外，近年來有許多新發明，年輕人比老年人更容易熟悉這些東西。例如，孫子可以教祖父如何使用網路。最後，老年人可以從年輕人身上學習到的最重要一點是，仍然有好多東西可以學習。求知慾不受年齡限制，我們絕對不要停下學習的腳步，自己要不斷求進步。

基於這些理由，我認為年輕人真的有一些寶貴的課程，可以教導老年人。我們應該從周遭的每個人身上，尋找可以學習的地方，而不只是向老年人學習而已。因為我們所擁有的知識各不相同，所以都可以從周遭的每個人身上學到東西，甚至從小孩身上。

【註釋】

bring up 教養（小孩）　　elder〔ˈɛldɚ〕*n.* 年長者
heed〔hid〕*n.* 注意　　***pay heed to*** 注意（= *pay attention to*）
undeniably〔ˌʌndɪˈnaɪəblɪ〕*adv.* 無可否認地
flexible〔ˈflɛksəbḷ〕*adj.* 有彈性的
approach〔əˈprotʃ〕*n.* 處理方法 < *to* >
preconception〔ˌprikənˈsɛpʃən〕*n.* 先入之見；成見
habitual〔həˈbɪtʃuəl〕*adj.* 習慣性的
deal with 處理　　valuable〔ˈvæljuəbḷ〕*adj.* 珍貴的
recent〔ˈrisṇt〕*adj.* 最近的　　Internet〔ˈɪntɚˌnɛt〕*n.* 網際網路
curiosity〔ˌkjurɪˈɑsətɪ〕*n.* 好奇心；求知慾

Quit	**Writing**

Do you agree or disagree with the following statement? Reading fiction (such as novels and short stories) is more enjoyable than watching movies. Use specific reasons and examples to explain your position.

▲

Cut

Paste

Undo

▼

127. The Pleasure of Reading Fiction

These days there are many forms of entertainment for us to choose from. Watching movies and reading fiction are two of the most popular free time activities. I enjoy both of them, but given the choice, I usually prefer to read fiction than watch a movie for the following reasons.

First of all, I can read a novel or short story at any time. I do not have to be at a theater or in front of a TV set at a certain time. I can even read when I have only a few spare minutes, *for example* while on a bus. I do not have to read the book from start to finish in one sitting. *Second*, I can read anywhere because books are portable. If the weather is fine, I can take my book outdoors, and when it is raining I can go to a coffee shop. *Most importantly*, I can take a more active part when reading a book than when watching a movie. The descriptions in the book require me to use my imagination to visualize the scene and the characters. When reading a book, I create my own interpretation of it, but when watching a movie I can only see the moviemaker's version of the events.

In conclusion, I prefer reading books to watching movies in my free time because reading gives me greater freedom and inspires my imagination more. Both activities allow me to experience a different world, but reading lets me make that world my own.

127. 閱讀小說的樂趣

　　現在有很多娛樂形式供我們選擇。看電影及讀小說，是兩種最受歡迎的休閒活動，我兩種都很喜歡，但如果要從中選擇，我通常寧願讀小說，而不要看電影，理由如下。

　　首先，我可以在任何時間讀長篇或短篇小說，我不需要在特定的時間，待在電影院或坐在電視機前。我甚至還可以在只有幾分鐘的空閒時間讀小說，例如在公車上。我不需要從頭到尾一口氣讀完整本書。第二，因為書本方便攜帶，所以我隨處都可以讀。如果天氣晴朗，我可以帶我的書到戶外，而下雨時，我可以去咖啡廳。最重要的是，跟看電影比起來，閱讀書籍時，我能夠扮演更主動的角色。對於書中的描述，我必須運用想像力，想像場景和人物。閱讀書籍時，我可以創造我自己的詮釋方法，但是看電影時，我只能看到電影製作人對於事情的看法。

　　總之，有空的時候，我寧願看書，也不要看電影，因為看書能給我較大的自由，更能激發我的想像力。兩種活動都能讓我體驗不同的世界，但是閱讀讓我可以創造一個屬於自己的世界。

【註釋】

fiction〔ˈfɪkʃən〕*n.* 小說　　form〔fɔrm〕*n.* 形式
entertainment〔ˌɛntəˈtenmənt〕*n.* 娛樂
given〔ˈɡɪvən〕*prep.* 如果有
prefer to + *V₁* + *than* + *V₂* 寧願 V₁，也不願 V₂
from start to finish 從頭到尾　　*in one sitting* 一口氣
portable〔ˈpɔrtəbḷ〕*adj.* 方便攜帶的
take a part 扮演一個角色 (= *play a part*)
active〔ˈæktɪv〕*adj.* 主動的　　imagination〔ɪˌmædʒəˈneʃən〕*n.* 想像力
visualize〔ˈvɪʒuəlˌaɪz〕*v.* 想像　　scene〔sin〕*n.* 場景
character〔ˈkærɪktə〕*n.* 人物；角色
interpretation〔ɪnˌtɜprɪˈteʃən〕*n.* 詮釋
moviemaker〔ˈmuvɪˌmekə〕*n.* 電影製作人
version〔ˈvɜʒən〕*n.* 意見；說法　　*in conclusion* 總之
inspire〔ɪnˈspaɪr〕*v.* 激發　　experience〔ɪkˈspɪrɪəns〕*v.* 體驗

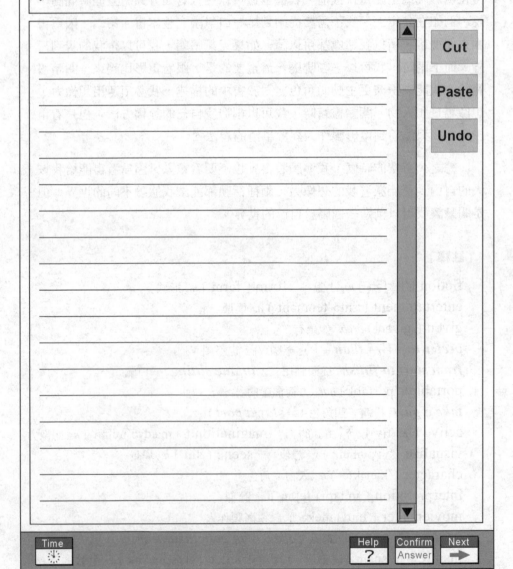

Quit   **Writing**

Some people say that physical exercise should be a required part of every school day. Other people believe that students should spend the whole school day on academic studies. Which opinion do you agree with? Use specific reasons and details to support your answer.

Cut

Paste

Undo

Time

Help
?

Confirm
Answer

Next

128. Exercise in School

There is no doubt that academic studies are a very important part of the school day. *However*, they are not the only thing that students should be learning. Schools should also be teaching students certain life skills so that they will be better able to get along in the world after they graduate. Following this reasoning, I believe that physical exercise should be a required part of every school day.

Mandatory physical exercise would benefit students in many ways. *First of all*, regular exercise is an important part of a healthy lifestyle. *However*, with their busy schedules, many students may not have the opportunity to exercise at home and so may become weaker. If schools allow students to do some physical activity every day, they will be happier and healthier students. *Second*, doing some sports during the school day will give the students a break and allow them to relax their minds. They will be able to return to their studies refreshed and with more energy to learn. *Finally*, by encouraging students to develop the habit of regular exercise, schools will help them stay fit and healthy all their lives.

As fitness is such an important ingredient of success, I believe that schools should require students to engage in some physical activity every day. It will not only be good for their bodies, but also for their minds. Happier and healthier students will do better at their academic studies and in life.

128. 校內運動

　　無疑地，課業學習在學校裏扮演一個非常重要的角色，然而，它們不是學生應該學的唯一事物。學校也應該教學生某些生活技能，讓他們畢業後在社會上，更能夠好好過日子。依照這樣的推論，我認為，運動在學校裏，應該是每天都需要的一部分。

　　強制做運動對學生有許多好處。首先，規律運動是健康的生活方式重要的一環。然而，由於課業繁忙，許多學生在家裏可能沒有機會運動，因此身體可能會變得較虛弱。如果學校讓學生每天都做體能活動，他們會更快樂、更健康。其次，在學校一整天，做點運動正好讓學生休息一下，也可以放鬆心情，再回到課業上時，精神會為之一振，更有精力學習。最後，藉由鼓勵學生培養規律運動的習慣，學校可以幫助學生永遠保持健康。

　　由於健康是成功非常重要的因素之一，我認為學校應該要求學生每天做一些體能活動。這不僅對他們的身體有好處，對他們的心理也有益。比較快樂、健康的學生，在課業學習和生活中，也會表現得比較好。

【註釋】

academic〔ˌækəˈdɛmɪk〕*adj.* 學術的　　***get along*** 進展；過日子

reasoning〔ˈriznɪŋ〕*n.* 推論　　physical〔ˈfɪzɪkl̩〕*adj.* 身體的

required〔rɪˈkwaɪrd〕*adj.* 必要的；必修的

mandatory〔ˈmændəˌtorɪ〕*adj.* 必要的；強制的

benefit〔ˈbɛnəfɪt〕*v.* 使獲益　　***first of all*** 首先（= *first*）

regular〔ˈrɛgjələ〕*adj.* 規律的

break〔brek〕*n.* 休息

refreshed〔rɪˈfrɛʃt〕*adj.* 恢復精神的

develop〔dɪˈvɛləp〕*v.* 培養　　fit〔fɪt〕*adj.* 健康的

fitness〔ˈfɪtnɪs〕*n.* 健康　　ingredient〔ɪnˈgridɪənt〕*n.* 因素

engage〔ɪnˈgedʒ〕*v.* 從事 < *in* >

Quit　　　　**Writing**

A university plans to develop a new research center in your country. Some people want a center for business research. Other people want a center for research in agriculture (farming). Which of these two kinds of research centers do you recommend for your country? Use specific reasons in your recommendation.

Cut

Paste

Undo

129. Business Research vs. Agricultural Research

Both agriculture and business are valuable fields to study and improve. No doubt a research center devoted to either would benefit my country. *However*, I believe that a business research center would be more valuable given the resources and direction of growth in my country.

My country is a technologically advanced and developed nation. While agriculture is still an important part of our economy, it is not an area of great growth as business is. Manufacturing and international trade are very important to my country now. Many people are employed in these fields and I believe that this is where our future lies. A research center devoted to business development would help us to better deal with international developments and to modernize our business practices in order to have the best chance of succeeding. International business is very competitive and it is, *therefore*, important to keep up with advances.

In conclusion, given the economic environment of my country and the importance of business to its future, I believe that we would benefit more from a research center devoted to business studies than one devoted to agriculture. Trade and international business are key components of our economy now and will be in the future.

129. 商業研究與農業研究

　　農業和商業都是很有價值，值得研究、改善的領域。無疑地，致力於二者中任一種的研究中心，都能使我國獲益。然而，我認為，由我國的資源和成長趨勢來看，商業研究中心可能較有價值。

　　我國是一個科技進步的已開發國家。雖然農業仍是經濟體系中重要的一部分，但這個領域的成長空間並不如商業大。製造業和國際貿易，現在對我國非常重要，許多人的工作都屬於這些領域，而且我認為，我們的未來必須仰賴這些領域。一所致力於商業發展的研究中心，能夠幫助我們更善於處理國際發展，使我們的貿易業務現代化，以得到最佳的成功機會。國際貿易競爭非常激烈，因此，不斷地進步是非常重要的。

　　總之，有鑑於我國的經濟環境，和商業對我國未來的重要性，我認為，商業研究中心比起農業研究中心，會讓我們受惠更多。貿易和國際商務，是我國現在和未來經濟的關鍵要素。

【註釋】

research〔rɪˋsɝtʃ ,ˋrisɝtʃ〕*n.* 研究

field〔fild〕*n.* 領域　　devoted〔dɪˋvotɪd〕*adj.* 致力於…的< *to* >

given〔ˋgɪvən〕*prep.* 考慮到　　resource〔rɪˋsors〕*n.* 資源

technologically〔͵tɛknəˋlɑdʒɪklɪ〕*adv.* 科技上地

advanced〔ədˋvænst〕*adj.* 先進的；進步的

economy〔ɪˋkɑnəmɪ〕*n.* 經濟

manufacturing〔͵mænjəˋfæktʃərɪŋ〕*n.* 製造業

lie〔laɪ〕*v.* 位於；存在　　***deal with*** 處理；應付

modernize〔ˋmɑdən͵aɪz〕*v.* 現代化　　practice〔ˋpræktɪs〕*n.* 業務

competitive〔kəmˋpɛtətɪv〕*adj.* 競爭激烈的　　***keep up with*** 跟上

advance〔ədˋvæns〕*n.* 進步

in conclusion 總之 (= *in brief* = *in short* = *in sum* = *in summary*)

key〔ki〕*adj.* 重要的；關鍵性的

component〔kəmˋponənt〕*n.* 要素；成分

Quit **Writing**

Some young children spend a great amount of their time practicing sports. Discuss the advantages and disadvantages of this. Use specific reasons and examples to support your answer.

Cut

Paste

Undo

Time

Help ?

Confirm Answer

Next →

130. Children and Sports

Many children spend their free time participating in a variety of sports, a practice which can bring both advantages and disadvantages to them. *For example*, practicing sports helps children develop both physically and mentally. They not only develop strong bodies but also valuable social skills such as teamwork and leadership. *Furthermore*, these advantages are likely to stay with them throughout their lives since people who adopt healthy habits early in life are more apt to keep them. *Finally*, practicing sports allows children to relax and to experience success in an area other than academic studies.

However, along with these advantages come several disadvantages. *One* is that if children spend too much time practicing sports, they may neglect other responsibilities, such as their studies. *Also*, some team sports are very competitive and care must be taken that children develop good sportsmanship along with their physical skills. *And last but not least*, not all children can be outstanding in sports and may become discouraged by failure. *Then*, they may avoid physical activity and not develop the healthy habit of exercise. *In conclusion*, I believe that the practice of sports is a good thing for children, but it should be done in moderation as part of a balanced education.

130. 兒童與運動

　　很多小朋友利用他們的空閒時間，參與各式各樣的運動，這種做法有好處，也有壞處。例如，運動有助於小朋友身體及心理的發展。他們不只鍛鍊強壯的身體，而且還培養寶貴的社交技能，像是團隊合作及領導才能。而且，這些好處可能會一輩子都受用，因為在早年就養成健康的習慣的人，比較容易保持這樣的習慣。最後，做運動能讓小朋友放鬆，並且在學業之外的領域，體驗成功。

　　然而，除了這些好處之外，也有一些壞處。其中之一就是，如果小朋友花太多時間運動，他們可能會忽視其他的責任，像是學業。此外，有一些團隊運動競爭非常激烈，所以一定要注意，小朋友除了體能技巧外，還要培養良好的運動家精神。最後一項要點是，並非所有的小朋友都可以在運動方面表現傑出，而且也可能因為失敗而感到氣餒，然後他們可能會逃避體能活動，不願去培養健康的運動習慣。總之，我認為運動的習慣對小朋友來說是一件好事，但是應該要適度，當作是均衡教育的一部份。

【註釋】

participate〔pɑrˈtɪsəˌpet〕v. 參與< in >　　*a variety of* 各式各樣的
physically〔ˈfɪzɪkl̩〕adv. 身體上　　mentally〔ˈmɛntl̩〕adv. 心理上
social〔ˈsoʃəl〕adj. 社交的　　teamwork〔ˈtimˈwɜk〕n. 團隊合作
leadership〔ˈlidɚˌʃɪp〕n. 領導能力
furthermore〔ˈfɜðɚˌmor〕adv. 此外　　adopt〔əˈdɑpt〕v. 採取
be apt to 傾向於　　*other than* 除了～之外
academic〔ˌækəˈdɛmɪk〕adj. 學術的
along with 伴隨；連同（= *together with*）
neglect〔nɪˈglɛkt〕v. 忽視
sportsmanship〔ˈsportsmənˌʃɪp〕n. 運動家精神
last but not least 最後一項要點是
outstanding〔ɑutˈstændɪŋ〕adj. 傑出的
practice〔ˈpræktɪs〕n. 習慣　　moderation〔ˌmɑdəˈreʃən〕n. 適度
balanced〔ˈbælənst〕adj. 均衡的

Quit　　　　　　**Writing**

Do you agree or disagree with the following statement? **Only** people who earn a lot of money are successful. Use specific reasons and examples to support your answer.

▲

Cut

Paste

Undo

▼

131. Money and Success

Most people dream of being a success in life. *However*, this does not mean the same thing to everyone. Many equate success with financial success and believe that only those who earn a lot of money can be considered successful. But there are other ways to measure success. *In my opinion*, it is definitely possible to be successful without earning a lot of money as long as one lives a meaningful life.

Some people find meaning in life simply by doing something they enjoy. They may or may not become wealthy, but they are very likely to lead a happy life. Others find meaning by making a contribution to the society. They may set a world record, cure a disease, create a beautiful work of art, or bring more convenience to everyday life. Still others find satisfaction in educating others, helping the poor, or raising a family. When the ones they nurture do well, they feel successful. Riches, *on the other hand*, do not guarantee happiness or meaning. No matter how wealthy a man is, he is unlikely to feel his life has been a true success if he is unhealthy, alone, or simply bored.

To sum up, there are many ways to measure a person's success, and material wealth is just one of them.　Some people really do find satisfaction and meaning in amassing a fortune for themselves and their heirs, and for them, this is a good way to measure their success.　*But* for other people, it is important to adhere to a more personal definition of success.　However we measure our own success, we must set our own goals and then strive to reach them.　Only in this way can we truly consider ourselves successful.

 學習新訊 •••

英文作文背不下來嗎？可背本公司出版的「托福、演講、英作文」。

131. 金錢與成功

　　大部分的人都會夢想成為成功的人，然而，對每個人而言，成功並不意味著相同的事情。很多人把成功視為金錢上的成功，並認為只有賺很多錢的人，才是成功的。但是，還有其他方式可以用來衡量成功。依我之見，就算沒有賺很多錢，只要過著有意義的生活，還是有可能會成功的。

　　有些人只要做自己喜歡做的事情，就能找到生命的意義。他們可能會變得有錢，也可能不會，但他們很可能過著快樂的生活。有些人藉由貢獻社會，找尋到意義，他們可能創造世界紀錄、治好疾病、創作出優美的藝術品，或者為日常生活帶來更多便利。還有些人在教育別人、幫助窮人、或養育子女的同時，得到滿足感。當他們養育的子女表現優異，他們就覺得很有成就。另一方面，財富並不保證會帶來快樂或意義。不論一個人多有錢，如果他不健康、孤單一人，甚至覺得無聊，就不可能覺得自己的生活很成功。

　　總之，要衡量一個人的成功，方式有很多，而物質上的財富只是其中之一。有些人真的會在為自己或其繼承人，累積財富的過程中，找到滿足及意義，對這些人而言，這是衡量成功的好方法。但對其他人而言，堅持個人對成功的定義更重要。不論我們如何衡量自己的成功，我們都必須設定自己的目標，然後努力去達成。唯有如此，我們才能真正達到自己想要的成功。

【註釋】

success〔 sək'sɛs 〕*n.* 成功；成功者
equate〔 ɪ'kwet 〕*v.* 視…為與～同等
financial〔 fə'nænʃəl 〕*adj.* 財務的　　measure〔 'mɛʒɚ 〕*v.* 衡量
definitely〔 'dɛfənɪtlɪ 〕*adv.* 一定
meaningful〔 'minɪŋfḷ 〕*adj.* 有意義的　　wealthy〔 'wɛlθɪ 〕*adj.* 有錢的
contribution〔 ˏkɑntrə'bjuʃən 〕*n.* 貢獻　　*set a record* 創紀錄
raise〔 rez 〕*v.* 撫養　　nurture〔 'nɝtʃɚ 〕*v.* 養育
riches〔 'rɪtʃɪz 〕*n. pl.* 財富　　*on the other hand* 另一方面
amass〔 ə'mæs 〕*v.* 累積　　fortune〔 'fɔrtʃən 〕*n.* 財富
heir〔 ɛr 〕*n.* 繼承人　　adhere〔 əd'hɪr 〕*v.* 堅持 < to >
definition〔 ˏdɛfə'nɪʃən 〕*n.* 定義　　strive〔 straɪv 〕*v.* 努力

Quit　　　　**Writing**

If you could invent something **new**, what product would you develop?
Use specific details to explain why this invention is needed.

Cut

Paste

Undo

132. A New Invention

The inventions of the last hundred years have brought us many advantages such as convenience, knowledge, entertainment and even longer and healthier lives. Although we already have wonderfully convenient lives compared to those of our ancestors, I believe we all still dream of new ways to improve our lives. What would I invent that could be of benefit to society? If possible, I would develop a new transportation device that could instantly and inexpensively transport a person from one location to another.

This device may sound like a science fiction toy, but I believe it would have several advantages. ***First of all***, it would save people a great deal of time. Currently, many city people spend an hour or more each day just commuting between home and work. ***And*** when we consider how much time we spend traveling between towns or even across oceans, the advantage of this device is obvious. People would be able to get where they want to go without wasting a minute and without the fatigue that long-distance travel entails. This would make people more productive and our society more prosperous.

Another benefit of this device would be a decrease in environmental pollution. Our present transportation systems burn great amounts of fossil fuels that pollute the atmosphere.

This contamination can lead to health problems and shorten lives. This, in turn, makes the society less productive. *So again*, this device could make us all more prosperous if it were invented. *Furthermore*, with no cars on the streets, there would be no parking problems and we would all have more green space to enjoy. More trees and open spaces would also help to clean up our atmosphere.

Finally, the new transportation device would save everyone a lot of money. There would be no need to buy cars or airline tickets. This would be a great equalizer, allowing people of all economic classes to move about the world freely. I believe that people would travel more as a result, not only for business but also for pleasure. Families could spend more time together and everyone could learn more about different cultures by seeing them firsthand. This would encourage more tolerance and harmony in the world, making it a better place for all of us.

To sum up, my invention would benefit society in many ways, including saving people time and money and improving the environment. Unfortunately, I do not have the ability to develop this device, but perhaps, in the future, someone else will. *But* whether or not my chosen invention is developed in my lifetime, I am bound to see great improvements of other kinds for no matter how many advantages man already possesses, he is always seeking new ways to improve his life. This is one of the reasons we are such creative and inventive people.

132. 一項新的發明

　　過去一百年來的發明，已經帶給我們很多好處，像是便利、知識、娛樂、甚至更長壽和更健康的生活。雖然和祖先比較起來，我們已經有出奇便利的生活了，但是我們仍夢想著，可以有改善生活的新方法。我要發明什麼，才能造福社會呢？如果可能的話，我想要研發出一種新的運輸裝置，讓人快速地往返各地，而且不會太貴。

　　這種裝置聽起來也許很像科幻小說中的玩具，但是我認為它會帶來很多好處。首先，它可以替人們省下很多的時間。目前，很多住在城市的居民，每天上下班的通勤時間，就要一個多小時，所以當我們考慮到往來各城鎮或橫越海洋所花的時間，這項發明的好處更是顯而易見。人們將可以到自己想去的地方，一分鐘都不浪費，同時也可免除長途旅行的舟車勞頓。這會讓我們更有生產力，社會更繁榮。

　　這項裝置的另一個好處是，可以減少環境污染。我們目前的運輸系統會燃燒大量石化燃料，污染大氣層。這種污染會導致健康問題，並縮短壽命。這必然也會降低社會的生產力。所以，如果發明了這項裝置，我們會因此更加繁榮。此外，一旦街上沒有了車子，也就不會有停車問題，而我們也能享有更多的綠地。有更多的樹木和開放空間，也有助於使大氣層更乾淨。

　　最後，這項新的運輸裝置可以替大家省下一大筆錢。因為不必買車或買機票，所以這項新裝置，能讓不同階層的人，自由地環遊全世界，大大地促進經濟上的平等。相信到時候，大家都會因為工作需要，或是休閒娛樂，更常旅行。家人可以有更多的時間相處，每個人也可以用親眼目睹的方式，更加了解不同的文化，這樣會使全世界的人更加相互包容，並且更和諧，讓大家能擁有更美好的世界。

　　總之，我的發明在很多方面都能使社會受益，包括節省時間、金錢，以及改善環境。不幸的是，我並沒有發明這項裝置的能力，不過，未來或許就有人能辦到了。但是在我有生之年，不論我想要的這項發明會不會出現，我一定要目睹其他發明帶來的卓越進步，因為不論人類已經有多少因發明帶來的好處，我們還是會不停地找尋可以改善生活的新方法。這就是人類會如此富有創造力和發明能力的原因。

【註釋】

invention〔ɪn'vɛnʃən〕*n.* 發明　　advantage〔əd'væntɪdʒ〕*n.* 好處

compared to 與…相比　　ancestor〔'ænsɛstɚ〕*n.* 祖先

dream of 夢想　　benefit〔'bɛnəfɪt〕*n.* 益處　*v.* 使獲益

develop〔dɪ'vɛləp〕*v.* 研發　　device〔dɪ'vaɪs〕*n.* 裝置

instantly〔'ɪnstəntlɪ〕*adv.* 立即地　　*science fiction* 科幻小說

first of all 首先 (= *first* = *in the first place*)

currently〔'kɝəntlɪ〕*adv.* 目前　　commute〔kə'mjut〕*v.* 通勤

obvious〔'abvɪəs〕*adj.* 明顯的　　fatigue〔fə'tig〕*n.* 疲勞

entail〔ɪn'tel〕*v.* 使人承擔；需要

prosperous〔'praspərəs〕*adj.* 繁榮的；順利的

fossil〔'fasḷ〕*n.* 化石　　fuel〔'fjuəl〕*n.* 燃料

fossil fuel 石化燃料 (如煤、石油、天然氣等)

atmosphere〔'ætməsˏfɪr〕*n.* 大氣層

contamination〔kənˏtæmə'neʃən〕*n.* 污染　　*in turn* 必然也

furthermore〔'fɝðɚˏmor〕*adv.* 此外

equalizer〔'ikwəlˏaɪzɚ〕*n.* 使相等的東西

firsthand〔'fɝst'hænd〕*adv.* 直接地　　tolerance〔'talərəns〕*n.* 寬容

harmony〔'harmənɪ〕*n.* 和諧　　*to sum up* 總之

lifetime〔'laɪfˏtaɪm〕*n.* 一生

be bound to + *V.* 一定 (= *be sure to* + *V.*)

possess〔pə'zɛs〕*v.* 擁有　　seek〔sik〕*v.* 尋求

creative〔krɪ'etɪv〕*adj.* 有創造力的

inventive〔ɪn'vɛntɪv〕*adj.* 有發明才能的

Writing

Quit

Do you agree or disagree with the following statement? A person's childhood years (the time from birth to twelve years of age) are the most important years of a person's life. Use specific reasons and examples to support your answer.

Cut

Paste

Undo

Time

Help
?

Confirm
Answer

Next

133. The Importance of Childhood

While it is true that we learn and develop throughout our lives, it is during childhood that we learn the most essential things and develop the most important qualities of our characters. *Therefore*, I believe that the years from birth to age twelve are the most important years of a person's life. The following are my reasons.

First, it is during childhood that our basic characters are formed. The values that we are taught and the experiences we have at that time will affect us for the rest of our lives. If we learn the value of kindness and honesty at an early age, we will likely be kind and honest adults. *Second*, when we are children we are very impressionable. Whatever we are exposed to during these years will have a great effect on us. *Therefore*, it is important to take care with a child's education. *Third*, children are more adaptable and open to new ideas than adults. Once we have developed certain traits in our childhood, it is difficult to change them when we are adults. *And* it is at this time that we are most open to new ideas and new ways of thinking. Our vision of the world, once formed, is also difficult to change.

Given these reasons, there is no doubt that the childhood years are very important. They are the time when our basic character and beliefs are formed. A person's experience and education during these years will affect him all his life.

133. 童年的重要

　　雖然我們的確在一生中，會不斷地學習與發展，但學習非常重要的事物，以及培養人格中最重要的特質，卻是在童年時期。因此我認為，從出生到十二歲的這段時期，是人生中最重要的。我的理由如下。

　　首先，我們基本的人格，是在童年時期形成的。童年時期所學到的價值觀及當時的經驗，會對我們日後有很大的影響。如果我們在幼年時期就學習了仁慈與誠實的價值，那麼長大以後，就可能會成為仁慈而且誠實的人。其次，我們在小時候，可塑性很強，當時所接觸到的一切，會對我們有很大的影響。因此，注意幼兒教育是非常重要的。第三，小孩比大人適應力強，而且較容易接受新的想法。一旦我們在童年時期培養了某些特點，長大以後就很難改變。在這個時期，我們最容易接受新的想法和新的思考方式，而且如果我們對外界的看法一旦形成了，也是很難改變的。

　　基於這些理由，童年時期無疑是非常重要的。在童年時期，我們形成了基本的人格以及信念。這段期間的經驗及教育，將會影響我們的一生。

【註釋】

childhood（'tʃaɪld,hʊd）*n.* 童年時期
throughout（θru'aʊt）*prep.* 遍及
essential（ɪ'sɛnʃəl）*adj.* 必要的；不可或缺的
quality（'kwɑlətɪ）*n.* 特質　　character（'kærɪktə）*n.* 性格
form（fɔrm）*v.* 形成　　values（'væljuz）*n. pl.* 價值觀
impressionable（ɪm'prɛʃənəbl̩）*adj.* 可塑性強的；易受影響的
be exposed to 接觸　　effect（ɪ'fɛkt）*n.* 影響
take care 小心；謹慎　　adaptable（ə'dæptəbl̩）*adj.* 適應力強的
be open to 容易接受～　　certain（'sɝtn̩）*adj.* 某個；某些
trait（tret）*n.* 特點　　vision（'vɪʒən）*n.* 看法
given（'gɪvən）*prep.* 考慮到　　***there is no doubt that*** 無疑地
belief（bɪ'lif）*n.* 信念

| Quit | **Writing** |

Do you agree or disagree with the following statement?　Children should be required to help with household tasks as soon as they are able to do so.　Use specific reasons and examples to support your answer.

▲

Cut

Paste

Undo

▼

134. Household Tasks

In every household there are many tasks that must be done on a regular basis. It is my belief that performing these tasks is the responsibility of all members of a family, including the children. *Also*, each member of the family benefits when the tasks are completed. *Therefore*, I agree that children should be required to help with household tasks as soon as they are able to do so.

Household tasks are a family responsibility and children are part of the family. Each should do tasks that are appropriate for his age and abilities. Performing these tasks allows children to contribute to the well-being of the family and feel that they are vital members. Household tasks can also teach children many things, such as responsibility, cooperation, and the importance of doing a job well. *In addition*, children can learn independence through doing household chores. These are all important characteristics to develop not only because the children may have to do such chores by themselves later in life, but because these traits will benefit them in everything they do. By learning to take responsibility at home, they can learn to be responsible at school and at work.

To sum up, I believe that asking children to do household chores will benefit them later in life. They will take the lessons they learn — responsibility, cooperation and independence — with them for the rest of their lives.

134. 家　事

　　每個家庭都有許多必須經常做的工作，我認為，做這些工作是所有家庭成員的責任，包括小孩在內。而且，當這些工作完成時，家中每個人都會受益。因此，我同意，孩子們只要有能力，就應該要求他們幫忙做家事。

　　家事是家庭的責任之一，而孩子也是家庭的一份子。每個人都應該做適合自己年齡和能力的工作。做這些工作，讓小孩能夠對全家的幸福有貢獻，並且會覺得，他們是家中非常重要的成員。家事也可以教導孩子許多事情，如責任感、合作精神，以及把工作做好的重要性。此外，透過做家事，小孩也可學會獨立。這些都是小孩必須培養的重要特質，不只是因為他們在日後的生活中，可能必須自己去做這些雜事，而且也是因為這些特質，對他們做任何事都有幫助。藉著學習負起做家事的責任，他們可以學習到，在學校以及工作上，也要負責任。

　　總之，我認為，要求孩子做家事，對他們日後的生活會有幫助。他們將會一輩子牢記所學到的事情 —— 責任感、合作精神，和獨立。

【註釋】

household〔'haʊs,hold〕*n. adj.* 家庭的

regular〔'rɛgjələ〕*adj.* 經常的

on a regular basis 經常地（= *regularly*）

perform〔pə'fɔrm〕*v.* 做　　benefit〔'bɛnəfɪt〕*v.* 獲益

appropriate〔ə'propriɪt〕*adj.* 適合的

contribute〔kən'trɪbjut〕*v.* 貢獻 < *to* >

well-being〔'wɛl'biɪŋ〕*n.* 幸福　　vital〔'vaɪtl̩〕*adj.* 非常重要的

cooperation〔ko,apə'reʃən〕*n.* 合作　　*in addition* 此外

independence〔,ɪndɪ'pɛndəns〕*n.* 獨立　　chore〔tʃor〕*n.* 雜事

household chores 家事

characteristic〔,kærɪktə'rɪstɪk〕*n.* 特質（= trait〔tret〕）

to sum up 總之

Quit　　　　Writing

Some high schools require all students to wear school uniforms. Other high schools permit students to decide what to wear to school. Which of these two school policies do you think is better? Use specific reasons and examples to support your opinion.

135. School Uniforms

Some high schools require their students to wear uniforms, while other schools allow students to wear what they like. Both of these policies have certain advantages and disadvantages. *However*, I believe that it is better to require students to wear uniforms to school for the following reasons.

First, requiring school uniforms equalizes students. Those who come from poorer families and cannot afford expensive and fashionable clothes will not feel uncomfortable among their peers. *Second*, when students are dressed the same way, they feel more as though they are part of a group. This can encourage pride in their school and in each other. *Third*, students do not have to worry about what to wear to school, which can save them time and help them focus on their studies. *And finally*, school uniforms can save students and their families' money as well.

Given the above, I think most people would agree that requiring school uniforms is a good idea. Although students are not as free to express themselves through their clothing, I believe that the advantages of uniforms outweigh this concern. School uniforms allow students to worry less about their appearance and concentrate more on their schoolwork.

135. 學校制服

　　有些學校要求學生穿制服，而有些學校則允許學生穿自己喜歡的衣服。這兩種政策都各有利弊。然而，我認爲最好要求學生穿制服上學，理由如下。

　　首先，要求穿制服，能使學生一律平等。那些家境較貧寒，買不起昂貴、時髦衣服的同學，在同儕之間，就不會覺得不自在。其次，當學生穿得都一樣時，他們比較會覺得像是群體的一份子，這樣可以激勵大家以學校爲榮，以彼此爲榮。第三，學生不需要煩惱該穿什麼衣服上學，這樣可以節省時間，幫助他們專注於課業。最後，學校制服也可以節省學生及其家人的金錢。

　　基於上述的理由，我認爲大多數的人都會同意，要求穿學校制服是個不錯的主意。雖然學生不能自由地藉由穿著來表現自己，但我認爲制服的優點勝過這一項考量。學校制服讓學生比較不需要擔心自己的外表，而且更能專注於學業。

【註釋】

uniform〔'junə,fɔrm〕 *n.* 制服　　require〔rɪ'kwaɪr〕 *v.* 要求
policy〔'pɑləsɪ〕 *n.* 政策
advantage〔əd'væntɪdʒ〕 *n.* 優點；好處
disadvantage〔,dɪsəd'væntɪdʒ〕 *n.* 缺點；壞處
equalize〔'ikwəl,aɪz〕 *v.* 使平等
fashionable〔'fæʃənəbl〕 *adj.* 時髦的　　peer〔pɪr〕 *n.* 同儕
as though 就好像 (= *as if*)
pride〔praɪd〕 *n.* 驕傲；自豪 < *in* >
focus on 專注於　　***as well*** 也 (= *too*)
given〔'gɪvən〕 *prep.* 考慮到；有鑑於
outweigh〔aut'we〕 *v.* (重要性)比～更大
concern〔kən'sɝn〕 *n.* 關心的事　　***concentrate on*** 專心於

Quit　　　**Writing**

Do you agree or disagree with the following statement? Playing a game is fun only when you win. Use specific reasons and examples to support your answer.

Cut

Paste

Undo

Time

Help
?

Confirm
Answer

Next

136. **Win or Lose, Games Are Fun**

We often hear the expression, "It's not whether you win or lose, but how you play the game, that is important." *But* no matter how many times they hear it, some people still find it difficult to accept defeat. They "play to win" and, if they lose, often feel upset with themselves or others. To such people, games are no fun unless they win. *In my opinion*, they are missing the point of games because we can gain a lot by playing them even when we lose.

Playing games brings us a lot of fun in several ways. *First of all*, it is something we do with others, so it provides us with companionship. *Furthermore*, playing games often allows us to meet people who have the same interests as we do. *Second*, we can test and challenge ourselves when we play games. Rather than worry about defeating our opponent, we can concentrate on improving our own performance. *In this way*, we are bound to get satisfaction from the game. *Third*, we can learn from the people we play with. When we play with others who are more skilled or knowledgeable than we are, we can observe their actions and improve our own skills.

The above are just three of the ways that we can have fun when playing games with others. *However*, in order to have fun, it is important to remember that winning is not always the most important goal of a game. *In conclusion*, if we take care to develop good sportsmanship and take a more relaxed attitude toward the outcome of the game, we will certainly enjoy ourselves more when playing.

136. 不論輸贏，比賽就是很好玩

我們常聽到一句話：「輸贏並不重要，重要的是比賽的過程。」但不論聽過這句話多少次，有些人就是難以接受失敗。他們是「比賽是爲了要贏」，如果輸了，通常會對自己或別人感到生氣。對這些人而言，比賽要獲勝才有樂趣。依我之見，這些人不了解比賽的意義，因爲只要參加比賽，即使輸了，我們都會很有收穫。

參加比賽在很多方面都帶給我們樂趣。首先，因爲我們是跟其他人一起合作，所以我們能藉此和別人培養友誼。此外，比賽通常能讓我們認識志趣相投的人。第二，我們可以在比賽時，考驗與挑戰自己。我們能專注於改善自己的表現，而非擔憂要如何打敗對手，這樣我們就能在比賽中獲得滿足。第三，我們可以跟對手學習。當我們與其他技巧更好，或懂得更多的人競賽時，我們可以觀察他們的動作，進而改善自己的技能。

以上這三點，能讓我們在跟他人比賽時獲得樂趣。然而，爲了要獲得樂趣，我們必須牢記獲勝並非比賽最重要的目標，這一點是很重要的。總之，只要我們注意，要培養良好的運動家精神，並且對比賽結果抱持較輕鬆的態度，我們絕對能在比賽時，覺得更有樂趣。

【註釋】

expression〔ɪk'sprɛʃən〕 *n.* 說法；辭句
defeat〔dɪ'fit〕 *n.* 失敗　*v.* 擊敗　　point〔pɔɪnt〕 *n.* 意義；重要性
first of all 首先　　companionship〔kən'pænjən,ʃɪp〕 *n.* 友誼
furthermore〔'fɝðɚ,mor〕 *adv.* 此外　　challenge〔'tʃælɪndʒ〕 *v.* 挑戰
opponent〔ə'ponənt〕 *n.* 對手　　*be bound to* + *V.* 一定
skilled〔skɪld〕 *adj.* 技術熟練的
knowledgeable〔'nɑlɪdʒəbl̩〕 *adj.* 有知識的
observe〔əb'zɝv〕 *v.* 觀察　　*in conclusion* 總之
not always 不一定（= *not necessarily*）　　*take care* 小心；注意
sportsmanship〔'sportsmən,ʃɪp〕 *n.* 運動家精神
relaxed〔rɪ'lækst〕 *adj.* 輕鬆的　　outcome〔'aut,kʌm〕 *n.* 結果

Quit　　　　**Writing**

Do you agree or disagree with the following statement? High schools should allow students to study the courses that students want to study. Use specific reasons and examples to support your opinion.

Cut

Paste

Undo

137. Elective Courses

The requirements of school systems differ from place to place. In some high schools students follow a strict program of study, while in others they have the freedom to choose some of their courses. *In my opinion*, elective courses are an important part of a complete high school education. *Therefore*, I believe that it would be beneficial for all students to be able to choose some of their courses.

One reason for my belief is that choosing from a variety of courses would allow students to explore new areas of study. They may discover a new talent or interest and broaden their horizons. *Another* reason is that when students choose their own courses they take more responsibility for them and really try to do well. They will be more motivated to learn the material they want to learn. A *final* reason is that making such choices in high school will help to prepare the students for their university lives, when they will have to make many such decisions.

In conclusion, it is my belief that students benefit from being able to choose courses they are interested in. *Of course*, they must still take some required subjects, but the addition of elective courses would enable them to receive a more well-rounded education. *Furthermore*, they might be fortunate enough to discover a lifelong interest at an early age.

137. 選修課程

　　學校制度的要求各地都不同。在有些高中，學生必須遵守非常嚴謹的課程規劃，而在有些高中，學生則有選擇部分課程的自由。依我之見，選修課程是完整高中教育裡的重要一環，因此，我認為，讓所有學生能夠自己選擇部分課程，對他們是很有益處的。

　　我會如此認為，原因之一在於，開放各種課程讓學生選擇，使他們有機會探索新的學習領域，他們或許會發現自己新的天份或興趣，並拓展自己的視野。另一個原因是，當學生自行選修課程時，他們要為自己負更大的責任，並且真的要努力好好表現。他們會更有動機，去學習自己想學的內容。最後一個理由是，在高中時期做這樣的選擇，能幫助學生對大學生活有所準備，因為上大學後，他們將必須做很多這樣的決定。

　　總之，我認為，學生會因為能夠選修自己感興趣的課程而獲益。當然，他們仍然必須修一些必修科目，但增加了選修科目，將使他們能夠接受更多元的教育。此外，他們也許能夠很幸運地，在早年就發現自己終生的興趣。

【註釋】

elective〔ɪˋlɛktɪv〕*adj.* 選修的
requirement〔rɪˋkwaɪrmənt〕*n.* 要求；必要條件
differ from place to place 各地都不同
beneficial〔͵bɛnəˋfɪʃəl〕*adj.* 有益的　　　***a variety of*** 各式各樣的
explore〔ɪkˋsplor〕*v.* 探索；探究　　broaden〔ˋbrɔdn̩〕*v.* 拓展
horizons〔həˋraɪzn̩z〕*n.pl.* 知識範圍
motivate〔ˋmotə͵vet〕*v.* 給予動機
benefit〔ˋbɛnəfɪt〕*v.* 獲益 < *from* >
required〔rɪˋkwaɪrd〕*adj.* 必修的　　addition〔əˋdɪʃən〕*n.* 增加物
well-rounded〔ˋwɛlˋraundɪd〕*adj.* 通才的；多才多藝的
furthermore〔ˋfɝðə͵mor〕*adv.* 此外
lifelong〔ˋlaɪf͵lɔŋ〕*adj.* 終生的

Quit　　　　　　　**Writing**

Do you agree or disagree with the following statement? It is better to be a member of a group than to be the leader of a group. Use specific reasons and examples to support your answer.

Cut

Paste

Undo

138. Be a Leader

Every group, no matter how large or small, has a leader. The leader may be recognized officially and given a title, or may be an informal, de facto leader, simply acknowledged as the one who always makes the decisions. Being a leader entails more responsibility than being an ordinary member of a group. Perhaps this is why some people feel that it is better to be a member than a leader. *But* I disagree because, along with its responsibilities, leadership brings many advantages.

The advantages of being a leader include the opportunity to make a greater contribution to the group, to test one's limits and discover strengths and weaknesses, and to gain valuable experience and develop skills. *First*, it is the leader who often determines the course that a group will take. *Therefore*, the leader has the chance to carry out his vision and to contribute his ideas to the group. *Second*, the leader of a group will have ample opportunity to discover what he is good at and what skills he needs to develop. *Finally*, leading a group is a valuable experience which can be applied to many other situations in life. A leader naturally develops communication and organizational skills which can help him succeed in other endeavors in the future.

With all of these advantages, it is obvious that leading a group can be a positive experience. Although there is always the risk of failure, if we do not face this risk, we cannot progress. The leader of a group is in a unique position to test himself, to grow and advance, and to learn from both his successes and failures.

138. 當一個領導者

　　團體不論大小都有領導者。這位領導者也許是經正式認可，而且有個頭銜，也許只是個被大家認定的決策者，這種人雖是非正式的領導者，但卻也是實質的領導者。當個領導者必須比團體中的一般成員，負更多的責任，也許這就是為什麼有些人認為，當個普通成員比當個領導者好。但我卻不同意這一點，因為領導雖肩負責任，卻也有很多好處。

　　當個領導者的好處包括，有機會對團體做更大的貢獻，可以考驗一個人的極限，發現自己的優缺點，並且還能獲得寶貴的經驗與發展技能。首先，領導者通常能決定一個團體的行動方針。因此，領導人物有機會去實現他的想法，將自己的意見提供給整個團體。其次，一個團體的領導者，會有很多機會，去發覺他真正擅長的領域，與必須培養的技能。最後，領導一個團體，是個非常寶貴的經驗，這樣的經驗能應用在生活中的其他方面。領導者會自然而然地培養出溝通與組織的技巧，而這能幫助他日後在做其他的事情時，能夠成功。

　　因為有這麼多的優點，所以很明顯地，領導一個團體是個很正面的經驗。儘管總是會有失敗的風險，但如果不面對風險，就無法進步。一個團體的領導者處於十分獨特的地位，能夠考驗自我，獲得成長與進步，也能從失敗與成功當中學習。

【註釋】

recognize〔ˈrɛkəgˌnaɪz〕v. 正式承認；認可
de facto〔dɪˈfækto〕adj. 事實上的
acknowledge〔əkˈnɑlɪdʒ〕v. 承認 < as >
entail〔ɪnˈtel〕v. 需要　　**along with**　連同；伴隨
leadership〔ˈlidɚˌʃɪp〕n. 領導的地位　　strength〔strɛŋθ〕n. 優點
weakness〔ˈwiknɪs〕n. 缺點　　determine〔dɪˈtɝmɪn〕v. 決定
course〔kors〕n. 路線；方向　　**carry out**　實現
vision〔ˈvɪʒən〕n. 看法　　ample〔ˈæmpḷ〕adj. 大量的；充足的
apply〔əˈplaɪ〕v. 應用 < to >
organizational〔ˌɔrgənəˈzeʃənḷ〕adj. 組織的
endeavor〔ɪnˈdɛvɚ〕n. 努力　　obvious〔ˈɑbvɪəs〕adj. 明顯的
positive〔ˈpɑzətɪv〕adj. 正面的；
progress〔prəˈgrɛs〕v. 進步（= advance〔ədˈvæns〕）
unique〔juˈnik〕adj. 獨特的

Writing

Quit

What do you consider to be the most important room in a house? Why is this room more important to you than any other room? Use specific reasons and examples to support your opinion.

Cut

Paste

Undo

Time

Help ?

Confirm Answer

Next

139. The Most Important Room in the House

Every room in the house has its function and it is difficult to imagine life without one of them. *However*, there is one room that I believe is truly indispensable because it is the center of the life of the household. That room is the kitchen.

The kitchen is always a warm room where the family like to gather. There always seems to be some kind of activity going on — cooking, eating, talking and even studying. It is an informal room and everyone feels comfortable in the kitchen. My family and I always eat our meals at the kitchen table unless we have company. *So*, the kitchen represents family time. Most of the family conversations seem to take place in the kitchen, too. *And*, of course, there is always something good to eat in the kitchen. It is the food center of the house and food is indispensable to the family.

For these reasons, the most important room in the house, and my personal favorite, is the kitchen. It represents the center of the family and is, *therefore*, the center of the house.

139. 房子裏最重要的空間

　　房子內的每個空間都有其功能，很難想像若缺少任何一間，生活會變得怎麼樣。但是，我認為其中有個空間，是真的不可或缺的，因為它是家庭生活的中心，那就是廚房。

　　廚房總是個溫暖的地方，家人喜歡聚在那裡。那裡似乎時時都有活動在進行 —— 做飯、用餐、談話，甚至唸書。那是一個輕鬆的場所，每個人在廚房都會感到很舒適。除非有訪客，不然我和家人總是喜歡在廚房的餐桌上用餐。所以廚房代表了全家人相聚的時光。家人彼此的交談，大部分也都是在廚房進行的。所以廚房裡當然總是有好吃的東西。廚房是家中的食物中心，而食物是家庭不可或缺的一部分。

　　基於這些理由，房子內最重要的空間，而且也是我個人最偏愛的地方，就是廚房了。廚房代表家庭的中心，也就是房子的中心。

【註釋】

function〔'fʌŋkʃən〕*n.* 功能　　imagine〔ɪ'mædʒɪn〕*v.* 想像
indispensable〔͵ɪndɪ'spɛnsəbl̩〕*adj.* 不可或缺的
household〔'haʊs͵hold〕*n.* 家庭
gather〔'gæðɚ〕*v.* 聚集　　***go on*** 進行
informal〔ɪn'fɔrml̩〕*adj.* 非正式的；輕鬆的
meal〔mil〕*n.* 一餐　　company〔'kʌmpənɪ〕*n.* 訪客；同伴
represent〔͵rɛprɪ'zɛnt〕*v.* 代表　　***take place*** 發生
favorite〔'fevərɪt〕*n.* 最喜歡的人或物

Quit　　　**Writing**

Some items (such as clothes or furniture) can be made by hand or by machine. Which do you prefer — items made by hand or items made by machine? Use reasons and specific examples to explain your choice.

Cut

Paste

Undo

140. Items Made by Hand

In today's mass-produced, machine-made world, it's refreshing to find items of necessity that are still handmade. Things like clothing and furniture for example. I am a little old-fashioned and prefer to buy things handmade.

There's a level of quality that can only be achieved when something is handmade. *For example*, a machine cannot possibly replicate the intricate weaving and design of a hand-woven Persian rug nor can a machine capture the subtle irregularities in the finish of hand-carved wooden furniture. Things handmade tend to last longer than machine-made items as well. By definition, a mass-produced, machine-made product is meant to last only a few years. There would be no money for the corporations to make if their products last an eternity. *However*, the downside of handmade items is that they tend to be much more expensive than mass-produced goods.

Although handmade goods are much more durable and convey a special feeling to the buyer knowing that a master craftsman had his hands in creating it, they are often prohibitively expensive and not for the masses.

140. 手工製品

在現今大量生產、機器製造的世界，找到仍是手工製的必需品，是令人振奮的事情，例如衣服和家具。我是個有點傳統的人，比較喜歡買手工製品。

某種程度的品質，唯有手工製的東西才能達到。例如，機器不可能複製手織的波斯地毯，所呈現的複雜精細的織工和圖案設計，也無法捕捉到用手雕刻而成的木製家具成品，所呈現的精巧的不規則變化。手工製品的壽命往往也比機器製品來得久。當然根據定義，大量生產、機器製造的的產品，就是只能維持幾年的壽命而已。如果產品可以一直無限期地使用，那公司就沒有錢可以賺了。然而，手工製品的缺點，就是它們通常比大量製造的產品貴很多。

雖然手工製品比較耐用，也傳達給購買者一種特別的感覺，知道手工精湛的工匠創造這個成品所展現的才能，但是它們的價錢經常是貴得驚人，不是一般大眾可以負擔的。

【註釋】

mass-produced〔'mæsprə,djust〕adj.（使用機器）大量生產的
machine-made〔mə'ʃin,med〕adj. 機器製的
refreshing〔rɪ'frɛʃɪŋ〕adj. 使人耳目一新的
necessity〔nə'sɛsətɪ〕n. 需要　handmade〔'hænd,med〕adj. 手工製的
level〔'lɛvl̩〕n. 水準；程度　replicate〔'rɛplɪ,ket〕v. 複製
intricate〔'ɪntrəkɪt〕adj. 複雜精細的　weave〔wiv〕v. 編織
hand-woven〔'hænd'wovən〕adj. 以手織機編織的
Persian〔'pɝʒən , 'pɝʃən〕adj. 波斯的　rug〔rʌg〕n. 地毯
capture〔'kæptʃɚ〕v. 捕捉　subtle〔'sʌtl̩〕adj. 微妙的
irregularity〔,ɪrɛgjə'lærətɪ〕n. 不規則的事物　finish〔'fɪnɪʃ〕n. 成品
hand-carved〔'hænd'kɑrvd〕adj. 以手工雕刻的
by definition 在定義上；當然（諷刺用法）
corporation〔,kɔrpə'reʃən〕n. 公司
eternity〔ɪ'tɝnətɪ〕n.（似乎無止境的）漫長時間
downside〔'daʊn'saɪd , 'daʊn,saɪd〕n. 不利；缺點
durable〔'd(j)ʊrəbl̩〕adj. 耐用的　convey〔kən've〕v. 傳達
master〔'mæstɚ〕adj. 精通的　craftsman〔'kræftsmən〕n. 工匠
hand〔hænd〕n. 才能；技巧
prohibitively〔pro'hɪbɪtɪvlɪ〕adv.（費用）過高地　*the masses* 大眾

Quit　　　　　Writing

If you could make one important change in a school that you attended, what change would you make? Use reasons and specific examples to support your answer.

_____

_____

_____

_____

_____

_____

_____

_____

_____

_____

_____

_____

_____

_____

_____

_____

_____

_____

_____

Cut

Paste

Undo

Time

Help ?

Confirm Answer

Next →

141. An Important Change at School

A school is an important place to students. It is where they spend the majority of their time during their school years. *Therefore*, it is important that the school provide a good environment for the students to develop both mentally and physically. *For this reason*, if I could make one change to the school I attend, I would add a large, modern gymnasium.

One reason I support the building of a modern gym is that physical education class is very important to the well-being of students. It provides us not only with exercise, but with a break from the mental rigors of our studies. *However*, without a large enough gym, we must often cancel our P.E. class when the weather is bad and more classes must share the indoor space. A new gym would solve this problem. *Another* reason I would like to have a new gym is that more modern athletic facilities would allow us to practice a wider variety of sports. This would appeal to those students who are not physically active because they find the current sports that we play boring or difficult. In developing the lifelong habit of exercise, it is important for everyone to find something he enjoys. *Finally*, a big, new gymnasium could be used for other events as well, such as class assemblies and performances.

For the reasons given above, I believe that a large, modern gymnasium would be a valuable addition to my school. It would encourage more students to exercise and allow them to do so on a more regular basis. *In addition*, it could be used by many school organizations and clubs for a variety of purposes. *Therefore*, I believe it is a practical suggestion.

141. 學校的重大改變

　　學校對學生而言,是個重要的地方,也是學生在求學期間,待最久的地方。因此,學校應該提供一個良好的環境,供學生發展身心,這是很重要的。基於這個理由,如果我能改變我所就讀的學校,我會增設一座大型的現代化體育館。

　　我支持興建一座現代化體育館的理由是,體育課對學生的健康是非常重要的。體育課不僅讓我們有機會運動,還能讓我們遠離耗盡心力的學業,獲得暫時的抒解。然而,如果沒有一座夠大的體育館,我們常會因為天氣不好,或有其他更多的班級要共用室內空間,而取消體育課。一座新的體育館就能解決這個問題。另一個我想擁有一座新體育館的理由是,更現代化的體育設施,能讓我們從事更多各式各樣的運動,如此便能吸引那些認為現在做的體育活動過於無聊或困難,而不太熱衷於運動的學生。在培養終生運動的習慣時,讓每個人都能找到自己所熱愛的運動,是很重要的。最後,一個大型且新穎的體育館,也可用來舉辦其他大型活動,如班級集會或各項表演。

　　基於以上的理由,我認為增添一座大型且現代化的體育館,對我的學校而言,是很有價值的。這會鼓勵更多學生運動,而且還能讓他們更定期地運動。此外,還可以供許多校內團體或社團,舉辦各種不同性質的活動。因此,我認為這是個相當實用的建議。

【註釋】

majority〔məˋdʒɔrətɪ〕*n.* 大多數　　mentally〔ˋmɛntḷɪ〕*adv.* 心理上
physically〔ˋfɪzɪkḷɪ〕身體上
gymnasium〔dʒɪmˋnezɪəm〕*n.* 體育館 (= *gym*)
physical education 體育 (= *P.E.*)
well-being〔ˋwɛlˋbiɪŋ〕*n.* 健康　　break〔brek〕*n.* 休息
rigor〔ˋrɪgɚ〕*n.* 艱苦　　athletic〔æθˋlɛtɪk〕*adj.* 運動的
facilities〔fəˋsɪlə͵tɪz〕*n. pl.* 設施
appeal to 吸引　　active〔ˋæktɪv〕*adj.* 活躍的
current〔ˋkɝənt〕*adj.* 目前的　　lifelong〔ˋlaɪf͵lɔŋ〕*adj.* 終生的
event〔ɪˋvɛnt〕*n.* 盛大活動　　assembly〔əˋsɛmblɪ〕*n.* 集會
addition〔əˋdɪʃən〕*n.* 增加物 < *to* >
on a regular basis 定期地 (= *regularly*)
organization〔͵ɔrgənəˋzeʃən〕*n.* 組織　　club〔klʌb〕*n.* 社團
practical〔ˋpræktɪkḷ〕*adj.* 實用的

Quit　　　**Writing**

A gift (such as a camera, a soccer ball, or an animal) can contribute to a child's development. What gift would you give to help a child develop? Why? Use reasons and specific examples to support your choice.

Cut

Paste

Undo

Time

Help
?

Confirm
Answer

Next

142. **The Best Gift for a Child**

All parents are concerned with their children's development, and seek many ways to stimulate them intellectually and instill in them good values. There are many valuable things that parents can give their children which will contribute to their development. They may be as elaborate as a computer or as simple as a ball. *In my opinion*, the best gift for a child is an animal because it will help them develop many important values.

The most important value is responsibility. When a child has a pet, he is in charge of that animal's health and happiness. *Moreover*, it is a lifelong responsibility. Unlike a toy, a pet cannot be discarded when the child becomes bored with it. *Another* important trait that a pet can help a child develop is consideration for others. When he sees how his behavior affects his pet, he may become more compassionate and considerate. *Finally*, a pet is a good companion for a child. It may teach him the value of having and being a loyal friend.

In conclusion, I believe that a child can learn many valuable lessons from the experience of owning a pet. Animals may not be able to speak, but they may be the best teachers when it comes to things like responsibility, compassion and friendship. If it is possible for parents to give their child an animal to care for, it will prove to be a very meaningful gift.

142. 給兒童最好的禮物

　　所有的父母都關心孩子的發展，因此就會尋求許多能激發孩子智力的方法，以及灌輸他們良好的價值觀。父母親有很多珍貴的事物可以給予他們的小孩，有助於他們成長。這些東西也許像電腦一樣複雜，或像球一樣簡單。我認為送小孩最好的禮物，就是動物，因為這樣能幫助他們培養許多很重要的價值觀。

　　最重要的價值觀就是責任感。當小孩養寵物時，他就必須對寵物的健康與快樂負責，而且，這是一輩子的責任。寵物不像玩具，就算小孩玩膩了，也不能丟棄。另一個重要特點是，寵物能讓小孩學會多替別人著想。當他知道自己的行為會對寵物產生何種影響時，他也許就會變得更有同情心，而且體貼。最後，寵物還是兒童的良伴。這會讓他知道擁有忠實的朋友與對朋友忠實的重要。

　　總之，我認為兒童可以從養寵物的經驗中，學到很多寶貴的事情。也許動物不能說話，但一提到責任感、憐憫與友情，寵物就是最好的老師。如果可能，應該給小孩一隻動物讓他照顧，這一定會是非常有意義的禮物。

【註釋】

concerned〔kən'sɝnd〕adj. 關心的　　seek〔sik〕v. 尋求
stimulate〔'stɪmjə,let〕v. 刺激
intellectually〔,ɪntḷ'ɛktʃʊəlɪ〕adv. 在智力方面
instill〔ɪn'stɪl〕v. 灌輸　　values〔'væljuz〕n. pl. 價值觀
contribute〔kən'trɪbjut〕v. 貢獻；有助於 < to >
elaborate〔ɪ'læbərɪt〕adj. 複雜的　　pet〔pɛt〕n. 寵物
in charge of 負責管理　　lifelong〔'laɪf,lɔŋ〕adj. 一生的
discard〔dɪs'kɑrd〕v. 拋棄　　trait〔tret〕n. 特點
consideration〔kən,sɪdə'reʃən〕n. 體貼；關心 < for >
compassionate〔kəm'pæʃənɪt〕adj. 有同情心的
considerate〔kən'sɪdərɪt〕adj. 體諒的
companion〔kəm'pænjən〕n. 同伴　　loyal〔'lɔɪəl〕adj. 忠實的
in conclusion 總之　　when it comes to 一提到
compassion〔kəm'pæʃən〕n. 同情　　care for 照顧
prove to be 結果是　　meaningful〔'minɪŋfḷ〕adj. 有意義的

Quit　　　　　　**Writing**

Some people believe that students should be given one long vacation each year. Others believe that students should have several short vacations throughout the year. Which viewpoint do you agree with? Use specific reasons and examples to support your choice.

Cut

Paste

Undo

Time

Help
?

Confirm
Answer

Next

143. Student Vacations

In many countries students enjoy one long vacation a year, but in others they do not. Originally, the long vacation was necessary due to seasonal conditions. It was too hot, too rainy or too cold and snowy to go to school. This is still the case in some developing countries, but in most places in the world, progress has made it possible to keep schools open year round. *So* is the traditional long vacation beneficial for students, or should they be given several shorter breaks throughout the year? *In my opinion*, it would be better for students to have more short vacations for several reasons.

First, students must work very hard at their studies. If they work for too long without a break, they may become overtired and discouraged. They may lose their enthusiasm for learning. *Second*, a very long vacation is not necessary. Students can recharge their energy in a few days rather than weeks. *Furthermore*, many students do not use a long vacation wisely and just waste their time instead of doing something meaningful. *And last but not least*, vacations give students time to explore other interests and perhaps apply what they have been learning to the real world. If they are always focused on their studies, they may lose touch with what is happening in their society. *In conclusion*, I believe that students today would benefit more from several short vacations than they do from a single long one.

143. 學生的假期

在很多國家，學生一年享有一次漫長的假期，但在有些國家則沒有。本來，必須放長假是因爲季節的因素，如天氣太熱、雨季太長，或者天氣太冷、會下大雪，而無法上學。在有些開發中國家，情況仍是如此，但在多數地區，已經有所進步，讓學校有可能全年無休。所以，是按照傳統放長假對學生有益，還是學生應該在一年當中，有好幾個短暫的假期？依我之見，基於幾個理由，學生最好擁有比較多的短暫假期。

首先，學生必須非常用功唸書。如果他們唸書的時間太長，而沒有休息的話，他們可能會過度疲勞，且心情沮喪。他們可能會喪失學習的熱忱。第二，一段很長的假期是沒有必要的。學生可以在幾天之內恢復精力，而不用好幾個禮拜的時間。此外，很多學生沒有好好利用長假，他們只是浪費時間，而不是從事有意義的活動。最後一項要點是，假期讓學生有時間去探索其他興趣，而且或許能把自己所學的，應用在眞實的生活裡。如果他們總是專心於學業，可能就會對社會上所發生的事情一無所知。總之，我認爲對現在的學生而言，放好幾次短假，比放一次長假，會更有益處。

【註釋】

originally〔ə'rɪdʒənlɪ〕*adv.* 起初；原本　　snowy〔'snoɪ〕*adj.* 下雪的

case〔kes〕*n.* 事實　　***a developing country*** 開發中國家

progress〔'prɑgrɛs〕*n.* 進步　　***year round*** 全年

beneficial〔ˌbɛnə'fɪʃəl〕*adj.* 有益的　　break〔brek〕*n.* 休息時間

enthusiasm〔ɪn'θjuzɪˌæzəm〕*n.* 熱忱

recharge〔ri'tʃɑrdʒ〕*v.* 再充電；使再充滿

furthermore〔'fɝðəˌmor〕*adv.* 此外

last but not least 最後一項要點是

explore〔ɪk'splor〕*v.* 探索　　apply〔ə'plaɪ〕*v.* 應用〈*to*〉

focus〔'fokəs〕*v.* 使集中〈*on*〉　　touch〔tʌtʃ〕*n.* 接觸

benefit〔'bɛnəfɪt〕*v.* 獲益〈*from*〉　　single〔'sɪŋgl̩〕*adj.* 單一的

Writing

Would you prefer to live in a traditional house or in a modern apartment building?　Use specific reasons and details to support your choice.

Cut

Paste

Undo

Time

Help
?

Confirm
Answer

Next

144. A Traditional House

These days, most people in modern cities live in apartment buildings, myself included. There are many advantages to apartments. *For example*, they are convenient and require less maintenance than a house, and they are usually much less expensive than a traditional house. *In addition*, traditional houses have some disadvantages. They often lack modern amenities and may need to be adapted to fit more modern lifestyles. *However*, despite these disadvantages, I would still prefer to live in a traditional house than a modern apartment for the following reasons.

One, a traditional house usually offers more space than a modern apartment. It is not only roomier inside, but may also have a garden. *Two*, it is unique and allows the owners to express their individuality. Too often, apartments are exact duplicates of each other and leave little room for creativity in decoration. *Three*, a house provides its owners with more privacy and a quieter environment. There are no neighbors directly above, below and next-door to disturb them. *Last but not least*, living in a traditional house is a way to preserve our culture. The architecture of the past can tell us a lot about how people before us lived and encourage us to maintain our traditions. Too often these fine old buildings are torn down to make way for modern apartment blocks.

In conclusion, I believe that the advantages of living in a traditional house outweigh its disadvantages. By choosing to live in one, I might have to put up with a few inconveniences, but I would gain space, quiet, and privacy. *Furthermore*, I would be saving an important part of our cultural heritage for the next generation to enjoy. In our efforts to advance our society and live more convenient lives, we should not ignore the value of our past.

144. 傳統式的房子

　　近來，現代都市的大部分居民都住在公寓大樓裡，包括我自己在內。住公寓有許多好處，例如，公寓很方便，而且和獨棟的房子比起來，不太需要保養，而且通常公寓的價格比房子便宜很多。此外，傳統式的房子有一些缺點，通常會缺乏現代化的設備，而且可能需要改裝，以適應較現代化的生活方式。然而，儘管有這些缺點，但基於下列理由，我還是寧可住傳統式的房子，而不願住在現代化公寓。

　　第一，傳統式的房子通常能提供比現代化的公寓更大的空間。不只是屋內的空間較寬敞，可能還會有個花園。第二，傳統式的房子具獨特性，能讓屋主表達自己的個性。公寓的設計經常是完全一模一樣，因此在裝潢上發揮創意的空間很小。第三，房子能提供屋主保有更多的隱私，以及較安靜的環境。房子的正上或正下方及隔壁，都沒有鄰居干擾。最後一項要點是，住傳統式的房子能保存我們的文化。舊式的建築物可以告訴我們，前人的生活情況，並鼓勵我們要維持本身的傳統。這些精緻的老建築物常會遭到拆毀，以挪出空間興建現代的公寓大樓。

　　總之，我認爲住在傳統式的房子的優點，勝過其缺點。選擇住在這樣的房子裡，我可能必須忍受一些不方便，但是我能獲得寬敞的空間、安靜，以及隱私。此外，我能保存文化遺產的重要部分，留給下一代欣賞。在我們努力促進社會的進步，及過著便利生活的同時，我們不應該忽視過去的重要性。

【註釋】

traditional〔trəˈdɪʃənḷ〕adj. 傳統的　　***these days*** 最近
apartment〔əˈpɑrtmənt〕n. 公寓
maintenance〔ˈmɛntənəns〕n. 維護；保養
amenities〔əˈmɛnətɪz〕n. pl. 設施　　adapt〔əˈdæpt〕v. 使適合
roomy〔ˈrumɪ〕adj. 寬敞的
individuality〔ˌɪndəˌvɪdʒʊˈælətɪ〕n. 個性
duplicate〔ˈdjupləkɪt〕n. 複製品　　privacy〔ˈpraɪvəsɪ〕n. 隱私（權）
last but not least 最後一項要點是　　preserve〔prɪˈzɝv〕v. 保留
tear down 拆毀　　***make way to*** 讓出地方給～
block〔blɑk〕n. 一排房屋　　outweigh〔aʊtˈwe〕v. 比…更重要
put up with 忍受　　heritage〔ˈhɛrətɪdʒ〕n. 遺產；傳統
advance〔ədˈvæns〕v. 使進步

Some people say that advertising encourages us to buy things we really do not need. Others say that advertisements tell us about new products that may improve our lives. Which viewpoint do you agree with? Use specific reasons and examples to support your answer.

▲

Cut

Paste

Undo

▼

145. Advertising

Advertising is a very big business these days. Billions of dollars are spent every year to persuade customers to buy one brand of product rather than another. We are all exposed to such advertisements every day and their effect on us cannot be denied. While it is true that some advertisements do provide useful information about new products, I believe that their primary effect is to encourage people to buy things that they don't really need.

First of all, most advertising does not introduce a brand-new product. *Instead*, it is designed to persuade consumers that one company's product is superior to that of another company. *Second*, when a product is new, the advertising is often designed to create demand for it. *In other words*, its goal is to convince potential buyers that this new product is really necessary, whether or not it actually is. *Third*, many advertisements are image ads, designed to sell people luxury products. The ads imply that by buying such products the consumer will gain something else such as happiness, respect or love. These ads not only try to sell things that people do not really need, but promise something that cannot be bought. *Finally*, if there is new information about a product or development, people will hear about it through word of mouth, and *in my opinion*, this is a more reliable source of information.

While it can be argued that advertising is sometimes useful to consumers who may want to compare different brands, I believe its overall effect is to get people to buy things that they don't need. That is not to say that the advertisements are deceptive. They are simply designed to create a need for the product among consumers. *Therefore*, we should all look at advertisements with a critical eye in order to avoid buying things that are not necessary.

145. 廣　告

　　最近廣告已成為非常大的事業。每年花在廣告上的經費都有好幾十億美元，以說服顧客買某個品牌的產品，而不買別家的。我們每天都接觸這一類的廣告，而它們對我們的影響是不可否認的。雖然某些廣告的確提供了關於新產品的有用資訊，但我認為，它們的主要功用，就是鼓勵大家去買一些不是真的很需要的東西。

　　首先，大多數的廣告並不會介紹一個全新的產品。相反地，廣告設計的用意，是要說服消費者，某家公司的產品，比另一家好。其次，當推出一項新產品時，廣告的目的，常是要創造對這項產品的需求。換句話說，它的目標，就是要說服可能的購買者，相信這項產品真的是必需品，無論是否真的如此。第三，很多廣告都是形象廣告，目的是要將奢侈品銷售給大家。這種廣告會暗示，買了此類產品的消費者，會得到其他的東西，如快樂、尊敬或愛。這些廣告不只會試著銷售一些，人們並不是真的很需要的東西，而且也會保證你得到某樣買不到的東西。最後，如果有與產品或發展相關的新資訊，人們會口耳相傳，我認為，這才是比較可靠的資訊來源。

　　雖然有人認為，廣告有時能夠幫助那些想要比較不同品牌產品的消費者。但我認為，廣告整體的效果，就是要人們購買自己不需要的東西。這並不是說，廣告都是騙人的。它們的目的，只是要讓消費者對這項產品產生需求。因此，我們都應該用批判性的眼光來看待廣告，以免買到不需要的東西。

【註釋】

advertising〔'ædvɚ͵taɪzɪŋ〕*n.* 廣告　　billion〔'bɪljən〕*n.* 十億
persuade〔pɚ'swed〕*v.* 說服　　brand〔brænd〕*n.* 品牌
be exposed to 接觸　　deny〔dɪ'naɪ〕*v.* 否認
primary〔'praɪ͵mɛrɪ〕*adj.* 主要的
brand-new〔'brænd'nju〕*adj.* 全新的
instead〔ɪn'stɛd〕*adv.* 取而代之　　***be designed to*** 目的是為了
consumer〔kən'sjumɚ〕*n.* 消費者　　***be superior to*** 優於
convince〔kən'vɪns〕*v.* 使相信　　potential〔pə'tɛnʃəl〕*adj.* 可能的
image〔'ɪmɪdʒ〕*n.* 形象　　luxury〔'lʌkʃərɪ〕*adj.* 奢侈的；豪華的
by word of mouth 口耳相傳　　reliable〔rɪ'laɪəbl̩〕*adj.* 可靠的
source〔sors〕*n.* 來源　　argue〔'ɑrgju〕*v.* 主張
overall〔'ovɚ͵ɔl〕*adj.* 全部的　　deceptive〔dɪ'sɛptɪv〕*adj.* 欺騙的
critical〔'krɪtɪkl̩〕*adj.* 批判性的　　eye〔aɪ〕*n.* 眼光

Quit

Writing

Some people prefer to spend their free time outdoors. Other people prefer to spend their leisure time indoors. Would you prefer to be outside or would you prefer to be inside for your leisure activities? Use specific reasons and examples to explain your choice.

Cut

Paste

Undo

Time

Help
?

Confirm
Answer

Next
→

146. Spending Time Outdoors

Leisure time is important to all of us, for everyone needs time to relax. Fortunately, in this modern age there is a wide variety of leisure time activities for us to choose from. Some, such as reading, painting or playing a musical instrument, may be done indoors. Others, like basketball or hiking, are pursued outside. My preference is for outdoor leisure activities for the following reasons.

For one thing, as a student, I spend much of my time indoors listening to lectures or studying texts. It is important for me to have a change of scene in order to refresh my mind and renew my energy. Spending some time outdoors each day actually improves my ability to study. *For another*, outdoor activities allow me to improve my health. Outdoors I can exercise and get some fresh air. This will give me the physical strength to keep on working. *Finally*, the activities that I like to do most are best done outside. They include sports like basketball and swimming and going for walks. I find these activities not only healthy, but relaxing.

For all of the above reasons, I prefer outdoor activities to indoor ones. After a long day of studying, I would rather get out and get some fresh air than stay inside and play video games or watch TV. Outdoor activities allow me to both improve my health and relax my mind. *Therefore*, I think they are the best choice for me.

146. 從事戶外活動

　　休閒時間對我們而言非常重要,因爲每個人都需要有時間放鬆。幸運的是,現代社會有很多各式各樣的休閒活動讓我們選擇。有些活動,如閱讀、繪畫或演奏樂器,都可以在室內進行;而有些活動,如棒球或健行,就只能在戶外進行。我因爲以下的理由,所以比較喜歡從事戶外活動。

　　首先,身爲學生,我大部分的時間都待在室內聽老師上課,或是讀教科書,因此,能夠有機會轉換環境,以恢復精神或體力,對我而言是很重要的。每天花點時間在戶外活動,確實能增進我唸書的效果。另一個原因是,戶外活動可以增進我的健康。在戶外,我可以做運動,而且能呼吸到新鮮空氣,這會讓我增強體能,可以繼續工作。最後,我最喜歡的活動,都適合在戶外進行,包括像籃球、游泳,以及散步。我覺得這些活動不僅有益健康,而且還能讓人放鬆。

　　基於以上這些理由,我喜愛戶外活動,甚於室內活動。在一整天長時間唸書後,我寧願出去呼吸新鮮的空氣,也不願意待在室內玩電動玩具或看電視。戶外活動既能讓我增進健康,又能放鬆心情。因此,我認爲對我來說,那是最好的選擇。

【註釋】

leisure time 空閒時間　　*a variety of* 各式各樣的
musical instrument 樂器　　hiking〔'haɪkɪŋ〕*n.* 健行
pursue〔pə'su〕*v.* 從事
preference〔'prɛfərəns〕*n.* 嗜好;優先選擇
for one thing…for another~ 一則…再則~
lecture〔'lɛktʃɚ〕*n.* 講課　　text〔tɛkst〕*n.* 教科書 (= *textbook*)
a change of scene 環境的改變　　refresh〔rɪ'frɛʃ〕*v.* 使恢復精神
renew〔rɪ'nju〕*v.* 使恢復　　energy〔'ɛnədʒɪ〕*n.* 精力
go for a walk 去散步 (= *take a walk*)
would rather + V₁ + *than* + V₂ 寧願 V₁,而不願 V₂
get out 出去 (= *go out*)　　*video game* 電動玩具

Quit　　　　　　**Writing**

Your school has received a gift of money. What do you think is the best way for your school to spend this money? Use specific reasons and details to support your choice.

Cut

Paste

Undo

147. A Windfall for the School

To receive an unexpected gift of money would be a happy thing. It would mean freedom to indulge in luxuries that were previously unaffordable. *However*, it would also mean taking on the responsibility of spending the money in the best way. This is especially true when the fortune does not come to an individual, but to an institution such as a school. If my school were to receive a gift of money, what would be the best way to use it? *In my opinion*, it would be to buy up-to-date computer equipment for students to use.

Buying computer equipment would be the best choice for several reasons, but the following are the two most important. *First*, it would allow all the students in the school to have access to computers when they do research or write reports. As it is now, some students have computers at home while others do not, and this gives the former an unfair advantage. *Second*, the chance to learn how to use up-to-date computer hardware and software would be a great advantage to all students. No matter what career they pursue in the future, they will most likely have to be computer literate. Nowadays, knowledge of computers is as an important part of our education as history and mathematics.

To sum up, buying computer equipment would be the best use of a gift of money to my school because it would bring important benefits to students. *Moreover*, unlike such things as athletic equipment or musical instruments, it would benefit all students equally since computers are something that all students must use. In this computerized age, computer literacy is essential and it is never too early to give students this advantage.

147. 學校的意外之財

　　意外地獲贈一筆錢是件很快樂的事,因爲這就表示,可以自在地把錢揮霍在以前買不起的奢侈品上。但是,這也意味著,必須負責妥善地選擇使用這筆錢的方式。當這筆錢送給像學校這樣的機構,而不是個人時,更是如此。如果我的學校獲得這種餽贈時,什麼才是最好的運用方式呢?我的看法是,要買最新的電腦設備供學生使用。

　　購買電腦設備是最好的選擇,理由有很多,以下所列舉的,是其中兩個最重要的原因。首先,這能讓全校學生做研究或寫報告時,都能使用電腦。事實上,現在有些學生家裡有電腦,而有些學生卻沒有,這讓家中有電腦的人佔了不公平的優勢。其次,讓學生有機會學習如何使用最新的電腦硬體與軟體,對所有的學生都有很大的好處。不論他們將來從事哪一行,都很有可能必須要會使用電腦。現在,電腦知識已經像歷史及數學一樣,都是我們教育中重要的一部分了。

　　總之,學校最好能用獲贈的金錢購買電腦設備,這樣做會帶給學生很多重要的好處。而且,不像體育設施或樂器,電腦能讓所有的學生都獲得相同的好處,因爲所有的學生都用得到電腦。在這電腦化的時代,電腦知識是必要的,而且讓學生有這樣的好處,是永遠不嫌早的。

【註釋】

windfall〔ˈwɪndˌfɔl〕*n.* 意外之財

indulge〔ɪnˈdʌldʒ〕*v.* 沉迷於 < *in* >　　luxury〔ˈlʌkʃərɪ〕*n.* 奢侈品

previously〔ˈprivɪəslɪ〕*adv.* 以前

unaffordable〔ˌʌnəˈfɔrdəbḷ〕*adj.* 負擔不起的　　***take on*** 承擔

fortune〔ˈfɔrtʃən〕*n.* 一大筆錢　　institution〔ˌɪnstəˈtjuʃən〕*n.* 機構

up-to-date〔ˈʌptəˈdet〕*adj.* 最新的

access〔ˈæksɛs〕*n.* 使用權 < *to* >　　research〔ˈrisɜtʃ〕*n.* 研究

the former (兩者中)前者　　unfair〔ʌnˈfɛr〕*adj.* 不公平的

advantage〔ədˈvæntɪdʒ〕*n.* 優勢;好處　　pursue〔pəˈsu〕*v.* 從事

literate〔ˈlɪtərɪt〕*adj.* 通曉…的　　***to sum up*** 總之

athletic〔æθˈlɛtɪk〕*adj.* 運動的　　***musical instrument*** 樂器

literacy〔ˈlɪtərəsɪ〕*n.* 通曉…的能力

essential〔əˈsɛnʃəl〕*adj.* 必要的

Quit　　　　　　**Writing**

Do you agree or disagree with the following statement? Playing games teaches us about life. Use specific reasons and examples to support your answer.

Cut

Paste

Undo

Time

Help
?

Confirm
Answer

Next

148. Playing Games Teaches Us About Life

Games have played an important role in nearly every culture throughout history. They are not only a source of amusement, but also an important way of learning. Long ago, games simulated real-life situations and developed skills useful in hunting and warfare, important activities at that time. Today, games can still teach us a lot about life.

For example, children often play games in which they take on adult roles. This kind of play helps them to prepare for their future lives. More organized games can teach us how to work as a team and get along with others. Games can also teach us how to win and lose gracefully. *In addition*, they can instill a sense of sportsmanship and fair play in young people that will be useful in all their future endeavors. *Finally*, although hunting and fighting techniques are no longer as essential, games can still help us develop certain practical skills. These skills may be physical or intellectual, such as the logical thinking developed by more mentally challenging games.

In short, whatever type of game people play, they get more from it than just entertainment and relaxation. Games can help us develop abilities that will assist us in other activities in life. *Therefore*, they are an invaluable way of learning about life.

148. 從遊戲中學習人生

　　自古以來，遊戲幾乎在每一種文化當中，都扮演著很重要的角色。它們不只是娛樂的來源，也是學習的一種重要方式。很久以前，遊戲模擬眞實生活的情境，以便在當時的重要活動中，如打獵及戰鬥，培養有用的技巧。現在，遊戲仍然可以教導我們許多與生活有關的事情。

　　舉例來說，在遊戲中，小朋友經常扮演大人的角色，這種遊戲能幫助他們爲未來的生活做準備。更有組織的遊戲，可以教我們如何像團隊一樣工作，和其他人如何相處。遊戲同時也可以教我們如何優雅地面對輸贏。此外，遊戲可以灌輸年輕人運動家精神，以及公平比賽的觀念，而這些觀念，在他們未來努力的過程中是很有用的。最後，雖然打獵和戰鬥技巧不再那麼必要，遊戲仍然可以幫助我們發展一些實用的技巧。這些技巧可能是體能上，或智力上的技巧，例如藉由較費腦力的益智遊戲，就可以培養邏輯思考的能力。

　　總之，無論人們玩什麼遊戲，他們獲得的不只是娛樂和放鬆。遊戲可以幫助我們，培養有助於我們在日常生活中，參加其他活動的能力。因此，遊戲是學習生活很寶貴的方法。

【註釋】

throughout history 自古以來　　amusement〔əˋmjuzmənt〕*n.* 娛樂
simulate〔ˋsɪmjəˏlet〕*v.* 模擬　　real-life〔ˋrɪəlˋlaɪf〕*adj.* 眞人眞事的
warfare〔ˋwɔrˏfɛr〕*n.* 戰爭　　***take on*** 採用
organized〔ˋɔrgənˏaɪzd〕*adj.* 有組織的　　***get along with*** 和～相處
gracefully〔ˋgresfəlɪ〕*adv.* 優雅地　　instill〔ɪnˋstɪl〕*v.* 灌輸
sense〔sɛns〕*n.* 感覺；觀念
sportsmanship〔ˋsportsmənˏʃɪp〕*n.* 運動家精神
fair〔fɛr〕*adj.* 公平的　　endeavor〔ɪnˋdɛvɚ〕*n.* 努力
technique〔tɛkˋnik〕*n.* 技術　　essential〔əˋsɛnʃəl〕*adj.* 必要的
intellectual〔ˏɪntḷˋɛktʃʊəl〕*adj.* 智力的　　logical〔ˋlɑdʒɪkḷ〕*adj.* 邏輯的
challenging〔ˋtʃælɪndʒɪŋ〕*adj.* 使人思考的　　***in short*** 簡言之；總之
entertainment〔ˏɛntɚˋtenmənt〕*n.* 娛樂　　assist〔əˋsɪst〕*v.* 協助
invaluable〔ɪnˋvæljəbḷ〕*adj.* 珍貴的

Quit	**Writing**

Imagine that you have received some land to use as you wish. How would you use this land? Use specific details to explain your answer.

Cut

Paste

Undo

149. Receiving Some Land

In this crowded city there are few resources more valuable than open land. As businesses continue to expand and more people move here in search of jobs, it becomes more difficult to find any space not occupied by a building of some kind. For most people, owning a traditional house with a garden is an impossible dream. ***Instead***, they live in high-rise apartment complexes. If I received a gift of land, I would build my dream house, but also open a portion of the land to those who wish to enjoy a garden but cannot afford their own.

My land would be divided into three sections. The first and smallest portion would contain my own house. Perhaps this is a bit selfish, but someone must reside there to oversee the activities on the rest of the land. The remaining land would be divided into two equal parts. The first would be devoted to gardens, but I would not design these gardens myself. ***Instead***, I would allow nearby residents or school groups to sign up for a small section and plant it with whatever they liked. This would allow many people to indulge in the hobby of gardening and preserve this disappearing art. We could even have annual floral and landscaping competitions. The final part of the land would be left in its natural state, for I feel that this is also a form of beauty worth preserving.

The above plan would allow a greater number of people to enjoy the piece of land that I received. It would also help to promote and preserve the art of gardening as well as keep people in contact with nature. ***For all of these reasons***, I believe that my plan would be a good use of the land.

149. 獲得一些土地

　　在這擁擠的都市裡，很少有資源會比空曠的土地更寶貴。因為商業不斷地擴張，且有更多人湧入求職，要找沒被某個建築物佔據的空間，是愈來愈困難了。對大部分的人而言，擁有一間有庭院的傳統房屋，是不可能實現的夢想。因此他們就退而求其次，住在高樓大廈裡。如果別人送我一塊土地的話，我會建造我夢寐以求的房屋，還會把土地的一部份，開放給希望能享受庭園樂趣，但卻負擔不起的人。

　　我的土地將分成三個區域。我的房子會建在第一區，也是最小的部分。也許這有點自私，但一定要有人住在那裡，才能監督到在其他區土地上所進行的活動。剩下的土地會分成兩個同樣大小的區域。第一區會用來蓋庭園，但是我不會自己設計，相反地，我會請附近的居民或學校團體認養一小塊，然後種他們自己喜歡的任何植物。這樣可以讓居民盡情享受園藝之樂，並保存這種日漸消失的技藝。我們甚至還可以每年舉行花藝與景觀設計的競賽。最後一塊土地將保持原始的風貌，因為我認為這也是一種值得保存的美感。

　　以上的規劃可以讓更多人享受我所獲贈的土地。這也可以協助提倡及保存園藝技術，還能讓人們接近大自然。基於以上的理由，我相信我的計畫是這塊土地最好的利用方式。

【註釋】

open〔'opən〕adj. 空曠的　　expand〔ɪk'spænd〕v. 擴充

in search of 尋找　　occupy〔'ɑkjə,paɪ〕v. 佔據

instead〔ɪn'stɛd〕adv. 取而代之　　high-rise〔'haɪ'raɪz〕adj. 高層建築的

complex〔'kɑmplɛks〕n. 複合式建築物　　portion〔'porʃən〕n. 部分

reside〔rɪ'zaɪd〕v. 居住　　oversee〔,ovɚ'si〕v. 監督

devote〔dɪ'vot〕v. 把…用於 < *to* >　　*sign up for* 經報名獲得

remaining〔rɪ'menɪŋ〕adj. 剩下的　　resident〔'rɛzədənt〕n. 居民

indulge〔ɪn'dʌldʒ〕v. 沉迷於　　gardening〔'gɑrdn̩ɪŋ〕n. 園藝

preserve〔prɪ'zɝv〕v. 保存　　annual〔'ænjuəl〕adj. 一年一度的

landscaping〔'lænd,skepɪŋ〕n. 景觀美化　　state〔stet〕n. 狀態

competition〔,kɑmpə'tɪʃən〕n. 比賽　　promote〔prə'mot〕v. 提倡

Quit

Writing

Do you agree or disagree with the following statement? Watching television is bad for children. Use specific details and examples to support your answer.

Cut

Paste

Undo

▲

▼

Time

Help
?

Confirm
Answer

Next
➡

150. The Effects of Television on Children

A debate is raging in America on the merits of television and its influence on children. 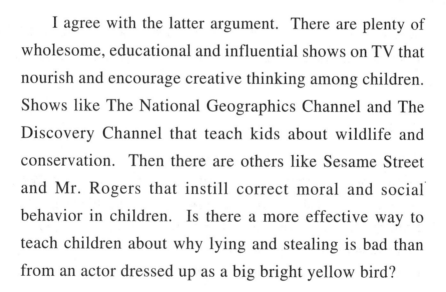 Critics contend that the violence being depicted on television is a primary cause for rising juvenile delinquents. Others say that it's the parents' responsibility, not the broadcasters to monitor what children are being exposed to on TV.

I agree with the latter argument. There are plenty of wholesome, educational and influential shows on TV that nourish and encourage creative thinking among children. Shows like The National Geographics Channel and The Discovery Channel that teach kids about wildlife and conservation. Then there are others like Sesame Street and Mr. Rogers that instill correct moral and social behavior in children. Is there a more effective way to teach children about why lying and stealing is bad than from an actor dressed up as a big bright yellow bird?

Although television these days is peppered with shows that are geared toward adults, there are plenty of other shows on TV that are healthy, fun and educational to children. It is the parent's responsibility to choose which ones are good for their kids and which ones are not.

150. 電視對兒童的影響

　　有關電視的價值及對兒童的影響,在美國所造成的爭論十分激烈。批評者強調說,電視上所呈現的暴力,是導致青少年犯罪增加的主要原因。有人則說,那是父母,而不是電視台的責任,要負責監督兒童觀看什麼樣的電視節目。

　　我同意後者的論點。有很多有益且具有教育性,也深具影響力的電視節目,支持並鼓勵兒童發展創造思考的能力。像是「國家地理頻道」與「發現頻道」,教育兒童關於野生動植物和保育的知識。還有其他的節目,例如「芝麻街」和「羅傑斯先生」,灌輸兒童正確的道德和社會行為。要讓兒童知道為什麼說謊和偷竊是不好的行為,有比從裝扮成鮮黃色大鳥的演員身上學到,更有效的方式嗎?

　　雖然現今的電視充滿了為了迎合成人喜好的節目,還是有很多其他電視節目,對兒童而言是健康的、有趣,而且富有教育性的。父母有責任選擇什麼樣的電視節目對自己的小孩有益,什麼樣的節目有害。

【註釋】

debate〔dɪˋbet〕*n.* 討論;辯論　　rage〔redʒ〕*v.* 激烈進行

merit〔ˋmɛrɪt〕*n.* 價值;優點　　critic〔ˋkrɪtɪk〕*n.* 批評家;評論家

contend〔kənˋtɛnd〕*v.* 堅決主張;聲稱　　depict〔dɪˋpɪkt〕*v.* 描述

primary〔ˋpraɪ͵mɛrɪ〕*adj.* 主要的　　rising〔ˋraɪzɪŋ〕*adj.* 上升的

juvenile delinquent 青少年罪犯

broadcaster〔ˋbrɔd͵kæstɚ〕*n.* 電視臺　　monitor〔ˋmɑnətɚ〕*v.* 監督

expose〔ɪkˋspoz〕*v.* 使接觸到 < *to* >

wholesome〔ˋholsəm〕*adj.* 有益的　　nourish〔ˋnɝɪʃ〕*v.* 培育;支持

wildlife〔ˋwaɪld͵laɪf〕*n.* 野生動植物

conservation〔͵kɑnsɚˋveʃən〕*n.* 保育

instill〔ɪnˋstɪl〕*v.* 灌輸 < *in* >　　moral〔ˋmɔrəl〕*adj.* 道德的

dress up as 裝扮成　　pepper〔ˋpɛpɚ〕*v.* 使佈滿 < *with* >

be geared toward 為了迎合…的喜好

Quit　　　　　　**Writing**

What is the most important animal in your country? Why is the animal important? Use reasons and specific details to explain your answer.

Cut

Paste

Undo

Time

Help
?

Confirm
Answer

Next
➡

151. The Most Important Animal in My Country

In some countries, the most important animal is a national symbol, *for example* the giant panda in China and the bald eagle in the United States. In others it is an endangered species such as the black rhino or Bengal tiger. My country also has symbolic animals that people consider important. For an endangered species we have the Taiwan black bear, and for an important symbol we might choose the mythical dragon. It not only represents good luck and fortune, but is also associated with water, something which is very important to people living on an island. Although these are both good choices, I do not think either of them is the most important animal in my country. *Rather*, I advocate a much more lowly animal, the pig, as the most significant to my country because it is not just a positive symbol, but also very useful.

The main reason that I choose the pig is that, *in my opinion*, the country's most valued animal does not need to be graceful or cuddly, but rather beneficial to the average person. To my mind, utility is more important than symbolism, and the pig is a very useful animal. *First of all*, pig farming is still an important industry in Taiwan.

Although we are now a highly developed and modern society, our agricultural roots are still important, and farming is a vital source of livelihood for many people in the countryside. *Second*, pork is one of the most popular foods in my country. It is important in traditional Chinese cooking and is a relatively inexpensive source of nutrition.

Although the pig is important primarily as a source of food, it also has some symbolic value. While it is regarded by many people as a dirty and stupid animal, the pig is far from unintelligent. *On the contrary*, it is quite clever. *In addition*, the pig is an important symbol in the Chinese zodiac. People born in the year of the pig are likely to be happy and lucky with money. *Thus*, it is a positive symbol in my country.

Considering all of these factors, I believe the pig is a logical and honorable choice for the most important animal in my country. It may not be as majestic as the American bald eagle or as lovable as the Australian koala, but considering its utility, cleverness and status as a representative of happiness and fortune, it is, *all in all*, a good choice.

151. 我國最重要的動物

　　在有些國家，最重要的動物就是該國的象徵，如中國的熊貓與美國的白頭鷹。在其他國家，就是瀕臨絕種的動物，如黑犀牛或孟加拉虎。我國也有大家認為很重要，具有象徵性的動物。以瀕臨絕種的動物而言，我們有台灣黑熊，但如果要選國家重要的象徵，我們也許會選擇神話故事中的龍，龍不僅是好運與財富的象徵，而且還跟水有關，這對住在島嶼上的人來說，是相當重要的。儘管這兩個都是不錯的選擇，我卻不認為牠們是我國最重要的動物。相反地，我會支持較卑賤的動物「豬」，作為我國最具代表性的動物，因為牠不僅有正面的象徵意義，還非常具有實用價值。

　　對我而言，我會選擇豬的主要理由是，全國最有價值的動物，不需要很優雅或很可愛，而應該是對一般人都很有用處的。在我的心目中，實用性比象徵意義更重要，而豬就是一種很有用的動物。首先，養豬在台灣仍是一項很重要的產業，雖然我們已經是個高度發展的現代化社會，農業的根基仍是非常重要的，而且在鄉下，農作仍是很多人賴以維生的主要方式。第二，豬肉是我國最普遍的食物之一，在傳統的中式料理中，是很重要而且較便宜的營養來源。

　　雖然豬的重要性，主要是在於食用價值，牠還是有其象徵意義上的價值。儘管很多人認為豬是一種既髒又笨的動物，但豬其實一點也不笨，相反地，牠們還相當聰明。而且，豬在中國十二生肖中，也是很重要的，生肖屬豬的人，比較有福氣與偏財運，因此豬在我國是個具有正面意義的象徵。

　　考慮到這些所有的因素後，我相信選豬作為我國最重要的動物，是合理而光榮的選擇。牠也許不像美國的白頭鷹一樣威嚴，或像澳洲無尾熊那樣可愛，但考慮到牠的實用性、聰明，以及具有代表福氣跟財富地位後。總之，豬絕對是個很好的選擇。

【註釋】

giant〔'dʒaɪənt〕*adj.* 巨大的　　panda〔'pændə〕*n.* 熊貓

giant panda 大熊貓（= *panda* ）　　***bald eagle*** 白頭鷹

endangered species 瀕臨絕種的動植物

rhino〔'raɪno〕*n.* 犀牛（= rhinoceros〔raɪ'nɑsərəs〕）

Bengal〔bɛŋ'gɔl〕*n.* 孟加拉　　mythical〔'mɪθɪkḷ〕*adj.* 神話的

dragon〔'drægən〕*n.* 龍　　associate〔ə'soʃɪˌet〕*v.* 聯想 < *with* >

rather〔'ræðɚ〕*adv.* 相反地

advocate〔'ædvəˌket〕*v.* 主張；擁護　　lowly〔'lolɪ〕*adj.* 卑微的

significant〔sɪg'nɪfəkənt〕*adj.* 重要的；意義重大的

positive〔'pɑzətɪv〕*adj.* 正面的　　valued〔'væljʊd〕*adj.* 有價值的

graceful〔'gresfəl〕*adj.* 優雅的　　cuddly〔'kʌdlɪ〕*adj.* 可愛的

beneficial〔ˌbɛnə'fɪʃəl〕*adj.* 有益的

average〔'ævərɪdʒ〕*adj.* 一般的　　utility〔ju'tɪlətɪ〕*n.* 實用

to one's mind 依某人之見

symbolism〔'sɪmbḷˌɪzəm〕*n.* 象徵意義；象徵性

first of all 首先　　farming〔'fɑrmɪŋ〕*n.* 養殖業；農業

roots〔ruts〕*n.pl.* 根源　　vital〔'vaɪtḷ〕*adj.* 非常重要的

livelihood〔'laɪvlɪˌhʊd〕*n.* 生計

relatively〔'rɛlətɪvlɪ〕*adv.* 比較上　　nutrition〔nju'trɪʃən〕*n.* 營養

primarily〔'praɪˌmɛrəlɪ〕*adv.* 主要地　　***be regarded as*** 被視為

far from 一點也不　　***on the contrary*** 相反地

zodiac〔'zodɪˌæk〕*n.* 黃道十二宮　　***Chinese zodiac*** 中國十二生肖

considering〔kən'sɪdərɪŋ〕*prep.* 考慮到；就⋯而論（= *given* ）

logical〔'lɑdʒɪkḷ〕*adj.* 合理的　　honorable〔'ɑnərəbḷ〕*adj.* 光榮的

majestic〔mə'dʒɛstɪk〕*adj.* 有威嚴的

lovable〔'lʌvəbḷ〕*adj.* 可愛的　　koala〔kə'ɑlə〕*n.* 無尾熊

status〔'stetəs〕*n.* 地位

representative〔ˌrɛprɪ'zɛntətɪv〕*n.* 代表　　***all in all*** 總之

Quit   **Writing**

Many parts of the world are losing important natural resources such as forests, animals, or clean water. Choose **one** resource that is disappearing and explain why it needs to be saved. Use specific reasons and examples to support your opinion.

▲

Cut

Paste

Undo

▼

152. Save the Forests

These days we often hear about the importance of our natural resources. In many countries they are disappearing at a rapid rate and environmentalists are urging people everywhere to protect their air, water, forests, wildlife, and so on. It is difficult to choose just one natural resource to save, but *in my opinion*, saving the forests should be the top priority.

First of all, forests help to preserve other natural resources such as water, air, and animals. Without forests, the land cannot hold water as well. This means that in a heavy rain hillsides will collapse, causing great damage. Not only that, but without the protection of trees, the nutrient-rich topsoil will be washed away and nothing will be able to grow on the land. Trees also help to clean the air by absorbing carbon dioxide and producing oxygen. *And*, of course, forests are the natural habitat of many wild animals. Without them, these animals will not be able to survive. *Another* reason to preserve our forests is that large numbers of trees can help to mitigate the greenhouse effect by absorbing solar radiation. *And finally*, forests are a place where people can get close to nature, and if they learn to love nature, they will want to preserve all the earth's natural resources.

All of the earth's natural resources are important, and we should all work to save them. The reason that I choose the forests as the most important is because they help us in so many ways. By saving the forests, I believe we can save the planet.

152. 拯救森林

現在我們經常聽到天然資源的重要性。在許多國家,天然資源正在快速消失中,環保人士向全世界的人呼籲,要保護空氣、水、森林、野生動植物等資源。要只選一樣資源加以保護,是很困難的,但依我之見,應該要優先考量拯救森林的事。

首先,森林有助於保存其他的天然資源,像是水、空氣,以及動物。若沒有森林,土壤就無法涵養水份,這意謂著下大雨的時候,山坡會崩塌,造成極大的損害。不僅如此,如果沒有樹木的保護,富含養份的表土層就會被沖刷掉,土地就長不出任何東西。樹木還會吸收二氧化碳,製造氧氣,有助於淨化空氣。而且森林當然是很多野生動物的自然棲息地,若沒有森林,這些動物將無法生存。另外一個要保存森林的理由是,大量的樹木可以吸收太陽幅射,緩和溫室效應的影響。最後一點,森林是人類可以接近大自然的地方,如果人類學會愛護大自然,就會想保存地球上所有的天然資源。

地球上所有的天然資源都很重要,我們應該共同努力去拯救它們。我會選擇森林為最重要的資源,是因為森林在很多方面都對我們有益。藉由拯救森林,我相信我們也能夠拯救地球。

【註釋】

forest〔ˈfɔrɪst〕n. 森林　　　*these days* 最近
natural resources 天然資源
environmentalist〔ɪn͵vaɪrənˈmɛntl̩ɪst〕n. 環境保護論者
urge〔ɝdʒ〕v. 呼籲　　wildlife〔ˈwaɪld͵laɪf〕n. 野生動植物
top priority 最優先考慮的事　　preserve〔prɪˈzɝv〕v. 保存
hillside〔ˈhɪl͵saɪd〕n. 山坡　　collapse〔kəˈlæps〕v. 崩塌
nutrient〔ˈnjutrɪənt〕n. 養分　　topsoil〔ˈtɑp͵sɔɪl〕n. 表土(層)
wash away 沖掉　　absorb〔əbˈsɔrb〕v. 吸收
carbon dioxide 二氧化碳　　oxygen〔ˈɑksədʒən〕n. 氧氣
habitat〔ˈhæbə͵tæt〕n. 棲息地　　survive〔səˈvaɪv〕v. 生存
mitigate〔ˈmɪtə͵get〕v. 緩和　　*the greenhouse effect* 溫室效應
solar〔ˈsolɚ〕adj. 太陽的　　radiation〔͵redɪˈeʃən〕n. 幅射
the planet 地球 (= *the Earth*)

Quit	**Writing**

Do you agree or disagree with the following statement?　A zoo has no useful purpose.　Use specific reasons and examples to explain your answer.

Cut

Paste

Undo

153. The Value of Zoos

It has been said that zoos no longer serve a useful purpose. I believe this statement may be based on the fact that we can now learn about animals in other ways, such as through television documentaries, books, and even travel to the animals' natural habitats. Others say that zoos are artificial environments that do the animals more harm than good. *In my opinion*, these arguments do have some merit but do not outweigh the advantages of zoos as centers for education and conservation.

The primary purpose of a zoo is to educate. It provides people with an opportunity to see live animals at close quarters. *Furthermore*, these are animals that most people would never see otherwise. They may be from areas that are far away or inaccessible. *Moreover*, they may be rare and difficult to see in the wild. While books and videos can provide people with information about such animals, nothing can equal the effect of seeing a live animal. Allowing people to see live animals, especially rare ones, can also help the zoo achieve another important goal — to promote conservation. People who feel a connection with animals are more likely to support programs to protect natural habitats and outlaw hunting. *In addition*, the zoo can take an active role by providing rare animals with a protected environment and working to increase their numbers.

In conclusion, there is no doubt in my mind that zoos still serve a vital function in today's society. They not only educate and conserve, but also allow people to experience a connection with animals. *And* it is this connection that may be the greatest benefit to both people and animals.

153. 動物園的重要

　　有人說動物園再也沒有用了，我想這種說法可能是因為，我們現在可以利用其他的方式來認識動物，例如經由電視上的紀錄片、書籍，甚至是前往動物天然的棲息地。還有人說，動物園是人造的環境，對動物們是弊多於利。依我之見，這些論點雖然的確有其價值，但仍比不上動物園可做為教育及保育中心的優點。

　　動物園的主要目的在於教育，讓人有機會近距離看到那些活生生的動物。而且，如果沒有動物園，大部分的人可能就看不到這些動物，牠們也許是來自很遙遠，或甚至無法到達的地方。此外，牠們或許很稀有，在野外很難看到。雖然書籍和錄影帶能提供我們，有關這些動物的資訊，但效果都比不上親眼目睹活生生的動物。讓人們能夠看到活生生的動物，尤其是稀有動物，也能幫助動物園達成另一項重要的目標——提倡保育。人們如果和動物們有感情，就更可能會支持那些保護天然棲息地和禁獵的計畫。此外，動物園可以提供稀有動物一個受到保護的環境，並且努力增加牠們的數量。

　　總之，我認為，動物園在現今社會中，無疑地仍具有非常重要的功能。它們不僅教育人們、保育動物，而且讓人們能夠感受到與動物之間的關連，而這樣的關連，可能對人類和動物而言，都是最大的好處。

【註釋】

serve〔sɝv〕v. 符合　　documentary〔͵dɑkjə'mɛntərɪ〕n. 紀錄片
travel〔'trævl̩〕v. 行進　　habitat〔'hæbə͵tæt〕n. 棲息地
artificial〔͵ɑrtə'fɪʃəl〕adj. 人造的
argument〔'ɑrgjəmənt〕n. 論點　　merit〔'mɛrɪt〕n. 價值；優點
outweigh〔aʊt'we〕v. 超越　　conservation〔͵kɑnsɚ'veʃən〕n. 保育
primary〔'praɪ͵mɛrɪ〕adj. 主要的
live〔laɪv〕adj. 活的　　*at close quarters* 非常接近
otherwise〔'ʌðɚ͵waɪz〕adv. 不那樣
inaccessible〔͵ɪnək'sɛsəbl̩〕adj. 無法到達的
rare〔rɛr〕adj. 稀有的　　*in the wild* 在野外
video〔'vɪdɪo〕n. 錄影帶　　equal〔'ikwəl〕v. 比得上
promote〔prə'mot〕v. 提倡　　program〔'progræm〕n. 計劃
connection〔kə'nɛkʃən〕n. 關係　　outlaw〔'aʊt͵lɔ〕v. 禁止
active〔'æktɪv〕adj. 積極的　　*in one's mind* 在某人看來
vital〔'vaɪtl̩〕adj. 非常重要的

Quit　　　**Writing**

In some countries, people are no longer allowed to smoke in many public places and office buildings. Do you think this is a good rule or a bad rule? Use specific reasons and details to support your position.

Cut

Paste

Undo

Time

Help ? 　Confirm Answer 　Next →

154. Smoking in Public Places

In recent years people's attitudes toward cigarette smoking have greatly changed. What was once seen as a sign of sophistication is now more likely to be looked down upon as a dirty habit. Some countries have gone so far as to ban smoking in many public places and office buildings. Although some people say that this limitation is a violation of their rights, the measure has received widespread support among non-smokers. *In my opinion*, it is a good rule for the following reasons.

The first and most important reason is that while limits on smoking restrict the rights of smokers, smoking itself impinges upon the rights of non-smokers. In a free society, we all have the right to engage in the activities we wish as long as we do not harm others. Studies have shown that second-hand smoke can have a detrimental effect on the health of non-smokers, so I agree that this is one activity which should be restricted. *Second*, aside from the long-term health effects of second-hand smoke, it can have very serious immediate consequences for those who are allergic to it.

In a public place we cannot know who may be allergic to our smoke so, for safety's sake, it is better not to smoke around others without their permission. ***Third***, the ashes and cigarette butts left behind by smokers are another form of pollution. They dirty our environment and, as taxpayers, we must all pay for the cleanup of our public places.

For all of the reasons above, I support the decision of some countries to ban smoking in public places and office buildings. Although it affects the right of smokers to enjoy their cigarettes where and when they wish, it is a decision for the greater good of society. We would all like to enjoy the right to do whatever we wish, but as members of a communal society we must recognize that our absolute rights end where they begin to impinge upon the rights of others.

154. 在公共場所吸煙

　　近年來，人們對抽煙的態度已經改變很多。抽煙曾被視爲是成熟的象徵，但現在可能已被貶爲不良的習慣。有些國家甚至在很多公共場所及辦公大樓禁煙。儘管有人說，這項限制違反了他們的權利，但此項措施已受到非吸煙者廣泛的支持。依我之見，基於下列理由，這是一項很好的規定。

　　第一個，而且是最重要的理由爲，雖然管制抽煙限制了吸煙者的權利，但抽煙本身危害了非吸煙者的權利。在自由社會裡，我們全都有權從事我們想參與的活動，只要在不傷害到別人的前提之下。研究顯示，二手煙對非吸煙者的健康有害，所以我同意這項行爲應受到限制。第二，除了二手煙對健康會造成長期的影響外，對於厭惡煙味的人而言，二手煙會造成立即性的嚴重後果。在公共場所，我們不知道有誰討厭煙味，所以爲了安全起見，在未經他人許可下，最好不要抽煙。第三，吸煙者留下的煙灰和煙蒂，是另一種形式的污染，它們會造成環境的髒亂，而且身爲納稅人，我們必須支付公共場所的清潔費用。

　　基於上述的理由，我支持有些國家的做法，禁止在公共場所及辦公大樓抽煙。雖然這會影響到吸煙者的權利，無法隨時隨地盡情吸煙，但對社會而言，卻是有利的決定。我們全都想要擁有做任何事情的權利，但身爲社會的一份子，我們必須了解，我們不受任何約束的權利，仍須以不侵害他人的權利爲限。

【註釋】

sophistication〔sə,fɪstɪ'keʃən〕n. 世俗；成熟
look down upon 輕視　　*go so far as to* + V. 甚至
measure〔'mɛʒɚ〕n. 措施　　ban〔bæn〕v. 禁止
violation〔,vaɪə'leʃən〕n. 違反　　restrict〔rɪ'strɪkt〕v. 限制
right〔raɪt〕n. 權利　　impinge〔ɪm'pɪndʒ〕v. 侵犯 < *upon* >
engage in 從事　　*second-hand smoke* 二手煙
detrimental〔,dɛtrə'mɛntḷ〕adj. 有害的　　*aside from* 除了～之外
consequence〔'kɑnsə,kwɛns〕n. 後果
allergic〔ə'lɝdʒɪk〕adj. 過敏的；對…極爲討厭的 < *to* >
for safety's sake 爲了安全起見　　permission〔pə'mɪʃən〕n. 許可
ash〔æʃ〕n. 灰　　butt〔bʌt〕n. 煙蒂　　*leave behind* 留下
dirty〔'dɝtɪ〕v. 弄髒　　communal〔kə'mjunḷ〕adj. 社會的；公有的
taxpayer〔'tæks,peɚ〕n. 納稅人
absolute〔'æbsə,lut〕adj. 不受任何約束的

Quit · **Writing**

Plants can provide food, shelter, clothing, or medicine. What is one kind of plant that is important to you or the people in your country? Use specific reasons and details to explain your choice.

Cut

Paste

Undo

155. An Important Plant

My country has a variety of plant life, including food crops such as rice and vegetables, wild plants such as the forests that protect our mountains, plants raised for their beauty, *for example*, flowers, and plants cultivated for their medicinal properties. All of these plants are important to us and to the balance of the ecosystem, but if I had to choose just one, I would choose tea.

One reason that I think tea is important to the people of my country is that it is an important crop. My country is well-known for its tea and we export great quantities of it every year. It is very important to our economy. *Another* reason that I think it is important is that different kinds of tea have different properties, some of which are very good for our health. *But* perhaps the most important reason that tea is so important to my people is that it is a significant part of our culture. Many people drink tea every day. We not only drink the tea but talk over tea. *Furthermore*, tea is important in many of our traditions and in our history.

The above reasons are why I choose tea as the most important plant to the people in my country. It plays a big part in our lives today and has done so throughout history. Nothing can replace tea in my country and that is why it is so important to us.

155. 一種重要的植物

　　我國有各式各樣的植物，其中有如稻米與蔬菜的糧食作物，也有野生的植物，如保護群山的樹林，也有供欣賞用而種植的植物，如花卉，還有些是因為有醫療價值而栽種的植物。這些植物對我們以及生態環境的平衡都很重要，但如果我只能選一種植物的話，我會選擇茶。

　　我認為茶對我國人民很重要的原因是，它是一種很重要的農作物。我國因為茶葉而聞名，每年我們都出口大量的茶葉，這對我們的經濟是非常重要的。另一個我認為它很重要的理由是，不同種類的茶葉，會有不同的特性，有些對我們的健康相當有益處。但茶葉對國人會那麼重要，其原因可能在於，它是我國文化中，非常重要的一部分。很多人每天都會喝茶。我們不只喝茶，還會邊喝茶，邊談話。而且，茶在我們許多的傳統與歷史中，都是非常重要的。

　　以上就是我將茶選為我國最重要的植物的理由。它在我們現在的生活中，扮演了十分重要的角色，而且自古以來也一直是如此。沒有東西可以取代茶葉在我國的地位，這就是為什麼，茶對我們而言是如此地重要。

【註釋】

a variety of 各種不同的 (= various (ˈvɛrɪəs))
plant life （全部）植物　　crop (krɑp) *n.* 農作物
rice (raɪs) *n.* 稻米　　wild (waɪld) *adj.* 野生的
raise (rez) *v.* 種植　　cultivate (ˈkʌltəˌvet) *v.* 栽培
medicinal (məˈdɪsən̩) *adj.* 藥物的　　property (ˈprɑpɚtɪ) *n.* 特性
balance (ˈbæləns) *n.* 平衡　　ecosystem (ˈikoˌsɪstəm) *n.* 生態系統
well-known (ˈwɛlˈnon) *adj.* 有名的　　export (ɪksˈport) *v.* 出口
quantity (ˈkwɑntətɪ) *n.* 數量　　economy (ɪˈkɑnəmɪ) *n.* 經濟
significant (sɪgˈnɪfəkənt) *adj.* 重要的　　*talk over tea* 邊喝茶邊談話
furthermore (ˈfɝðɚˌmor) *adv.* 此外　　big (bɪg) *adj.* 重要的
play a ~ part in 在…扮演～角色　　*throughout history* 自古以來
replace (rɪˈples) *v.* 取代 (= *take the place of*)

Quit　　　**Writing**

You have the opportunity to visit a foreign country for two weeks. Which country would you like to visit?　Use specific reasons and details to explain your choice.

Cut

Paste

Undo

156. Visiting a Foreign Country

Traveling to foreign countries gives us an opportunity to experience another culture and broaden our horizons. We can learn a great deal about the world and about ourselves through travel. Given the opportunity to visit another country, I would choose to go to mainland China. Although it is not far from my own country, there are several reasons I want to see it.

First of all, China has a long cultural history and, as I'm Chinese, this is especially relevant to me. Seeing important historical sights such as the Great Wall, Forbidden City and the terracotta soldiers of Xian would help me to better understand my own history and culture. *Second*, China is a country that is undergoing rapid development. Cities such as Shanghai and Guangzhou are modern and growing fast. I think I could learn a lot from the advances the Chinese have made in China. *Last but not least*, mainland China offers great natural beauty to the visitor. Being such a large country, it has a variety of climates and topography. I would like to see the beautiful mountains and coast, as well as the deserts and great grasslands that cannot be found in my own country.

To sum up, I believe that mainland China has a great deal to offer a visitor. It has both cultural and historical relics as well as vibrant, modern cities. I would enjoy seeing not only the historical sights, but also the way of life in this rapidly changing country. *Therefore*, the foreign country that I would choose to visit first is mainland China.

156. 出　國

　　到國外旅行，讓我們有機會體驗不同的文化，並拓展我們的眼界。透過旅行，我們能多了解世界和自己。如果有機會到國外，我會選擇去中國大陸。雖然中國大陸離我國不遠，但還是有一些理由讓我想去那裡看看。

　　首先，中國大陸是個擁有悠久文化與歷史的國家，因此對身為中國人的我而言，覺得關係特別密切。去看重要的歷史古蹟，如萬里長城、紫禁城與西安的兵馬俑，能讓我更加了解自己的歷史與文化。第二，中國大陸現在正處於快速發展的時刻。有些都市，如上海與廣州，都已相當現代化，而且成長快速，我想我可以從中國大陸人民的進步中，學到很多東西。最後一項要點是，中國大陸有很多壯麗的自然美景，可供觀光客欣賞。因為中國大陸的幅員遼闊，所以有各種不同的氣候與地形。我想去看我國所沒有的景色，如美麗的高山與海岸，以及沙漠與大草原。

　　總之，我相信中國大陸有很多值得遊歷的地方，有歷史文化悠久的遺跡，也有充滿生機的現代化都市。我不只想欣賞歷史古蹟，也想看看在快速變遷的國家中，人們的生活方式。因此，中國大陸會是我出國旅遊第一個想去的國家。

【註釋】

foreign〔'fɔrɪn〕*adj.* 國外的

horizons〔hə'raɪzn̩z〕*n.pl.* 知識範圍；眼界

given〔'gɪvən〕*prep.* 如果有　　*mainland China* 中國大陸

first of all 首先　　relevant〔'rɛləvənt〕*adj.* 有關的< *to* >

historical sights 歷史古蹟　　*the Great Wall* 萬里長城

forbidden〔fɚ'bɪdn̩〕*adj.* 被禁止的

terracotta〔'tɛrə'katə〕*adj.* 陶土製的　　undergo〔ˌʌndɚ'go〕*v.* 經歷

advance〔əd'væns〕*n.* 進步　　*last but not least* 最後一項要點是

a variety of 各式各樣的　　topography〔to'pagrəfɪ〕*n.* 地形

desert〔'dɛzɚt〕*n.* 沙漠　　grassland〔'græsˌlænd〕*n.* 草原

to sum up 總之　　relics〔'rɛlɪks〕*n.pl.* 遺跡

vibrant〔'vaɪbrənt〕*adj.* 充滿活力的

Writing

Quit

In the future, students may have the choice of studying at home by using technology such as computers or television or of studying at traditional schools. Which would you prefer? Use reasons and specific details to explain your choice.

_____

_____

_____

_____

_____

_____

_____

_____

_____

_____

_____

_____

_____

_____

_____

_____

_____

_____

_____

_____

Cut

Paste

Undo

157. The Advantages of Studying at Traditional Schools

In recent years the way that we learn has been greatly affected by modern technology. *For example*,   it is now possible to get a wider range of information more quickly by using computers. It is possible that in the future students will not have to attend school at all. They will be able to study at home using computers or televisions. Many students may prefer this, but I would still prefer to attend classes in a traditional school.

One important reason for my preference is that we learn more in school than just our academic subjects. We also learn how to work with other people, and this is one skill that I think is very difficult to develop by means of a computer course. *Another* reason is that I enjoy the social environment of the school. I have made many good friends at my school and do not think these relationships could be replaced by faceless communication via a computer. *Finally*, going to school forces me to be more disciplined than studying at home. I fear that if I have to control my own time at home, I may study inefficiently.

For all of the above reasons, I prefer attending traditional school classes to taking courses through the computer at home. *Therefore*, although I appreciate all the benefits that modern technology brings to students, I would use it to assist me in my studies rather than depend on it for my entire education.

157. 就讀傳統學校的優點

近幾年來，我們的學習方式，大大地受到現代科技的影響。例如，現在我們可以藉由使用電腦，更快速地取得更廣泛的資訊。在未來，學生可能根本就不必去學校上學了，他們可以使用電腦或電視，在家學習。許多學生也許比較喜歡這樣，但我寧願到傳統的學校上課。

我會這樣選擇，一個很重要的理由是，我們在學校所學的，不只是學科而已，我們也學習，如何與他人合作，而這個技巧，我認為是很難藉由電腦培養的。另一個理由是，我喜歡學校裏的社交環境。我在學校交了很多好朋友，而且我認為我們的友誼，是不能被無法面對面溝通的電腦取代的。最後，去學校上學比在家讀書，更能強迫我守規矩。我怕我如果在家自行安排時間，讀書可能沒有效率。

基於以上的理由，我寧願到傳統的學校上學，也不願在家裏利用電腦上課。因此，雖然我也很欣賞現代科技帶給學生的種種優點，我寧願用電腦來輔助學習，而不是依賴它來完成所有的教育。

【註釋】

traditional (trə'dɪʃənḷ) adj. 傳統的　　range (rendʒ) n. 範圍
preference ('prɛfərəns) n. 偏愛；優先選擇
academic (ˌækə'dɛmɪk) adj. 學術的
relationship (rɪ'leʃənˌʃɪp) n. 關係　　replace (rɪ'ples) v. 取代
faceless ('feslɪs) adj. 看不見臉的
via ('vaɪə) prep. 藉由 (= by means of)　　force (fors) v. 強迫
disciplined ('dɪsəplɪnd) adj. 遵守紀律的
inefficiently (ˌɪnə'fɪʃəntlɪ) adv. 沒有效率地
take courses 選讀課程　　appreciate (ə'priʃɪˌet) v. 欣賞
benefit ('bɛnəfɪt) n. 利益；優點　　assist (ə'sɪst) v. 協助
entire (ɪn'taɪr) adj. 全部的

Quit　　　　　**Writing**

When famous people such as actors, athletes and rock stars give their opinions, many people listen.　Do you think we should pay attention to these opinions?　Use specific reasons and examples to support your answer.

Cut

Paste

Undo

▲

▼

158. Should We Pay Attention to the Opinions of Famous People?

Famous people, such as athletes, actors, and other entertainers, are often interviewed by the press. They not only answer questions about their careers and personal lives, but also often give their opinions on issues of the day. The public tends to give more consideration to the views of the famous than it does to the opinions of more ordinary people. Should we give greater weight to these opinions? *In my opinion*, we should not, for the following reasons.

First, famous people are not necessarily well informed about the issues under discussion. While everyone has a right to express his opinion, a willingness to speak does not imply knowledge. *Furthermore*, a famous person may be an authority in his field, but that does not mean he is also an expert in others. *For example*, an actor who plays a doctor on TV is probably not a true authority on medical matters.

Second, a famous person may not be impartial. *Rather*, he may have financial or other motives for the opinions he espouses. This is particularly true when some type of product endorsement is involved. A good example of this would be an entertainer who proclaims the benefits of a certain product when he has, *in fact*, never even tried it.

Third, a reliance on the opinions of famous people may prevent us from thinking for ourselves. We should all develop the ability to evaluate facts and reach our own conclusions. While there is no harm in listening to the opinions of others, we must realize that our situations are often very different. What may be true or beneficial for one person, may not be so for another. This is especially true in the case of famous people who, due to their wealth and fame, live in circumstances that are very different from those of ordinary people.

To sum up, we would be better off learning to evaluate situations and reach our own conclusions than relying on the opinions of others, no matter how well-known. Listening to the views of other people is a good way to gather information and come to our own decisions. *However*, we should not accept the opinions of others blindly. *Instead*, we must consider their knowledge and motivation. Famous people have the power to draw attention to a certain message that might not otherwise be heard, but we must still determine the validity of the message for ourselves.

158. 我們是否應該注意名人的意見？

　　像運動員、演員以及其他的藝人，這樣的名人常會有媒體訪問他們。這些名人不僅會回答有關他們的工作，以及個人生活的問題，通常還會對時下的一些議題，提出自己的看法。民衆對名人的意見，會比一般人所提的意見，更加認眞的思考。我們是否應該比較重視名人的意見呢？就我的觀點而言，大可不必如此，以下就是我的理由。

　　首先，名人不見得會對所討論的議題有充分的了解。儘管每個人都有表達意見的權利，但有表達的意願，不代表就具備知識。此外，這位名人也許在他的專業領域是個權威，但這不表示，他在其他領域也是專家。舉個例子，一個在電視上扮演醫生的演員，在醫學領域內，可能就不是個眞正的權威。

　　第二，名人不見得會保持公正。相反地，他可能因爲金錢或其他動機，而擁護某種意見，這一點特別適用於對某種產品的背書保證上。藝人可能從來沒用過某種產品，卻宣稱使用之後好處很多，這就是一個很好的例子。

　　第三，依賴名人的意見可能會使我們無法獨立思考。我們應該培養能自己評估事實，並得出結論的能力。雖然聽別人的意見沒有什麼壞處，但我們必須了解，每個人的情況通常都不盡相同。對某人而言是正確的或有利的，不見得就適用於其他人，這點在名人的身上尤其貼切，因爲他們擁有一般人所沒有的財富與名聲，其生活環境更是和一般人大不相同。

　　總之，我們最好要學會如何評估情況，並得到自己的結論，而不是只依賴別人的意見，不論那個人多有名。聽取別人的意見是獲取資訊，與做出決定一個很好的方法，但我們不應該盲目地接受別人的意見。相反地，我們必須考量他們的知識與動機。名人有能力，可以吸引人們注意原本不會被注意的訊息。但我們仍必須自己評斷這些訊息是否確實。

【註釋】

athlete〔'æθlɪt〕*n.* 運動員

entertainer〔ˌɛntɚ'tenɚ〕*n.* 藝人   interview〔'ɪntɚˌvju〕*v.* 採訪

the press 新聞界   issue〔'ɪʃju〕*n.* 議題

of the day 當時的   consideration〔kənˌsɪdə'reʃən〕*n.* 考慮

weight〔wet〕*n.* 重要性   ***not necessarily*** 未必

informed〔ɪn'fɔrmd〕*adj.* 消息靈通的

under discussion 討論中的   willingness〔'wɪlɪŋnɪs〕*n.* 樂意

imply〔ɪm'plaɪ〕*v.* 暗示；意味著

furthermore〔'fɝðɚˌmor〕*adv.* 此外

authority〔ə'θɔrətɪ〕*n.* 權威；專家

field〔fild〕*n.* 領域   matter〔'mætɚ〕*n.* 事情

impartial〔ɪm'parʃəl〕*adj.* 公正的   rather〔'ræðɚ〕*adv.* 相反地

financial〔faɪ'nænʃəl〕*adj.* 財務的   motive〔'motɪv〕*n.* 動機

espouse〔ɪ'spauz〕*v.* 擁護

endorsement〔ɪn'dɔrsmənt〕*n.* 背書；保證

involve〔ɪn'valv〕*v.* 牽涉   proclaim〔pro'klem〕*v.* 宣稱

benefit〔'bɛnəfɪt〕*n.* 優點   reliance〔rɪ'laɪəns〕*n.* 信賴 < *on* >

prevent sb. ***from*** + ***V-ing*** 使某人無法～

evaluate〔ɪ'væljəˌet〕*v.* 評估   ***reach a conclusion*** 下結論

beneficial〔ˌbɛnə'fɪʃəl〕*adj.* 有益的

circumstances〔'sɝkəmˌstænsɪz〕*n. pl.* 環境

to sum up 總之   ***be better off*** 情況較佳

motivation〔ˌmotə'veʃən〕*n.* 動機

otherwise〔'ʌðɚˌwaɪz〕*adv.* 否則

determine〔dɪ'tɝmɪn〕*v.* 決定   validity〔və'lɪdətɪ〕*n.* 確實性

Quit   Writing

The twentieth century saw great change. In your opinion, what is **one** change that should be remembered about the twentieth century? Use specific reasons and details to explain your choice.

Cut

Paste

Undo

Time

Help ?

Confirm Answer

Next →

159. The Most Important Change of the 20th Century

There were a great many changes in the twentieth century. They affected everything from the political composition of the world to how long we can expect to live. *As a result*, our lives are very different from those of our great-grandparents. It is difficult to say which of these great changes should be remembered most but, *in my opinion*, the invention of the computer is a good candidate, for it has affected our lives in so many ways.

One effect of the computer has been its impact on communication. Thanks to the Internet and computer-controlled satellites, it is now quick and cost-effective to communicate over great distances. This has made the world smaller and has had a great influence on business, leading to greater productivity worldwide. *Another* great effect of the computer is that it has changed the way we live our daily lives. It has made it a simple task to find and manage information and has brought us countless conveniences. Most of us deal with computers in one way or another every day. *Finally*, the development of computer technology has made possible a host of other scientific advances. Computers are used to save lives in hospitals, find new sources of energy under the sea and explore outer space. There seems to be no end to what computers can help us do.

In short, the computer has had such a great impact on so many areas of our lives that I feel its invention was the most memorable change of the twentieth century. No other product or event has affected so many people. Its influence is felt around the world and will only continue to grow in the future.

159. 二十世紀最重要的改變

　　二十世紀有很多重要的變革。這些變革的影響層面很廣泛，從政治結構到人類平均壽命的長短。因此，我們與上上代的生活有極大的差異。很難說有哪些重大的變革是應該被牢記的，但就我而言，電腦的發明是個不錯的選擇，因為它在很多方面都影響了我們的生活。

　　電腦影響的其中一個層面，就是對通訊的衝擊。由於網際網路與電腦控制衛星的出現，現在遠距離的通訊，已經非常快速而且划算，這使得世界變得更小，而且對商業有很大的影響，也讓全球的生產力增加了。電腦的另一個影響是，它改變了我們的日常生活方式。電腦讓資訊尋找及管理，成為簡單的事情，這帶給我們非常多的便利。我們大部份的人，每天或多或少都會使用到電腦。最後，電腦科技的發展，造就了許多其他科學上的進步。電腦被用來救活醫院裡的病人、尋找海底的新能源，以及探索外太空。電腦的助益似乎是多到數不清。

　　總之，電腦對我們生活的許多層面，都造成了很大的影響，因此我認為這項發明是二十世紀最值得紀念的變革。沒有其他產品或事件，曾影響這麼多人。它的影響力在世界各地都可以感受得到，而且在未來還會持續不斷增強。

【註釋】

century〔'sɛntʃərɪ〕 *n.* 世紀　　***a great many*** 許多的 (= *many*)

composition〔ˌkɑmpə'zɪʃən〕 *n.* 組成；結構

great-grandparents〔ˌgret'grænd͵pɛrənts〕 *n. pl.* (外) 曾祖父

candidate〔'kændə͵det〕 *n.* 候選人

impact〔'ɪmpækt〕 *n.* 影響；衝擊

thanks to 由於　　satellite〔'sætḷ͵aɪt〕 *n.* 人造衛星

cost-effective〔'kɑstə͵fɛktɪv〕 *adj.* 划算的

worldwide〔'wɝld'waɪd〕 *adv.* 在全世界

countless〔'kauntlɪs〕 *adj.* 數不清的　　***deal with*** 與～相處

in one way or another 以某種方式　　host〔host〕 *n.* 許多 < *of* >

advance〔əd'væns〕 *n.* 進步　　source〔sors〕 *n.* 來源

explore〔ɪk'splor〕 *v.* 探索　　area〔'ɛrɪə〕 *n.* 方面

memorable〔'mɛmərəbḷ〕 *adj.* 值得紀念的；難忘的

Quit　　　**Writing**

When people need to complain about a product or poor service, some prefer to complain in writing and others prefer to complain in person. Which way do you prefer? Use specific reasons and examples to support your answer.

▲

Cut

Paste

Undo

▼

160. Complaining About a Product

It is unfortunate, but sometimes we buy a product that is defective or does not live up to its promise. At times like these we need to inform the company of the problem through a formal complaint. Some people prefer to make complaints in writing while others prefer to make them in person. I prefer the latter for several reasons.

First of all, making a complaint in person allows two-way communication. *Therefore*, there is less chance of a misunderstanding. When talking face to face with someone I can explain myself clearly and also answer any questions that he may have. *Second*, making a complaint personally is much more direct and efficient. It is more likely that my problem will be solved quickly when I speak to someone directly than when I only make a written complaint. *Last but not least*, I prefer to deal with a real person rather than a faceless company. I think that when a company is willing to talk to me about my problem it shows that it cares and takes my complaint seriously.

Because direct communication is more efficient and exact, I prefer to make complaints in person. *In this way* I can receive a speedy answer and know whether the company takes my problem seriously or not.

160. 抱怨產品

　　說來遺憾，但有時候我們會買到有瑕疵，或與廣告內容不符的產品，發生這種情況時，我們必需透過正式的申訴管道，通知這家公司這項產品的問題。有些人比較喜歡用書面的方式申訴，有些則比較喜歡親自去投訴。基於下列一些理由，我選擇後者。

　　第一，親自去投訴才能雙向溝通。因此，發生誤會的機率就會比較少。當和人面對面時，我可以清楚說明自己的意思，並且回答他們可能會提出的任何問題。第二，親自投訴比較直接又有效率。我直接去找個人談，跟我只是做個書面申訴比較起來，我的問題比較可能獲得迅速解決。最後一項要點是，我比較喜歡和活生生的人打交道，而不是身份不明的公司團體。我認為當一家公司願意跟我談我的問題，就表示它很在乎，同時會認真看待我的申訴。

　　因為直接溝通比較有效率而且明確，所以我寧可選擇親自去申訴。這樣子我可以得到迅速的回應，並且知道這家公司是否會認真看待我的問題。

【註釋】

complain〔kəm'plen〕v. 抱怨；申訴
unfortunate〔ʌn'fɔrtʃənɪt〕adj. 不幸的
defective〔dɪ'fɛktɪv〕adj. 有瑕疵的
live up to 符合…的標準；不辜負（期望）
promise〔'prɑmɪs〕n. 保證；承諾
at times 有時候　　inform〔ɪn'fɔrm〕v. 通知＜ *of* ＞
formal〔'fɔrml̩〕adj. 正式的　　complaint〔kəm'plent〕n. 抱怨；申訴
in person 親自（= *personally* ）　　*the latter* （兩者中）後者（↔ *the former* ）
first of all 首先　　misunderstanding〔͵mɪsʌndə'stændɪŋ〕n. 誤會
face to face 面對面　　efficient〔ɪ'fɪʃənt〕adj. 有效率的
deal with 和～打交道
faceless〔'feslɪs〕adj. 沒有個性的；身份不明的
be willing to 願意　　*take sth. seriously* 認真看待某事
speedy〔'spidɪ〕adj. 迅速的

People remember special gifts or presents that they have received.
Why? Use specific reasons and examples to support your answer.

Cut

Paste

Undo

161. **Why People Remember Special Gifts or Presents**

Most people can remember at least one special gift that they once received. It may have been expensive, or it may have had very little monetary value. It may have been something that they had longed for or something unexpected. It may have come from a beloved person or a complete stranger. Whatever kind of gift it was, it was remembered long after the occasion and perhaps even after the gift itself had disappeared. Why do we remember such special gifts? I believe it is because the meaning of the gift was greater than the gift itself. The following are some examples.

Many kinds of gifts are unforgettable. One type of memorable gift is one that somehow changes our lives. For example, we might receive something we greatly need or something that introduces us to a new interest. Other gifts have great meaning because of the person who gives them to us. A gift from a loved one has great sentimental value that exceeds the value of the gift itself. Likewise, a gift from a respected or famous person may be valued because he took notice of us. Finally, a gift may be special and memorable because it is given to us on an important occasion, such as our graduation or wedding. It then reminds us of this special event in the future.

In conclusion, the value of special gifts is usually emotional rather than monetary. This sentimental value is impossible to measure, and the gifts are often irreplaceable. They may remind us of a special occasion or person or a turning point in our lives. In some way these gifts touch our heart and are, therefore, important to and memorable for us.

161. 爲什麼人們會記得特別的禮物

　　大部分的人，至少都會記得一件他們曾經收過的特別禮物。那份禮物也許非常昂貴，或者可能沒什麼金錢上的價值；也許是自己渴望已久的東西，或者是一個意外的驚喜；也許是摯愛的人所送的，或者來自於一個陌生人。無論那是一件什麼樣的禮物，即使是年代已經久遠，甚至禮物本身都已消失，還是令人難忘。那麼爲什麼我們還會記得這些特別的禮物呢？我相信是因爲禮物所代表的意義，大於禮物本身。以下就是一些例子。

　　有很多種禮物是令人難忘的，其中，有一種是會以某種方式，改變我們的生活，例如，我們也許會收到某樣我們非常需要的東西，或是讓我們有新的興趣的禮物。有些禮物則是因爲送禮者的身份，而意義非凡。收到摯愛的人所送的禮物，其蘊含的心意大於禮物本身。同樣地，我們會在乎受尊崇的人或名人所送的禮物，那是因爲他們注意到我們。最後，禮物之所以特別難忘，可能是因爲它是在重要的場合送的，例如畢業典禮或結婚典禮，在往後的日子裡，這份禮物會使我們想起這特別的一刻。

　　總之，特別禮物的重要性，通常是情感方面，而非金錢上的價值。這種情感上的價值是無法衡量的，而這樣的禮物也是無法取代的。它們能讓我們回想起特別的場合、人物，或人生的轉捩點。在某種程度上，這些禮物能讓我們感動，因此對我們而言，是非常重要，而且難忘的。

【註釋】

monetary〔'mʌnə,tɛrɪ〕*adj.* 金錢的

long for 渴望　　beloved〔bɪ'lʌvd〕*adj.* 心愛的

occasion〔ə'keʒən〕*n.* 場合

unforgettable〔,ʌnfə'gɛtəbl̩〕*adj.* 難忘的（= *memorable*）

somehow〔'sʌm,haʊ〕*adv.* 以某種方式

introduce〔,ɪntrə'djus〕*v.* 使認識

sentimental〔,sɛntə'mɛntl̩〕*adj.* 情感的　　exceed〔ɪk'sid〕*v.* 超過

likewise〔'laɪk,waɪz〕*adv.* 同樣地　　value〔'væljʊ〕*v.* 重視

in conclusion 總之　　measure〔'mɛʒə〕*v.* 衡量

irreplaceable〔,ɪrɪ'plesəbl̩〕*adj.* 不可替代的　　***turning point*** 轉捩點

touch〔tʌtʃ〕*v.* 觸動；感動

Some famous athletes and entertainers earn millions of dollars every year. Do you think these people deserve such high salaries? Use specific reasons and examples to support your opinion.

▲

Cut

Paste

Undo

▼

162. The High Salaries of Athletes and Entertainers

Highly paid athletes and entertainers are a fortunate and privileged group. Few people can earn so much money for what they do, and at times this seems unfair. This is especially so when someone who makes meaningful contributions to a field such as medicine or education remains largely unrecognized and poorly compensated. Many people consider the work of athletes and entertainers frivolous by comparison. Do they deserve such high salaries? *In my opinion*, they must; otherwise, society would not choose to give them so much money.

Although the salaries of athletes and entertainers seem exorbitant, there are valid reasons why they receive them. *First of all*, they work in a free market. If what they did was not valued by society, they would not be so well-paid. It must also be considered that entertainers do make a contribution to society because they amuse people and help them to relax and forget their troubles. *Second*, athletes and entertainers, no matter how talented, invest a lot in training for their careers. *And*, unlike other more conventional professions, success is by no means guaranteed or even likely. When they choose to pursue sports or the arts full-time, they make a gamble, and such high salaries could be considered the reward for this risk. ***Last but not least***, athletes and entertainers are excellent role models for young people. They demonstrate that it is possible to pursue a dream and beat the odds. They inspire many children to pursue their own dreams, and the possibility of a high salary may be an important part of the incentive.

To sum up, although the salaries of some professional athletes and entertainers seem excessive, there are convincing reasons why they receive them. Their contributions to society may not seem as important as those of scientists, doctors and statesmen, but they are valued by the general public. If they were not, we would not pay them so well.

162. 運動員與演藝人員的高所得

　　高所得的運動員與演藝人員，都是幸運且享有特權的一群人。很少有人能像他們一樣，工作能賺那麼多錢，有時候似乎顯得不太公平。這種情形在諸如醫學或教育這些領域中，有人雖有很大的貢獻，卻大都沒有得到認可，而且報酬微薄時，顯得更為不公平。很多人認為相較之下，運動員與演藝人員的工作微不足道。他們真的應該得到這麼高的收入嗎？在我看來，他們應該要獲得這麼高的收入，否則社會大眾就不會選擇給他們這麼多錢了。

　　儘管運動員與演藝人員的收入高得似乎有點離譜，但之所以如此，是有原因的。首先，他們是在一個自由市場工作，如果他們的表現不受到社會大眾的重視，就不會有那麼高的收入。大家必須考慮到，演藝人員的工作對社會有貢獻，因為他們娛樂大家，幫助人們放鬆心情並忘卻煩惱。第二，運動員與藝人，不論多有天份，都必須為了他們的工作而投注很多心力接受訓練。而且，不像其他傳統職業，他們是不一定會成功的。當他們選擇從事職業的運動員或演藝人員時，就必須下賭注，而如此高的所得，就是承擔這種風險的報酬。最後一項要點是，運動員與藝人是年輕人絕佳的榜樣，因為他們證明，不但可以去追求夢想，而且會有意想不到的成功。他們激勵許多孩子追求自己的夢想，而且獲得高所得的可能性，也是個重要的誘因。

　　總之，儘管有些職業運動員與演藝人員的所得，似乎是過高，但他們能拿這麼多錢，還是有令人信服的理由。他們對社會的貢獻也許不如科學家、醫生，以及政治家那麼重要，但仍然受到社會大眾的重視。如果不是的話，大家也不會讓他們賺那麼多錢了。

【註釋】

athlete〔'æθlit〕 *n.* 運動員　　entertainer〔,ɛntɚ'tenɚ〕 *n.* 演藝人員

privileged〔'prɪvḷɪdʒd〕 *adj.* 有特權的　　***at times*** 有時候

unfair〔ʌn'fɛr〕 *adj.* 不公平的

contribution〔,kɑntrə'bjuʃən〕 *n.* 貢獻 < *to* >

field〔fild〕 *n.* 領域　　largely〔'lɑrdʒlɪ〕 *adv.* 大部分

unrecognized〔ʌn'rɛkəg,naɪzd〕 *adj.* 未被承認的

compensate〔'kɑmpən,set〕 *v.* 補償；給予報酬 < *for* >

frivolous〔'frɪvələs〕 *adj.* 不重要的　　***by comparison*** 比較之下

exorbitant〔ɪg'zɔrbətənt〕 *adj.* 過高的

valid〔'vælɪd〕 *adj.* 有根據的；令人信服的

value〔'vælju〕 *v.* 重視　　***first of all*** 首先

talented〔'tæləntɪd〕 *adj.* 有才能的

well-paid〔'wɛl'ped〕 *adj.* 待遇優厚的

invest〔ɪn'vɛst〕 *v.* 投資 < *in* >

conventional〔kən'vɛnʃəṇḷ〕 *adj.* 傳統的

profession〔prə'fɛʃən〕 *n.* 職業　　***by no means*** 絕不

guarantee〔,gærən'ti〕 *v.* 保證　　pursue〔pɚ'su〕 *v.* 從事；追求

full-time〔'ful'taɪm〕 *adv.* 全職地

gamble〔'gæmbḷ〕 *n.* 賭博；冒險

last but not least 最後一項要點是

role model 模範　　demonstrate〔'dɛmən,stret〕 *v.* 證明

odds〔ɑdz〕 *n.* 勝算；成功的可能性

beat the odds 獲得出乎意料的成功　　inspire〔ɪn'spaɪr〕 *v.* 激勵

incentive〔ɪn'sɛntɪv〕 *n.* 動機；誘因

to sum up 總之　　professional〔prə'fɛʃəṇḷ〕 *adj.* 職業的

excessive〔ɪk'sɛsɪv〕 *adj.* 過度的

convincing〔kən'vɪnsɪŋ〕 *adj.* 令人信服的

statesman〔'stesmən〕 *n.* 政治家　　***pay sb. well*** 給某人很高的酬勞

Writing

Quit

Is the ability to read and write more important today than in the past? Why or why not? Use specific reasons and examples to support your answer.

Cut

Paste

Undo

163. The Importance of Literacy

Literacy, the ability to read and write, is even more important in today's world than it was in the past. Years ago, many people did not know how to read or write and yet were able to live successful lives. Society was more strictly divided by occupation. *That is*, a farmer's son would most likely grow up to be a farmer and a merchant's son, a merchant. Not every occupation required the ability to read and write, and as people did not often aspire to change their employment, many did not need to be literate. *Furthermore*, neither education nor printed material was widely available. Most people did not read for recreation, but instead talked, sang, or played games. *In short*, literacy was not an essential thing for many people in the past.

In our own time, the situation is very different. Without the ability to read and write, it is difficult to succeed. *For one thing*, our society is much more open and people can choose the career that they want to pursue. *However*, many careers are now closed to those who are not literate. *Moreover*, literacy is necessary in daily life, no matter what one's occupation is. More information is disseminated in written form, such as newspapers and advertisements. Without the ability to read, one would not even be able to pay bills and would always be dependent on others. *Also*, education is widely available, but one needs the ability to read and write in order to pursue it. *And finally*, a man who is not literate in our society is looked down upon and will rarely earn others' respect no matter how good he is at other things. *For all of these reasons*, I believe that the ability to read and write is more important now than ever.

163. 識字的重要性

　　識字能力，也就是讀寫的能力，在現今的世界，比過去重要得多。多年前，有許多人不懂得讀書寫字，卻也能夠很成功。當時的社會是依照職業有較嚴格的區分，也就是說，農夫的兒子，很有可能長大之後就成為農夫；商人的兒子日後也會是商人。並非每種職業都需要讀寫能力，而且人們通常不會渴望要改變職業，所以許多人不需要識字。此外，當時的教育和印刷資料也都不普及。大部分人的娛樂不是閱讀，而是聊天、唱歌，或玩遊戲。簡言之，在過去，識字能力對很多人而言，並不是必要的。

　　在我們現在的時代，情況已大不相同了。沒有讀書寫字的能力，是很難成功的。首先，我們的社會較為開放，人們可以選擇自己想從事的職業。然而，現在許多職業，並不歡迎不識字的人。此外，識字能力在日常生活中也是必須的，無論從事哪一種職業。有更多的資訊是用書寫的形式散播出去的，例如報紙和廣告。如果無法閱讀，可能連付帳單的能力都沒有，必須總是依賴別人。而且，現在教育普及，一個人需要讀寫能力，才能受教育。最後，不識字的人，在社會上會被瞧不起，就算其他方面再擅長，也很少能贏得別人的尊敬。基於這些理由，我認為，現在讀寫能力比從前更加重要。

【註釋】

literacy〔'lɪtərəsɪ〕n. 識字　　strictly〔'strɪktlɪ〕adv. 嚴格地

divide〔də'vaɪd〕v. 區分　　occupation〔,ɑkjə'peʃən〕n. 職業

that is 也就是說（= *that is to say*）　　merchant〔'mɝtʃənt〕n. 商人

aspire〔ə'spaɪr〕v. 渴望　　employment〔ɪm'plɔɪmənt〕n. 職業

literate〔'lɪtərɪt〕adj. 識字的　　furthermore〔'fɝðə,mor〕adv. 此外

printed〔'prɪntɪd〕adj. 印刷的　　available〔ə'veləbḷ〕adj. 可獲得的

recreation〔,rɛkrɪ'eʃən〕n. 娛樂　　*in short* 簡言之（= *in brief*）

essential〔ɪ'sɛnʃəl〕adj. 必要的　　*for one thing* 一則；一來

pursue〔pə'su〕v. 追求；從事

disseminate〔dɪ'sɛmə,net〕v. 散佈；傳播

in written form 以書寫的形式

dependent〔dɪ'pɛndənt〕adj. 依賴的〈on〉

look down upon 輕視　　rarely〔'rɛrlɪ〕adv. 很少

be good at 擅長

Quit　　　　**Writing**

People do many different things to stay healthy. What do you do for good health? Use specific reasons and examples to support your answer.

Cut

Paste

Undo

164. Staying Healthy

There is no denying the importance of health. Without it, it is
difficult to live a happy life no matter
how much money or success one has. *However*, many
people neglect their health. They develop unhealthy
habits such as smoking or overeating, lead sedentary
lives or succumb to the pressures of modern life. *As a
result*, they develop serious but preventable diseases.
In order to maintain our good health and lead lives that
are as fulfilling as possible, it is important to take some
steps. Those mentioned below are what I do to stay
healthy.

The *first* step I take is to keep regular hours and
stick to a healthy, balanced diet. This is not always
easy to do in today's fast-paced society, but it is the
basis of good health. Our bodies need sufficient
nutrition and rest in order to function well and resist
illness. The *second* step I recommend is to get regular
exercise. This does not mean we have to run marathons
or join expensive fitness centers. Studies have shown
that even moderate exercise, such as walking, can
have great benefits for our health if done on a regular

basis. ***Third***, I suggest seeing a doctor for an annual checkup. Most of us do not think too much about our health until we feel that something is wrong. ***However***, a doctor can often diagnose problems before they become serious enough to be apparent to us. ***Last but not least***, I take time to relax and renew my spirits and mental energy every day. This is just as essential as physical exercise because our mental state often has a profound influence on our physical health. As the saying goes, "A sound mind in a sound body."

There are many things that we can do to stay healthy. The above steps are only a few suggestions. The important thing is to value our health and not neglect it. This means making healthy habits a part of our everyday life. There is no need to dwell on our health or take precautions against every disease known to man. If we simply develop a healthy way of living we are bound to live healthier, more satisfying lives.

164. 保持健康

健康的重要性是不可否認的。如果不健康，一個人不管多有錢或多有成就，都很難過著快樂的生活。然而，就是有很多人忽視自己的健康。他們養成像是抽煙或飲食過度的壞習慣，整天賴著不動，向現代生活的壓力屈服，因而得到嚴重，但原本可預防的疾病。為了要保持良好的健康，和盡量能充分發揮自我能力的生活，採取一些步驟是很重要的。而下列提到的，便是我用來維持健康的方法。

我所採取的第一個步驟，就是作息規律、保持健康均衡的飲食。在現今步調快速的社會，這種做法未必容易，可是這卻是良好健康的基礎。我們的身體需要足夠的營養和休息，才能夠維持正常的運作功能，抵抗疾病的威脅。我推薦的第二個步驟，就是規律運動。這並不是說我們得跑馬拉松，或是加入收費昂貴的健身中心。研究顯示，就算是像走路這種適度的運動，只要規律地做，也能對我們的健康有很大助益。第三，我建議去看醫生，每年做一次健康檢查。我們大部份的人除非感覺身體不舒服，否則根本不會太注意自己的健康。然而，醫生可以在我們發覺自己病情惡化之前，先診斷出哪裡有毛病。最後一項要點是，我每天會花時間好好放鬆，來恢復我的精神和腦力。因為我們的心理狀態通常對身體健康有很深遠的影響，所以和體能運動一樣，都是很重要的。就好比俗話說：「健全的心靈，在於健全的身體。」

我們可以用很多方法來保持健康。以上的步驟只是一些建議而已。最重要的還是要珍惜自己的健康，不要忽視它，也就是說，要讓健康的習慣成為每天生活的一部份。不過也沒必要一天到晚想著健康問題，或是想採取一切預防疾病的措施。只要我們養成健康的生活方式，就一定可以過著更健康，而且更令人滿意的生活。

【註釋】

There is no denying~ ～是不可否認的（ = *It is impossible to deny~* ）

neglect〔nɪˈglɛkt〕v. 忽略　　develop〔dɪˈvɛləp〕v. 養成

sedentary〔ˈsɛdn̩ˌtɛrɪ〕adj. 經常坐著的；少動的

succumb〔səˈkʌm〕v. 屈服 < *to* >　　develop〔dɪˈvɛləp〕v. 得（病）

preventable〔prɪˈvɛntəbl̩〕adj. 可預防的

fulfilling〔fʊlˈfɪlɪŋ〕adj. 能充分發揮能力的　　***take steps*** 採取步驟

keep regular hours 作息正常規律　　***stick to*** 堅持

balanced〔ˈbælənst〕adj. 均衡的　　diet〔ˈdaɪət〕n. 飲食

not always 不一定（ = *not necessarily* ）

fast-paced〔ˈfæstˈpest〕adj. 步調快速的

sufficient〔səˈfɪʃənt〕adj. 足夠的　　nutrition〔njuˈtrɪʃən〕n. 營養

function〔ˈfʌŋkʃən〕v. 運作　　resist〔rɪˈzɪst〕v. 抵抗

recommend〔ˌrɛkəˈmɛnd〕v. 推薦

marathon〔ˈmærəˌθɑn〕n. 馬拉松賽跑　　***fitness center*** 健身中心

moderate〔ˈmɑdərɪt〕adj. 適度的　　benefit〔ˈbɛnəfɪt〕n. 益處

on a regular basis 定期地（ = *regularly* ）

annual〔ˈænjʊəl〕adj. 一年一度的　　checkup〔ˈtʃɛkˌʌp〕n. 健康檢查

diagnose〔ˌdaɪəgˈnoz〕v. 診斷　　apparent〔əˈpærənt〕adj. 明顯的

last but not least 最後一項要點是　　renew〔rɪˈnju〕v. 使恢復

essential〔əˈsɛnʃəl〕adj. 必要的　　***mental state*** 精神狀態

profound〔prəˈfaʊnd〕adj. 深刻的　　***as the saying goes*** 俗話說

sound〔saʊnd〕adj. 健全的　　value〔ˈvæljʊ〕v. 重視

dwell on 老是想著　　precaution〔prɪˈkɔʃən〕n. 預防措施

be known to sb. 爲某人所知

be bound to + *V.* 一定（ = *be sure to* + *V.* ）

Quit　　　　　**Writing**

You have decided to give several hours of your time each month to improve the community where you live. What is one thing you would do to improve your community? Why? Use specific reasons and details to explain your choice.

Cut

Paste

Undo

165. Volunteering

A community is made up of a group of people. *And* it depends on those people for its existence. It is possible for people to live in close proximity and fail to be a community. That is because the word community implies communal action. It is neighbors working together to create a better place to live. *Therefore*, it is important for us all to contribute our efforts to our community. If I have several hours of time each month to do so, I will work toward creating and preserving green spaces in my community.

I feel that preserving green space is a worthy endeavor that would be of great value to my community. It is especially important because I live in an urban community. The open spaces and parks are limited in the city and are too often sacrificed for further development. Working to protect these spaces and to establish new parks would be a way to conserve one of the community's scarce resources. *Furthermore*, providing green spaces for the residents of my neighborhood would increase the feeling of community and improve relationships among neighbors. This is because attractive parks would encourage people to get out and socialize with others in a relaxed atmosphere. *In addition*, by beautifying the neighborhood, it would provide the residents with more contact with nature. This would encourage them to exercise and lead healthier lives.

The above are just some of the advantages of having green spaces and parks in a community. Because it is so beneficial to the community, that is how I will choose to devote my free time. *In this way*, I hope to make a meaningful contribution to my neighborhood and to my neighbors.

165. 擔任義工

　　社區是由一群人組成的，其存在就仰賴這一群人。人們可能住得很近，但卻不能形成一個社區，因為社區這個字，是指有共同行動的意思，也就是鄰居們須共同努力，創造一個更好的生活環境。因此，大家都要為我們的社區貢獻一己之力，這是很重要的。如果每個月我能貢獻幾小時的時間，我會努力創造和保留我們社區的綠地。

　　我覺得保留綠色空間對社區很有價值，而且是值得努力的事。因為我住在市區，所以這一點顯得格外重要。城市裡的空地和公園不但有限，而且還常常被犧牲，以作進一步發展之用。努力保護這些空間，並且興建新的公園，是一個保存社區稀有資源的方法。此外，提供附近居民綠色空間，也可以增進社區居民的感情，並改善鄰居之間的關係。因為有吸引人的公園，大家就會想出去走走，在輕鬆的氣氛下和其他人互相來往。此外，藉著美化鄰近地區，能讓居民更有機會接觸大自然。這會使他們更想運動，過更健康的生活。

　　上述只是社區保有綠色空間，以及公園的一部分好處而已。因為這對社區助益很多，所以我打算把空閒時間都花在這上面。藉由這個方式，我希望能夠為我的社區及鄰居，做些有意義的貢獻。

【註釋】

volunteer (ˌvɑlən'tɪɚ) v. 自願服務
community (kə'mjunətɪ) n. 社區
be make up 由～組成　　existence (ɪg'zɪstəns) n. 存在
proximity (prɑk'sɪmətɪ) n. 接近　　*fail to + V.* 未能
imply (ɪm'plaɪ) v. 暗示
communal ('kɑmjʊnḷ , kə'mjunḷ) adj. 公共的；共同的
contribute (kən'trɪbjut) v. 貢獻 < to >　　*work toward* 努力達到
preserve (prɪ'zɝv) v. 保存　　space (spes) n. 空地
worthy ('wɝðɪ) adj. 值得的　　endeavor (ɪn'dɛvɚ) n. 努力
urban ('ɝbən) adj. 城市的　　open ('opən) adj. 空曠的
sacrifice ('sækrəˌfaɪs) v. 犧牲　　further ('fɝðɚ) adj. 更進一步的
scarce (skɛrs) adj. 稀有的　　resident ('rɛzədənt) n. 居民
socialize ('soʃəˌlaɪz) v. 交往　　atmosphere ('ætməsˌfɪr) n. 氣氛
beautify ('bjutəˌfaɪ) v. 美化　　beneficial (ˌbɛnə'fɪʃəl) adj. 有益的
devote (dɪ'vot) v. 奉獻　　*free time* 空閒時間
meaningful ('minɪŋfḷ) adj. 有意義的

Quit　　　**Writing**

People recognize a difference between children and adults. What events (experiences or ceremonies) make a person an adult? Use specific reasons and examples to explain your answer.

Cut

Paste

Undo

Time

Help
?

Confirm
Answer

Next

166. Experiences or Events Making One an Adult

If you were asked to differentiate between adults and children, how will you respond? The obvious thing will be to look at them physically. But there are other things such as experiences and ceremonies that determine whether a person is an adult.

For example, one of the privileges to being an adult is getting your driver's license. Nearly all countries require that drivers satisfy a minimum age requirement before they can get their licenses. Another experience open only to adults is voting. Governments will not let children decide the fate of a nation when they can barely tie their own shoelaces. Perhaps the most ceremonial experience and coming of age practice is marriage. Adults get married while children attend the wedding dinner.

Experiences such as marriage and voting are serious events in life. Only mature adults are able to handle the responsibilities and significance of these events. Being able to participate in these things is what separates children from adults.

166. 讓一個人成爲成人的經驗或事件

如果你被問及成人和小孩的區別爲何，你會怎麼回答？顯然就是觀察身體上的差異。但是還有其他事情，像是經驗和儀式，可以決定一個人是否是成人。

例如，成人的基本權利之一，就是取得汽車駕照。幾乎所有國家都要求，駕駛人要符合最低年齡的要求，才能取得駕照。另外一個唯有開放給成人的經驗，就是投票。小孩子自己連鞋帶都不大會綁了，政府當然不會讓他們決定國家的命運。或許最正式的經驗和已成年才會有的行爲，就是結婚。成人才能結婚，而小孩子則只能參加婚禮晚宴。

像是結婚和投票的經驗，是人生的重要大事。唯有成熟的成人才能負起這些事情的責任，並了解其意義。是否可以參與這些事件，就是小孩和大人的區別。

【註釋】

differentiate〔ˌdɪfəˈrɛnʃɪˌet〕v. 區別 < between >

obvious〔ˈɑbvɪəs〕adj. 明顯的　　physically〔ˈfɪzɪkl̩ɪ〕adv. 身體上

ceremony〔ˈsɛrəˌmonɪ〕n. 儀式；典禮

determine〔dɪˈtɜmɪn〕v. 決定　　privilege〔ˈprɪvlɪdʒ〕n. 特權

driver's license 駕駛執照 (= *license*)

satisfy〔ˈsætɪsˌfaɪ〕v. 符合 (要求)

minimum〔ˈmɪnəməm〕adj. 最小的；最低的

requirement〔rɪˈkwaɪrmənt〕n. 要求；規定　　*be open to* 開放給

voting〔ˈvotɪŋ〕n. 投票　　fate〔fet〕n. 命運

barely〔ˈbɛrlɪ〕adv. 勉強；幾乎沒有　　*tie one's shoelaces* 綁鞋帶

ceremonial〔ˌsɛrəˈmonɪəl〕adj. 儀式上的；正式的

come of age 到達法定成人年齡 (通常是十八或二十一歲)

practice〔ˈpræktɪs〕n. 習俗；做法

serious〔ˈsɪrɪəs〕adj. 重要的；須認眞對待的

mature〔məˈt(j)ʊr〕adj. 成熟的

significance〔sɪgˈnɪfəkəns〕n. 重要性

participate in 參與　　separate〔ˈsɛpəˌret〕v. 區別 < from >

Writing

Quit

Your school has enough money to purchase either computers for students or books for the library. Which should your school choose to buy — computers or books? Use specific reasons and examples to support your recommendation.

Cut

Paste

Undo

Time

Help
?

Confirm
Answer

Next
→

167. Computers Versus Library Books

Most schools have to deal with the problem of limited resources. There is only so much money, and it must be divided up between different school programs. This often means that difficult choices must be made. In the case of computers versus library books, I think that everyone would agree that both are valuable resources for students. ***However***, given the current state of technology and the changes in how people communicate and find information, I believe that a school should spend its money on purchasing computers for students to use rather than more library books.

One reason for my opinion is that knowledge of computers is increasingly important in today's society. Without this knowledge, a graduate may find it difficult to work well or even find a job. In view of the necessity of computer proficiency these days, I believe that schools should make every effort to make students familiar with computers. ***Another*** reason is that the way people research problems and communicate with each other has greatly changed in the last decade. It is now possible to find information quickly and efficiently by using a computer. ***In addition***, students can write up their findings and send them to others via computer. Having every resource book available in the school library may no longer be necessary.

In conclusion, it is my belief that computers are an important resource for students today. They cannot replace books, but they can help students learn in a very effective and efficient way. ***Therefore***, I think that schools should spend more money on computer equipment than on library books.

167. 電腦與圖書館藏書

　　許多學校必須面對資源有限的問題。經費有限，又必須要分配給不同的學校課程計劃，這通常意味著，必須做很困難的抉擇。在電腦與圖書館藏書之間，我想大家都會同意，這二者對學生而言，都是很珍貴的資源，然而，若考慮到目前科技發展的情況，以及人們彼此溝通和找尋資訊方式的改變，我認為，學校應該花錢購買電腦，以供學生使用，而非添購圖書館的藏書。

　　我會抱持這樣的看法，原因之一在於，電腦知識在現今社會中，愈來愈重要。沒有這樣的知識，學生畢業時可能會覺得，想好好工作都有困難，或甚至找不到工作。有鑑於現在大家都必須精通電腦，故我認為，學校應該盡力讓學生熟悉電腦的操作。另一個理由是，在過去十年內，人們研究問題，和彼此溝通的方式，已有很大的改變。現在，藉由使用電腦，能更快速、更有效率地取得資訊。此外，利用電腦，學生能夠將研究成果寫得更為詳盡，並且用電腦傳送給其他人。學校圖書館必須具備各種參考資料書籍的情況，可能已不再需要了。

　　總之，我相信，電腦對現今的學生而言，是一項非常重要的資源，它們無法取代書籍，但卻能幫助學生用非常有效果，而且有效率的方式學習。因此，我認為，學校方面應多花一些經費購買電腦設備，而非圖書館藏書。

【註釋】

deal with 應付 (= cope with)　　　resource〔 rɪˈsors 〕n. 資源
divide〔 dɪˈvaɪd 〕v. 劃分　　program〔ˈprogræm〕n. 課程；計劃
versus〔ˈvɝsəs〕prep. ～對～　　valuable〔ˈvæljuəbl̩〕adj. 珍貴的
given〔ˈgɪvən〕prep. 考慮到　　current〔ˈkɝənt〕adj. 目前的
state〔 stet 〕n. 狀態　　purchase〔ˈpɝtʃəs〕v. 購買 (= buy)
graduate〔ˈgrædʒuɪt〕n. 畢業生　　in view of 有鑑於
proficiency〔prəˈfɪʃənsɪ〕n. 熟練　　make every effort to 非常努力
research〔rɪˈsɝtʃ〕v. 研究　　decade〔ˈdɛked〕n. 十年
efficiently〔əˈfɪʃəntlɪ〕adv. 有效率地　　write up 更詳細地寫
via〔ˈvaɪə〕prep. 藉由　　equipment〔ɪˈkwɪpmənt〕n. 設備

Quit　　　　　**Writing**

Many students choose to attend schools or universities outside their home countries. Why do some students study abroad? Use specific reasons and details to explain your answer.

	Cut
	Paste
	Undo

Time

Help 　Confirm Answer 　Next

168. **Why Students Study Abroad**

Attending high school or university a-broad is very expensive. Not only that, but students may also experience homesickness when away from their families for so long. *But* despite this, studying abroad is still very popular. That is because there are several advantages to receiving an education overseas.

One advantage is that living abroad for a period of time allows students to experience a different way of life and broaden their horizons. When they return to their own country they will have a wider base of experience to draw on. *Another* advantage is that living abroad is a wonderful chance for students to develop their foreign language skills. When a student wants to learn another language well, nothing can take the place of living among native speakers of that language. A *third* advantage of overseas studies is that students can pursue interests and areas of study that may not be available in their own countries. *And finally*, by studying abroad students learn how to take care of themselves in a very different environment and so develop greater confidence and independence.

With all these advantages it is easy to see why many students choose to attend schools or universities abroad. They believe that such an experience will help them to develop both academically and personally. They will then be able to apply the skills and knowledge they have gained abroad in their home countries.

168. 學生爲什麼要出國唸書

　　到國外就讀高中或大學十分昂貴。除此之外，學生要離開家人這麼久，可能還會想家。但是儘管如此，出國留學的現象仍然很普遍，因爲在國外接受教育有一些好處。

　　第一個好處是，在國外住一段時間，可以讓學生體驗不同的生活方式，並拓展眼界。這些學生回到自己的國家後，會有比較廣泛的經驗基礎可以利用。另一個好處是，住在國外對學生而言，是培養他們外語技巧很好的機會。當學生想要學好另一種語言時，最好的方法就是置身於以該語言爲母語的人群中。出國留學的第三個好處是，學生可以追求在自己國家無法發展的興趣，以及學習領域。最後，藉由出國留學，學生能學習如何在一個截然不同的環境中，照顧自己，藉此培養更多自信心，並且更獨立。

　　有這些好處，所以爲什麼很多學生選擇出國唸書或上大學，是很容易理解的。他們認爲，這樣的經驗將有助於他們在學術上及個人的發展。之後他們就可以在自己的國家，運用他們在國外所獲得的技巧和知識。

【註釋】

abroad〔əˋbrɔd〕adv. 到國外　　advantage〔ədˋvæntɪdʒ〕n. 好處

homesickness〔ˋhomˏsɪknɪs〕n. 鄉愁；思鄉病

overseas〔ˋovɚˋsiz〕adv. 到國外　adj. 國外的

broaden〔ˋbrɔdn̩〕v. 拓展

horizons〔həˋraɪzn̩z〕n.pl. 知識範圍；眼界　　base〔bes〕n. 基礎

draw on 利用　　***take the place of*** 取代（= *replace* ）

native〔ˋnetɪv〕adj. 本國的　　pursue〔pɚˋsu〕v. 追求

available〔əˋveləbl̩〕adj. 可獲得的

confidence〔ˋkɑnfədəns〕n. 信心

independence〔ˏɪndɪˋpɛndəns〕n. 獨立

academically〔ˏækəˋdɛmɪkl̩ɪ〕adv. 學術上　　apply〔əˋplaɪ〕v. 應用

Quit	Writing	

People listen to music for different reasons and at different times. Why is music important to many people? Use specific reasons and examples to support your choice.

Cut

Paste

Undo

Time

Help ?　Confirm Answer　Next →

169. Why Music Is Important to People

Music plays a very important role in our lives, and it is important in every cul- ture. People listen to many kinds of music, and they listen to it for different reasons at different times. The following are some examples of how and why people listen to music.

One reason people listen to music is to relax and enjoy themselves. *In this case*, everyone will listen to the music that he likes best. *However*, most people like a variety of music and will choose the type which best suits their current mood. *Another* reason people listen to music is to create a certain atmosphere. *For example*, soft music can create a peaceful or romantic atmosphere and help people to calm down. Energetic music, *on the other hand*, can inspire people to work or play harder. *Finally*, people also use music to signal certain events. *For example*, the wedding march means that a bride is about to walk down the aisle, while playing Pomp and Circumstance is a sign that a group of students have just graduated.

Whatever reason people have for listening to music, there is no doubt that music plays an important role in our lives. It can help us relax or give us energy. It can also tell us that something important is happening. It is difficult to imagine what life would be like without music. It has been with us since man first learned how to make sounds, and it will be with us far into the future.

169. 音樂爲何對人們很重要

音樂在我們的生活中扮演很重要的角色，而且在每個文化中都很重要。人們聽很多種音樂，而且在不同的時間，因爲不同的原因而聽音樂。下面有些例子，可說明人們聽音樂的原因和方式。

聽音樂的理由之一，是爲了放鬆及娛樂。在這種情況下，人們就會聽自己最喜歡的音樂。然而，大多數的人都喜歡聽各式各樣的音樂，所以會選擇最適合他們當時心情的音樂來聽。人們聽音樂的另一個理由，是爲了營造某種氣氛。例如，柔和的音樂可以創造平和或浪漫的氣氛，有助於讓人獲得平靜。另外一方面，動感的音樂可以鼓舞人更努力工作，或玩得更盡興。最後，人們也會用音樂來表示特定的事件。例如，播放結婚進行曲，就表示新娘即將步上紅毯；而演奏驪歌，則代表有一群學生剛剛畢業了。

不論人們聽音樂的理由爲何，無疑地，音樂在我們的生活，扮演了重要的角色。它能夠幫助我們放鬆，讓我們充滿活力，也可以告訴我們，剛剛發生了什麼大事。很難想像生活中如果沒有音樂，會是什麼樣子。自從人類知道如何發出聲音之後，音樂就一直伴隨著我們，在很久很久之後，也將是如此。

【註釋】

play a role in 在…扮演一個角色　　case〔kes〕*n.* 情況
a variety of 各式各樣的　　suit〔sut〕*v.* 適合
current〔'kʒənt〕*adj.* 目前的　　mood〔mud〕*n.* 心情
atmosphere〔'ætməs,fɪr〕*n.* 氣氛　　*calm down* 平靜下來
energetic〔,ɛnə'dʒɛtɪk〕*adj.* 充滿活力的　　inspire〔ɪn'spaɪr〕*v.* 激發
signal〔'sɪgnḷ〕*v.* 表示　　event〔ɪ'vɛnt〕*n.* 事件
march〔martʃ〕*n.* 進行曲　　bride〔braɪd〕*n.* 新娘
be about to + *V.* 即將　　aisle〔aɪl〕*n.* 走道
pomp〔pamp〕*n.* 盛大　　circumstance〔'sʒkəm,stæns〕*n.* 隆重儀式
Pomp and Circumstance 驪歌　　sign〔saɪn〕*n.* 象徵
graduate〔'grædʒu,et〕*v.* 畢業　　far〔far〕*adv.* 久遠地

Quit　　　**Writing**

Groups or organizations are an important part of some people's lives. Why are groups or organizations important to people? Use specific reasons and examples to explain your answer.

	Cut
	Paste
	Undo

Time

Help　?　Confirm　Answer　Next　→

170. The Importance of Groups and Organizations

Most people belong to at least one group or organization. These groups of people include social clubs, special interest groups, sports teams, classmates and workmates. Such organizations play an important part in people's lives today because they provide both material and personal benefits.

Both formal and informal organizations can provide their members with material benefits. *For example*, membership in an exercise class offers the benefit of improved health. *In addition*, organizations which work toward a specific goal, such as passing legislation or improving a neighborhood, allow people to achieve that goal more efficiently by working together. *Finally*, some organizations provide special benefits that are reserved for members, *for example* a music or book club in which the members exchange materials or receive special discounts.

Most organizations also provide personal benefits, the most important of which is a sense of belonging. When people choose to ally themselves with a group, that becomes part of their identity. In the group, they can find people of like-minded interests and feel like part of a team. This gives the members both companionship and the opportunity to share their feelings with sympathetic listeners. *Moreover*, trying out different groups enables people to discover their interests and clarify their goals. Through this process they can find out where they best fit in.

In conclusion, organizations and informal groups of people are important in our lives because they provide us with many advantages. They help us clarify our goals and interests and find the support we need to pursue them effectively. *More importantly*, in this increasingly impersonal society, they give us companionship and a sense of belonging.

170. 團體與組織的重要

　　大部份的人都會至少分屬於一個以上的團體或是組織。這些團體包括了社交聯誼的俱樂部、特殊興趣的團體、運動團隊、同班同學，以及同事。現在這些組織，在每個人的生活中，都扮演了重要的角色，原因就在於，它們能提供實質上以及個人的好處。

　　正式與非正式的組織，都能提供其會員實質的好處。舉例來說，參加運動課程的會員，能有改善健康的好處。此外，針對某些特定目標運作的組織，像是爲了要通過法規，或是改善社區的組織，就能透過團隊合作，更有效地達成目標。最後，有些組織是提供會員獨享的好處，例如音樂俱樂部或讀書會，會員可以互相交換資料，或是享有特別的優惠折扣。

　　大部份的組織也提供個人好處，其中最重要的，就是歸屬感。當人們選擇加入某個團體時，這種關係便成了個人身份的一部份。在團體中，他們能夠找到志趣相投的人，感覺自己是團體的一份子，讓會員不但擁有友誼，同時也有機會和能夠產生共鳴的聽衆，分享自己的感覺。此外，多方嘗試不同的團體，有助於發現自己的興趣所在，並認清自己的目標。透過這種過程，每個人都能找到最適合自己的團體。

　　總之，因爲這些組織和非正式團體，能帶給我們很多好處，所以它們在我們的生活中十分重要。它們幫助我們認清自己的目標和興趣，也使我們得到支持，這是在追求目標和興趣時所必需的。更重要的是，在現今這個愈來愈沒有人情味的社會裡，團體能給我們友誼和歸屬感。

【註釋】

sports〔sports〕*adj.* 運動的

workmate〔'wɜk,met〕*n.* 同事（= *co-worker* = *colleague*）

play a part in 在…扮演～角色

material〔mə'tırıəl〕*adj.* 具體的

benefit〔'bɛnəfıt〕*n.* 利益；好處

membership〔'mɛmbə,ʃıp〕*n.* 會員資格

in addition 此外　　*work toward* 努力達成

specific〔spı'sıfık〕*adj.* 特定的

legislation〔,lɛdʒıs'leʃən〕*n.* 法規　　achieve〔ə'tʃiv〕*v.* 達成

reserve〔rı'zɜv〕*v.* 保留 < *for* >

discount〔'dıskaʊnt〕*n.* 折扣　　ally〔ə'laı〕*v.* 使結盟

identity〔aı'dɛntətı〕*n.* 身份

like-minded〔'laık'maındıd〕*adj.* 志趣相投的

companionship〔kəm'pænjən,ʃıp〕*n.* 夥伴關係；友誼

sympathetic〔,sımpə'θɛtık〕*adj.* 有同感的

try out 試驗　　clarify〔'klærə,faı〕*v.* 使清楚

fit in 適合　　*in conclusion* 總之

pursue〔pə'su〕*v.* 追求　　effectively〔ı'fɛktıvlı〕*adv.* 有效地

increasingly〔ın'krisıŋlı〕*adv.* 愈來愈

impersonal〔ım'pɜsnḷ〕*adj.* 沒有人情味的

Quit **Writing**

Imagine that you are preparing for a trip. You plan to be away from your home for a year. In addition to clothing and personal care items, you can take **one** additional thing. What would you take and why? Use specific reasons and details to support your choice.

Cut

Paste

Undo

Time

Help ?

Confirm Answer

Next ➡

171. Packing for a Year Abroad

The opportunity to travel for one year is a dream for many people, myself included. It would be a wonderful chance to explore different cultures and expand my horizons. *However*, a year away from home would not be without hardship and would require careful planning. I would not be able to carry much more than the necessary clothing and personal effects. If I could take only one additional thing, it would be a picture of my family and hometown.

The primary reason I would take a photograph would be to remind myself of where I come from. I have no doubt that a year-long trip would be full of excitement and novelty. I would be exposed to a great many new ideas and social customs. *However*, I would not want to forget my own culture or those who depend on me, and the picture would help to remind me of what is important. *Another* important reason I would take a photograph of my family would be to console myself when I felt homesick. I have no doubt that even with all the exciting new sights to see and interesting people to meet, there would be times when I would miss my family. Seeing their faces would remind me that they were still there for me and help me to feel closer to them. *Finally*, I would like to share my life and culture with the people I meet abroad. Showing them a photograph of my home and family would be a wonderful way to do this.

In conclusion, a photograph of my family and hometown would be the most valuable thing to me on a long trip abroad. It would remind me not only of my home, but also of those who are most important to me. It would ease feelings of loneliness and homesickness and serve as a way to introduce my culture to others. *Therefore*, I believe it would be my best companion on the journey.

171. 打包行李，出國一年

　　有機會能夠旅行一年是很多人的夢想，當然我也不例外，這將是探索不同文化和拓展眼界的大好機會。然而，離家一整年不可能不碰到困難，所以需要仔細規劃。我最多只能帶些必需衣物和個人用品。如果還能再帶一樣東西，我會選一張家人和家鄉的照片。

　　我會帶這張照片的主要原因，是因為它會提醒我來自何處。無疑地，這趟為期一年的旅程會充滿刺激和新奇，我會接觸到很多很多的新思想和社會風俗。然而，我並不想忘掉我自己的文化，或是那些信賴我的人，而這張相片有助於提醒我，什麼才是最重要的。另一個我會帶著全家照片的重要原因，就是它可以在我想家時，給我安慰。因為就算可以看到那麼多讓人興奮的新奇景點，以及認識有趣的人，我想還是一定會有想家的時候。看見家人的臉，會讓我想起他們仍然在等我回去，而我也會覺得離他們比較近。最後一個原因是，我想和那些在國外認識的朋友，分享我的生活和文化，而讓他們看一張我家鄉和家人的照片，會是一個很棒的方法。

　　總之，一張全家人和家鄉的照片，會是我這趟國外長途旅程中最珍貴的東西，不但會讓我想到家鄉，也會讓我想起那些對我而言，最重要的人。這張照片會排解我的寂寞和鄉愁，也可以拿來向別人介紹我的文化。因此，我相信它會是我這趟旅程中最好的夥伴。

【註釋】

expand one's *horizons* 拓展某人的眼界

hardship〔ˈhɑrdʃɪp〕*n.* 辛苦　　*personal effects* 私人所有物

additional〔əˈdɪʃənḷ〕*adj.* 額外的　　primary〔ˈpraɪˌmɛrɪ〕*adj.* 主要的

novelty〔ˈnɑvḷtɪ〕*n.* 新奇　　*be exposed to* 接觸

a great many 許多的　　console〔kənˈsol〕*v.* 安慰

homesick〔ˈhomˌsɪk〕*adj.* 想家的　　sight〔saɪt〕*n.* 景色

serve as 充當　　companion〔kəmˈpænjən〕*n.* 同伴

Quit　　　　　**Writing**

When students move to a new school, they sometimes face problems. How can schools help these students with their problems?　Use specific reasons and examples to explain your answer.

▲

Cut

Paste

Undo

▼

172. **Helping New Students Adjust**

Moving to a new school inevitably involves making some adjustments. A transfer student often has to adapt to a very different environment with unfamiliar rules, teaching styles and norms of behavior, all without the support of the classmates he or she has grown up with. Considering these factors, it is not at all unusual for a new student to feel a bit like an outsider at first. *However*, some students have more trouble adjusting than others. *But* this does not have to be the case. Schools can help new students to solve these problems and even to avoid them in the first place in the following ways.

First, the school should provide orientation programs for new students. With information about academic requirements, school regulations, activities, clubs and sources of help, new students could avoid many problems. *Second*, a peer mentor program would help new students to feel at home more quickly. By assigning other students to assist the transfer students on a one-to-one basis, the school would provide them with a valuable source of support and information. *Third*, individual counseling services should be made available to those students who find that they still have trouble making the adjustment to the new environment.

To sum up, the most important way to help transfer students adjust to their new environment is to ensure that they do not feel alone. Schools should take steps to assist the new students before problems arise. Orientation programs, peer mentors and individual counseling are all effective ways to do so. By implementing them, the school will help new students through the difficult process of adjustment.

172. 幫助新生適應環境

　　換到一所新學校，不可避免地，必須做些調適。轉學生常常得在沒有一起長大的同學幫忙下，去適應一個規則、教學方式和行為規範都不熟悉，且非常不同的環境。考慮到這些因素後，新生剛開始，或多或少會覺得自己像個局外人，這種感覺是很常見的。然而，有些學生比其他學生更難適應環境，可是這種情況是可以避免的。學校可以幫助新生解決這些問題，甚至可以在一開始，就以下面的方法來避免這些問題。

　　首先，學校應提供新學生新生訓練。若是擁有關於學業方面的規定、校規、活動、社團和尋求協助的管道等的相關資訊，新學生就可以避免很多問題。第二、同儕輔導計劃會讓新生更快熟悉環境。透過指派另一個同學擔任輔導員，以一對一的方式來協助轉學生，學校就能提供他們一個重要支持和資訊來源。第三、個別諮詢服務應該開放給那些在適應新環境方面，仍感困難的學生。

　　總之，幫助轉學生適應新環境，最重要的方法就是，要確保他們不會覺得孤立無援。學校應該在問題發生之前，就採取幫助新生的步驟。新生訓練、同儕輔導員，和個別諮詢，都是相當有效的方法。藉著推行這些措施，學校將能幫助新生，渡過困難的適應過程。

【註釋】

adjust〔ə'dʒʌst〕v. 適應　　inevitably〔ɪn'ɛvətəblɪ〕adv. 不可避免地

involve〔ɪn'vɑlv〕v. 包含；牽涉

transfer student 轉學生　　***adapt to*** 適應（= *adjust to*）

norm〔nɔrm〕n. 規範　　outsider〔'aʊt'saɪdɚ〕n. 局外人

in the first place 首先　　orientation〔‚orɪɛn'teʃən〕n. 新生訓練

academic〔‚ækə'dɛmɪk〕adj. 學業的

requirement〔rɪ'kwaɪrmənt〕n. 要求；規定

regulation〔‚rɛgjə'leʃən〕n. 規定　　peer〔pɪr〕n. 同儕

mentor〔'mɛntɚ〕n. 輔導員；指導者

program〔'progræm〕n. 計劃　　assign〔ə'saɪn〕v. 指派

one-to-one adj. 一對一的　　counseling〔'kaʊnslɪŋ〕n. 輔導

to sum up 總之　　ensure〔ɪn'ʃʊr〕v. 確保

assist〔ə'sɪst〕v. 協助　　arise〔ə'raɪz〕v. 發生

implement〔'ɪmplə‚mɛnt〕v. 實施

Quit — **Writing**

It is sometimes said that borrowing money from a friend can harm or damage the friendship. Do you agree? Why or why not? Use reasons and specific examples to explain your answer.

Cut

Paste

Undo

Time

Help **?** Confirm Answer Next ➡

173. Borrowing Money from a Friend

There is a common saying, "Neither a borrower nor a lender be." *In my opinion*, this is sound advice because the cause of many disagreements is money. Even among good friends, who would willingly share whatever they have, borrowing money can lead to problems. *As a result*, borrowing or lending money has cost many people a friendship. Why is this so? There are several reasons.

First, when friends ask favors of us, we like to oblige them. This may be why some people lend others money when they really cannot afford to do so or when it is inconvenient for them. *Then*, after they have parted with their money, they begin to feel regret and to blame their friends for their feelings. *Second*, people have different concepts of money. What may be a small sum to one person may be a significant amount to another. *Also*, different people have different ways of spending and saving money. When friends borrow money from each other, these differences may become more obvious and lead to friction. *Finally*, people also have different conceptions of time. What may seem like timely repayment to the borrower may not seem so to the lender. *And* in the case of friends, terms for borrowing money are usually not spelled out in advance because such an act seems unfriendly. The result may be worry, distrust, or hurt feelings, all of which are detrimental to a friendship.

Given all the disadvantages above, I have to agree that borrowing money from a friend may damage the friendship. Because people have different ideas and feelings about money, it is best to make any lending agreement clear to both parties. *However*, friends are often reluctant to do this. The result is too often a broken friendship. *Therefore*, as far as friends are concerned, I believe it is best to be neither a borrower nor a lender.

173. 向朋友借錢

常言道：「既不要做負債者，也不要做債主。」在我看來，這是一個明智的建議，因為很多的紛爭就是因錢而起。即使是願意分享一切的好朋友，借錢也是會引發問題。因此，跟別人借錢或者借錢給別人，都會傷感情。為什麼會這樣呢？以下就是一些可能的原因。

首先，當朋友請我們幫忙時，我們會想要答應幫他，這也就是為什麼有些人其實負擔不起，或是不方便借錢給別人時，卻還是把錢借出去。當他們把錢借出去之後，就開始後悔，也會因此開始責怪他們的朋友。第二，每個人對錢的看法不一樣。對某些人來說是小錢，可能在其他人眼中卻是很龐大的數目。而且，每個人花錢和存錢的方式也不同，所以當朋友互相借貸時，這些差異就會變得更明顯，然後導致摩擦。最後一點就是，每個人對時間的觀念也不盡相同。借方覺得適當的還錢時間，對貸方而言，不一定能夠接受。而且朋友之間的金錢往來，通常不會事先講好借貸的相關條件，因為這樣的行為常常會被看成不夠朋友。這樣子的結果可能會產生擔憂及不信任感，甚至會有受傷的感覺，而這些都會破壞原本的友誼。

考慮到上述這麼多的缺點後，我必須同意，向朋友借錢的確會損害友誼。因為每個人對錢的看法和感覺都不一樣，所以借貸雙方最好做出彼此都清楚明白的協議。然而，朋友之間通常不太願意這麼做，而結果往往就是友誼破裂。因此，就朋友而言，我認為最好就是不向別人借錢，也不要借錢給別人。

【註釋】

borrower〔'bɑroɚ〕*n.* 借方　　lender〔'lɛndɚ〕*n.* 貸方；出借者

sound〔saʊnd〕*adj.* 正確的；合理的

disagreement〔,dɪsə'grimənt〕*n.* 分歧；爭論

oblige〔ə'blaɪdʒ〕*v.* 答應⋯的請求　　cost〔kɔst〕*v.* 使喪失

ask a favor of sb. 請某人幫忙　　*part with* 花掉

concept〔'kɑnsɛpt〕*n.* 觀念　　regret〔rɪ'grɛt〕*n.* 後悔

blame〔blem〕*v.* 把⋯歸咎於

significant〔sɪg'nɪfəkənt〕*adj.* 相當大的

obvious〔'ɑbvɪəs〕*adj.* 明顯的　　friction〔'frɪkʃən〕*n.* 摩擦

conception〔kən'sɛpʃən〕*n.* 觀念　　timely〔'taɪmlɪ〕*adj.* 適時的

repayment〔rɪ'pemənt〕*n.* 償還

terms〔tɝmz〕*n. pl.* 條件；條款　　*spell out* 詳加說明

in advance 事先　　distrust〔dɪs'trʌst〕*n.* 不信任

detrimental〔,dɛtrə'mɛntl̩〕*adj.* 有損的 < *to* >

given〔'gɪvən〕*prep.* 考慮到

disadvantage〔,dɪsəd'væntɪdʒ〕*n.* 壞處 (↔ *advantage*)

agreement〔ə'grimənt〕*n.* 協議　　party〔'pɑrtɪ〕*n.* 一方

reluctant〔rɪ'lʌktənt〕*adj.* 勉強的；不願意的

as far as ～ is concerned 就～而言

Quit　　　**Writing**

Every generation of people is different in important ways. How is your generation different from your parents' generation? Use specific reasons and examples to explain your answer.

Cut

Paste

Undo

Time

Help
?

Confirm
Answer

Next
➡

174. My Generation

The world is constantly changing and so are the people in it. With each generation we see important developments that affect the way we think and live our lives. ***Therefore***, it is not surprising that each generation of people is different from the one before, and my generation is no exception. My peers and I differ from our parents in several important ways, including our view of the world and our expectations of the future.

People my age usually have a more global outlook than their parents. Unlike the previous generation, we have been exposed to a wide variety of information about the world from a very young age. We have benefited from technological advances such as satellite communications and the Internet. These have truly made the world a global village and we have been greatly influenced as a result. We are not only concerned about our traditional way of life, but also about how life is lived around the world.

Our expectations of the future are also different. This is due mainly to the greater prosperity and peace that we have known. Few of us have suffered true economic hardship and most take a good education and high standard of living for granted. Although we are willing to work hard to succeed, we also value our leisure time. We are more likely to spend money on recreational activities than start saving for our old age in our youth. Our prosperity has made us more materialistic than our parents, but also more carefree.

Given our different circumstances, it is not surprising that we are so different from the previous generation. Our parents may shake their heads and worry over these changes, but no doubt their parents did the same. Rather than worry about what the next generation is coming to, I believe it is smarter to look for and appreciate the advantages in these developments.

174. 我們這一代

　　世界不斷在改變，世界上的人也是如此。每一個世代中，我們都可以看到一些重要的發展，它們會影響著我們的思考方式和生活方式。因此，每個世代的人和上一代的人大不相同，這一點也不令人驚訝，而我們這一代也不例外。我跟我的同儕們對於某些重要的事情，就和父母的觀念不同，其中包括我們的世界觀，和我們對未來的展望。

　　我們這一代的人，通常比父母有更寬廣的世界觀。不像上一代的人，我們在很年輕的時候，就已經接觸到很多各式各樣的世界資訊。我們因科技的進步而獲益，如衛星通訊和網際網路。這些科技確實使世界成為一個地球村，而我們也因此受到很大的影響。我們不僅關心自己傳統的生活方式，也關心現今全世界的生活方式。

　　我們對未來的展望也不同。這主要是因為我們經歷過繁榮和平的景況。我們之中，很少有人真正經歷過經濟困難，而大部分的人都把良好的教育和高生活水準，視為理所當然。雖然我們願意努力工作，以求功成名就，但是我們也很重視休閒時間。我們比較可能把錢花在娛樂活動上，而不會在年輕時，就開始儲存我們的養老金。繁榮的生活使我們比父母更重視物質生活，也使我們更無憂無慮。

　　如果考慮到我們與父母之間的差異，那麼我們這一代和上一代大不相同，就沒什麼好驚訝的了。我們的父母或許會搖頭嘆氣，擔心這些變動，但毫無疑問地，他們的父母也做過同樣的事。與其擔心下一代會變成什麼樣子，我認為不如期待，並欣賞這些發展所帶來的好處，這會是更明智的做法。

【註釋】

generation〔ˌdʒɛnəˈreʃən〕 *n.* 世代

constantly〔ˈkɑnstəntlɪ〕 *adv.* 不斷地

peer〔pɪr〕 *n.* 同儕　　view〔vju〕 *n.* 看法

expectation〔ˌɛkspɛkˈteʃən〕 *n.* 期待

global〔ˈglobḷ〕 *adj.* 全球的　　outlook〔ˈaʊtˌlʊk〕 *n.* 展望；看法

previous〔ˈprivɪəs〕 *adj.* 之前的　　*be exposed to* 接觸

a variety of 各式各樣的（= various〔ˈvɛrɪəs〕）

benefit〔ˈbɛnəfɪt〕 *v.* 獲益 < *from* >

advance〔ədˈvæns〕 *n.* 進步　　satellite〔ˈsætḷˌaɪt〕 *n.* 衛星

communications〔kəˌmjunəˈkeʃənz〕 *n.pl.* 通訊

Internet〔ˈɪntɚˌnɛt〕 *n.* 網際網路

be concerned about 關心　　prosperity〔prɑsˈpɛrətɪ〕 *n.* 繁榮

hardship〔ˈhɑrdʃɪp〕 *n.* 困難

take…for granted 視…為理所當然

willing〔ˈwɪlɪŋ〕 *adj.* 願意的　　value〔ˈvælju〕 *v.* 重視

recreational〔ˌrɛkrɪˈeʃənḷ〕 *adj.* 娛樂的

in one's youth 在某人年輕的時候

materialistic〔məˌtɪrɪəlˈɪstɪk〕 *adj.* 物質主義的

carefree〔ˈkɛrˌfri〕 *adj.* 無憂無慮的　　given〔ˈgɪvən〕 *prep.* 考慮到

circumstances〔ˈsɝkəmˌstænsɪz〕 *n.pl.* 情況

shake one's head 搖頭；表示不同意

rather than 與其…（不如）　　*come to* 結果是

appreciate〔əˈpriʃɪˌet〕 *v.* 欣賞

advantage〔ədˈvæntɪdʒ〕 *n.* 好處；優點（↔ *disadvantage*）

Quit　　　　　　**Writing**

Some students like classes where teachers lecture (do all of the talking) in class. Other students prefer classes where the students do some of the talking. Which type of class do you prefer? Give specific reasons and details to support your choice.

Cut

Paste

Undo

175. The Benefits of Class Participation

Different teachers have different styles of teaching. Some prefer to deliver a prepared lecture, while others expect some participation from their students. *Likewise*, some students learn best in the former situation, while others do so in the latter. Sometimes the style of teaching is dictated by the subject matter, but at others the teacher has some discretion as to how much interaction he or she will encourage or allow. Perhaps the best learning environment is one in which the preferred styles of teacher and students match. For me, that is a class in which the teacher encourages class participation.

I prefer to participate in class for several reasons. *One* is that student participation makes the class more lively and interesting. I can hear not only my teacher's opinions on a subject, but also those of my classmates. This often leads to a meaningful discussion. *Another* reason is that I believe the teacher can better understand the students when they interact with him or her in class.

Rather than wait for exam results to indicate how much the students have absorbed, the teacher can know immediately whether the students understand what he or she is talking about. *Last but not least, in my opinion*, I can acquire more knowledge in this kind of class. The teacher is a valuable resource, and asking questions in class allows me to make the best use of this resource. I can ask more in-depth questions and satisfy my curiosity.

With all of these advantages, I am convinced that a class that encourages student participation is the best learning environment for me. I can not only learn more, but also enjoy learning it. Expressing my opinions in class and listening to those of the other students helps me to think more deeply about the material. *In this way*, I do not just learn facts, but learn how to use them as well.

175. 課堂參與的好處

　　不同的老師有不同的教學風格。有的老師偏好上課時照本宣科，講授事前預備好的內容，有的老師則期望學生能參與課程。同樣地，有的學生在前者的環境下學習效果最佳，而有的學生則適合後者的學習環境。有時候教學方式是依授課主題而定，但在有些情況，老師會斟酌是否要鼓勵，或考慮要有多少的互動程度。也許最好的學習環境，就是剛好老師與學生想要的方式不謀而合。對我來說，最好的情況就是，老師會鼓勵課堂參與。

　　我偏愛課堂參與，是基於幾個理由。其中一個原因是，學生的參與讓課堂更有活力，也更有趣。我不但可以聽到老師對某一主題的意見，也可以聽到同學們的看法，如此一來，常會形成一個很有意義的討論。另一個原因就是，當學生與老師在課堂上互動時，老師能藉此更加了解學生。老師藉由課堂參與，就能立即知道學生明不明白上課的內容，不用等到測驗結果出來，才知道學生到底吸收了多少。最後一項要點是，在我看來，這種課能讓我獲得更多知識。老師是很寶貴的資源，因此在課堂中發問，我就能充份利用這項資源，並提出更深入的問題，來滿足我的求知慾。

　　由於有這麼多項好處，我深信，就我而言，鼓勵學生參與的課程，是最好的學習環境。我不但能學到更多，也能在這樣的學習過程中得到樂趣。在課堂上發表意見，和聽取其他同學的看法，有助於讓我更深入思考課程內容。如此一來，我不僅能獲得知識，也知道該如何學以致用。

【註釋】

participation〔pɑrˌtɪsə'peʃən〕*n.* 參與

lecture〔'lɛktʃɚ〕*n.* 授課　　likewise〔'laɪkˌwaɪz〕*adv.* 同樣地

former〔'fɔrmɚ〕*adj.*（兩者中）前者的

latter〔'lætɚ〕*adj.*（兩者中）後者的

dictate〔dɪk'tek〕*v.* 要求；支配

discretion〔dɪ'skrɛʃən〕*n.* 考慮；斟酌　　*as to* 關於

interaction〔ˌɪntɚ'ækʃən〕*n.* 互動

preferred〔prɪ'fɝd〕*adj.* 被喜愛的

match〔mætʃ〕*v.* 相配；適合　　lively〔'laɪvlɪ〕*adj.* 生動的

meaningful〔'minɪŋfḷ〕*adj.* 有意義的

interact〔ˌɪntɚ'ækt〕*v.* 互動　　*rather than* 與其…（不如）

indicate〔'ɪndəˌket〕*v.* 指出；顯示

absorb〔əb'sɔrb〕*v.* 吸收

last but not least 最後一項要點是

acquire〔ə'kwaɪr〕*v.* 獲得

valuable〔'væljuəbḷ〕*adj.* 珍貴的

resource〔rɪ'sors〕*n.* 資源

in-depth〔'ɪn'dɛpθ〕*adj.* 深入的

curiosity〔ˌkjʊrɪ'ɑsətɪ〕*n.* 好奇心

convinced〔kən'vɪnst〕*adj.* 確信的　　*as well* 也（= *too*）

Quit

Writing

Holidays honor people or events. If you could create a new holiday, what person or event would it honor and how would you want people to celebrate it? Use specific reasons and details to support your answer.

Cut

Paste

Undo

Time

Help
?

Confirm
Answer

Next

176. A New Holiday

Holidays are important in every culture. They usually honor important people
or historic events. They are not only times

to celebrate, but also serve to remind us of what is important
in our society. To choose a new holiday is not easy. There
have been many great people throughout history and many
important events. ***Therefore***, if I had the opportunity to
establish a new holiday, I would do something completely
different. Rather than honor a person or a human event, I
would choose to celebrate man's most loyal companions —
pets.

In my opinion, establishing a National Pet Day is a good
idea for two very important reasons. ***First***, it would remind us
of how important animals are to us — not just cats and dogs
and other common household pets, but also animals such as
horses and those raised in captivity in zoos and animal parks.
All of them provide us with a connection to the natural world.
In addition, our personal pets give us companionship,
devotion and affection. ***Second***, a holiday in honor of our pets
would remind us of our responsibilities toward them. Too
often these days pets are taken for granted or even neglected
when their owners become too busy to pay much attention to
them. This is poor repayment for their devotion to us. A
holiday in their honor would encourage people to recognize
the important role their pets play in their lives.

As for how this holiday should be observed, I have several suggestions. *One* is that people simply play with their pets and get reacquainted with them if this is something they have not done in a while. If people do not own their own pets, they could take their children to a zoo to help them realize the importance of animals in the world. *Another* suggestion is that people take their pets to a veterinarian. It is important for animals to have checkups and receive necessary vaccinations. This will help to ensure a long and healthy life for them and is perhaps the best gift an owner can give to his or her pet. *Finally*, if a family has room in their home for a pet, I suggest that they visit a local animal shelter and adopt one. There are many cats and dogs that have been abandoned and would appreciate a loving home.

These are my suggestions for a new holiday. Although it may seem a little unconventional when compared with holidays that honor important statesmen or religious figures, it would serve to make people recognize an important part of our lives that is too often neglected — the world of animals. *Moreover*, it is a holiday that everyone can participate in no matter what his or her religious beliefs or political views. *Therefore*, I believe that a National Pet Day would be a valuable addition to our list of holidays.

176. 一個新節日

　　節日在每個文化中，都很重要，通常節日是爲了紀念重要的人物，或歷史事件。節日不僅是慶祝的時刻，也能夠提醒我們，在我們的社會裡，什麼才是重要的。選出一個新的節日並非易事。自古以來，我們已經有很多偉人以及重要事件，因此，如果我有機會可以訂定一個新的節日，我會做出很不一樣的選擇。我不會選擇紀念某人或某個與人相關的事件，而是會讚揚人類最忠實的朋友 —— 寵物。

　　依我之見，基於兩個非常重要的理由，訂定國定寵物節是個不錯的主意。首先，這個節日可以提醒我們，動物對我們而言是多麼重要 —— 不只是貓和狗，以及其他常見的家中寵物，還有像是馬和飼養在動物園籠子裡及野生動物園的動物，這些動物全都能提供我們和大自然接觸的管道。此外，我們私人的寵物會帶給我們友誼、奉獻，及熱愛。第二個理由是，紀念寵物的節日能提醒我們對牠們的責任。現今常見的狀況是，寵物被視作理所當然的東西，甚至當主人太忙碌，而無法花心思在牠們身上時，這些寵物常遭到忽略。寵物全心全意地對待我們，卻換得差勁的對待。一個紀念牠們的節日，可以鼓勵人們重視寵物在生活中所扮演的重要角色。

　　至於該如何慶祝這個節日，我有幾個建議。其一就是和寵物玩，並且重新認識牠們，如果你已經有一段時間沒這麼做的話。如果你沒有養寵物，則可以帶小孩到動物園，幫助小孩了解動物在這個世界的重要性。另一個建議就是，帶自己的寵物去看獸醫。動物接受健康檢查，以及接種必要的疫苗，是很重要的。如此，便有助於確保動物能活得久、活得健康，這或許是主人可以送給寵物的最佳禮物。最後一個建議是，如果家中有空間養寵物的話，我建議大家到當地的動物收容所看一看，收養一隻動物。有很多貓和狗遭到遺棄，牠們會很感謝你提供溫暖的家。

　　這些是我對新節日的建議。雖然這節日和紀念偉大的政治家，或宗教人物的節日比起來，有點不合傳統，但這個節日可以讓人們發現我們生活中經常忽略的一個重要部分 —— 也就是動物界。此外，這是個衆人皆可參與的節日，不論宗教信仰或政治理念爲何。因此，我認爲在我們既有的節日外，加上「國定寵物節」會是個富有價值的新節日。

【註釋】

historic〔hɪs'tɔrɪk〕*adj.* 歷史上有名的　　event〔ɪ'vɛnt〕*n.* 事件

serve〔sɜv〕*v.* 符合；供…使用　　*remind sb. of sth.* 提醒某人某事

throughout history 自古以來　　*rather than* 與其…（不如）

honor〔'ɑnɚ〕*v.* 向~致敬　　loyal〔'lɔɪəl〕*adj.* 忠心的

companion〔kəm'pænjən〕*n.* 同伴　　pet〔pɛt〕*n.* 寵物

household〔'haʊs,hold〕*adj.* 家庭的　　raise〔rez〕*v.* 養育

captivity〔kæp'tɪvətɪ〕*n.* 囚禁　　*animal park* 野生動物園

in addition 此外　　connection〔kə'nɛkʃən〕*n.* 連結

companionship〔kəm'pænjən,ʃɪp〕*n.* 友誼；同伴關係

devotion〔dɪ'voʃən〕*n.* 奉獻　　affection〔ə'fɛkʃən〕*n.* 愛

in honor of 紀念　　*take…for granted* 視…爲理所當然

neglect〔nɪ'glɛkt〕*v.* 忽略　　repayment〔rɪ'pemənt〕*n.* 回報

recognize〔'rɛkəg,naɪz〕*n.* 認可　　*as for* 至於

observe〔əb'zɜv〕*v.* 慶祝（節日等）

get reacquainted with 重新認識

veterinarian〔,vɛtərə'nɛrɪən〕*n.* 獸醫（= *vet*）

checkup〔'tʃɛk,ʌp〕*n.* 健康檢查

vaccination〔,væksn̩'eʃən〕*n.* 疫苗接種

adopt〔ə'dɑpt〕*v.* 收養　　abandon〔ə'bændən〕*v.* 抛棄

appreciate〔ə'priʃɪ,et〕*v.* 感激

unconventional〔,ʌnkən'vɛnʃənl̩〕*adj.* 非傳統的；不按慣例的

compared with 與~相比　　statesman〔'stetsmən〕*n.* 政治家

figure〔'fɪgjɚ〕*n.* 人物　　world〔wɜld〕*n.*（生物）界

participate〔pɑr'tɪsə,pet〕*v.* 參與 < *in* >

belief〔bɪ'lif〕*n.* 信仰　　valuable〔'væljəbl̩〕*adj.* 珍貴的

addition〔ə'dɪʃən〕*n.* 增添物

Quit   **Writing**

A friend of yours has received some money and plans to use all of it
either
- to go on vacation
- to buy a car

Your friend has asked you for advice. Compare your friend's two
choices and explain which one you think your friend should choose.
Use specific reasons and details to support your choice.

	Cut
	Paste
	Undo

177. A Vacation vs. a Car

If my friend had to choose between taking a vacation and buying a new car, it would be a difficult decision to make. *On the one hand*, vacations are important because they help us relax and replenish our energy. They can also be good opportunities for learning or personal growth. A car, *on the other hand*, is a useful tool which can make our lives more convenient. Although the choice is difficult, I would advise my friend to purchase a car for the following reasons.

First of all, the benefit of owning a car will last years rather than weeks. My friend would be able to enjoy the car long after any vacation was over. *Second*, a car is very useful and owning one would make my friend's life more convenient. Although the purchase of a new car would not immediately relieve as much stress as a vacation, it could reduce the pressure my friend feels in daily life by saving him time. *Last but not least*, it would be possible for him to buy a car and still go on vacation. My friend could plan a cheaper vacation and travel to his destination in his new car.

The choice between a vacation and a car is indeed a difficult one. *However*, I believe that purchasing a car would be the right choice for my friend to make. It would provide him lasting benefit and make his life easier and less stressful on a daily basis. *In the end*, a car is more useful than a vacation.

177. 渡假與買車

　　如果我的朋友要在渡假和買新車之間，做一個選擇，這將是個很困難的決定。一方面，假期很重要，因爲可以幫助我們放鬆，補充活力。假期也可能是學習，或是讓個人成長的機會。而另一方面，車子是很有用的工具，可以使我們的生活更便利。雖然要做選擇很困難，但是我會勸我的朋友買車，理由如下。

　　首先，擁有一部車的好處會維持數年，而非只有幾週。我的朋友在任何假期結束後，仍然能夠長期地享受有車的優點。其次，車子很有用處，擁有一部車，可以使我朋友的生活更便利。雖然買新車不像渡假，能夠立刻減輕那麼多壓力，但買車節省時間，可以讓我的朋友減少日常生活中所感受到的壓力。最後一項重點是，買了車，仍然可以去渡假。我的朋友可以計劃比較便宜的行程，並且開著新車前往目的地。

　　假期和新車之間，的確是一個困難的選擇，然而，我相信，買車才是我朋友該做的正確抉擇。這可以給他長久的好處，使他的生活較輕鬆，並且能減少每天的壓力。車子終究是比假期更有用。

【註釋】

replenish〔rɪ'plɛnɪʃ〕v. 補充　　advise〔əd'vaɪz〕v. 勸告
purchase〔'pɝtʃəs〕v., n. 購買　　relieve〔rɪ'liv〕v. 減輕；緩和
stress〔strɛs〕n. 壓力（= *pressure*）
last but not least 最後一項要點是
destination〔ˌdɛstə'neʃən〕n. 目的地　　indeed〔ɪn'did〕adv. 的確
lasting〔'læstɪŋ〕adj. 持久的　　benefit〔'bɛnəfɪt〕n. 利益；好處
stressful〔'strɛsfəl〕adj. 充滿壓力的　　*on a daily basis* 每天
in the end 最後；終究

Writing

Quit

The 21st century has begun. What changes do you think this new century will bring? Use examples and details in your answer.

_____

_____

_____

_____

_____

_____

_____

_____

_____

_____

_____

_____

_____

_____

_____

_____

_____

_____

Cut

Paste

Undo

Time

Help
?

Confirm
Answer

Next
➡

178. **What the 21st Century Will Bring**

Mankind has made great progress since scientific exploration began, and this progress seems to be accelerating. In the last hundred years we have seen inventions that have not only greatly improved our lives but changed the very way we live. There is no reason to believe that this rapid progress will not continue into the 21st century. While there is no way to predict exactly what our scientists and entrepreneurs will come up with, there are indications that advances will be made in certain areas. The following are some examples.

First, advances will continue to be made in the field of medicine that will allow people to live longer and healthier lives. In developed countries today most people already have a lifespan that would have been unusually long a hundred years ago. Steady progress has been made in the eradication of disease and this should continue in the next 100 years. *In addition*, biotechnology in the field of genetics may someday allow us to develop bodies that are stronger and free of inherited defects. Perhaps we will even be able to clone ourselves. No matter what form these advances take, it is highly likely that we will greatly extend our lifespan in the new century.

Second, new technology has already brought people around the world closer. This trend will continue in the

21st century as communication becomes more efficient and affordable. Countries and their peoples have formed stronger bonds both economically and politically, as in the recent development of the European Union. Perhaps some day in the future there will cease to be national boundaries. *However*, one side effect of this globalization is that many characteristics of individual cultures will be lost. Sadly, by the end of the century, some languages and art forms may only be found in museums.

Third, we can expect a growing population and demands for a higher standard of living to put increasing pressure on the earth's resources. We have already seen some of the effects of this pressure in the form of pollution and global warming. It is likely that these trends will also continue and that more damage to the environment will be done. *On the other hand,* perhaps we will find more efficient ways to make use of the available resources or develop alternative forms of energy. *In that case*, we may live in better harmony with nature.

The scenarios above are just three of the many possible changes that this new century will bring. We can expect to see great advances in many fields, including medicine, communications, trade, transportation and production. Although there may be problems in the future, our ingenuity and inventiveness will help us to deal with them.

178. 二十一世紀會有何進展

從科學探索發展以來，人類就已經有了長足的進步，而進步的速度似乎愈來愈快。在過去的一百年中，我們看到許多發明出現，這些發明不僅大大地改善了我們的生活，而且也改變了我們的生活方式。我們沒有理由不相信，這樣迅速的進步會持續到二十一世紀。雖然我們沒有辦法精確地預測，科學家和企業家會想出什麼新點子，但有跡象顯示，某些領域將會有進步。以下是一些例子。

第一，醫學領域會持續進展，那將使人類活得更久，而且更健康。在現今的已開發國家裡，大多數人的壽命跟一百年前的人比起來，已經算是很長壽了。在疾病的根除方面，已經有了穩定的進步，未來的一百年應該還會持續進步。此外，也許有一天，遺傳學這項生物科技，會使人類的身體更強壯，而且沒有遺傳上的缺陷。或許我們將來甚至能夠複製自己。不管是哪一種形式的進步，非常可能的是，我們在新的世紀裡，將大幅延長我們的壽命。

第二，新的科技已經使世界上的人更接近。這個趨勢會持續到二十一世紀，因為通訊變得更有效率，而且一般人更負擔的起。國與國之間，以及人民與人民之間，不論在經濟上和政治上，都會更緊密地結合，就像歐盟最近的發展一樣。或許將來有一天，這世界將沒有國界的存在。但是，全球化有一個副作用，那就是各個文化的特性將會消失。遺憾的是，在世紀末的時候，有一些語言和藝術形式，或許只能在博物館裡找到。

第三，我們可以預計人口會增加，人類會追求更高的生活水準，導致地球資源承受更大的壓力。我們已經看到這種壓力所導致的一些結果，如污染和全球暖化。這種趨勢可能也會持續，而且可能會對環境造成更大的破壞。可是就另一方面來說，或許我們會找到更有效的方法，來利用可獲得的資源，或是發展出其他形式的能源。如此，我們才能與大自然更和平共處。

以上的設想，只是新世紀可能會帶來的變動中的三項。我們預期在許
多領域都會有很大的進步，包括醫學、通訊、貿易、交通，和生產方式。
雖然未來可能會有難題產生，但是我們的創造力和發明力，將會幫助我們
解決問題。

【註釋】

mankind〔'mæn,kaɪnd〕n. 人類

progress〔'prɑgrɛs〕n. 進步（= advance〔əd'væns〕）

exploration〔,ɛksplə'reʃən〕n. 探索

accelerate〔æk'sɛlə,ret〕v. 加速進行

entrepreneur〔,ɑntrəprə'nɜ〕n. 企業家　　***come up with*** 提出；想出

indication〔,ɪndə'keʃən〕n. 跡象　　field〔fild〕n. 領域

lifespan〔'laɪf,spæn〕n. 壽命　　steady〔'stɛdɪ〕adj. 持續的

eradication〔ɪ,rædɪ'keʃən〕n. 根除

biotechnology〔,baɪotɛk'nɑlədʒɪ〕n. 生物科技

genetics〔dʒə'nɛtɪks〕n. 遺傳學　　***free of*** 無…的

inherited〔ɪn'hɛrɪtɪd〕adj. 遺傳的　　defect〔dɪ'fɛkt〕n. 缺陷

clone〔klon〕v. 複製　　***take…form*** 以…形式出現

extend〔ɪks'tɛnd〕v. 延長　　trend〔trɛnd〕n. 趨勢

efficient〔ə'fɪʃənt〕adj. 有效率的

affordable〔ə'fɔrdəbl̩〕adj. 負擔得起的　　people〔'pipl̩〕n. 民族

bond〔bɑnd〕n. 聯結　　recent〔'risn̩t〕adj. 最近的

cease〔sis〕v. 停止　　boundary〔'baʊndərɪ〕n. 邊界

side effect 副作用　　globalization〔,globəlaɪ'zeʃən〕n. 全球化

characteristic〔,kærɪktə'rɪstɪk〕n. 特性

resource〔rɪ'sors〕n. 資源　　***in the form of*** 以…形式

global warming 全球暖化　　alternative〔ɔl'tɜnətɪv〕adj. 替代的

harmony〔'hɑrmənɪ〕n. 和諧　　scenario〔sɪ'nɛrɪ,o〕n. 情節；設想

ingenuity〔,ɪndʒə'nuətɪ〕n. 創造力

inventiveness〔ɪn'vɛntɪvnɪs〕n. 發明才能　　***deal with*** 處理

| Quit | **Writing** |

What are some of the qualities of a good parent? Use specific details and examples to explain your answer.

Cut

Paste

Undo

| Time | Help | Confirm | Next |
| | ? | Answer | → |

179. A Good Parent

Becoming a parent is a great responsibility. Children depend on their parents not only for their material needs, but also for guidance and emotional support. Because parents have such a great effect on their children's lives and futures, it is important that they take this responsibility seriously and do their best to be good parents. A good parent is many things, but what follows are the characteristics that I think are most important.

First of all, good parents must know how to set limits for their children. They will not only protect them from danger but also help them to develop patience and self-control. ***Second***, parents should spend time with their children. Only by spending time with them can the parents really know what their children think and feel. They will also discover their children's strengths and weaknesses and, in this way, be better able to help them develop the skills that they need. ***More importantly***, parents must talk to their children. Only in this way can they keep the lines of communication open. ***Third***, good parents are supportive and encourage their children to dream and to pursue their dreams. Rather than impose their own preferences on their children, parents should help them to set and realize their own goals. ***Last but not least***, good parents should be a good example to their children. Children are very observant and believe the actions of their parents more than their words. If parents want their children to hold certain values, they must demonstrate these values themselves.

The above are only a few of the many ways that parents can be nurturers and role models to their children. They must know what values are important to them and concentrate on passing these on to their sons and daughters. ***Most importantly***, parents should see their children as unique individuals with their own talents and dreams. When they can see the good in their children and encourage it, parents will help them to reach their full potential.

179. 稱職的父母

要成為稱職的父母是一項重大的責任。小孩依賴父母，不僅是在物質上的需求，還有父母所給予的指導，以及情感上的支持，因為父母對小孩的生活及未來影響非常大，所以很重要的是，父母應該以認真的態度看待這許多特點，但下列特色是我認為最重要的。

首先，稱職的父母，必須知道如何為他們的子女設限，這點將不僅保護小孩免於危險之外，也有助於小孩培養耐心及自制力。第二點，父母應該花時間和小孩相處，唯有和小孩相處，父母才能真正知道子女的想法及感受。他們也能發現小孩的優缺點，如此一來，將更能幫助小孩培養他們所需的技能。更重要的是，父母必須跟小孩說話，唯有如此，才能讓溝通之門永遠敞開。第三點，稱職的父母會給予小孩支持，且鼓勵小孩懷抱夢想，並勇於追求。父母與其把自己的偏好強加在小孩身上，不如幫助小孩設定自己的目標，並加以實現。最後一項要點是，稱職的父母應該是子女的好榜樣。小孩的觀察力很敏銳，會認為父母的所作所為，比所說的話要更有說服力。如果父母希望小孩具有某些價值觀，他們就必須表現出他們認同這些價值觀。

上述只是父母成為養育者及小孩的模範，許多方法中的其中一些。父母必須知道哪些價值觀是重要的，並且全心全意地把這些價值觀傳遞給他們的子女。最重要的是，父母應該把小孩視為獨特的個體，他們有各自的才能及夢想。若父母能夠知道子女的長處為何，並加以激發，將有助於小孩充份發揮他們的潛力。

【註釋】

material〔məˈtɪrɪəl〕*adj.* 物質的　　guidance〔ˈgaɪdn̩s〕*n.* 指導

emotional〔ɪˈmoʃən̩l〕*adj.* 情感的

take* sth. *seriously 認真看待某事

be many things 有很多特性

characteristic〔ˌkærɪktəˈrɪstɪk〕*n.* 特點

self-control〔ˌsɛlfkənˈtrol〕*n.* 自制

strength〔strɛŋθ〕*n.* 優點（↔ *weakness*）

line〔laɪn〕*n.* 管道

supportive〔səˈpɔrtɪv〕*adj.* 支持的；給予幫助的

pursue〔pɚˈsu〕*v.* 追求　　***rather than*** 與其…（不如）

impose〔ɪmˈpoz〕*v.* 強加…於＜ *on* ＞

preference〔ˈprɛfərəns〕*n.* 偏愛　　realize〔ˈrɪəˌlaɪz〕*v.* 實現

last but not least 最後一項要點是

example〔ɪgˈzæmpl̩〕*n.* 榜樣

observant〔əbˈzɝvənt〕*adj.* 觀察力敏銳的

values〔ˈvæljʊz〕*n. pl.* 價值觀

demonstrate〔ˈdɛmənˌstret〕*v.* 示範

nurturer〔ˈnɝtʃərɚ〕*n.* 養育者　　***role model*** 模範

pass on 傳遞＜ *to* ＞　　***see* A *as* B** 把 A 視為 B

potential〔pəˈtɛnʃəl〕*n.* 潛力

Quit **Writing**

Movies are popular all over the world. Explain why movies are so popular. Use reasons and specific examples to support your answer.

Cut

Paste

Undo

Time

Help ?

Confirm Answer

Next →

180. The Popularity of Movies

Movies have long been popular all over the world. People not only go to see movies, but also talk about them and read about them. They seem to be an important part of most people's lives. Even though there are many other forms of entertainment available now, most people still enjoy going to see a movie. I believe there are several reasons for their continued popularity.

First of all, movies allow viewers to escape into another world for a couple of hours. This is especially apparent during times of trouble. *For example*, movies were never more popular than during the Great Depression, and moviegoers continue to flock to escapist movies in poor countries such as India. At such times people seem to prefer happy, even silly movies that let them forget their problems for a while. *But* movies can also challenge the mind and reflect both popular opinion and dissenting views. *Thus*, they become an important topic of conversation. *Finally*, going to see a movie is a shared experience, different from watching a video or DVD at home. Movies allow people to connect with others in a way that other forms of entertainment do not.

For all these reasons, I believe that the popularity of movies will continue no matter what other forms of entertainment are invented. They allow people to explore other worlds and take them out of their own lives for a short time, and there are few people who can resist such an experience.

180. 電影受歡迎的原因

　　長久以來，電影在世界各地都很受歡迎。人們不僅會去看電影，而且也會談論及閱讀與電影有關的資料。電影似乎是大多數人的生活中，很重要的一部份。即使現在已有許多其他類型的娛樂，但大多數的人，仍然喜歡去看電影。我認為，電影能持續受歡迎，有好幾個理由。

　　首先，電影能讓觀眾逃入另一個世界，停留幾個小時。這種現象在困難時期特別明顯。例如，電影在經濟大恐慌時期是最受歡迎的，而在較貧窮的國家，如印度，看電影的人持續蜂擁到電影院，想逃避現實。在這段時期，人們似乎比較喜歡愉快，甚至是有點愚蠢的電影，因為這樣能讓他們暫時忘卻煩惱。但是，電影也可以發人深省，並且反映一般的輿論及不同的意見。因此，電影成了談話的重要主題。最後，看電影是一種可以和他人分享的經驗，這和在家看錄影帶或是 DVD 不同。電影能讓人們互相聯繫，這是其他娛樂方式所無法做到的。

　　基於這些理由，我認為無論發明什麼其他種類的娛樂，電影受歡迎的情況，會持續下去。電影能讓人們探索其他的世界，並帶領人們短暫地脫離現實生活，很少有人能夠抗拒這樣的經驗。

【註釋】

popularity〔ˌpɑpjəˈlærətɪ〕 *n.* 受歡迎

entertainment〔ˌɛntɚˈtenmənt〕 *n.* 娛樂

available〔əˈveləbḷ〕 *adj.* 可獲得的

viewer〔ˈvjuɚ〕 *n.* 觀眾　　***a couple of*** 幾個（= *several*）

apparent〔əˈpɛrənt〕 *adj.* 明顯的

depression〔dɪˈprɛʃən〕 *n.* 不景氣；蕭條

the Great Depression 經濟大恐慌（指 1929-1939 年發生於美國和其他國家的經濟大衰退）　　moviegoer〔ˈmuvɪˌgoɚ〕 *n.* 看電影的人

flock〔flɑk〕 *v.* 蜂擁；聚集　　escapist〔əˈskepɪst〕 *adj.* 逃避現實的

silly〔ˈsɪlɪ〕 *adj.* 愚蠢的　　challenge〔ˈtʃælɪndʒ〕 *v.* 考驗～的能力

challenge one's ***mind*** 促使某人動腦筋　　reflect〔rɪˈflɛkt〕 *v.* 反映

popular opinion 輿論　　dissenting〔dɪˈsɛntɪŋ〕 *adj.* 不同意的

shared〔ʃɛrd〕 *adj.* 共同的　　video〔ˈvɪdɪ‚o〕 *n.* 錄影帶（= *video tape*）

connect〔kəˈnɛkt〕 *v.* 結合；使有關係＜ *with* ＞

explore〔ɪkˈsplor〕 *v.* 探索　　resist〔rɪˈzɪst〕 *v.* 抗拒

Quit　　　　**Writing**

In your country, is there more need for land to be left in its natural condition or is there more need for land to be developed for housing and industry? Use specific reasons and examples to support your answer.

Cut

Paste

Undo

181. **The Need to Preserve Land**

The land on earth is a limited resource.
This is especially true in Taiwan, an island
country with a dense population. *As a result*,

there is often fierce debate between those who want to develop
land for residential and industrial use and those who want to
leave it in its natural state. *In my opinion*, there is a greater
need to preserve some of the land in my country in its natural
condition than to develop it.

One reason for my position is that we have already developed
a great deal of the land in my country. Much of the remaining
land is mountainous and unsuitable for development due to its
instability. *Furthermore*, deforestation of the forests would
damage the environment, causing landslides and other hazards.
Another reason is that the largely urban population needs a
natural retreat. Without such areas the people would lose
contact with nature and perhaps their concern for the environment.
Finally, these beautiful natural areas not only attract tourists
from around the country and from abroad, but also support
endangered species of plant and animal life. Their loss would
be a loss for all mankind.

For the above reasons, I believe that my country should
set aside more of the remaining undeveloped land as nature
preserves. *In this way* we will be able to conserve our natural
resources, protect the environment and ensure that future
generations have the ability to experience nature. As for the
demands of industry and residential developers, I believe that we
are technologically advanced enough to find more efficient ways
to use the land we have already developed.

181. 我們必須保存土地

　　地球上的土地是一項有限的資源，這對於人口稠密的島國台灣而言，尤其貼切。因此，想要開發土地做為住宅用地和工業用地的人，便常常與想要維持土地自然風貌的人，有激烈的爭論。依我看來，保留我國部份區域，維持其自然風貌，要比開發土地，來得有必要。

　　以我的立場來看，其中一個原因是，我國已開發了大部份的土地。大多數未開發的土地則多是山區，或是因為地質不穩而不適合開發的地區。此外，砍伐森林會破壞環境，導致山崩和其他的危險。另一項原因是，大量的都市人口，需要一個回歸自然的空間。一旦失去了這些土地，人們會喪失與自然的接觸，甚至可能不再關心自然環境。最後一點，這些美麗的自然地區，不但能吸引國內外的觀光客，也同時提供了瀕臨絕種的生物生存的空間，倘若這樣的地區消失了，將對全人類造成一大損失。

　　基於以上種種理由，我認為我國應該保留更多未開發土地，作為自然保護區。這樣我們才能夠保存天然資源並保護環境，以確保後代子孫能夠體驗大自然。至於那些工業及房地產開發商的需求，我相信我們的科技已經夠進步，能夠找出更有效率的方法，來使用那些已經開發的土地。

【註釋】

resource〔rɪ'sors〕*n.* 資源　　dense〔dɛns〕*adj.* 稠密的
fierce〔fɪrs〕*adj.* 激烈的　　debate〔dɪ'bet〕*n.* 辯論；討論
residential〔ˌrɛzə'dɛnʃəl〕*adj.* 居住的　　state〔stet〕*n.* 狀態
preserve〔prɪ'zɝv〕*v.* 保存　*n.*（動植物）保護區
position〔pə'zɪʃən〕*n.* 態度；立場
remaining〔rɪ'menɪŋ〕*adj.* 剩下的
instability〔ˌɪnstə'bɪlətɪ〕*n.* 不穩定性
deforestation〔dɪˌfɔrɪs'teʃən〕*n.* 砍伐森林
landslide〔'lænd,slaɪd〕*n.* 山崩　　hazard〔'hæzəd〕*n.* 危險
retreat〔rɪ'trit〕*n.* 退隱處　　***endangered species*** 瀕臨絕種的動植物
set aside 保留　　conserve〔kən'sɝv〕*v.* 保存
ensure〔ɪn'ʃur〕*v.* 確保　　***as for*** 至於　　demand〔dɪ'mænd〕*n.* 需求
developer〔dɪ'vɛləpɚ〕*n.*（房地產）開發者
advanced〔əd'vænst〕*adj.* 進步的　　efficient〔ɪ'fɪʃənt〕*adj.* 有效率的

Quit　　　Writing

Many people have a close relationship with their pets. These people treat their birds, cats, or other animals as members of their family. In your opinion, are such relationships good? Why or why not? Use specific reasons and examples to support your answer.

Cut

Paste

Undo

182. Pets Are Not Family

Many people around the world keep pets. They may be common goldfish, cats, dogs, or something more exotic like a snake or pot-bellied pig. Whatever animal one chooses as a pet, it can offer companionship and affection. It is natural that people should become very attached to their pets. *However*, some go so far as to consider them members of the family, such as a son or daughter, sister or brother. *In my opinion,* this is not a good practice for several reasons.

One is that pets cannot stay with us forever. *Generally*, they live much shorter lives than people. They may also easily get lost or run away. A person who considers his pet a child or sibling might have trouble accepting this fact. He may not be able to keep the importance of this relationship in perspective and suffer greatly. *Another* more important reason is that pets cannot truly reciprocate our feelings or communicate with us as people can. *Thus*, it is a one-way relationship as far as the deep feelings go and is, *therefore*, shallower than the relationships we can have with other people. A *third* reason is that developing such close relationships with pets can get in the way of real relationships with others. Someone who feels his emotional needs are met by a cat or dog may fail to reach out to other people and establish more meaningful relationships.

In conclusion, while pets can be a wonderful addition to a family, it is not appropriate to view them as substitutes for real family members. They can offer companionship, but not the meaningful communication and emotions that help to develop a real relationship. *Therefore*, it is important to keep our relationships with our pets in perspective. *Otherwise*, we may suffer feelings of loss that are out of proportion and fail to connect with other people in meaningful ways.

182. 寵物並不是家人

　　全世界有很多人養寵物。有的可能是一般的金魚、貓狗，或是像蛇或大肚豬，這種具有異國風味的寵物。不論選那種動物當寵物，動物都會和你作伴並培養感情，因此自然而然地，人們會對他們的寵物懷有感情。然而，有的人甚至已經視寵物為家庭的一份子，像是子女或兄弟姐妹一般。在我看來，基於幾項理由，這種情況並不是個好現象。

　　其中一個理由是，寵物不可能永遠待在我們身邊。一般說來，寵物的壽命比人類短許多。他們很容易就會走失或逃跑。把寵物視為孩子或兄弟姐妹的人，可能不大能接受這種事實，也可能因未能以正確的態度來看待這種關係，而非常痛苦。另外一個更重要的理由是，寵物並不能真的像人一樣，對我們的感情有所回報，或是與我們溝通。因此，這只是單向地付出許多感情，這比起我們與其他人建立的關係，膚淺許多。第三個理由是，和寵物培養如此親密的關係，可能會阻礙我們和其他人建立真實的關係。那些覺得需要透過貓狗來滿足其情感需求的人，可能沒有辦法向外接觸其他人，建立更具意義的關係。

　　總之，雖然寵物可能是家中很棒的增添物，可是若視牠們為真正的家庭成員，就不太妥當了。牠們雖然能陪伴我們，卻無法和我們進行有意義的溝通和情感交流，這些才能有助於發展真正的關係。因此，用正確的眼光來看待我們和寵物的關係是很重要的。否則，我們可能承受超乎常理的失落感，同時也無法以有意義的方式，和其他人建立關係。

【註釋】

keep a pet 養寵物

exotic〔ɪgˈzɑtɪk〕*adj.* 奇異的；有異國風味的

snake〔snek〕*n.* 蛇

pot-bellied〔ˈpɑtˌbɛlɪd〕*adj.* 大肚皮的

companionship〔kəmˈpænjənʃɪp〕*n.* 同伴情誼

affection〔əˈfɛkʃən〕*n.* 愛；感情   *be attached to* 喜歡；依戀

go so far as to + *V.* 甚至   practice〔ˈpræktɪs〕*n.* 做法

sibling〔ˈsɪblɪŋ〕*n.* 兄弟姐妹

have trouble + *V-ing* ～有困難

keep sth. in perspective 以正確的眼光看待某事

reciprocate〔rɪˈsɪprəˌket〕*v.* 報答   *as far as ~ goes* 就～而言

shallow〔ˈʃælo〕*adj.* 淺的   *get in the way of* 妨礙

meet〔mit〕*v.* 滿足   *fail to* + *V.* 無法

reach〔ritʃ〕*v.* 努力爭取   *reach out to sb.* 對某人傾心

in conclusion 總之   addition〔əˈdɪʃən〕*n.* 添加物

appropriate〔əˈproprɪɪt〕*adj.* 適當的   *view…as~* 視…為～

substitute〔ˈsʌbstəˌtjut〕*n.* 代替品 < *for* >

out of proportion 不成比例；不合理 (↔ *in proportion*)

connect〔kəˈnɛkt〕*v.* 溝通；聯繫 < *with* >

Quit　　　　　**Writing**

Films can tell us a lot about the country where they were made. What have you learned about a country from watching its movies? Use specific examples and details to support your response.

▲

Cut

Paste

Undo

▼

183. **Learning from Films**

Films are popular in almost every country in the world. They offer entertainment, escape and even information to millions of people. Some themes, such as love, family relationships and war, are universal. *However*, the films of different countries have some unique characteristics that can tell us something about the culture that inspires them. After seeing movies from the United States and from India, I know more about the societies of these two countries.

American movies often feature futuristic high technology as part of the story. This tells me that Americans are interested in creating a future that is more progressive and convenient. The movies are also often filled with violence, and violence is often seen as a means of solving problems. This may reflect a belief in the importance of power and that "might is right." *Lastly*, many American films show a clear differentiation between good and evil. From this I believe that Americans prefer clear answers to problems. Perhaps this is a reflection of the directness of the society.

In contrast with American films, Indian movies often appear unsophisticated and simplistic. The sets are inexpensive and the story line is predictable, yet the films are overwhelmingly popular. The audience seem to especially like the improbable song and dance numbers. Perhaps this is due to the difficult life that many people in India lead. For a small amount of money they can forget their troubles and be part of a better world. *In addition*, the themes of these movies usually center around family and the impact of modern life on traditional values. From this I have learned that cultural traditions are still very strong in India.

In conclusion, films are not only an important form of entertainment, but can tell us a great deal about the cultures that they reflect. They can tell us what is important to the people who made them and who watch them. They can also tell us about the hopes and aspirations of their creators. They are truly a reflection of our societies.

183. 從電影中學習

電影幾乎在全世界所有國家都很受歡迎。電影可以提供幾百萬人娛樂、逃避的空間，甚至資訊。有些主題，像愛情、家庭關係與戰爭，是很普遍的。然而，不同國家的電影，都有其特色，能讓我們知道是什麼樣的文化，會激發出這樣的電影。在看過美國與印度的電影後，我對這兩個國家的社會，有更深入的了解。

美國電影的特色是常將極其先進高科技，作為故事情節的一部分。從這一點可知，美國人對於創造一個更進步而且便利的未來，是很有興趣的。電影通常也充斥著暴力，而暴力也常被視為解決問題的方法。這可能就反映出，他們認為力量很重要，以及「強權即是公理」。最後，在很多美國電影中，善惡是黑白分明的。由此可知，美國人比較喜歡有明確答案的問題，也許這也反映了美國社會的率直。

跟美國電影比起來，印度電影通常顯得沒那麼世故，而且單純。電影的布景便宜，而且劇本的情節容易預測，但是電影卻非常受歡迎。觀眾特別喜歡看那些穿插很多看起來很不真實的歌舞節目的電影，也許是因為印度的人，大多生活都很困苦，只要花一點小錢，就可以讓他們暫時忘卻煩惱，進入一個更好的世界。此外，這些電影的主題通常都以家庭與現代生活對傳統價值觀的衝擊為中心。由此可知，文化傳統在印度仍然是非常根深蒂固的。

總之，電影不僅是一項重要的娛樂形式，而且還會大幅度地反映出電影所根植的文化。電影能使我們知道，對製作與觀賞這些電影的人而言，什麼是重要的，也讓我們知道，創作者的希望與抱負。電影的確能反映我們社會的原貌。

【註釋】

film〔fɪlm〕*n.* 電影　　escape〔ə'skep〕*n.* 逃避（現實）；解悶

theme〔θim〕*n.* 主題　　universal〔ˌjunə'vɝsḷ〕*adj.* 普遍的

unique〔ju'nik〕*adj.* 獨特的

characteristic〔ˌkærɪktə'rɪstɪk〕*n.* 特色

inspire〔ɪn'spaɪr〕*v.* 激發；給予靈感

feature〔'fitʃə〕*v.* 以…為特色

futuristic〔ˌfjutʃə'rɪstɪk〕*adj.* 極其先進的

progressive〔prə'grɛsɪv〕*adj.* 進步的

means〔minz〕*n.* 方法　　right〔raɪt〕*n.* 公理

reflect〔rɪ'flɛkt〕*v.* 反映　　might〔maɪt〕*n.* 強權

differentiation〔ˌdɪfəˌrɛnʃɪ'eʃən〕*n.* 區分

directness〔də'rɛktnɪs〕*n.* 率直　　*in contrast with* 與…相比

unsophisticated〔ˌʌnsə'fɪstɪˌketɪd〕*adj.* 單純的；不世故的

simplistic〔sɪm'plɪstɪk〕*adj.* 過分簡單化的

set〔sɛt〕*n.* 布景　　*story line* 故事情節

predictable〔prɪ'dɪktəbḷ〕*adj.* 可預測的

overwhelmingly〔ˌovə'hwɛlmɪŋlɪ〕*adv.* 壓倒性地

improbable〔ɪm'prɑbəbḷ〕*adj.* 不大可能的；未必真實的

number〔'nʌmbə〕*n.* 節目之一；演唱歌曲　　*in addition* 此外

center around 以～為中心　　impact〔'ɪmpækt〕*n.* 衝擊；影響

values〔'væljʊz〕*n.pl.* 價值觀

aspiration〔ˌæspə'reʃən〕*n.* 渴望；抱負

Quit	**Writing**

Some students prefer to study alone. Others prefer to study with a group of students. Which do you prefer? Use specific reasons and examples to support your answer.

▲

Cut

Paste

Undo

▼

184. Studying with Others

All students must spend a great deal of time studying, and each has a method that works best for him. Some prefer to study very hard without interruption, while others like to take frequent breaks. Some students would rather study by themselves, while others do better in a group. As for me, I prefer to study with a group of students rather than study alone. The following are some of the reasons why.

First, when I study with others, I can benefit from their knowledge. When one student comes across something he doesn't understand, the others can help him right away. *In this way*, we save time and also expand our knowledge. *Second*, when students study in a group they can encourage one another. I, for one, always study longer and with more enthusiasm when I have friends to cheer me on. *Last but not least*, studying with others makes this work more fun for me. I not only complete my homework, but also spend time with my friends.

In short, I would rather study with others than study on my own because it is a more efficient and effective method for me. *Furthermore*, it can be interesting and fun to hear what others have to say on the same subject. My study partners always give me new ideas and new ways of looking at problems. *Therefore*, studying with others broadens my mind.

184. 與其他人一起唸書

　　所有的學生都要花很多時間唸書，而且每個人都有最適合自己的一套方法。有些人喜歡一股作氣，不受打擾地認眞唸書，而有些人喜歡多作休息。有些學生喜歡自己唸，而有些則喜歡一群人一起唸書。對我來說，我比較喜歡跟一群學生一起唸書，而不喜歡自己一個人唸。以下這些就是我的理由。

　　首先，當我跟其他人一起唸書時，我可以吸收他人的知識而獲益。當某個學生遇到不了解的問題時，其他人可以馬上幫他，如此一來，可以節省時間，並且擴展知識。其次，當一群學生在一起唸書時，可以互相鼓勵。就拿我來說，當有朋友鼓勵我時，我總是能夠唸得更久，而且更有熱忱。最後一項要點是，跟其他人一起唸書，讓我覺得更有趣。我不只完成了作業，還能跟朋友相處。

　　總之，我比較喜歡跟別人一起唸書，而不是單獨一個人唸，因為這對我來說，是個比較有效率，而且有效果的方法。此外，聽聽別人對同一主題的說法，也是很有趣的。我的讀書夥伴總是提供新觀點，以及對問題的新看法給我。因此，和別人一起唸書，會拓展我的心智。

【註釋】

interruption 〔,ɪntəˈrʌpʃən〕 n. 打斷

frequent 〔ˈfrikwənt〕 adj. 經常的　　break 〔brek〕 n. 休息

would rather 寧願　　**as for** 至於

prefer to + V_1 + **rather than** + V_2 比較喜歡 V_1，甚於 V_2

benefit 〔ˈbɛnəfɪt〕 v. 獲益 < *from* >　　**come across** 碰巧遇到

right away 立刻　　expand 〔ɪkˈspænd〕 v. 擴展

for one 舉例來說　　enthusiasm 〔ɪnˈθjuzɪ,æzəm〕 n. 熱忱

cheer sb. **on** 鼓勵某人　　**on** one's **own** 獨自 (= *alone*)

efficient 〔ɪˈfɪʃənt〕 adj. 有效率的

effective 〔ɪˈfɛktɪv〕 adj. 有效果的　　broaden 〔ˈbrɔdn̩〕 v. 擴展

Quit　　　　　**Writing**

You have enough money to purchase either a house or a business. Which would you choose to buy? Give specific reasons to explain your choice.

Cut

Paste

Undo

Time

Help ?　Confirm Answer　Next →

185. **The Advantages of Owning a Business**

Given the opportunity, most people would be delighted to purchase a house or business of their own. Choosing between the two would be very difficult. One provides security while the other offers opportunity. If I were able to purchase only one, I would choose to buy a business because of the chance it would give me to grow and succeed.

There are several reasons why I think purchasing a business would be a better choice for me. *First of all*, I would have the opportunity to improve the business and make it more valuable. Usually, the only way to increase the value of a house is to wait for the market to rise and then sell it. *Second*, if I were successful in my business, I would then have enough money to also buy a house. *In this way*, I could have both. *Finally*, I am still young and so can afford to take the risk of choosing a business over a house. If I should be so unfortunate as to fail in my business, I believe that I am resourceful enough to recover.

In short, a business is a better choice for me than a house because I am at a point in my life when I can afford to take some risks. The opportunity to own a business is also an opportunity to grow. If I am successful, I will gain both profits and experience; if I fail, I will still gain experience. *But* if I do not take the chance, I will gain neither. *After all*, nothing ventured, nothing gained.

185. 擁有事業的好處

　　假如有機會的話，多數人會買一棟自己的房子或事業。要在這兩者之中選一個，是件很困難的事。一個提供安全感，而另一個則提供機會。如果我只能選擇一個的話，我會選擇有自己的事業，因為我會因此有機會成長與成功。

　　有很多理由讓我覺得，擁有自己的事業，對我而言，是更好的選擇。首先，我會有機會改善事業，讓它變得更有價值。而通常要讓房價升值的唯一方法，就是等到房價上漲，然後再出售。其次，如果我事業有成，就會有足夠的錢買房子了。這樣一來，我就能兩樣都擁有。最後，我還年輕，可以承擔做生意而不買房子的風險。如果不幸生意失敗，我相信我還有足夠的應變能力，可以從失敗的挫折中恢復過來。

　　總之，有個事業對我而言，是比買房子更好的選擇，因為我仍然處於能承擔風險的人生階段。擁有自己事業的機會，也是個讓自己成長的機會。如果我成功了，兩樣好處我都有，而且還能獲得經驗；如果不幸失敗了，至少我獲得了經驗。但如果我不願冒險，就什麼都得不到。畢竟，不冒險，沒有收穫（不入虎穴，焉得虎子）。

【註釋】

given〔'gɪvən〕 *prep.* 如果有　　delighted〔dɪ'laɪtɪd〕 *adj.* 高興的

purchase〔'pɝtʃəs〕 *v.* 購買　　security〔sɪ'kjurətɪ〕 *n.* 安全感

first all of 首先　　improve〔ɪm'pruv〕 *v.* 改善

valuable〔'væljuəbl̩〕 *adj.* 有價值的

market〔'markɪt〕 *n.* 市場；行情　　rise〔raɪz〕 *v.* （價格）上漲

resourceful〔rɪ'sorsfəl〕 *adj.* 足智多謀的；善於應變的

afford〔ə'fɔrd〕 *v.* 負擔得起　　***take a risk*** 冒險

recover〔rɪ'kʌvɚ〕 *v.* 自…中恢復　　***in short*** 總之

profit〔'prafɪt〕 *n.* 利潤　　venture〔'vɛntʃɚ〕 *v.* 冒險

Nothing ventured, nothing gained. 【諺】不入虎穴，焉得虎子。

給校長的一封信

親愛的校長：

　　大家最常問我的問題是，爲什麼你年紀那麼大，經濟情況那麼好，還這麼拼命工作？因爲工作使我快樂，**因爲我還有一個心願沒有達成**。全世界非英語系國家的人，學了多年的英文，還是不會說，「啞巴英語」是世紀大癌症，是人類必須解決的問題。

　　我教英文近50年，發現英文老師無法教學相長是最大的問題。就像空中小姐，最大的痛苦，不是在飛機上工作有多勞累，也不是隨時有生命危險，而是每天每天地工作，沒有從工作中學到東西。**18歲的年輕人沒有學習，就和80歲的老人一樣內心空虛**。我在工作中學習，所以每天都很快樂。今年73歲，叫我回到70歲、50歲、30歲、20歲，我都不願意，因爲不斷在發明創造，一年比一年進步，朋友也越來越多，當然不想回到過去。

怎麼樣讓老師快樂？

　　好的老師不管你給他多少錢，你多愛他，他都可能想離開，因爲在教書中學不到東西，沒有進步。那些外國人編的教材，如 Oxford 出版的 "Let's Go I" 中的 "Is this a book?" 這一類的話，背了一輩子都用不到，這樣學下去，老師痛苦，孩子也痛苦。不如背「一口氣背會話」中的 *Great to see you.*（很高興見到你。）*So good to see you.*（看見你眞好。）*What's going on?*（有什麼事發生？）這三句話天天都用得到，也可以隨時主動對他人說，可以說一句、兩句，也可以一次說三句。要背，就要背用得到的句子。老師一面教、一面學，背多了，老師自己英語最流利，有成就感，當然快樂。

如何讓孩子愛上課？

　　我們有一位同學叫陳少崙，是台北市百齡國小六年級學生。他來「劉毅英文」補了一年，什麼課都上，除了上兒童英語以外，還上國中、高中及多益課程，結果多益考了 925 分，超過大學畢業生，還在「2017年高中英文單字大賽」中得到第 3 名，獲得台幣壹萬元獎金。所以，小孩子如果只上兒童英語，到了國中一年級，他就會離開，到

別的升學補習班。**開一家補習班一定要 K13**，從小學到高中、成人的課程都有，讓優秀的同學可以越級上課。小學就把國中、高中的單字背完，又會說話，又會演講，到處表演，家裡、學校都會以他爲榮幸。

解決「啞巴英語」的方法

1. **要有足夠的單字量**：英文使用中的單字有 17 萬 1,476 個，每個字又有多個意思，任何人都沒辦法背下來。「高中 7000 字」是常考、常用的單字，以它爲目標就對了。我們有：

   ① 「小學生英語字彙輕鬆背」

   ② 「國中 2000 字輕鬆背」

   ③ 「高中常考 3500 字輕鬆背」
   用分類和比較的方式，背起來輕鬆。如：「職業・工作」這一類中，我們背：profession-professional-professor，美籍老師唸一遍，同學跟著唸一遍，只要不斷聽錄音，就記得了。

   ④ 「第 6 級單字輕鬆背」：「高中 7000 字」分爲 6 級，第 6 級最難，教這些單字，老師受益最大。有了訣竅，老師教起來輕鬆、很快樂，同學背了最難的部份，其他就變簡單了。

2. **要背 10 篇演講稿**：小孩子兩歲開始說話，媽媽說一句，孩子跟著說一句。三歲可以開始學英文，不需要教，**只要媽媽學英文，小孩就會受到影響**。我之所以對英文那麼有興趣，就是因爲小時候看到我媽媽在學英文，每天早上聽張澍教授的英文廣播。

   這本小冊子中的兩篇英語演講稿：1.「**英文自我介紹**」(Self-Introduction)，背完一輩子用得到。小孩會寫字以後，可以叫他默寫，背完英文背中文。2.「**向父母致敬的演講**」(A Speech to Honor Parents)，這篇演講非常感人，百善孝爲先。**學會感謝，一生都幸福**。家中如果請客時，孩子就可以背這篇演講稿給他們聽。另外還有「**給父母的一封信**」，可讓同學先唸中文給父母聽。學會話從背演講開始，背了一篇演講稿，模仿美籍播音員的腔調，終生說起話來就像美國人。

劉毅　敬上
2017 年 9 月 16 日

托福網路獨立寫作 185 篇
Internet-Based TOEFL
Writing Test

定價：780 元

主　　　編/劉　毅
發　行　所/學習出版有限公司　　☎ (02) 2704-5525
郵 撥 帳 號/05127272 學習出版社帳戶
登　記　證/局版台業 2179 號
印　刷　所/裕強彩色印刷有限公司
台 北 門 市/台北市許昌街 10 號 2 F　☎ (02) 2331-4060
台灣總經銷/紅螞蟻圖書有限公司　　☎ (02) 2795-3656
本公司網址/www.learnbook.com.tw
電 子 郵 件/learnbook@learnbook.com.tw

2017 年 12 月 1 日初版

4713269382584

因為有您，劉毅老師
心存感激，領路教育

　　「領路教育」是2009年成立的一家以英語培訓為主的教育機構，迄今已經發展成為遍佈全國的教育集團。這篇文章講述的是「領路教育」與臺灣教育專家劉毅老師的故事。作為「一口氣英語」的創始人，劉毅老師一直是「領路教育」老師敬仰的楷模。我們希望透過這篇文章，告訴所有教培業同仁，選擇這樣一位導師，選擇「一口氣英語」，會讓你終生受益。

劉毅老師與「領路教育」劉耿董事長合影

一、濟南年會，領路教育派七位老師參加培訓

　　2014年4月，劉毅老師在濟南組織了「第一屆一口氣英語師訓」，這是「一口氣英語」第一次在大陸公開亮相。「領路教育」派出7位老師趕往濟南參加，因為團隊表現優異，榮獲了最優秀團隊獎，Windy老師還獲得了師訓第一名。劉毅老師親自為大家頒發了證書，並且獎勵了Windy老師往返臺灣的機票費用。他希望更多的優秀老師，能夠更快地學到這個方法，造福更多學生。這一期對大陸老師的培訓，推動了兩岸英語教育的交流，也給大陸英語培訓，注入了全新的方式和動力。

二、效果驚人，「領路教育」開辦「一口氣英語班」

　　培訓結束後，「領路教育」很快組織並開設了「暑假一口氣英語演講班」。14天密集上課，孩子們取得的成效令人驚訝！孩子獲得了前所未有的自信！苦練的英文最美，背出的正確英文最自信。孩子們回到學校，走上講臺，脫口而出英文自我介紹時，留給整個課堂的是一片驚訝，和雷鳴般的掌聲！這也讓我們對劉毅「一口氣英語」的教學效果更加信服。

三、Windy老師成為劉毅一口氣英語培訓講師

　　自此，我們開始著手開了更多的「一口氣英語」班級，越來越多的區域出現了非常多優秀的「一口氣英語」老師。「領路教育」逐漸發明了一套「一口氣英語」班級的激勵系統，特色的操練方式和展示的配套動作。由於在「領路教育」有了成功的教學實踐，Windy老師收到劉毅老師的邀請，作為特邀講師，協助「一口氣英語」在各地的師訓工作。

四、連續三場千人講座，助推劉毅一口氣英語的全國傳播

　　2016年10月18日，在「領路人商學院週年慶典暨千人峰會」的同時，「領路教育」順利組織了劉毅「一口氣英語」在長沙的首屆師訓，劉毅老師親臨現場授課，並且接連在長沙、太原、武漢三地開展「劉毅一口氣英語千人講座」，向學生、家長展示「一口氣英語」學習效果，場場爆滿，反應熱烈！